RAVES FOR CATHERINE SPANGLER AND *SHIELDER!*

"With a stunning debut novel, *Shield* Catherine Spangler has shown she is a brilliant n oice in futuristic romance!"

—Janelle Taylor, Bestselling Author of
Lakota Winds

"Ms. Spangler's words are so powerful you can feel, smell, and hear her characters as she brings about a stunning story. Fantastic! Five Bells!"

—*Bell, Book and Candle*

"Catherine Spangler has created an unforgettable world of chaos, revenge, redemption, and passion, set among the stars. *Shielder* is a captivating tale that you won't want to put down . . . a fast-paced, action-packed romance that will leave you wanting more. Ms. Spangler is a new star on the romance horizon."

—Compuserve Romance Reviews

MORE PRAISE FOR *SHIELDER!*

"Catherine Spangler has skillfully told the story of two passionate and unforgettable characters. *Shielder* is wonderful!"

> —Victoria Chancellor, bestselling author of
> *A Cry At Midnight*

"Intriguing, imaginative, and HOT. Catherine Spangler takes us to a new dimension in her debut novel, *Shielder*."

> —Kathy Baker, Waldenbooks

"*Shielder* sweeps you into a whirlwind of passion, betrayal, and transcending love."

> —Nancy Cane, award-winning author of
> *Keeper of the Rings*

"Catherine Spangler has given lucky readers a tale of sacrifice, redemption, and triumph against insurmountable odds."

> —Kristen Kyle, award-winning author of *Nighthawk*

FIRST KISS

Chase couldn't resist moving to Nessa's side, squatting down to eye level. Her eyes widened at this invasion into her personal space. Her delicate scent, compliments of recent bathing, tantalized him, increasing the pressure in his loins. But her eyes pushed him over the edge—dark liquid pools unconsciously reflecting a response she didn't yet recognize. That, and her full mouth, which quivered oh-so-enticingly. He couldn't resist. Leaning forward, he pressed his lips to hers.

She jerked back as if she'd been struck. Grasping her shoulders, Chase pressed his assault, teasing her lips with his tongue. She was new and sweet . . . and totally ignorant of how to respond.

Heat roared through him like a wildfire. The urgent need to ravage her mouth, to fill his hands with those small breasts, warred with common sense. She was too innocent for this, and his actions way out of line. By the Spirit, what was he doing?

He wrenched away, gasping for breath and sanity. Certain Nessa would be as shocked as he at his behavior, he wouldn't have been surprised if she fled the cockpit.

She didn't. Starting at him, her face flushed, she raised trembling fingers to her lips. "That was a kiss," she whispered inanely.

"Have you never been kissed, Nessa?"

"I thought . . ." She paused, her brow furrowing. "I . . . isn't kissing part of mating?"

Chase cursed himself. He strode to his chair and sat down, willing his obvious physical reaction to subside.

"Would you kiss me again?"

He spun around in his chair. "What?"

Nessa rose and walked over to him. "Kiss me."

To, Mary Jane and her
sister & the Wonderful
Farmers Branch
Catherine Spangler

Shielder

CATHERINE SPANGLER

LOVE SPELL BOOKS   NEW YORK CITY

For James, my wonderful and loving husband. Your unwavering faith and support over the years made this book possible. Too much!

And for Diane, Jennifer, and Linda, the other three "Musketeers." Your vision and encouragement helped create the reality. Thank you.

LOVE SPELL®

April 1999

Published by

Dorchester Publishing Co., Inc.
276 Fifth Avenue
New York, NY 10001

ISBN 0-505-52304-3

Printed in the United States of America.

Chapter One

Only one object adorned the pitifully small grave.
A toy. A pretend phaser, crudely fashioned from bi-
nea wood.

Once again, the spirit of death had shown no
compassion, no discrimination in choosing its
prey. The Orana virus had performed the evil purpose the Controllers intended. Their latest victim
was a young child, barely four seasons old.

She did not care! She could not care. . . .

Feelings, emotions, were something Nessa had
buried deep inside, eons ago. Yet, if she felt anything—anything at all—it would be for the children, the ones who had not yet learned to despise
her.

Sinking into a crouch, she rested her head
against the barrier separating the living from those
who have passed on. The damp wind plastered wisps
of her roughly shorn brown hair against her cheek.

Her leg throbbed in protest against the pressure and the dampness. She ignored the pain, as she had every day these last ten seasons.

There was no time to dwell on her grievous shortcomings, not when the future of her entire race lay at stake. The Controllers had created a weapon more horrible, more devious than any fusion cannon or photon torpedo: a deadly virus, capable of breaching and destroying a Shielder's only protection against them, a natural mind barrier.

Nessa pushed herself upright, stretching to find relief from the aching stiffness. Shivering, she hugged her worn tunic closer to her thin body. She limped away from the burial grounds and into the main compound, territory normally forbidden to her.

Outside the assembly hall entrance she paused, gathering her courage. She already knew why the Council had adjourned the meeting inside—and what must be done. She turned for another look at the barren terrain that was both her home and her prison. If the Council accepted her offer, she might never again see the distant mountains or the ever-present haze drifting around them.

Taking a fortifying breath, Nessa entered the assembly. Built within a massive cave, the hall was large enough to hold every citizen of the Shielder colony. Even the press and heat of so many bodies couldn't completely dispel the damp coolness pervasive to all the caves and dwellings in the colony. The dim lighting from the solar lanterns added little in the way of comfort or warmth.

Fortunately, the entrance lay at the rear of the

hall, so no one noticed her presence. At the far end, the Council members sat upon a raised dais around a massive half-circle of stone. The Council head, Captain Ranul san Mars, stood explaining the crisis. Nessa slipped to the side of the crowd, where she could observe her father speaking.

"Our situation is critical. Five more colonists have been infected. We can delay no longer. We must take a sample of the Orana virus to our laboratory at Sonoma. It's the only Shielder facility capable of developing an antidote," Captain san Mars told the gathering. "As if that isn't challenge enough, there's another problem. With the Controllers' agents scanning most interstellar space vehicles, the virus must be transported via a live host to prevent detection."

The crowd reacted audibly as his meaning sank in. The virus would be carried within the volunteer's body. Preferably someone dispensable, Nessa thought.

Someone such as herself.

"The person must be able to man a star-class ship," Commander Jarek san Ranul added. "Only a star class is capable of the trek."

Nessa drank in the sight of her brother, pride momentarily dimming her inner turmoil. Jarek displayed the calm, controlled assurance befitting a future Council head, the position he would inherit from their father. He represented everything she would never be.

"Do we have any volunteers?" Captain san Mars scanned the faces of the Shielders grouped around the hall. They shifted their feet nervously, shaking their heads and shrugging.

Elder Gabe san Ardon stepped forward. "I'll go. My fighting skills are waning and I'm an old man. Let me carry the virus."

Murmurs of protest swept the room. Everyone respected the elder, a knowledgeable and skillful battle tactician. Most certainly they would prefer Nessa's alternative. Fear surged through her, followed by a flare of determination. No matter how disfigured she might be, no matter how flawed, she was still a Shielder, sworn enemy of the Controllers. She would never be allowed into combat against them, but she could still contribute to the cause. Resolute, she shoved her way to the front of the crowd.

"Don't sacrifice someone of value. Send me instead."

Startled gasps of outrage and horror filled the room as the crowd around her hastily parted and pressed back a safe distance. Nessa ignored them, but Ranul's icy gaze pierced her bolstered bravado.

"You know you are not allowed here," he stated coldly. "Get out, or I will have you removed."

Not just her father's callous words, but also his granite expression, wrenched Nessa deep inside. No love, no warmth, no sign of concern—of any feeling at all—for his only daughter, showed on his face. Sometimes she thought even hatred would be preferable to this frigid indifference.

She almost forgot her purpose here, tormented by the unanswered litany of questions rising from her soul. *Spirit of Being, why me?* She pushed aside the futile question. Adrenaline pounded through her body, but she managed to meet Ranul's glare evenly. "You have no other use for me, Captain."

"Aye, you are right about that. Not only are you useless to this colony, but your presence only upsets its members." Ranul glowered accusingly at Jarek.

Mutterings of agreement rose around Nessa. There was no need to put Ranul's thoughts into words, she knew what they were thinking. She shouldn't be alive to plague the colony, partaking of their pitifully few resources—and wouldn't be, if it hadn't been for Jarek.

Clenching her hands tightly at her side, she drew herself up to the fullest of her slight height. "Then let me carry the virus to Sonoma."

"Foolishness!" Elder Gabe scoffed. "The girl's not right in the head, we all know that. She couldn't possibly pilot a ship."

"Gabe's right," Mara, a female soldier, agreed. "Possessed as she is, she probably couldn't get to Sonoma, much less communicate with the technicians there."

"She's crazy, that's what she is."

"Get her out of here before she jinxes us."

Derisive opinions echoed around the hall. Through it all, Nessa forced herself to stand quietly, to give no outward sign of recognition to the barbs. She'd heard them many times before.

With an angry slash of his arm, Ranul silenced the protestors. "Enough! It's agreed we can't let a simpleminded girl who knows not the first thing

13

about starships carry the virus to Sonoma. Nessa! Leave now."

"I know how to pilot a starship. I've flown one many times." Nessa turned toward her brother. "Tell them, Jarek."

All eyes focused on Jarek, who shook his head warningly at Nessa. "Her offer is unacceptable. I'm one of your best pilots. I will go."

She knew he wanted to protect her, as he had for so long now. As he had when the members of the colony voted to have her euthanized after her first seizures, which had caused the accident that crippled one of her legs. Afraid to die, she'd allowed him to intervene on her behalf. At the time, Nessa had despised herself for her cowardice. But no more.

"Let this wretched life have some worth," she pleaded to her brother. "By the Spirit, Jarek, let me contribute like everyone else."

Jarek stared at her a long moment, finally dropping his head in resignation. He turned to Ranul with a sigh. "She does know how to fly a starship, sir. I taught her. I took her with me on solo reconnaissance missions. She's an adequate pilot."

Shock etched Ranul's face, followed by a flush of anger. "You had no right. But we'll deal with that matter later. Right now, we have more pressing concerns." His gaze settled on Nessa, assessing her.

"So, you can pilot a ship, and you volunteer to carry a sample of the virus to Sonoma?"

Her heart careened on a runaway course, driven both by trepidation and excitement. "Yes, I volunteer."

"And you are aware the virus will be implanted

within your body and that you will develop an active case of Orana within one moon cycle?"

Her throat constricted, but she pressed on. "Yes."

"I assume you are also aware that those with Orana lose the function of their mind shields, leaving them defenseless against the Controllers. Within days after shield loss, they die a hideous death."

"I understand fully."

Ranul contemplated her a moment longer, then turned to the Council members. "We could preprogram the ship's destination and lock out override. Then she wouldn't be able to alter the course. She'd just have to monitor the basic ship functions. I vote aye."

Three of the four Council members on his right raised their hands in agreement. Two of the four on his left also raised their hands. Ranul nodded. "It is decided then. Leonessa dan Ranul will carry the virus to Sonoma."

Cries of outrage and protest swept the hall. Ranul silenced them once again with a motion of his arm. "It has been decided. Unless one of you wants the honor of being implanted with Orana. Who will come forward?"

His challenge deflated the crowd's displeasure. They dispersed, considerably subdued. As awareness of her victory set in, the strength deserted Nessa's good leg. She stumbled and almost fell, but Jarek caught her. "I wish you wouldn't do this," he told her.

She raised her eyes to his concerned expression. "I have to," she whispered. "I can no longer endure this existence."

For she had likely just signed her death warrant.

*   *   *

Clutching her bundle against her, Nessa approached her mother. Her belly throbbed where the Orana virus had been injected, and the crude fabric of her pilgrim's tunic, even rougher than her usual clothing, scraped against her skin. Ranul and Jarek had concocted her disguise of a pilgrim traveling to Zirak to pay homage at the goddess Shara's shrine.

It was a clever idea, since Zirak was only two days' light travel from Sonoma. Many pilgrims went there this time of year. Her disguise would easily deceive the Anteks, who patrolled all airspace for the Controllers.

But Nessa wasn't thinking of her masquerade as she approached Meris. Although she had hardly spoken with her mother these ten seasons past, a compelling need drew her now. With her world about to change forever, the possible end of her life looming, Nessa yearned for the comfort only a mother could provide. It was childish, she knew, but then, she'd been just a child the day her parents had turned their backs on her.

It was harsh, but it was the reality of Shielder existence everywhere in the galaxy. The Controllers had driven the Shielders into the most destitute corners of space. With so few resources available, necessity dictated survival of the fittest. Parents shared their meager supplies and limited energies only with their healthy offspring. There was no time to mourn those euthanized or left behind to die.

It was a difficult reality for a girl of twelve seasons to understand. Even after ten seasons, the pain of desertion lingered like a festering wound.

Meris maintained the weapons for the colony's combat units. Intent on the rocket launcher she was cleaning and inspecting, she appeared oblivious to her daughter's presence. Nessa watched her work. With efficiency, Meris quickly dismantled then reassembled the launcher.

Gray had not yet streaked her limp and faded brown hair. Yet despite the fact that she was not an old woman, deep lines scored her face, the result of Liron's unrelenting weather and the severe living conditions her people endured.

"Meris." Nessa stepped forward, unable to bring herself to use the familial title. She no longer had that right.

Her mother's head snapped up, her gaze narrowing. She set the launcher down with a clank. "What do you want?"

"I'm getting ready to depart for Sonoma."

Meris drew herself up to a regal height Nessa would never reach. "So I heard. Why are you here?"

Why, indeed? Had she expected her mother to greet her with open arms? To wish her well?

Nessa struggled to find words, which did not come readily to her. Normal conversation had ceased for her ten seasons ago. Outside the sounds of nature, her world was one of enforced, silence, broken only by brief, clandestine visits with her brother Jarek; or Council meetings she overheard through furtive monitoring of the computer system. Or when the younger children, forgetting the dire warnings that she was possessed, ventured near her solitary quarters and sometimes even spoke to her.

"I wanted to tell you good-bye."

Meris stared at her, seemingly unmoved. With a glimmer of insight, Nessa thought perhaps the only way a parent could turn her back on her child was by forcing herself to no longer care. Her parents had certainly succeeded.

"Well, you've said it," Meris stated gruffly. "Be off with you, then." She whirled and strode into the hut behind her.

That was that. Fighting waves of despair, Nessa slid her burlap pack on her back and trudged away. Her mother would feel differently when she returned with an antidote for the virus. They all would.

Once out of sight of Meris, she stopped and pulled the pack off of her back. It shook as she unhooked the closures. When she opened the flap, a fuzzy head popped out. Four beady black eyes stared at her. Chatters of greeting filled the air, and a long furry body squirmed out. "Turi! Get back in there." She scooped the lanrax into her arms. "I just wanted to check on you."

Turi immediately nestled against her chest, nuzzling her neck. His frantic chattering calmed to a series of contented clicks. With a sigh, he rested his head on her shoulder.

Jarek had given Turi to Nessa two seasons ago. Lanraxes were small, endearing mammals that bonded for life with only one owner, usually the first person to place their scent on them. Turi had bonded with Nessa instantly. And other than her

brother, the creature provided her sole companion-
ship.

"Nessa! Wait up!"

She turned to see Jarek hurrying down the hill.
He grinned when he saw the lanrax. "I'm glad
you're taking Turi. He'll be good company on the
trip."

Nessa stroked Turi's soft fur. He was one of the
few joys in her life. She couldn't leave him, although she refused to think what might happen to
him if she didn't make it to Sonoma in time.

"I wanted to see you off," Jarek said.

"Oh." She was so accustomed to being an outcast,
it hadn't occurred to her that anyone would concern himself with her departure.

"Come, let me escort you to your ship." He fell
into place beside her. They headed toward the
cliffs, where deep caves carved into the steep rock
expanses hid the colony's ships. They walked in silence, lost in their own thoughts.

After a short climb up a steep embankment, they
entered the cave where Nessa's ship stood ready.
The transport shuttle had seen better days. It didn't
appear very space worthy. Given the importance of
her mission, Nessa had expected a military class
ship. Oh well. At least the shuttle was a model capable of light speed.

"I'm sorry this vessel is so old," Jarek apologized.
"But we feared a defense interceptor or scout ship
would raise suspicions. Pilgrims traveling to a
shrine wouldn't be likely to travel in such ships."

Nessa nodded, pushing back her disappointment.

"Your computer has been preprogrammed with flight instructions," he continued. "The ship will operate on auto pilot and fly directly to Sonoma. You won't have to do anything except monitor the equipment." He grasped her shoulders and turned her to face him. Turi hissed protectively, alarmed at this intrusion by another person into Nessa's personal space.

"Nessa, listen to me. Maybe I was wrong to allow you free reign of Liron's computer system. You're probably more knowledgeable about computer programming than anyone in the colony. We both know you're capable of overriding this ship's computer and disabling the flight instructions. I'm asking you not to do that. Let the autopilot do its job and fly the ship. I don't want you taking any unnecessary chances. You should reach Sonoma in one week, three weeks ahead of full incubation."

Barring any number of unforeseen problems, Nessa thought. Four weeks. She only had four weeks before Orana would ravage her body. She didn't plan on taking any chances. "I'll leave the computer alone, Jarek. When I reach Sonoma safely, I'll send word."

He didn't look reassured. "I wish you hadn't volunteered for this mission. Elder Gabe had already offered. He's old, and has lived a full life. You should have kept quiet, and remained here where you're safe."

"I don't want to be safe. What good is safe when I have no life? I want to help our people."

"And you think *they* will honor you for your efforts?" Jarek gestured toward the direction of the colony.

He knew her well. She had long fantasized about again becoming an accepted member of the Shielder colony. Of regaining love and respect from her parents. They were dreams best left unspoken.

She turned toward the shuttle. "I'd better be off."

"Wait." Jarek withdrew a small pouch from his tunic. "Even though your ship will travel directly to Sonoma, I want you to take these, in case you need them for any reason."

Nessa heard the clink of precious coins as he pressed the pouch into her hand. Her heart swelled at his generosity and sudden tears glazed her eyes.

"Thank you," she whispered shakily. "Good-bye, brother."

Jarek dabbed at the moisture in his own eyes. "The Spirit be with you, sister. Take great care."

Then he did something no one had done since Nessa's first seizure.

He hugged her.

Chapter Two

She was stranded in space.

Only two days out, the main stardrive quit functioning. Nessa had no expertise in repairing stardrives, but it wouldn't have mattered if she had. A search of the ship's storeroom revealed no spare parts. Spaceships of any kind were in short supply among Shielders, much less parts.

Ships seldom traveled this area of the sector. She would have to send out a distress signal, even though transmitting any signal presented risks. She could attract space pirates, Anteks—or worse—Controllers.

But she had no choice. Her only other option was to wait for the Orana to incubate fully. That would solve the problem of her miserable existence, but it wouldn't help her people. Genuine fear gnawed at Nessa, and realizing how badly she wanted to live surprised her.

She activated the signal.

Two days passed before a ship responded. Nessa was crouched in front of the open stardrive casing, studying a technical schematic, when the incoming message alert activated. She scrambled to the control panel. Before answering the hailing ship, she studied the sensor readings.

The approaching ship appeared much larger than her shuttle, possibly three or four times its size. Although the sensors classified the ship as a private long-range cruiser, they also indicated it was loaded to the hilt with advanced scanning equipment and armaments. Nuclear rockets, particle accelerators, laserlances, and more.

Only Controllers or their agents were allowed to operate spaceships so equipped in this sector. Dread settled over Nessa, but she knew she had to answer the hail or raise suspicions. She opened voice communication.

"Who are you and what are you doing in this sector?" a male voice demanded over the communicator. It was a deep, resonant, arrogant voice. Not the wavering, whispery utterance of a Controller, But the voice could belong to an Antek.

"I'm Nessa Ranul," she answered, dropping the dan from her name. Only Shielders used the system of naming sons and daughters after their fathers. "I'm on a pilgrimage to Zirak to honor our mother goddess Shara."

"Turn on your video transmitter."

With trembling hands, Nessa did so, then raised the hood of her pilgrim robe over her head, grateful that her colony's computer had provided thorough files on the cult worship of Shara. She pressed the pad, watching the screen. No visual appeared. The man had not turned on *his* transmitter. He could see her, but she couldn't see him. She stood stiffly while he completed his one-way perusal.

She jumped when he suddenly barked, "Why is your distress signal on? Are you ill or injured?"

His curtness offended her. Although she couldn't see the man, Nessa quickly decided she didn't like him. She stared levelly at the videocorder. "My star-drive is inoperable. I need assistance repairing my ship."

He snorted contemptuously. "Pilgrim, your ship looks older than the Ziraki sun. I don't have the parts you'd need for repairs, and I doubt they would be for sale anywhere. When I get to the next star base, I'll send a tow ship for you."

Alarm edged aside Nessa's intensifying dislike for the man. With the Orana incubating inside her, she couldn't wait for a tow ship. If her ship couldn't be repaired, she needed a ride to the nearest transport base where Jarek's coins could ensure her passage to Sonoma. "It could take days for a ship to get here," she argued, struggling to keep her voice calm. "I can't wait that long."

"I don't have time to play rescuer. A ship will be here in a week. If you're low on supplies, I can give you some. What do you need? Be quick about it."

A week! Full-blown panic surged through her. Nessa gripped the console, searching for words to convince this insolent, cold person to help her without revealing her identity. "I can't wait a week. I need to get to the shrine of Shara. I must be there

24

for the eclipse. Please, you have to help me."

"I don't have to help anyone, pilgrim. If you don't need supplies, I'm on my way."

"No, wait!" Tremors shook Nessa, and she feared she'd have a seizure then and there. Sucking in a deep breath, she willed herself to calm. "The eclipse coinciding with the festival of Shara occurs only once every fifty seasons. I'll never again have this opportunity to receive the full blessing of the goddess."

She paused, mentally sorting through arguments. "Take me with you. You can leave me at the star base. I'll catch a transport from there. Please. This is very important."

A long, tortuous interval of silence ensued. "How many are aboard your ship?" he finally demanded.

Nessa hesitated, surprised. His scanners should have provided him that information.

"Answer me, pilgrim. How many?"

"Just one."

"That's odd. I'm picking up two life forms. I don't give passage to people I can't trust. No deal."

Her thoughts whirled. His readings made no sense, unless—Turi. "I also have a pet on board," she told the man. "But he's the only other living creature on the ship. I swear on the goddess."

"I don't give a flying meteorite about your goddess." An irritated sigh rumbled over the com line. "But since you foolishly carry no viable armament, you probably won't last the week against pirates if I leave you here. Prepare for boarding."

Relieved, she sagged against the console, easing the weight off her throbbing leg. The arrogant voice thundered through the com again. "You may bring only what you can carry. I'm not a freighter service. And be fast about it. We leave in five minutes."

Startled, she bolted upright. Seeing no need for further discussion, she nodded and cut the visual. She rushed to gather her few belongings. The pouch with the coins went into the inside pocket of her tunic. She slipped her magnasteel dagger, her only weapon, into her boot.

She filled a large knapsack with her meager food supply. Turi went, chattering in protest, into a smaller pack. "Hush," she told him. "Not a peep out of you."

Her last act was to erase all records from the computer. No information that might lead to Liron could be left behind. The Controllers were known to offer rewards for information that led to the destruction of Shielder colonies.

As she finished wiping the ship's memory clean, she felt the thud of a ship docking with hers. Her rescuer—whoever he was—had arrived.

Nessa slipped the small pack with Turi over one shoulder, then picked up her supplies. She faced the airlock as the panel slid open. The man stepping through the panel towered over her, but he wasn't an Antek. The apelike Anteks were stupid brutes. She sighed in relief, realizing her rescuer's obvious intelligence should have negated that possibility in her mind. The innate ability to sense her own kind—which all Shielders possessed—told her he wasn't a Shielder either.

He was massive, broad of shoulder and through the chest. The black flightsuit stretched taut across his muscled frame emphasized his size. Cold gray eyes pinned her to the spot, glaring at her from a harsh, chiseled face. Dark-blond hair brushed against his collar and shoulders. Distracted by his appearance, she realized belatedly that he held an activated phaser trained on her.

He moved rapidly for his size, striding to her and skimming her with a hand scanner. His sudden loud sneeze sent her heart pounding even faster. "Blazing hells, the dust in here! Your air filtration system must not be working properly." Scowling fiercely at her as if that was her fault, he resumed scanning. "Remove your weapon."

Defiance was risky, but Nessa hesitated giving up her only protection. "What weapon?"

His eyes narrowed to silver slits. "The weapon in your boot, pilgrim. Don't play games with me. One more deception from you and I'll leave you here to rot. Is that clear?"

She nodded, slipping out the dagger and offering it to him. He slid the scanner into his flightsuit and took her weapon, his large hand engulfing hers. He sneezed again.

Muttering under his breath, he whirled and strode to the open stardrive. He squatted and peered inside. After a moment, he released a low whistle. "The primary driver coil is cracked right down the middle. The whole unit will have to be overhauled. This ship isn't going anywhere."

He rose and sneezed again. "By the fires of the Abyss, your polluted air is going to suffocate me. We'll finish this on my ship. Come on, get moving." Picking up Nessa's bag of supplies, he swung behind her, prodding her toward the airlock. Well aware of the phaser still trained on her, she moved to do his bidding.

But her leg, stiff from her standing so long, refused to cooperate. It collapsed and she pitched forward. The man snaked an arm around her and yanked her up before she hit the floor.

"What's wrong?" he demanded.

His arm pressed upward against her breasts like a steel band. Mortified, Nessa balanced on her good leg and tried to pry his arm away. It didn't budge.

"Nothing's wrong," she gasped, still tugging. "I tripped."

He released her and she almost stumbled again. "Try to be less clumsy. Let's go."

Nessa started forward. Her leg held the weight this time, although she couldn't control her limp. He didn't comment; but then, he was too busy sneezing—three times—before they got through the airlock into his ship.

He closed the hatch, then lowered her supplies to the floor. His relentless gaze settled on her again. "What's wrong with your leg?"

Nessa didn't discuss her injury with anyone, not even Jarek. "Nothing. I'm just stiff from standing so long."

He sneezed and shook his head angrily. "That's what I get for stopping," he muttered, taking her arm. "Over here, pilgrim. No one enters my ship without being decontaminated first."

"What's that?" she asked warily, digging in her heels.

He gave an impatient jerk, pulling her toward a

panel. "Just some sterilizing rays that remove germs and dirt." He stopped in front of the panel, pointing to her tunic. "Take off that filthy rag. I'll clean it in the conclave. If that doesn't do the job, it's refuse."

Nessa clutched her tunic, panic rising swiftly. She had never bared her body to anyone. "I will not. You can't destroy this. I have nothing else to wear."

He started to speak, then sneezed again—twice. She noticed his eyes beginning to water. "By the gods!" he snarled. "You try my patience, lady. And you brought that polluted air in here with you. Either that, or something on you is irritating my allergies." He jerked up her bag of supplies and began rifling through it.

Allergies? This incredible specimen of a warrior had allergies? Nessa found his behavior bewildering. And her people thought *she* was crazy. Tossing the supplies down, he spun her toward him. "Let me see the other bag."

Turi was in that bag. "No." Nessa tried to hang on to the knapsack, but he wrested it from her grasp. He raised the flap and Turi popped out, hissing angrily.

"A lanrax! You brought a frigging lanrax on my ship. I knew you were trouble the minute I saw your wretched excuse of a space vehicle." He hauled Turi from the sack by the scruff of his neck.

"That's the last time I stop to help anyone!" he roared. "By the gods, a pilgrim with a lanrax. It's not staying here." He strode down the corridor, sneezing repeatedly. Turi writhed and snarled, to no avail.

Catherine Spangler

"What are you doing?" Alarmed, Nessa limped behind, cursing her leg for slowing her down.

Halting, he opened a window airlock and stuffed Turi in. "I'm allergic to lanraxes—*very* allergic. Any lanrax crossing my path regrets it. I'm jettisoning this creature out of here."

"No!" Frantic, Nessa lunged forward and grabbed his arm before he could push the eject pad. "You can't jettison him into space. He'll die!"

A diabolical grin spread across the man's face. "Exactly."

Hysteria flooded her. Losing all restraint, she threw herself against him, screaming. "Nooo! You can't do this. You don't understand . . . he's all I have. Please don't do this. Please . . . don't . . . *He's all I have!*"

Sudden streaks of light flashed behind her eyes and she felt the beginning spasms rock her body. *No, no! Not now . . .*

It was her last conscious thought.

"It's about time you came around." The gruff voice penetrated the edge of Nessa's consciousness, but she didn't respond. Although a life alone in the wilderness had trained her to sleep lightly and awaken instantly, the seizures always left her sluggish and disoriented. And for some reason she couldn't quite grasp, she didn't want to wake up.

A faint hum vibrated over her forehead. "Come now, pilgrim, I know you can hear me. Open your eyes."

She knew the commanding, arrogant voice from

somewhere. . . . No, she didn't want to remember that voice. She shook her head.

"Still trying my patience. How about this: Either open your eyes or get a stimulant injection."

Her eyes flew open. Steel-gray eyes, set in a cold face etched with disapproval, stared back. Him. His black-clad bulk filled her field of vision, making avoidance impossible. Memory returned—every excruciating detail of the moments before her blackout.

Turi. Grief slashed like a sharp blade through her body. She arched her back in agony. He had jettisoned Turi. She clenched her eyes shut against the pain. Tension curled through her and light sparked behind her eyelids.

"Oh, no, you don't." A sharp twinge pierced her neck and the tightness flowed out of her muscles immediately. Limp, she sagged to the surface beneath her. But although her body was relaxed, her thoughts flowed clearly. The seizure. He must have stopped it.

Amazed, she opened her eyes again. He watched her, a frown on his face. His gaze shifted to the medical monitor he was scanning over her chest. Over the metallic blanket covering her bare chest. Her tunic was gone! As she struggled to absorb this information, he set the monitor aside.

"What just upset you so badly that you almost sent yourself into another episode? I assume it's not my face, since you didn't react this way when you first saw me."

The painful memory rushed back, forming a burning knot in her chest. Grasping the blanket in her fists, she silently glared at the man responsible for Turi's demise.

His golden brows shot up as his gaze moved to the knotted cover. "There you go again." His warm hand slid over her cold fist. "Don't tell me all this stress is over a worthless lanrax."

Her stricken expression must have been answer enough. He shook his head in disgust. Moving back, he motioned toward the opposite wall. "That particular lanrax?"

Her head whirled to the side. There in a plexi-shield case, Turi stared back at her, very much alive. He was plastered against the side, his mouth opening and closing in indignant protest. The case must have been soundproof, since she couldn't hear his chattering.

She nodded, overwhelmed by relief, her eyes glued to her pet. As the immediate joy of discovering Turi unharmed faded, worry about her predicament resumed. She shifted her gaze to the man. He wasn't sneezing and his eyes were no longer red. What was he planning now?

He seemed to read her thoughts. "Don't worry, pilgrim. That worthless creature is safe." He shot a damning glare at Turi. "As long as he's in the case, the dander is contained. I figure it's easier to let him live than to revive you from a seizure every five minutes." A determined expression crossed his face. "Now, about these seizures. How long have you been having them?"

Shame and humiliation engulfed her. No. She couldn't bear to go through this again. To go though the degradation and disgrace. If he thought

Shielder

she was possessed . . . he might jettison *her*. Jarek wasn't around to protect her this time. Scrambling upright, she grabbed at the blanket, barely preventing it from slipping off her chest.

"There's nothing wrong with me."

She started to get down from the table, but he moved at light speed, grabbing her waist and pinning her there. His eyes bored into hers. "My examination and medical monitor say differently. Not just these episodes, but your leg—"

"My leg is fine," Nessa insisted, struggling in earnest now. He restrained her easily, but she continued thrashing, mindless from rushing adrenaline. "There's nothing wrong with my leg! It's fine, it's fine, it's—"

"Stop it! I saw your leg, Nessa. And I want to know why it wasn't tended."

She slumped back, trembling uncontrollably. "There's nothing wrong with me," she whispered.

He stared at her, his expression incredulous. He eased his tight grasp. "Your leg could have been repaired. And you should receive treatment for your seizures."

She focused her gaze on her clenched hands. "I'm fine now, I tell you."

"There's no shame because you have seizures. You have a condition—a medical condition that has a name—and a treatment. You don't have to suffer these episodes. And there are surgical procedures that can help your leg."

Nessa refused to listen, refused to accept what he was saying. She had survived too long by convincing herself that she was okay, or at least functional.

33

She didn't dare dwell on farfetched hopes beyond her reach. She shook her head in denial. "I can get by. Just take me to the nearest star base. Then you'll be rid of me."

He exhaled angrily and released her. "Fine."

He took her tunic from a nearby cabinet and tossed it to her. "I sterilized this while you were *resting*, as you choose to call it. Get dressed. Join me in the cockpit when you're done. It's at the end of the corridor. We'll discuss the rules of this ship. Believe me, there are plenty."

The panel whisked shut behind him. Nessa slid from the table, avoiding the sight of her scarred leg. Still trembling, she fumbled into her tunic, her cold hands clumsy. One thought dominated her mind— her rescuer knew about her intolerable flaws. He hadn't seemed particularly upset, but he might react later when he had time to reconsider the facts.

Perhaps his mocking suggestion of a cure for her seizures was his way of reacting, a cruel response, but consistent with his personality. He hadn't displayed any inclination to help thus far; her plight appeared but an irritating inconvenience to him.

He might decide not to help at all. He might just turn her in to the nearest Controller prison. Fear churned in Nessa's chest. She had to find a way to check his navigational system and ensure he was indeed headed to the closest star base. But there was no time now. He awaited her in the cockpit.

Her attention turned to Turi, still silently protesting from inside his container. She placed her palm against the cool plexishield, noting the filtered air vents on the sides. Turi flattened even more, trying to reach her through the barrier. She hesitated to release him. It was probably safer for him to remain in the case, especially if his containment averted further sneezing episodes from their host.

"Sorry, Turi. I have to leave you here for now. But I'll be back." Nessa glanced around the room. Gleaming, antiseptic white walls of cabinets filled two sides. The table she'd vacated ran half the length of the third wall. Only it looked more like a bed than a table, with one end slightly elevated. A computer screen headed that end.

A counter skirted part of the fourth wall, where Turi's case rested. An array of equipment lined the counter and the inset in the backdrop. A huge instrument took up the rest of the floor space beside the counter. Its broad base angled upward into a metal column almost as tall as Nessa, with a double eyepiece centered in it. Upon closer inspection, she identified it as a scanning electron microscope. She'd seen a picture of one while browsing Liron's computer data files. They were used mainly in medical research. This room must be a laboratory or sick bay.

"I don't remember giving you permission to snoop, pilgrim. I'm waiting for you. Now." The arrogant voice booming over the intercom jolted Nessa from her speculation. There was probably a videoviewer as well as the intercom in the room. She hastily located her boots.

When she tried to pull on the first one, she found her pouch of coins stuffed inside. She'd forgotten all about the money. Relief rushed through her. At least her rescuer wasn't a thief, whatever else he might be. She stuffed the pouch back into her tunic pocket and pulled on her boots.

The panel opened automatically at her approach. She stepped into a corridor twice as wide as any on Shielder ships. It was cleaner and brighter, too, illuminated by glowing light strips running along both the top and bottom of the walls. Fresh, temperate air issued from overhead vents.

Nessa walked slowly down the corridor, craning her neck to see every detail. An electronic hum emanated from an alcove ahead on her left. As she approached, she realized the alcove was actually a small chamber. A man stood just inside, watching her. Of medium height, with short blond hair and intense green eyes, he wore an expensive-looking tunic and leggings.

"Well, well, what have we here?" he drawled, looking her over. "You don't look like a wanted person to me."

Nessa gaped at him. She had assumed her rescuer was traveling alone. "Who are you?"

"Nathan Long, at your service," he answered with a graceful sweep of his hand and a small bow. He straightened, his eyes calculating as they again swept her from head to toe. "I'd be delighted to foster an acquaintance with such a lovely lady. If you'd be so kind as to deactivate this force field, we could get to know each other better. The deactivation pad is to your right."

Knowing full well no man would ever find her attractive, Nessa ignored his charming smile. "You're a prisoner?" She eyed his cubbyhole curiously. She'd never seen a ship's brig before. A narrow bunk and hygiene facilities were all it contained.

Nathan sighed dramatically. "I'd prefer to think of it as temporary custody. What's your name? You look like you might need some assistance yourself. If you'd release me, I could—"

"You could rot in the blazing hells of Nasdor," a deep voice rang out.

Nessa whirled. Her rescuer strode toward them, scowling. He halted mere millimeters away, forcing her to tilt her head to look up at him. His gaze speared the prisoner. "As a matter of fact, you will burn in agony, Long. I'll make certain of it."

The prisoner shrugged indifferently. "I doubt that, McKnight. You don't have anything on me. No proof. Just your deranged hallucinations."

So her rescuer had a name. McKnight. Nessa rolled it around in her mind. McKnight bared his teeth in a feral grin. "Oh, yeah? Then why do you suppose the Controllers have a galaxy-wide call out for your capture? One with a reward of five thousand miterons attached?"

At the mention of the Controllers, a shiver wracked Nessa's body. Nathan wasn't unaffected either; apprehension flitted across his face, but rapidly changed to arrogance. "Just a little misunderstanding, McKnight. I'll be freed quickly. You'll regret the day you crossed my path."

"I'll have no regrets when you suffer a slow, painful death," McKnight growled. Grabbing Nessa's arm, he pivoted and marched toward the end of the corridor, dragging her with him, heedless of her stumbling gait.

"Getting pretty desperate, aren't you?" Nathan sneered after them. "I didn't think females were your type. She's pretty scrawny, but she doesn't look like a boy to me."

McKnight stiffened, his rage almost palpable in the room. He maintained his silence however but quickened their pace. Breathless, Nessa noted three more brig cubicles as she limped along behind him. A prison ship! This must be a Controller prison ship. Which meant McKnight was one of their designated agents.

He halted before the panel next to the airlock—the same one he had demanded she enter when they boarded the ship. "You still need to go through decontamination, along with your possessions. All of them. Wait here." Whirling, he strode back down the corridor, entering the area Nessa had just vacated.

Having never experienced decontamination, she stared at the panel warily. A flashing light a few feet to the right of the panel drew her attention to a computer screen inset in the wall. The screen displayed a spacescape. Looking closer, she recognized the computer as an OCIS-6000 model, the latest in technology. She had read about them, but never dreamed she would actually see one.

She touched the screen reverently. Instantly the image rippled, replaced by a gallery of holograms. Faces—rows of faces. Beneath each hologram were listed physical characteristics of each person, their last-known location, and the reward offered for their capture and delivery to the Controller prison base on Alta. At the bottom of the screen, a map depicted the entire quadrant, with flashing cursors on all the last-known locations.

The full implication of the data hit Nessa just as the panel down the corridor slid open. Frozen with horror, she stared at McKnight coming toward her, the heavy plexishield case containing Turi resting easily on one arm.

The prisoner in the brig, the computer information, McKnight's sense of urgency, all pointed to one thing. He wasn't just a Controller agent. No, he was something far worse.

This man McKnight was a shadower. A bounty hunter.

And in this quadrant so cruelly ruled by the Controllers, Shielders were the prey.

Chapter Three

Holding the lanrax against her chest, Nessa rocked back and forth on the bench. She buried her face against the creature's midnight blue fur as it chattered softly. Observing the decontamination chamber from the cockpit viewer, Chase was oddly reminded of a mother and child. Preposterous. The lanrax was an animal, not an infant.

Yet as he watched the seemingly mutual exchange of comfort, Nessa's frantic plea echoed in his mind. *You don't understand . . . he's all I have!* A vision of her eyes, huge and dark in her pale face, flashed before him; eyes that had briefly opened a doorway into a well of loneliness and pain.

He knew pain when he saw it. Knew it intimately.

He understood how it felt, more shattering than a laser blast to the gut. How it tasted, the bitterness of despair and impotence. How it smelled—most especially how it smelled; rancid fear, charred and decaying flesh. How it looked, contorting once-beautiful faces as death's merciless claws ripped the soul from the body.

Chase leaped from his chair and pivoted away from the images on the view screen—and in his mind. This ragtag pilgrim was of no concern to him. The whole universe was filled with unfortunates. He had no time for any of them.

Yet Nessa's mutilated leg, her seizures, her obvious poverty, continued to haunt him. He'd been tempted to jettison her tunic, a pitiful excuse for even a rag, along with her boots, which were riddled with holes and too large for her feet. She hadn't been filthy, but she hadn't been clean either. The decontamination chamber would take care of that problem.

But it wouldn't fix the disruption to his plans. Chase balled his hands into fists, nagged by misgivings he had harbored when he first intercepted her distress signal. True, Nessa hadn't given him any real cause for concern, but he made it a point to be suspicious of everyone. Her ship had been stranded right in his flight path. Coincidence? Or one of Dansan's attempts to decoy him?

Not that he'd allow anything—or anyone—to deter him. Nessa had no weapons, nor could she access his ship operations. Instinct told him she posed no real threat. Even so, he'd find out everything he could about her. He'd watch her every move until he deposited her at Star Base Intrepid, four days away.

The beep of the subspace transceiver drew his

attention. He punched the com pad. "State your message."

"You were supposed to contact me at fifteen hundred hours, McKnight. Sudden memory lapse, old man?"

Curse it all. Taking care of Nessa, he'd forgotten about Sabin. The one person who would never let him slide. "A small delay, Travers. I've got Nathan Long. Caught him stowing away on a freighter headed for the Verante constellation."

"Well, son of an Antek. Long's been evading shadowers for as long as I can remember. How'd you get a fix on him?"

"Let's just say he double-crossed one of his closest associates. The associate was only too willing to disclose Long's location."

"I've got a lead on a max-level offender in Alta's sector. A lot of reward miterons riding on this one. Since I'll be traveling near the prison base, I can take Long and turn him in," Sabin offered. "Where do you want to hook up?"

"I heard Dansan's been spotted on Saron. I'm headed there now, but I'm two days out." Good thing the pilgrim was in decon, Chase thought. She wouldn't appreciate the delay in their flight schedule.

"You've had more false leads on Dansan than Alta has moons. You never give up, do you?"

The ever-present pain and hatred spilled from Chase's soul. No, he'd never give up. Although well aware of his obsession with Dansan, Sabin had no inkling of Chase's real reason for pursuit. Chase intended to keep it that way. His partner might not buy the explanations, but he knew when to mind his own business. "You know how it is, Travers. I could use the miterons."

"Okay, where are you headed after Saron?"

"Star Base Intrepid. I have to deliver something."

"Intrepid. That would work," Sabin mused. I can pick up more supplies while I'm there."

"Not to mention a lengthy visit to the Pleasure Dome," Chase retorted.

"Yeah, right. Moriah would dismember me and feed the parts to the Anteks if I set foot there. But you should try it, old man. It would do wonders for your sour disposition. I can meet you at Intrepid, but it'll have to be fast, so I can get to Alta. Can't let some other shadower get my quarry and collect all those miterons."

"Intrepid it is, then. I'll need a day on Saron, so give me five days. Contact me before you enter the star base orbit and I'll transmit my coordinates. Signing off." Chase disconnected the signal, then returned to the decon viewer.

He studied Nessa critically. She'd told him she was twenty-two seasons of age. She was little for an adult female, and way too thin. With her narrow hips and small breasts, she could even be mistaken for a boy, dressed in the right clothing. How long since she'd had enough to eat? he wondered. The scant supply of food she'd brought with her wouldn't feed a child for a week.

The strong pull to come to her aid irritated him. He didn't have time to be concerned over the fate of one bedraggled waif and her mangy lanrax. Not when the annihilation of an entire clan cried out for revenge. With a disgusted grunt, Chase turned off the viewer. The sooner he got rid of his passenger, the better.

Just one quick stop first.

"You are not permitted access to any part of this ship, other than your quarters and the galley. You may enter the cockpit only with my permission. You're forbidden to talk to any prisoners I'm transporting."

Nessa nodded, unable to look away from McKnight's eyes. They glinted like magnasteel, taking on the hue of snowstorm clouds. No one except Jarek had made such direct eye contact with her in ten seasons, and she found it unnerving.

"No unnecessary conversation or senseless chattering. I abhor distractions. And that creature—" He pointed at Turi in his plexishield case. "It stays in the case at all times. Are we clear so far?"

His unwavering gaze seemed to bore through to her very soul. *Shadower*. This man was a bounty hunter. Outside of the Anteks, the Controllers' barbaric enforcers, shadowers were the scourge of the quadrant. They willingly underwent Controller psychic mind indoctrination for the sole purpose of receiving permission to hunt down criminals and collect the reward. It didn't matter to them whether or not the unfortunates they captured might be innocent. Nor did it matter that Controller prison facilities were purported to be more horrible than the Abyss. Gold was ultimately the bottom line. Once indoctrinated, a person no longer housed even a microbe of pity or concern. They knew only the compelling, cruel dictates of the Controllers.

"Answer me," McKnight demanded. "Are you clear on these rules?"

His harsh tone sent shivers through Nessa. He couldn't possibly know she was a Shielder, she told herself. She nodded again. "Yes."

"Most important of all, I'm the captain of this ship. I'm the absolute and final authority. My orders are to be obeyed at all times, immediately and without question. Any infraction of ship rules and you'll spend the trip in the brig. Understood?"

Even sitting, he cut an imposing figure, filling the large flight chair, crackling with vitality and authority. And the certainty he was a shadower added more peril to an already threatening situation.

Nessa twisted her hands in her lap, praying the tension invading her body wouldn't trigger another seizure. "I understand, Captain."

"Then see that you follow those rules."

He swiveled around and studied a computer screen, punching rapidly. He appeared to have dismissed her, but she had no idea where her quarters were. Reluctant to disturb him, she remained seated, quietly studying the cockpit. Her focus settled on the computer next to her chair.

OCIS-6000, the most advanced system in use. She'd read about the new computers on Liron's Information Access and Retrieval link, or IAR. They had only been available for a few moon cycles, yet here was one right in front of her. She longed to touch the keypad, to delve into data banks reputed to retrieve information almost as fast as light speed.

"What are you doing?"

The harsh question jolted her out of her reverie. The familiar feeling of guilt, even when she had done nothing wrong, swept through her. She jerked around, her heart hammering against her chest. "I was just looking at the computer. I've never seen an OCIS-6000."

His eyes narrowed. "Why would you be interested in my ship's computer?"

He obviously didn't trust her any more than she trusted him. Desperately she wished she could access the navigational system and reassure herself they were headed to the nearest star base rather than a Controller prison. But she couldn't afford to arouse McKnight's suspicions any further.

"I had heard about the new computers and was just curious about them. I'm sorry. I won't touch your computer."

"See that you don't." He rose from his chair, towering over her. "Come on. I'll show you to your quarters."

Nessa scrambled up awkwardly, resisting the urge to rub her stiff leg. She started to draw the heavy case with Turi into her arms. "I'll take that." McKnight brushed her arms away, then lifted the case easily in one muscular arm.

She found his size and strength intimidating, yet in an odd way, she also found it fascinating. Shielder men, although wiry and resilient, tended to be slighter in stature. They relied on speed and skill in battle rather than brawn.

She followed McKnight down the corridor. The cabin quarters lined the wall opposite from the brig cubicles. Nathan Long lounged near the force field of his brig, smiling insolently. Ignoring him, McKnight led Nessa to the second panel. She assumed the first was his quarters.

"Lighting on," he commanded as they entered the cabin. Lights blinked on. The room was compact but efficiently laid out. A bunk filled one wall, while shelves and a control panel for the room functions lined the second wall. Recessed storage drawers and an entry into a small lavatory occupied the third wall.

Nessa looked around the bright, cozy cabin. Although the room's accommodations were probably modest by McKnight's standards, to her they seemed luxurious. Her hut on Liron was primitive by comparison, and so had been her shuttle quarters.

The cabin's limited floor space forced her into close proximity to McKnight. As he eased around her to set Turi's case on the table, his leg brushed against her. The sensation of rock-hard muscles touching her sent an odd vibration through her body. She could feel the heat emanating from him, could inhale his unique scent.

Since her injury, Nessa's senses had sharpened, compensating for her lack of physical agility, giving her a highly attuned sense of smell. She found McKnight's scent an unfamiliar blend of clean skin and masculine essence; a far cry from the unwashed, sweaty bodies of male and female Shielders practicing their battle skills. And not at all unpleasant. She studied him, an odd warmth surging through her.

Frowning, he returned her perusal. Self-conscious, she fingered her tunic, wondering if her own smell, increased by scant opportunity to bathe and old clothing, offended him.

"The controls are voice-activated. You have lights, climate, and music. The lav also operates on voice control. You should find everything you need here." He turned to go, brushing past her again.

Nessa realized he hadn't covered such concerns as water or energy conservation. "Captain Mc-Knight."

He swung around, his glittering gaze making her feel foolish for even asking the obvious. "Yes?"

She swallowed. "What are the limits for light usage?"

His brows raised. "None. You may keep them on the entire ship cycle, for all I care. Anything else?"

Surprised but heartened by his answer, Nessa smoothed her tunic, hoping against hope he'd allow her access to a cleansing stall. "How about water usage?"

He shifted, seemingly impatient with her questions. "What about it?"

"I was wondering if I would be allowed use of the cleansing stall and what the water limit is."

His mouth quirked into a sardonic smile. "By all means, pilgrim, use the cleansing stall—please! Take all the water you need." He paused, apparently noting her expression. "That surprises you. All water used on this ship is recycled through filtration and biological sterilization; none is lost. Outside solar panels supplement the ship's internal power sources, so electricity is plentiful. Now, is that all?"

"Yes, Captain."

He strode to the entry, then swung back around. "Meet me in the galley at eighteen hundred hours."

Still distracted by the wonder of unlimited power and water, she blurted, "Why?"

"For the evening meal. It's best to keep standard ship hours, pilgrim. Makes the adjustment easier when you're back on terra firma."

He left before Nessa could point out that she had her own food. But she didn't know where he'd put her bag of supplies, and she'd have to ask him for it. Her growling stomach reminded her that she hadn't eaten since the previous day, but her hunger would have to wait. She must tread lightly with this suspicious shadower. She'd approach him at 18:00 hours and ask about her supplies then.

Meanwhile, she planned to take a long shower, with all the water—hot water—she wanted. She'd never dreamed she would experience such a luxury.

Glancing at the entry panel to be sure it was completely closed, she slid the lid to Turi's case back far enough to slip her arms inside. Immediately, he wrapped himself around one arm, chattering a greeting.

"Shhhh. Don't let him hear you. I have to close the lid in a minute. I know you're hungry, but I'll get our food soon." She stroked her pet, finding comfort in the warmth of another living thing.

Approaching the galley, Nessa heard sounds of activity from within. She stopped at the entrance. McKnight punched a sequence of buttons on a metal unit taking up most of the opposite wall. He

49

noticed her and gestured at her to come in. "Sit down."

He turned back to the wall unit. Nessa stood there, uncertain. He glanced around, his tawny eyebrows drawing together. "Sit," he repeated, the command in his voice unmistakable.

She slid onto a seat at a small table, folding her hands tightly together in her lap. "If I could have my supplies, I can eat in my quarters."

"You call those supplies? You don't have enough in that bag to keep a desert krat alive, much less a person."

Admittedly, her stores were meager and she should conserve them as long as possible. But hunger knotted her stomach and she feared if she didn't eat soon, she might faint. As if by magic, a loaf of bread appeared behind the plexishield panel in the wall unit. McKnight opened the shield and retrieved the bread, setting it on the table.

Enthralled, Nessa leaned forward. "You have a food replicator? How does it work?"

"You've never seen one before?" He punched more buttons before turning to face her. She shook her head. "Well, it's pretty complicated. Basically this system takes sterilized, organic particulate suspensions and converts them into solid food. It requires a lot of energy, but there's virtually no risk of unsafe bacteria, and the food is fortified with nutrients."

"Oh." Nessa eyed the replicator in awe. She didn't know much about bacteria, but McKnight seemed very concerned about them.

He retrieved a white, round item and set it on the

table, giving her something new to wonder about. "What's that?"

"You don't know what this is?"

She shook her head again, feeling terribly ignorant. She decided not to ask more questions, no matter how fascinating these replicated creations were.

"It's kerani cheese, pilgrim. Full of protein molecules."

"Oh." She studied the cheese. She'd read about it and knew it came from the milk of the kerani, a relatively common mammal on many planets. Since Liron's terrain couldn't support livestock, she'd never seen any kind of cheese.

In a few more minutes, two plant-based foods that McKnight called amar grain and canta beans made their way to the table. Nessa mentally hoarded their names and the information he imparted on them. The Shielder diet was a spartan one, composed mainly of bread made from wild grains, and the few greens and fruits that would grow in Liron's cool, damp terrain.

He placed two plates and eating utensils on the table before taking the chair opposite her. She watched in silence as he cut generous slices of the bread and kerani cheese onto both plates. He served equally generous portions of the other items. Then he shoved one plate across to her.

Without another word, he dug into the food in front of him, eating with obvious relish. Nessa stared at the food heaped on her plate. It was more than she ate in one day, maybe two. She reached out and touched the bread, finding it warm and soft. How many seasons since she'd had bread that wasn't hard and stale?

"Is something wrong?"

Nessa looked up at McKnight. He took another generous bite, his gaze fixed on her. She'd scavenged for sustenance so long, she couldn't conceive of anyone sharing his meal with her. He probably hoped to gain her trust, then trick her. She returned her hands to her lap. "You don't have to feed me. I have provisions."

His eyes never leaving hers, he took a drink from his tumbler, his throat working in his powerful neck as he swallowed. He set the drink down and pointed at her plate. "Your nourishment is right there. Eat."

The tempting smell of bread wafted up to tease Nessa's nose. Maybe one bite wouldn't hurt. She reached out, then hesitated, self-conscious with McKnight's intense stare impaling her.

"Eat." He pointed his utensil at her plate again.

Her stomach growled. She picked up the bread and took a tentative bite. It was soft and light, free of mold and grit. She couldn't remember when anything had tasted this good. Ignoring the urge to gulp every bit, she forced herself to chew slowly. She ate a few more bites, then reluctantly slipped the rest of the bread into her tunic while McKnight spooned more canta beans onto his plate.

She found the cheese chewy and tangy, with a unique flavor. She took a few nibbles before furtively pocketing that as well. She tasted small samples of the beans and grain, finding them nutty tasting and satisfying.

Having done away with two plates of food, McKnight leaned back in his chair, returning his attention to Nessa. "What planet are you from?"

What remaining appetite she had fled. She laid down her utensil. "I'm from the colony Delsan. It's on one of Halpern's moons." Fortunately, she'd done her homework and she believed her information was accurate. Many cult followers separated themselves from society, choosing to inhabit moons.

He appeared to digest this information. "What about your family? What kind of parents would allow a young, defenseless woman to roam the quadrant alone?"

Her family. Nessa's chest constricted. "I have no parents," she whispered, battling the pain of the past ten seasons. She noticed McKnight's eyes were no longer icy, but a deep gray, laced with an unexpected compassion.

"Have you no one, then?"

Thoughts of Jarek eased the ache in her chest. "I have a brother. He awaits word of my safe arrival."

"It's good to have someone."

His quiet comment struck a chord with Nessa. "What about your family?"

The warmth fled his eyes at light speed, replaced by frigid steel. "*My* family is not open for discussion. Ever. I'm the one who asks for information on this ship. I advise you to keep your questions to yourself."

Tension emanated from him. Her question had been totally innocent, but she'd managed to overstep her boundaries again. She rose from her chair.

"I haven't given permission for you to leave. Sit down. Now." His voice shook with anger and authority.

She sank onto the edge of her chair. "I'm sorry. I won't pry further. I request permission to go to my quarters."

He leaned back, some of the tension easing. "You haven't finished eating. And I have more questions."

"I'm not hungry anymore. I'd like to rest," Nessa hedged. She was too tired to match wits with McKnight right now.

He steepled his hands together on the table and studied them thoughtfully. After a moment he looked up, his eyes speculative. "Have you ever had caroba, pilgrim?"

She'd never seen such expressive eyes, capable of changing appearance in a single moment. Nessa wondered at his new game. "No. I've never heard of it."

"You haven't? We'll have to correct that right now."

He stood and began punching pads on the replicator. "I think you'll like caroba, pilgrim. It's quite delicious, and it will put some meat on your bones."

Positive he wasn't interested in her well-being, Nessa held her silence. A moment later, he set a plate of small, dark-brown squares in front of her. "Here you go. Try it."

Wary, she shook her head. "I'm not hungry."

"Oh, but this is worth the effort." Leaning forward until his face hovered only millimeters from hers, he plucked up a square and waved it beneath her nose. He was so close, she could see a thin band of gold around his pupils, and the faint gold flecks splashed like stars against the pale gray background of his eyes. "Smell it," he urged, his breath warm on her face.

She inhaled a rich, sweet odor. "Taste it." He pressed it against her lips and her mouth opened automatically. He shoved in the entire piece. "Go ahead. Eat it."

He didn't retreat a millimeter. Still mesmerized by his eyes, she chewed obediently—and instantly fell in love with caroba. It had the sweetest, most satisfying flavor she'd ever tasted. It seemed to flow from her mouth to her stomach and heart and lungs, and even to her lower body, filling her with a warm glow. Her eyes widened with appreciation.

McKnight smiled knowingly. "Like it?" He picked up another square and held it near her mouth. She leaned toward it eagerly. He backed away, taking the promised treat with him. "You can have the whole plate. After you answer my questions."

Narrowing her eyes, Nessa drew back, a surge of anger racing through her. The vehemence of her response surprised her. For ten seasons she'd been forced to subjugate anger and pain in order to survive. Maybe leaving Liron had freed those bonds, or maybe it was the stress of her current situation. Whatever the reason, her emotions had been as turbulent as a wormhole crossing ever since she'd met McKnight.

She was neither a child nor witless, and she was tired of being treated as such. But she was at this man's mercy, she reminded herself. Reacting foolishly might endanger her further. She met his challenging gaze and inhaled slowly. "I will answer your questions, Captain McKnight. You don't have to use childish tricks. All you have to do is ask."

He slid into his chair, an annoying, satisfied expression on his face. "Good. We understand each other. I ask and you answer. What happened to your leg?"

The tumult inside her intensified. Relentless as the chilling winds pervading Liron, he would give no respite until he had obtained the information he wanted from her. "My leg was injured in weaponry practice."

"What kind of weapon? How old were you?"

She didn't understand why he could possibly have any interest in her injury. What useful information could he gain? She focused her attention on the table, trying to bury the pain of the memory. "A laser sword. I was twelve seasons of age."

"A laser sword? I thought religious cults prohibited violence. Why were you using such a weapon, and at so young an age?"

There it was. He still didn't believe her story. She raised her gaze to her tormentor. "We would prefer to live our lives peacefully, by the teachings of Shara. But others in this quadrant live by attacking the weak and taking over their lands. To survive, we must defend ourselves."

"Why didn't you receive medical treatment for your injury?"

Here he sat, on the finest ship miterons could buy, surrounded by the latest technology and luxurious accommodations. He couldn't begin to comprehend the life of a Shielder. To understand what it was like living from hand to mouth; to always be in hiding from a lethal, all-powerful enemy. Never enough food or warm clothing or medicine.

"We are a very poor people. Medical treatment wasn't available."

McKnight leaned forward, resting his forearms on the table. "Where were you headed when I found you?"

"I already told you. To Zirak, for the Festival of the Eclipse."

He smiled grimly. "So you say. Why were you traveling alone? It seems odd that all of your cult wouldn't want to attend this momentous event."

Nessa had thought her story through several times. McKnight wouldn't trip her up. "True, all would have liked to attend the festival. But our numbers are few and the crops must be harvested, and our colony protected from attack. We could only spare one ship. So we drew lots, and I won. I'm the lucky pilgrim who will receive the blessing of Shara."

"Very lucky, indeed," he murmured. "Now you have no ship and no good way to get to Zirak."

Alarm sizzled through her. "What do you mean? You agreed to take me to a star base. Are you telling me you won't honor your word?"

He leaped to his feet. Planting his palms on the table, he leaned toward her. Fury set his face in a mask of granite. His eyes speared her like laser bolts. "I always honor my word. Unlike many of those from your quadrant who murder innocent people to further their own fortunes." He jerked up and stepped back. His icy gaze raked her contemptuously. "You'll get to Star Base Intrepid in due time. The meal is over. Return to your quarters."

He left the galley before Nessa could even respond. Stunned by the force of his reaction, she rose on shaking legs.

Scanning the corridor to be sure he was gone, she stuffed the rest of the precious caroba into her other pocket before seeking the haven of her quarters.

Chapter Four

Nessa glanced toward McKnight's cabin entry before hurrying to the computer screen by the decontamination unit. She'd used a piece of bread to prop her panel open just a crack—enough to observe when he finally turned in for a sleep cycle. Then she waited two long hours to be sure he was asleep. She also checked on Nathan Long as she slipped past his brig. He lay huddled on his bunk, his breathing deep and even.

At the computer, she turned and eyed McKnight's room's door panel again. She was taking a great risk, but his actions in the galley spurred her on. His unpredictable and volatile behavior had further heightened her distrust of him. She needed to know if they were really headed for Star Base Intrepid.

Hopefully basic ship data, such as navigational information, wasn't security coded. After all, McKnight was the only person accessing the system. Taking a deep breath, she touched the screen. The same three-dimensional holograms of wanted criminals she'd seen earlier rippled into view. Quickly, she punched the keypad to exit that program, then studied the directories that appeared.

She couldn't tell which one contained navigation. She touched the first directory. Not there. Ignoring the mounting tension tightening her chest and speeding up her heart, she touched another directory. No. Another directory, then another. Ah! There it was.

She located the navigation pod and accessed it. After perusing the options, she chose current destination status. As she suspected, it was a read-only file, but it confirmed her nagging fears. At the top of the screen, followed by a listing of exact directional coordinates, flashed the staggering blow: DESTINATION: SARON.

Nessa stared at the incriminating words, mounting terror slithering through her body. She racked her brain, trying to recall whether Saron had an Antek post on it. With her limited knowledge, she didn't even know if Saron was anywhere near Star Base Intrepid. She touched the screen to return to the directory and chose the option for specific plotting coordinates. She scrolled through the list: asteroids, moons, planets, then, finally, star bases. More scrolling through the names of bases: Alpha, Borean, Caldmar . . . Galen . . . Intrepid—

"What in the blazing hells do you think you're doing?" Two hands clamped around her upper arms, jerking her back and spinning her around.

McKnight glared down at her, rage etched upon his face.

Nessa gaped at him, her heart pounding so fiercely that she thought it might burst through her chest.

His lips pressed into a thin line and he shook her. "I asked you a question. What are you doing?"

His cold, controlled voice alarmed her more than it would have if he had shouted. "N-nothing," she stammered, grasping his arms to steady herself against the waves of adrenaline washing through her.

His eyes narrowed to silver slits. He shook her again. "Liar." He swung his head toward the screen and scanned it. "Well, well, Star Base Intrepid. Position coordinates." He returned his damning gaze to her, his brows almost meeting above his eyes.

"And what were you going to do with that information, pilgrim? Alter this ship's course? A futile attempt, I assure you. You'd never be able to access beyond read-only data."

"I wasn't trying to do that. I—I wanted to . . . I—" Nessa hesitated, realizing the futility of an explanation.

"Don't stop now, pilgrim. Tell me. Just what were you doing, sneaking into my computer system in the middle of sleep shift?"

She ignored the tremors rippling through her limbs. "We're not headed for Intrepid. Twice you've given me your word you'll take me there."

"I told you I'd get you there in due time," he snapped, all restraint apparently gone. "By the fires! You refuse to accept the fact that my word is good. I warned you what would happen if you gave me any trouble."

Her tremors increased with the force of his anger. The brig. He'd promised the brig if she crossed him. "I only wanted to know where we were headed. I must reach Sono—I mean Zirak—soon." Spasms in her limbs halted her. He said something, but the roar in her ears blocked his words.

A second later, she was sitting on the floor, McKnight pushing her head down between her legs. "Breathe!" she heard him yell above the internal din. "Take deep, slow breaths. Breathe, damn it!"

She tried to obey, but she couldn't drag any air into her constricted lungs. Gasping, she clawed at the gray mist closing around her, flailing her arms against a hard, immobile object. Then total darkness surrounded her.

Funny . . . she was lying on the floor. It was cold . . . and hard. Even her straw-stuffed mattress on Liron was more comfortable than this. But she'd left Liron. . . . Groggy, Nessa tried to sit up, but a strong hand against her chest forced her back down. "Don't get up yet. Lie still a few minutes."

She squinted at the form above her. It blurred, then came into focus. McKnight. She wondered if that scowl on his face ever went away. In sleep maybe . . . except she was beginning to doubt the man ever slept. That thought required too much energy to contemplate. She sank back, taking a deep breath. In a moment, her mind cleared enough for her to realize she must have had another seizure. By the Spirit, they were coming more frequently now.

"How are you feeling?" McKnight knelt beside her, a medical monitor in his hand. A medicine hypochamber lay on the floor next to him. She stared at it dumbly. "Nessa, I asked how you're feeling."

She returned her gaze to him. His scowl conveyed worry, she realized with sudden insight. Concern—about her. Amazed, she searched his face, finding confirmation of her startling discovery in the soft gray of his eyes. No, she had to be wrong. Only Jarek cared what happened to her.

"I'm okay." She struggled onto her elbows. He set the monitor down and slipped an arm beneath her shoulders. He eased her to a sitting position, keeping his arm firmly around her.

Except for her brother, Nessa had gone for ten seasons without anyone touching her. Yet now McKnight had crossed that unspoken barrier by placing his arm around her. She found his touch disconcerting. But at the same time, she savored the strength his support loaned her trembling body. She'd always recovered from her seizures alone, pulling herself up and back on her feet with painstaking slowness.

"How does that feel sitting up? Are you dizzy?" He retrieved the scanner and skimmed it over her.

"I'm fine." She stared past him up at the computer, thinking about the consequences of her actions. He would put her in the brig now. Would he let her have Turi with her? Surely he wouldn't leave Turi alone to starve. She'd have to convince him to spare her pet.

Resolute, she started to push to her feet. Her still shaky limbs refused to cooperate. She swayed and almost fell.

"I told you to wait. Little fool!" McKnight rose with her, sweeping her into his arms before she could gain her footing.

She couldn't remember ever having been held. The hardness of his chest amazed her, as did the intense warmth he radiated. She tried to look up at him, but he had her closely gathered against him, and she could see no more than the underside of his stubborn chin; the thickness of his muscular neck.

He strode down the corridor. Nessa tensed, preparing to be tossed into the cubicle next to Nathan Long. "I must keep Turi with me. Please."

"I certainly don't want that creature." His voice rumbled above her as he stopped at her cabin. Surprise swept through her when he carried her inside and lowered her onto her bunk.

She grabbed the mat, trying to anchor her whirling thoughts. "You brought me to my cabin."

He stepped back, his brows arched questioningly. "Would you prefer my cabin?"

His question confused her even more. Why would he suggest his cabin? "The brig," she blurted. "I thought—" She froze. *Fool! Keep quiet.*

Returning anger flared in his eyes. "Ah yes, the brig. That is where you belong, after blatantly violating orders." He leaned over the mat, placing a hand on either side of her shoulders. "That's where you should be. Rotting in the brig for disobeying the ship's captain."

Nessa felt crowded, unnerved by his massive presence. Her breath caught in her throat. "I didn't do anything wrong."

His steely gaze held her immobile. "I disagree. I told you to stay away from the computer, and you ignored me. It would simplify my life considerably to put you in the brig and leave you there. But I've decided to give you one more chance. I will have your word—again—that you'll observe the rules of this ship. And you will not touch the computer without my consent. Understood?"

Nessa nodded slowly, sensing her seizure had somehow tempered his decision. "Understood, Captain."

"Good." He rose and strode to the panel in two steps.

"Captain McKnight." She scrambled off the bunk, spurred by a strange need to express her gratitude. He turned as she stumbled toward him. His hand shot out, grabbing her elbow and steadying her. The scowl returned to his face.

"Don't you have the good sense to stay put until the effects of the seizure and medicine wear off?"

Nessa started to deny any aftereffects, but he cut her off with an angry wave of his hand. "I know, I know. There's nothing wrong with you. You just like to 'rest' in the middle of the corridor."

His vehemence surprised her. Save Jarek, no one had shown any concern for her welfare. Not her own people, her father, or even the woman who had given birth to her. But this man had. Hesitantly, she placed her hand on his arm. He tensed. Her hand looked small against the swell of his muscular forearm. She raised her gaze to unfathomable gray eyes.

"Thank you," she whispered, her throat strangely tight. She wasn't sure exactly what she was thanking him for—rescuing her from a stranded ship, treating her seizures, sparing Turi, providing food, or not imprisoning her. She only knew he'd done more for her in one day than family and friends had done in a lifetime. "Thank you, Captain McKnight."

Myriad emotions swept through his eyes. "Chase," he growled after what seemed an interminable silence.

"What?"

"My first name is Chase. I don't expect formality during off-duty hours. When we're in the cockpit, during work shifts, I'm Captain McKnight to you. But at meals and off duty, call me Chase."

His husky voice wrapped around her like a warm cloak. She took a step closer, inexplicably drawn to him. "All right . . . Chase."

He inhaled sharply, his arm stiffening again beneath her hand. She felt his tension increasing, although she couldn't imagine what she'd done to anger him now. But his eyes weren't cold as he stared down at her. They were molten, like melted silver.

He released her elbow, his hand sliding up her arm and over her shoulder. The breath froze in Nessa's lungs as he captured an unruly lock of hair near her chin and rubbed it between his fingers. Strange sensations skittered through her body.

He stopped abruptly, clenching his hand into a fist by his side. She stepped back, her heart palpitating an uncomfortable rhythm. All at once, the small cabin seemed much too crowded, much too warm.

She backed into the bunk. Her knees collapsed, and she sank down. Chase spun toward the entry. Her muddled senses cleared as he opened the panel, jarred to alert status by the memory of what she'd seen on the computer.

"Captain McKni—Chase, wait."

He pivoted, his expression fierce. "What?"

She knotted her hands in her lap. "Why did the computer say we're headed for Saron?"

His eyes glinted coldly. "Because we are."

The distance between them slammed back into place. Nothing had been resolved. Just the exchange of more meaningless words. "But what about Intrepid? You said—"

"I said you would reach Intrepid in due time, pilgrim," he interrupted. "That means by my time schedule—when I decide. No one questions my decisions on this ship." His frigid gaze warned her against challenging him.

Nessa heeded the warning. At least for then.

Morning shift came and went, and still the pilgrim didn't emerge from her cabin. He preferred it that way, Chase told himself. The troublesome waif would only be underfoot. After the way his unruly body had responded to her mere touch last night, the best solution would be for her to stay in her cabin the remainder of the trip.

His physical reaction to Nessa bothered him. He could probably attribute it to the fact he'd been a long time without a woman. But he shouldn't be reacting to an obvious innocent like Nessa, especially since she was vulnerable right now. He needed to distance himself from her and her problems.

Yet he kept remembering how pale she'd been after that blasted seizure, how shaky and fragile. Guilt assailed him. He possessed a fair amount of knowledge about her particular seizure disorder; enough to know he shouldn't have shaken her and yelled at her when he caught her at the computer. He knew enough to formulate a compound that would reduce the frequency of its occurrences. . . .

He shook that thought away before it reached completion. By the Spirit, he would never do research in a medical laboratory again.

But Nessa couldn't afford to suffer many more episodes. She was already wound tighter than a black hole, and much too thin. She needed to eat more. He hadn't returned her supplies. He had more than enough food to share, and she would need her own on the trip from Intrepid to Zirak. The bread and cheese she'd sneaked from her plate when she thought he wasn't looking wouldn't last long, especially if she shared it with that worthless lanrax.

Chase clicked on Nessa's cabin monitor, though leaving the visuals disengaged. Everyone deserved privacy in their own quarters, with the exception of criminals. He heard her moving around the room and talking to the creature, so he knew she was all right. He should leave her alone, but concern for her welfare gnawed at him.

68

He punched the com pad. "Nessa. Can you hear me?"

First a muffled sound, then, "Yes."

He waited for her to speak further, but got only silence. "Are you okay?"

"Yes." More silence.

He'd never have to worry about her chattering driving him to distraction, Chase thought wryly. She was the quietest female he'd ever encountered. "Good. Then you can join me for the midday meal in five minutes."

"I'd prefer to stay in my cabin. If you will give me my supplies, I'll eat from them."

Chase slapped his hand on the console and spun his chair around. He'd fought this battle once. He didn't intend to fight it the entire trip. Striding to her cabin panel, he sounded the tone once, then twice. No answer. He pounded on the panel. "Nessa, I'm coming in."

He opened the panel and entered. She stood in the center of the room. Her eyes widened with surprise, but she said nothing as he halted millimeters away. "Why didn't you answer the tone?"

Confusion replaced surprise in her eyes. "I didn't know what that sound was. What's the tone for?" she asked, taking a step back.

"You ring the tone when you want to enter someone's cabin. Then you wait until they tell you to come in."

"Oh." She stared past him at the panel, as if she could see how the tone worked.

He looked her over, noting her paleness. "What have you been doing in here all morning?"

"Not much." Her gaze slid to the plexishield case, where the creature held a piece of bread in a hind paw. It stopped eating long enough to hiss at Chase, then took another bite, glaring at him malevolently.

Chase looked around the cabin, realizing for the first time how bare the room was. The shelves were empty—no holographic games or puzzles. By design, the room did not have a computer monitor, so there were no reading disks. Nessa had been in here for hours, with nothing to do, and without a single complaint. But then, she was not one to complain. He glanced back at her, noticing the wariness in her eyes.

Blazing hells. She was afraid of him. After last night, who could blame her? But he preferred it that way, he reminded himself. He didn't know anything about his unwelcome guest. He couldn't afford to let his guard down, even for a minute. Still, he couldn't expect her to stay in this stark atmosphere for five more days.

Sighing in resignation, he gestured toward the panel. "Come on. Let's get you something to eat."

"But my supplies—"

"Either you eat with me or you don't eat at all," he interrupted firmly. "And if you'll cooperate, pilgrim, I'll do something for you." He stepped behind her, urging her toward the panel.

"What?" She stumbled slightly, then regained her balance. He noticed her limp appeared more pronounced today.

"I've decided to let you use the computer. But—" Chase held up his hand as she gasped and whirled around, pleased amazement shining on her face.

"But only for reading and games, to keep you occupied for the rest of the trip. Nothing else."

"Oh," she breathed, her eyes glowing with excitement. "Will I be able to link to Information Access Retrieval files?"

Her childlike joy cemented his decision. "I don't mind if you want to delve into IAR. Maybe you could do research for me."

"I would! Oh, I would. Can I use the computer right now?"

"Meal first." He grasped her shoulders, turning her and walking them both through the panel.

A few minutes later, watching her eager expression as she nibbled at her meal, more guilt nagged him. He had the knowledge to make her life easier. She didn't need to suffer seizures. Within a very short time, he could research her disorder and compound the appropriate preventative.

Panic raced through him. Spirit, anything but the lab. Until now, he'd successfully avoided it and, for the most part, the memories it dredged up. Until Nessa had boarded his ship. Until her seizures had forced him into the lab, once again to face his failures.

Stop it! he told himself sharply. Drawing a deep breath, he reeled in his emotions. Three seasons lay between him and the demons, three empty seasons. . . . He should be able to control his reactions by now.

Formulating a medication didn't require any great skill. He could do it easily. Besides, if he halted Nessa's seizures, then he wouldn't have to enter the lab again.

He would do it, immediately after the meal. Decided, Chase sat back in his chair. Oblivious to his inner turmoil or his covert observation, Nessa slipped the rest of her bread into her pocket.

Shaking his head, Chase repressed a smile. Odd, but he suddenly felt more lighthearted than he had in three seasons.

Chapter Five

Chase strapped a blaster and a phaser onto his utility belt. He appeared oblivious to Nessa's presence as he reached into the weapon vault for a pair of blast gloves. Pulling those on, he closed the vault, then strode toward the hatch. His actions strengthened her suspicion that he'd traveled to Saron to pursue a criminal.

Fingering the vial of capsules in her pocket, she followed him to the hatch. He'd offered them one ship cycle ago, claiming they would help prevent her seizures. While she knew better than to cling to false hopes, she had accepted the vial. She didn't truly believe anything could eradicate her affliction . . . yet she hadn't been able to resist swallowing a capsule this morning.

Right now, however, her attention focused on the fact that they'd just landed on Saron, with Chase preparing to leave the ship. Panic edged her thoughts, raising apprehension at this delay in reaching Sonoma.

She halted beside Chase as he snapped open the portal cover. "Captain McKnight."

"Yes?" he answered, his voice flat. He appeared distant, withdrawn.

Nessa recognized that withdrawal. She had seen it many times before, in Shielders preparing to go into battle against the Controllers or the Anteks. A shadower stalking a wanted criminal would need the same emotional distance. This was no game McKnight engaged in. The hunt could readily become a matter of life or death.

"How—how long will you be gone?"

He looked at her then, his eyes cold and expressionless. "As long as it takes."

Her breath froze in her chest. How could she possibly have allowed her perception of this man to soften? *Shadower!* He was a shadower. She must remember that, in spite of his surprising compassion and assistance, his indoctrination would assure her swift demise if he ever discovered her true birthright.

Slipping a visored helmet over his head, he punched the hatch control, then turned to her one final time. "I've programmed the brig force fields so you can't deactivate them. Stay away from Long. We'll take off as soon as I return."

He still didn't trust her, and probably never would. Well, she didn't trust him either, which made it imperative that she gain full access to his computer system. Realizing he waited for acknowledgment of his orders, Nessa nodded; then he strode out, the hatch whirring shut behind him.

"Nessa! Nessa, come here," Long wheedled from his cubicle.

Ignoring him, she hurried to the cockpit. She needed to find her supplies and her weapon; needed to exert control of all computer functions—just in case.

Delving into the computer, she began searching for the hidden files every system contained. It took some time, but she finally found what she was looking for. The PWL file, which contained the security codes and passwords necessary for accessing all operational ship functions. The heart and core of the computer.

As expected, the file was encrypted, but that didn't deter her. With Jarek's indulgent permission, she'd spent seasons secretly exploring Liron's computer system and accessing technical IAR files. Files that had taught her how to program—and more importantly, how to access—any information in a computer data bank.

For another hour, while she listened anxiously for the hatch tone heralding Chase's return, Nessa painstakingly created a program to decode the file. It might take days to fine-tune a program that could eventually break the code on the PWL; it would almost certainly take several trial-and-error adjustments. But she had nothing to lose and everything to gain.

Breathing a sigh of relief, she finally closed the file, her decryption program hidden and running. Then she searched the read-only files until she located full ship schematics. They led her to the location of Chase's general supplies.

General storage was located near the lab and, fortunately, not secured. Nessa searched through the shelves of blankets, food particle refills for the replicator, and tools. Weapons and money were kept under secured, coded locks at other locations on the ship. She found her bag of supplies, along with her knife.

She slipped the knife back into her boot and hid her bag in her cabin. Pleased with her accomplishments, she returned to the computer in the cockpit to browse IAR files until Chase returned. He had initially barred her from the cockpit without specific permission, but he'd rescinded the order when he'd granted her access to read-only computer information. Nessa settled in, anticipating an enjoyable interlude in IAR.

Some time later, she heard the hatch tone. She quickly exited her file on various religious cult beliefs and celebrations and left the cockpit.

Standing with his back to the hatch, Chase pulled off his gloves, then his visor, exposing bleeding scrapes on his face. Nessa was surprised to find him alone. She'd automatically assumed the trip to Saron had been in pursuit of a wanted felon. Scowling fiercely at her, Chase turned and headed down the corridor, yanking off his utility belt.

"Captain," she gasped when she saw the bleeding wound on his upper back, near his left shoulder blade. "What happened?"

"My sources were wrong," he growled, not breaking stride. "This trip was a total waste!"

Nessa hurried after him. "But what happened to your shoulder?"

He jerked to a halt and threw the helmet against the wall. "A damn Jaccian decided he wanted my weapons and any gold I might be carrying."

"Too bad he didn't want your head as well," Long sneered.

His jaw clenched tightly, Chase opened the weapon vault and tossed the phaser and blaster inside. Appalled at the blood oozing from his upper back, Nessa stepped closer.

"Captain, your shoulder—"

"I'll tend to it!" he snapped, pounding the vault pad. "Just leave me alone!"

"Let him bleed to death," Long advised.

Chase leveled a glare hotter than a nuclear explosion at the prisoner. "Shut up, Long, or I'll put you under for the remainder of the trip."

Chase strode to his cabin and opened the panel.

"Captain!" Nessa protested, alarmed he wasn't headed to the lab. "Your shoulder is bleeding heavily."

Chase stood ramrod stiff, his entire body radiating tension. "So?" he ground out, not turning.

"You can't let it go. Surely you have supplies in your lab for treating wounds?" she persisted, concern overriding the desire to avoid his wrath.

He turned his head and looked at her, his expression cold. "You let me worry about that, pilgrim."

Not at all squeamish, Nessa had treated Jarek's injuries more than once. "It will be hard for you to tend your back. I—I can help you."

Some of the tension eased from his shoulders. "Can you, now?"

"I can try." She hesitated, wondering why in the universe she was offering to help a shadower.

He sighed, swaying slightly. She realized the wound must have weakened him more than he would admit. Her conscience kicked in, reminding her of all he had done for her.

"You've assisted me so much, Captain. Please let me help in return."

"All right." Reluctantly, he turned toward the lab. "Let's get this over with."

In the lab, Nessa watched him gather an array of equipment on a motorized cart, moving efficiently despite his wound and the loss of blood.

Chase pointed to an inset wall receptacle. "Place your hands in that. When the beam cuts off, they'll be sterile."

He steered the cart to the exam table, then opened the seam of his flightsuit. "Have you ever used an infrared sterilizer?" He peeled his shirt off, detaching it from his pants and tossing it into the corner.

She stared at his bare chest, at the swells of muscle tapering down to a firm waist. Her gaze was drawn to his flat, pale brown nipples. "N-no."

He turned around and reached up, activating the switch on a metal box about the size of a videoviewer. In spite of the nasty wound, the sight of his broad shoulders, the powerful rippling across his back when he moved, sent a funny sensation churning through Nessa.

A metal arm lowered the unit above the exam

table. Chase levered himself onto the table, then lay face down. "Put on the medical gloves—they're on the cart. Then get one of the sterile cloths and the silver container off it," he instructed. "Pour some of the compound on the cloth and clean the blood away from the wound."

Nessa approached him. Even prone, his large body dominated the table. She marveled at how golden his skin was, how smooth, stretching over the solid wall of his back. Taut buttocks curved down to powerful thighs. The sudden temptation to touch his rear, to see if it was as firm as it looked, shocked her. Spirit, what was wrong with her?

Swallowing hard, she forced her attention back to the gaping wound. She followed Chase's instructions, carefully loosening the dried blood and blotting it away, along with the fresh blood oozing from the laceration. It looked like a phaser wound to her, although she'd only seen a few. It must have hurt, but Chase never flinched.

Calmly, he guided her through the procedure. She lowered the infrared sterilizer just above the wound and adjusted the settings. When the sterilizer beeped off, she deadened the skin with a spray from the cart. Then she placed a suture unit over the injury, listening to its odd hum as it sealed the edges of the wound together. All this advanced technology amazed and fascinated her, and she asked Chase numerous questions about these wonders.

Finally, she bandaged the wound, smoothing a self-adhesive fabric over it.

Chase's skin felt incredibly warm and smooth,

even through the gloves. She'd never touched anyone like this before. The fluttery feeling in her abdomen returned, and of their own accord, her fingers lingered over the swell of his shoulder. His scent wafted up to her sensitive nose, musk and male and blood, oddly stimulating. She inhaled deeply.

Was this what the desire to mate felt like? The inexplicable rush of emotions; this sensitivity to another person—how they looked, how they felt, their scent? She'd read about mating, of course, had seen her people embracing and kissing, from up among the rocks near her primitive hut on Liron.

Nessa had often longed for a normal life like the other colonists enjoyed. She recognized her yearnings as foolish and futile, but still, she'd wondered what it would be like to have a lifemate, to enter into the mating act, to bear children. . . . Pain slashed through her, and she unintentionally dug her fingers into Chase's shoulder.

"Damn!" Flinching for the first time, he turned his head and squinted up at her. "What in the blazing hells are you doing? Is that bandage on yet?"

She stepped back quickly, her heart skittering into an irregular beat. "Y-yes. I think it's done."

He swung himself up and shifted his legs over the edge. His sharp gaze scanned her. "Are you all right? You're flushed."

Her hand flew to her heated face. "I—I'm fine. But we need to tend to those scratches on your face."

"I can do that."

She suddenly, desperately, wanted to touch him

again. "No, let me. Do I use the compound in the silver flask?"

Grudgingly, he nodded, and she took another cloth and the flask from the cart. She found his face as fascinating as his body. The high, pronounced cheekbones, the two furrowed lines between his brows, the gold specks in his eyes, the full curve of his lips. She committed every detail to memory.

He jerked slightly as she cleaned the cuts, and she drew back, concerned. "Does it hurt?"

"Only when I fly too low."

"What?"

He grinned wryly and her heart danced again. "That's an old joke, Nessa. Haven't you ever heard it?"

She shook her head and returned her attention to the cuts. The heat Chase generated wrapped around her, along with his scent. He remained as silent as she, and by the time she finished, every nerve in her body stood on edge, and her skin tingled with odd sensations. She stepped back, at a loss for words.

He slid off the table and took the cloth from her hands. As always, his massive presence dwarfed her. "Thank you, Nessa. I'll clean up. Throw your gloves in the incinerator over there. You might want to sterilize your hands again."

She complied, watching him covertly while he put everything away. Was this breathless sensation she experienced at the sight of his bare skin and beautifully delineated muscles another aspect of the mating fever? Not that it made any difference, she told herself.

She had accepted long ago that she would never have a lifemate. Who would want a cripple who suffered from unexplainable and frightening seizures? Even without her defects, she'd still be undesirable. She was too thin, too plain.

It was best to keep her focus on her mission, to remember time was running out. Nessa shuddered, assailed by thoughts of what would happen if she failed. No, she refused to think about that now.

Instead, she headed toward the cockpit, where she could lose herself in IAR and the knowledge it offered; could read about far-off places, exotic animals, and myths of hidden treasures.

Where she could pretend—if only for a little while—that she was normal. And maybe just a little bit pretty . . . and desirable.

Chapter Six

Nessa's fingers flew over the keyboard. She paused to study the screen, her expression rapt as she scanned the data presented there. Distracted from plotting position coordinates to transmit to Sabin, Chase leaned back to watch her. Oblivious to his scrutiny, she soaked up the knowledge on the screen like a wilted corona plant absorbing water, her dark eyes shining with the wonder of discovery.

Without her usual mask of distrust, she looked almost pretty. Her face still held the gauntness of hardship, but her skin glowed with golden tones, and her short mahogany hair had some body and sheen to it. Obviously, she made use of the cleansing stall in her cabin's lav.

She leaned forward eagerly as the image on the screen changed. Regret swept through Chase. Once he'd been just as hungry for knowledge, eager to learn anything and everything. He'd been innocent and trusting and zealous in his desire to help others.

Once.

Now he knew better. Bitter hatred and self-accusation disintegrated the regret. He had learned the hard way—trust no one. And he'd been a fool to think he could ever be competent in his originally chosen profession. How many lives had been lost because of that self-centered delusion?

Chase gripped the console, a flood of memories churning through him. Anger and disgust burned in his gut. Dragging in a deep breath, he forced the memories away—for now. He turned his attention back to the orbit coordinates and relayed them to Sabin.

Fortunately, his partner had been willing to change the rendezvous point. When Chase had received word that Dansan had been seen on Calt, he'd immediately contacted Sabin, asking that they meet near Calt instead of Intrepid.

The coordinates sent, Chase tried to focus on other matters, but his attention kept returning to Nessa. Her fixation on the screen hadn't wavered. Giving up all pretense, he leaned back in his chair. "What has you so fascinated, pilgrim?"

She started, glancing at him guiltily. He knew she wasn't in any unauthorized section of the computer—she couldn't gain access to anything but general information without a security code. Only a person with considerable expertise would be able to locate the PWL file in this system—much less decode it. Nessa's guilty reactions must be the result of a lifetime of conditioning.

She glanced back at the screen, her face lighting up. "The planet Vilana. Is it true it rotates so fast that it has three sunrises and three moonrises every standard ship cycle?"

She presented an odd blend of suspicious distrust and childlike simplicity. Chase felt certain her life up to now had been harsh, yet she radiated innocence. He'd bet a thousand miterons she'd had minimal experience with men.

She acted skittish around him, yet at the same time, he sensed her growing awareness of him as a male. He recognized the subtle reactions; the way her eyes flared when he got close, the delicate flush of her skin, the tautening of the peaks of her breasts beneath her tunic.

Her budding sensuality had a startling effect on him. Even now, as she looked back at him, he hardened. Blazing hells. There was nothing overtly sexual about her; she certainly wasn't one of the sophisticated, experienced women he preferred. He willed back the ironclad control he normally exercised over his body. It just had been too long since he'd been with a woman. Sabin had been right—it was time for a visit to the Pleasure Dome when they arrived at Star Base Intrepid.

Still, he couldn't resist moving to Nessa's side, squatting down to eye-level. Her eyes widened at this invasion into her personal space. "It's true, pilgrim. Vilana has three sunrises and moonrises every single ship cycle. Too bad the weather is so foul and changeable. The heat scorches the land by day, while the nights are bitter cold. Three times a day. Hot, cold, hot, cold, hot . . ."

Her delicate scent, compliments of a recent bathing, tantalized him, increasing the pressure in his loins. But her eyes pushed him over the edge—dark liquid pools unconsciously reflecting a response she didn't yet recognize. That, and her full mouth, which quivered oh so enticingly. He couldn't resist. Leaning forward, he pressed his lips to hers.

She jerked back as if she'd been struck. Grasping her shoulders, Chase pressed his assault, teasing her lips with his tongue. She was new and sweet . . . and totally ignorant of how to respond.

Heat roared through him like a wildfire. The urgent need to ravage her mouth, to fill his hands with those small breasts warred with common sense. She was too innocent for this, and his actions were way out of line. By the Spirit, what was he doing?

He wrenched away, gasping for breath and sanity. Certain that Nessa would be as shocked as he at his behavior, he wouldn't have been surprised if she fled the cockpit.

She didn't. Staring at him, her face flushed, she raised trembling fingers to her lips. "That was a kiss," she whispered inanely.

Her absurd remark helped clear his head. He stood and moved a safe distance away. "Yes, that *was* a kiss. Have you never been kissed, Nessa?"

She rubbed her mouth, sadness entering her eyes. "Not since I was a child. My parents used to kiss me at sleep time. But that was many seasons ago."

Chase envisioned a young girl all alone, and unwelcome compassion flooded him. "Is that when you lost your parents?"

She drew a deep breath. He noticed her hands clenched in her lap, which he had come to recognize as a sign of tension. "You might say that." She raised one hand to her mouth again. "But they didn't kiss me here. I thought . . ." She paused, her brow furrowing. "I . . . isn't kissing part of mating?"

Chase cursed himself. Such an innocent would be easy prey once he dropped her at Intrepid. He didn't have time to educate an orphaned waif about sex. But he also didn't have the heart to throw her to the wolves of the universe. He struggled to keep his answer objective and impersonal.

"It is part of mating for most people. But many people enjoy kissing without mating. Do you understand what happens when people have intercourse, Nessa?"

Her deepening blush told him she had some knowledge. "I've read about mating, but I've never . . . um, I'm not sure exactly how it's done."

His body would like to show her. Chase strode to his chair and sat down, willing his obvious physical reaction to subside. He faced the console. "I'll locate some instructional material on the computer for you."

He awaited a barrage of questions. Although she hardly spoke at other times, when Nessa's curiosity was piqued, she interrogated him like an Antek would a prisoner.

"Would you kiss me again?"

He spun around in his chair. "What?"

Nessa rose and walked over. She gazed down at him, serious and intent. "Kiss me. The other one was so fast, I didn't have the chance to see what it's really like."

She touched his shoulder, and the blood pounded back into his lower body. "Nessa, I don't think—"

"Do you just press your mouths together?" she asked, bending down. He started to rise from the chair, but then her lips touched his, soft as Saija silk and as electrifying as a fully charged solar panel.

Blazing hells. He pulled her into his lap. Her weight there only intensified his need. He grasped her face, his gaze probing hers. "There's more to it than pressing your lips together. Open your mouth. Touch your tongue to mine."

Surprise reflected in her eyes as she considered this information. "But what about germs? I thought you said germs could be spread by—"

"To hell with germs." His mouth swooped down on hers, his tongue plundering between her lips. She gasped, then tried to accommodate him, opening her mouth too wide at first. But she proved to be an apt pupil, quickly adapting to his movements.

He kissed her thoroughly, unable to resist sweeping his hand up her rib cage, brushing his fingers against the side of one breast. By the Abyss, but it was firm, swelling at his touch. One of his own body parts expanded in response.

He slid his hand around, cupping the breast and teasing the nipple. Nessa started with a small cry, but he curled his other hand behind her head and recaptured her mouth. With a throaty little sound, she sank against him, and he moved his attention to the other breast.

The blood pooling in his lower extremities left him light-headed, devoid of common sense. Spirit, what would she do if he opened her tunic and pressed his mouth to one of those tender mounds? Or—

The docking tone blared through his consciousness, alerting him to the fact that Sabin's ship had just aligned with his. Fortunately, it stopped him from doing other aligning he would very much have regretted later.

"What is that?" Nessa pulled back, alarmed and flushed.

Chase took the opportunity to lift her off his lap and stand. "That's my associate, Sabin Travers. He's docking to pick up Long and take him to Alta."

It was a good thing a few more minutes would pass before the docking procedure was completed. That would allow his overheated body time to return to normal. He glanced at Nessa. Gingerly, she touched her swollen lips, then smoothed her tunic. The outline of puckered nipples assured him that she had been just as affected as he.

Even so, he couldn't allow this to happen again. It would be unconscionable to take advantage of her inexperience. Not only that, but he didn't want or need involvement with anyone. All his energies were focused on one thing, and one thing alone: revenge.

Nessa drew a deep breath. "Your associate?"

"Sabin and I frequently work together to track down criminals."

"Oh." She turned away, her body stiff.

He was unsurprised by the sudden tension radiating from her. Many people despised shadowers, or felt immensely uncomfortable around them. Chase shrugged. He didn't care what anyone thought. Emotion had no place in hunting blatant murderers.

He headed to the airlock to greet Sabin.

Another Shielder!

Awareness of a Shielder's presence struck Nessa like a lightning bolt. She whirled to see a man stepping into the cockpit, followed by Chase. His eyes, darker than a moonless night, locked on her. His body stiffened with the innate recognition all Shielders shared.

He stared at her, his inscrutable gaze skimming over her. Panic coursed through her. She grasped the control panel for support. Oh, Spirit! This man could undo everything in a single instant, simply by revealing her true identity. Once Chase knew she was a Shielder, he'd turn her over to the Controllers. The standard reward of five hundred miterons offered on every Shielder was too good for anyone to pass up.

She battled for breath, trying to clear her reeling mind. Chase's associate, a fellow shadower, was *a Shielder*. The implications threatened her balance. She gripped the console until her knuckles were colorless. He must be one of a number of Shielder traitors who found gold more alluring than the preservation of their own people. They were devil's spawn who routinely hunted and turned in their own kind.

The end loomed near. She had to escape . . . to flee. She cast her gaze wildly around the cockpit, looking for another exit and finding none. She reached toward her boot for her dagger.

"Nessa, are you all right?" Coming to her side, Chase raised her erect, then eased her rigid body into a chair. "You look like you're about to have a seizure."

Gasping, Nessa shot him a helpless look.

"Well, well, what have we here?" the devil's spawn inquired, swaggering forward.

She stared up at the man towering over her. Half a head shorter than Chase, leaner and sleeker, he had the build of a feline predator. His shoulder-length ebony hair was drawn behind his neck and tied with a cord. Like Chase, he dressed in solid black, from his flightsuit to a low-slung utility holster displaying two evil-looking blasters to his boots.

She tried to bolt out of the seat, but Chase pushed her back. "Stay there until you're not so shaky."

"What's this about seizures? Who is this woman?" the traitor persisted. His gaze raked her insultingly. "Or should I say girl?"

Chase straightened, his concerned gaze on Nessa. "She's a pilgrim on her way to the shrine of Shara on Zirak. Her ship broke down in the tenth sector. I couldn't repair it, so I'm giving her a ride to Intrepid."

"Really? A pilgrim, you say? How interesting."

Catherine Spangler

His eyes mocking, the traitor offered her his hand. "What is your name, *pilgrim?*"

She shrank back, frantically praying for a way out of this horrifying predicament.

Chase gestured toward his associate. "Nessa, this is Sabin Travers. He won't hurt you. You can answer him."

"Yes, Nessa, I'm most anxious to find out all about you."

She ignored the demon, focusing her desperate gaze on Chase. "I'm tired. I want to go to my cabin."

He studied her, a frown on his face. "Perhaps a rest would be good. You're very pale." He slid his hand beneath her elbow. "You're trembling."

"Poor *pilgrim*," Sabin goaded. "Why, I believe she's afraid of me."

Nessa scrambled to her feet, breaking free from Chase's hand and sidling around the two men. Refusing to look at either of them, she ran from the cockpit. Once in her cabin, she paced rapidly, rubbing her upper arms.

Certainly, Chase's associate would be telling him about her masquerade, would be revealing her true identity at this very moment. She had her dagger, but it offered little protection against two seasoned warriors—shadowers at that.

Watching her agitated movements around the chamber, Turi chattered anxiously. Heedless of Chase's disapproval, Nessa flung off the lid and grabbed the furry body against her. "Oh, Turi, Turi, what are we going to do?"

Escape appeared the obvious answer. And if that failed—if she faced incarceration and execution in

92

Shielder

a Controller prison, or a hideous death from Orana—then suicide. Nessa didn't know if she had the strength or the courage for that option. Escape now was the best choice.

Sabin Travers's ship should still be docked with theirs. If she could slip though the airlock and override his computer system, she might be able to flee.

But rational thought began returning and she knew that option wasn't feasible. Sabin's computer system might be sophisticated, requiring hours to locate the necessary codes to override the system. She sagged down on the bunk in despair. Turi curled his front legs around her neck.

Her entry panel slid open, and Sabin Travers stepped inside.

Nessa came to full alert, shoving Turi behind her and retrieving her dagger from her boot as she rose. Sabin leaned nonchalantly against the entry frame, his arms crossed over his chest.

"You really don't expect me to be intimidated by that pitiful weapon, do you, *pilgrim*?"

Her heart seemed lodged in her throat, the fierce pounding hindering clear thinking. To make matters worse, Turi leaped to her shoulder, painfully digging in his claws and hissing at the interloper.

The devil's spawn raised an ebony eyebrow. "What's this? A new secret weapon, a killer lanrax? I'm shaking in my boots."

Drawing a deep breath, Nessa backed slowly to the plexishield case and forcefully pried a protesting Turi from her shoulder. She stuffed him in the case and slammed the lid, all the while keeping Sabin in her sights. Gripping her dagger, she faced her antagonist. She drew another breath, concentrating on her early training as a junior combatant, before she'd become an outcast.

"I'll fight you to the death, traitor," she hissed.

"Now I'm really frightened," he taunted. "Of a scrawny, one-legged *pilgrim* I could crush with one hand."

He lunged forward, as rapid as a striking viper. He knocked the dagger from her hand, sending it sailing beyond reach. Grabbing her, he pressed her against the wall, holding her hands by her sides and stilling her flailing legs with his body.

"You have one leg that's useless and, as I understand it, you suffer from seizures. I find that very interesting. Why are you still alive?"

"I don't know what you're talking about," Nessa cried, her pride stinging along with her wrist.

"Oh, I'm sure you do, little fake. You would have been put out of your misery when you became a cripple in almost every Shielder colony in the quadrant. Tell me why you were spared."

The shame and humiliation of the past ten seasons burned inside her, spurring her to struggle. "Let me go."

He ignored her demand. "Tell me why you're involved in this masquerade and where you're really headed."

"Maybe I just want to travel through the quadrant without being hunted," she spat. "Especially by traitors like you."

His eyes, so black she couldn't distinguish the pupils, gleamed wickedly. "Things are not always what they seem, are they, *pilgrim?* But one fact is

certain: You're hiding something. And you've involved my partner in your scheme."

His face remained an impassive mask, and Nessa
found his concern for Chase very unlikely. She
heartily doubted he cared for anything beyond his
own material gain.

"I want nothing from *your partner* other than a
ride to the nearest star base."

"Somehow I find that hard to believe." He pressed
her harder against the wall, and she gasped. "However, since Chase has a temper and would be angry
if I interfered in his affairs, I'll leave him to deal
with you. But mark me well, *pilgrim*. I owe Chase
a great debt—one I can probably never repay. I'll
be in contact with him every ship cycle, and I will
make it my business to know your every move. If
you do anything—anything—to harm my partner,
you'll pay dearly."

He released her so suddenly that she almost
stumbled forward. Catching her balance, she cautiously moved away from him. "Are you going to
tell him the truth about me?"

He shrugged, straightening his flightsuit. "Maybe
I will and maybe I won't. That depends entirely on
you, Nessa—if that's your real name. You'd better
choose your actions carefully." He strolled to the
panel, then turned with an arrogant smile. "See you
at the evening meal."

Nessa stared at the panel after he'd gone, a sick
feeling in the pit of her stomach. She didn't trust
the traitor, or believe he'd keep his word. A man
who would turn his own people in for gold had no
honor. He would certainly betray her to Chase at

some point. But for now, she had no choice but to play along.

Even if the peril she faced had just increased ten-fold.

Chapter Seven

Nessa stood inside her cabin, watching Chase and Sabin through the open door. They had just finished transporting Nathan Long to Sabin's ship. The prisoner had been forcibly dragged away, yelling a string of foul curses and threats. Nessa felt relieved to be free of his odious presence.

She was just as anxious to be free of Sabin, of his knowing leers and threatening posturing. Hopefully, he would depart immediately, and they could continue on to Star Base Intrepid.

That hope was dispelled a moment later when Sabin said to Chase, "I want to go down on Calt with you, McKnight. Dansan always has guards around, and I don't want you walking into a possible trap alone."

Chase started toward the cockpit. "It won't be the first time I've gone after Dansan without backup."

"I'm well aware of your abilities. By the fires,

you're one of the best shadowers in this quadrant. All the same, I'd like to go along on this one."

Chase shrugged. "Suit yourself. I'm not too proud to accept assistance. Just remember, Dansan is mine."

Sabin slapped him on the back. "Good. Then I'll take my ship and meet you planetside. Rendezvous at Giza's, seventeen hundred hours ship time?"

Chase checked his watch and agreed. Sabin disappeared through the airlock, leaving Nessa stunned. She'd had no clue they'd altered course, much less traveled anywhere near a planet. With Sabin on the ship, she'd remained in her cabin, venturing out only when Chase insisted she join them for the midday meal.

She waited to be sure the airlock light went off before entering the corridor to look for Chase. She hurried toward the cockpit, almost colliding with him as he strode out. He steadied her with a hand on her shoulder.

"There you are. I was just coming for you. Get into the cockpit and strap in."

His words confirmed what she had just heard. She stepped back from his hand. "Where are we going?"

"To the planet Calt. We're right outside its orbital field."

A wave of despair washed over her. Chase had detoured the ship again—and her time was running out. She curled her hands into fists by her side. "You gave me your word, Captain. I have to reach Zirak soon, or miss the eclipse."

His eyes, cold and distant, bored into hers. "I

don't have time for dramatics. This ship operates on *my* schedule, not on the whims of a passenger. I'm tired of you questioning my authority. Get in the cockpit—now."

By the Spirit, what could she do? Her mind whirling like a Sharan dervish, she followed Chase into the cockpit. Once strapped securely in her seat, she watched mutely as he deftly guided the ship into orbit, then began the descent to Calt.

While he was on the planet, she would check the program decoding the PWL file. If she could access the security codes, she might have more options. If not . . . a new possibility suddenly occurred to her.

"Captain McKnight."

He frowned, his concentration wholly focused on the controls. "Quiet. We'll talk when we're planet-side."

Nessa waited impatiently, going over the newest alternative in her mind. It seemed an eternity before Chase landed the ship.

Exhaling loudly, he eased back in his chair. "Well, what is it?"

"Is there a transport station on Calt? If there is, I can catch a transport now."

He shook his head. "I don't think you understand what Calt is, Nessa. It's the bowels of the quadrant, a haven for criminals of the worst sort. Here they obtain new identities, ships, and supplies, anything gold can purchase."

Surely the Controllers would be aware of such a place, Nessa thought. "Then why don't the Anteks patrol Calt and arrest all the criminals?"

Chase smiled bitterly. "The Anteks are just as sus-

Catherine Spangler

ceptible to gold as other beings. They can be persuaded to look the other way. Calt has no commercial transport station. No decent being would want to visit this hellhole. Those who do arrive secretly, under the cover of darkness."

Her brief hope fled, and Nessa pushed back the nagging fear. She still had over two weeks, she reminded herself. She undid her safety harness and watched Chase prepare to leave the ship. Once again, he strapped on an array of weapons; a phaser, a blaster, a stunner, and an evil-looking short saber.

Ready to disembark, he turned to her. As he had done at Saron, he had withdrawn behind an invisible barrier, detaching himself with a frightening intensity. This was not Chase she faced, but a fierce, remote warrior, beyond react. A shadower, with no mercy.

A violent shiver passed through her, but he didn't seem to notice. "Don't respond to any hailings or open the hatch for any reason," he instructed tersely. "Be ready to strap in for takeoff the minute I return. Understand?"

"Yes."

He stopped at the hatch and pulled the porthole cover open to scan the area. Nessa got a glimpse of the sun beginning to rise over an arid expanse of sand littered with spaceships before he closed the portal. "Remember my orders." Opening the hatch, he slipped away like a wraith into the semidarkness.

She waited a few minutes to be certain he had left, then rushed to the computer. She accessed root

100

command and located her hidden program. It had not succeeded in decoding the PWL file. Battling abject frustration, she studied the system's response to her program. That gave her enough information to alter her commands and try a new path. She reworded the program, then exited.

She didn't doubt for a moment she might need the information in the file. If Chase proved to be untrustworthy and refused to take her to Star Base Intrepid, then she'd have to resort to more drastic options. Unfortunately, decoding the PWL file could take days. Even if she managed to confiscate some of Chase's weapons and overtake him, without the security codes, she couldn't operate his ship. Sabin added a new threat; he might reveal her Shielder identity at any time.

In view of Sabin's presence and the uncertainty of what Chase might do next, she needed to find a transport now. Nessa thought of the bag of coins in her pocket. Gold could buy anything, or so Chase had said. Surely it could buy her transport, even on Calt.

She rushed to her cabin and slipped Turi into his pack. She stuffed her hoarded cheese and bread into her bag of supplies. Returning to the hatch, she opened it and slipped outside before she could change her mind.

A blast of sweltering air slammed into her. The blazing sun peeking over the horizon blinded her momentarily, forcing her to squint until her eyes became used to the glare. Amazed, she stared at the varied array of ships that stretched as far as the eye could see. Obviously the outcasts of the universe found Calt a popular spot. Surely the owner of one of these ships could be persuaded to give her a ride to Sonoma.

Turning slowly, Nessa spied the outline of buildings in the distance. Slinging her pack onto her back, she began the trek to the settlement. The oppressive heat surrounded her, and beneath her heavy tunic, rivulets of sweat trickled over her skin. The walk to the settlement seemed to take forever, and her leg throbbed by the time she reached the outbuildings.

Nessa gazed around Calt, finding it bare and unimpressive. Debris littered the hard-packed sand, Stark, weathered structures were sprawled about haphazardly. Although they had no windows, they had numerous entry panels on each side, plenty of escape routes, she thought, something she could well understand.

The problem was, she didn't know how to go about finding transport. She decided to check each building to find a gathering or eating place, where she might blend with the crowd and find a willing pilot with a ship. But not a single being or living creature of any sort lurked in sight. Nothing stirred except small eddies of sand lifted by the arid wind.

The first two buildings Nessa came to appeared to be closed up. She couldn't read the strange language on the signs, so she had no idea what they were. Glancing down the deserted thoroughfare, she felt doubts creeping up. Where were the owners of all those ships back on the plain? And where were Chase and Sabin?

She forced her stiff leg to move and walked

around the second building. As she cleared the structure, she caught sight of a woman sitting on the steps of a third. Hunched over a mug clasped in her hands, the woman stared pensively toward the sunrise. Coppery waves of hair veiled most of her face and cascaded down her back. She appeared oblivious to Nessa, who moved forward cautiously, stopping near the steps.

Sensing her presence, the woman stiffened, swinging her head around. Nessa stared into beautiful, surprise-filled amber eyes. The mug slipped from the woman's hands, falling with a thud to the sand.

"Oh, my, you startled me." She rose gracefully, flipping her hair over her shoulders. "I wasn't expecting anyone this early and I'm afraid you've caught me unprepared. I'm not open yet, actually. I rarely have customers before midday." She rambled on in a low, melodic voice. Tall and slender, she wore a lightweight gold jumpsuit that emphasized her lithe body.

Nessa had never seen anyone so beautiful, and for a brief moment, she could only stare. But the urgency of her situation soon pushed to the forefront. "Excuse me, but do you know where I can hire a transport?"

The woman studied Nessa, taking in her ragged pilgrim's tunic. "A transport? How on Alta did you get here if you don't have a ship?" She came down the steps. "Why, you're just a child. Are you fleeing from someone who brought you here?" She turned to scan the area, then looked at Nessa again. "Who are you?"

Relief at finding someone who might be able to help surged through Nessa. "My name is Nessa Ranul, and I need to find transport to Zirak. Do you know anyone who would take me?"

The woman let out her breath in a sigh. "Not anyone who could be trusted. Are you in some sort of trouble?" She laughed musically, shaking her head. "What am I saying? Anyone who comes to this abyss is either in trouble or the cause of it." Taking Nessa's arm, she turned her toward the steps. "And from the looks of it, you've got a problem. Come inside and I'll get you some tea."

Disheartened, Nessa followed her up the steps. The woman had to be wrong; surely someone here could help her. The sight that greeted her eyes stopped her dead in her tracks. The room they stepped into was large and surprisingly light and airy, considering the grimness of the settlement outside.

Sunshine filtered in from high skylights, illuminating shelves upon shelves filled with all kinds of merchandise. Fabrics, jewelry, scented oils, crystal, clothing, boots, holograms, computer disks, even live plants, lined the walls. Nessa had never seen such a variety and quantity of goods. The enticing aroma of incense drifted through the air, while soft music filled the room.

Her hostess nudged her gently toward the back of the room. "Come on. I have a little alcove in the corner." She led Nessa through a wall of crystal bead strands into an area with a table and chairs and a small solar stove. "Have a seat."

She put water on to boil and pulled two mugs

from a cabinet decorated with inlaid crystal and lavender stone, chatting all the while. "I don't often have company, so I'm afraid I don't have much to offer you. But I do have some wonderful caroba from Elysia. The brutes around here wouldn't even begin to appreciate it. Now, where did I put that? Ah, here it is."

Half-listening, Nessa kept looking back at the main room, still amazed at the number of goods. The woman set two mugs of tea and a plate of caroba on the table, then slid into the opposite chair. "You're very quiet, aren't you?"

Nessa dragged her attention back to her hostess. "I'm sorry. That room . . . so many wonderful things."

The woman smiled. "Yes, it is pretty amazing, isn't it? Even on this dismal planet, people have gold and they're willing to spend it. My mercantile is the only place that provides goods other than the usual alcohol, drugs, space rations, weapons, or ship parts. It's surprising, but even the crudest criminal will buy rare and beautiful items."

She waved a slender hand toward the main chamber. "Saija silk from Verante, Calpernian crystal, Vilana gemstones. You name it, I have it. And they pay dearly for it. By the way, my name is Moriah. Pleased to meet you, Nessa." She extended her hand.

Hesitantly, Nessa offered her hand in return, unused to the courtesy. Moriah squeezed her hand warmly before releasing it. Leaning back in her seat, she sipped her tea, eyeing Nessa thoughtfully. "Now that the formalities are out of the way, why don't you tell me how you got here and why you need a transport."

Nessa plunged into her story. "I'm a pilgrim of Shara. I was traveling to Zirak for the Festival of the Eclipse when my ship broke down. A shadower rescued me, but he refuses to take me to a star base so I can get transport to Zirak."

Moriah's golden eyes widened. "A shadower? You've been traveling around the quadrant with a shadower? By the Spirit, you poor thing. It's no wonder you want to get away."

Nessa breathed a sigh of relief. Moriah understood her predicament and hopefully would help her.

Her hostess poured more tea into their cups. "How long have you been with this shadower?"

"About seven ship cycles. I must get away from him. If I don't get to Zirak soon, I'll miss the eclipse."

Moriah studied her closely. "Nessa, has this man hurt you in any way?"

Quite the opposite, in fact, Nessa thought. Chase had treated her seizures and insisted she eat well. He certainly hadn't acted in any manner she would have expected from a shadower. She shook her head. "No."

Concern etched Moriah's lovely features. "I know what most shadowers are like. You can tell me the truth, Nessa. I'll help you if I can. Has the man forced you to do anything against your will?"

Nessa had no idea what she meant. "I'm not sure."

Moriah leaned forward, placing her hand over

Nessa's. "Goodness, but you might be as innocent as you seem. Let me rephrase the question: Has he tried to mate with you?"

A heated flush spread across Nessa's face as she remembered Chase's kisses, his hand on her breast. "Well . . . not really. I mean, we haven't mated."

"That's a relief."

"He did kiss me." Now why had she blurted that out? Uncomfortable with the discussion, Nessa shifted her gaze from her hostess. She had no reason to mention the kissing; she couldn't imagine Chase ever wanting to repeat the experience. "But it probably won't happen again."

"What makes you think that?"

Nessa fingered her tattered tunic. "Just look at me. No man is going to want me."

Moriah squeezed her hand. "Why in the universe not?"

Why not, indeed. Nessa fought back her despair. Wasn't it obvious? "I'm not only unattractive—I have physical defects as well."

"You mean your limp?" Moriah scoffed. "That's nothing. Listen, Nessa, beauty isn't just a surface commodity. Looks can be bought. A good heart can't."

Nessa didn't bother to reveal the fact that she also had seizures. Nothing Moriah said could change the truth. She'd been told often enough by her own people how undesirable she was.

"This is very interesting," Moriah mused. "A shadower has spent seven cycles alone with you, and he's only kissed you. At least he's not a rapist, which is a good thing. Maybe his preferences veer away from females."

She leaned toward Nessa. "Who is this shadower?"

A chime sounded before Nessa could reply. "A customer at this hour?" Moriah stood and hurriedly gathered her hair and began winding it into a bun. "I always keep my hair up and wear a loose over-robe when I'm doing business, especially with these space scum. It keeps things more professional, and I certainly don't want to give them any ideas, if you know what I mean."

Nessa looked at her blankly, and the woman paused. "No, I guess you don't. Seven cycles with a shadower, and you're still innocent. Amazing."

Nessa watched, fascinated, as her hostess deftly tucked her glorious hair into a severe knot.

"Moriah? Where are you?" a familiar voice called out, and heavy footsteps approached the alcove.

Nessa's breath caught, the well-known sensation signaling another Shielder's presence jolting through her. She rose from her chair as Sabin came through the strings of crystal beads separating the alcove from the mercantile.

He halted when he saw Nessa. "What are you doing here?" he growled, then strode toward her.

Nessa grabbed the chair for support as her leg threatened to give out. By the Spirit, would she ever get away from this man? "Why aren't you with Chase?" she managed to ask.

"Why aren't you on the ship, where you belong?" he shot back.

"Wait just a minute here!" Moriah interjected.

Her eyes narrowed with suspicion, she marched over to Sabin and jabbed him in the chest. "How do you know Nessa? Do you know the son of an Antek who's dragging this poor girl all over the quadrant instead of taking her where she needs to go? If you do—"

"Mori, Mori!" Sabin took the hand stabbing him and lifted it to his lips. "I travel light years through the quadrant to reach you, and all I get for my efforts are harsh words. Aren't you glad to see me?" He kissed her hand.

She pulled free. "No. Especially if you're in cahoots with the shadower mistreating Nessa. I want to know what's going on."

"I had nothing to do with this, Mori. She's traveling with McKnight."

"Chase?" Moriah looked incredulously from Sabin to Nessa. "Is that true, Nessa?"

Nessa nodded, and Moriah seemed truly taken aback. "Chase McKnight. That explains a lot of things . . . I think." She tapped her cheek thoughtfully. "But he kissed you . . . ?"

"He kissed her?" Sabin scowled at Nessa. "Why, you little gold digger—Ouch!" he yelped, as Moriah punched him in the chest.

"This is not Nessa's doing. Chase is to blame here," she stormed. "Not only has he kept her on his ship against her will, but he refuses to take her to Zirak. He needs to be put in his place."

"And you're just the person to do it, Mori." Sabin rubbed his chest. "So stop taking it out on me, sweetheart. You like me, remember?"

Moriah sniffed. "Sometimes."

"Come on," Sabin wheedled, pulling her against him. "You're happy to see me. Admit it."

She didn't offer much resistance. "Not really."

Nessa watched them with interest. She sensed an underlying tension between the two that had nothing to do with their conversation. The tension didn't seem to be anger or enmity, really. More like the odd energy she experienced around Chase; similar to the sensations that left her breathless and her heart racing.

"Well then, maybe I'll just have to change your mind," Sabin said huskily.

He lowered his head, but Moriah turned her face. "We have an audience."

His accusing gaze shot to Nessa. "So we do." Heaving a sigh, he released Moriah. "Have you got anything for me?" he asked, his voice lower, more serious now.

Moriah glanced at Nessa. "Yes. The merchandise arrived two days ago. I'll get it for you." She slipped through an entry at the rear of the alcove, leaving Nessa alone with Sabin.

He immediately turned his attention on her. "Just what do you think you're doing, leaving the ship and wandering around Calt by yourself? Stars, this hellhole is dangerous for an armed man, much less a lone woman. Chase needs to lock you up."

"Chase needs to honor his word," Nessa retorted fiercely. "He promised to get me to a transport but shows no signs of doing so. I have to get to Zirak soon."

"What's your hurry? And don't give me that song and dance about the eclipse and the shrine of

Shara. I've never known a Shielder to be a cult member."

Not giving her a chance to reply, Sabin activated the com link on his wrist. "Hey, old man. I've got Nessa with me. Found her at Moriah's."

Nessa stood too far away to hear Chase's response, but she could well imagine what he might have to say about her leaving the ship against orders.

Sabin shook his head. "I have no idea. She was just sitting at Moriah's table, drinking tea like they were old friends." He listened a moment. "Okay. We'll meet you outside of Mori's in five minutes."

He punched off the com. The look he gave Nessa appeared sympathetic, but she knew better. "Well, *pilgrim*, I wouldn't want to be in your shoes when Chase gets here. He's not very happy with you right now."

"I'm not very happy with him, either," she replied with a bravado she didn't feel. Now she probably would spend the remainder of the trip in the brig.

Moriah returned just then, and Sabin moved to the end of the alcove with her. She handed him a computer disk and they talked in low voices.

Wondering if she might be able to give Sabin the slip, Nessa sidled through the beads into the main chamber and headed toward the entry.

"Don't even think about it," Sabin called after her. "Stay right there. Chase will be here in just a minute."

She sighed, realizing she could not elude Sabin and Chase when she didn't even know where to look for transport. Somehow, she didn't think Moriah would offer a haven from the two. She'd have to fall back on her computer program and see if she could access Chase's ship operations.

Resigned, she turned her attention to the vast array of goods in the mercantile. The brightly colored clothing interested her the most. A Saija silk robe in a deep russet color caught her eye. She couldn't help but stroke the whispery fabric. She'd never felt anything so soft.

"Beautiful, isn't it?" Moriah spoke quietly from behind her.

Nessa drew back. "I'm sorry. I shouldn't have touched it. I've never seen anything so fine."

"Saija silk is meant to be touched. No harm done." Smiling gently, Moriah patted her shoulder. "Nessa, you really need to go with Chase. He's one of the few shadowers who can be trusted to get you safely to your destination."

That might be true, Nessa thought, if she wasn't a Shielder. But if Chase discovered that fact, her days would be numbered. Prisoners in a Controller holding facility had short life spans indeed. And if she didn't get to Sonoma within the next few weeks, her life was over anyway. No, she couldn't depend on Chase for anything. She'd have to find another way, although for now, she had no choice.

She gave the robe one last glance, then turned back. "Thank you for the tea and the caroba, Moriah."

"Any time, little friend." Moriah offered her hand once more. "Good luck. I hope you see your eclipse and that your goddess smiles upon you."

Sabin grunted and rolled his eyes. "Fat chance,"

he muttered. He hugged Moriah, holding her close a long moment. "I don't know how long I'll be. We'll be stirring up the riffraff out there, so there might be some laser action. You be careful, Mori. Stay inside and don't take any unnecessary chances, you understand?"

"You worry too much, shadower. I can take care of myself."

"Be careful." Sabin repeated, his hands lingering on her hips as he released her. "Later."

"Promises, promises. Bye, Nessa."

Moriah watched Sabin and Nessa leave. They stepped out into the lifeless surroundings that seemed even bleaker to her after having been inside Moriah's wonderful store. The dusty thoroughfare remained deserted. Obviously, the inhabitants of Calt were late risers.

Sabin glanced around. "Where is McKnight? I guess we'll meet him halfway." Taking Nessa's arm firmly, he marched her toward the landing strip. The sun rose higher now, building the temperature to almost unbearable levels with its ascent. Heat waves created distorted images of the hodgepodge of ships, and as she struggled to keep up with him, she drew in a searing breath.

"Damn fool thing to do," Sabin muttered, pulling her along without any regard for her leg. "For a Shielder, you don't show much intelligence. I should just leave you alone out here and let the riff-raff finish you off. I don't have time to play protector to a crippled runt."

His words hit home with stinging accuracy. Nessa jerked back. "Why don't you just leave me, then? I'd rather deal with known criminals than a traitor."

Sabin swung around, grabbing her shoulders in a punishing grip. "Don't tempt me. If you were my responsibility, I'd have washed my hands of you long before now." He glanced up. "There's Chase."

Chase strode toward them, his rapid pace eating up the distance. He had on his helmet, with the visor raised. Sabin gripped Nessa's arm, as if afraid she might try to flee. The thought had definite appeal as Chase approached. He must be furious with her, yet his expression showed nothing.

He stopped beside them, hardly sparing her a glance. "Thanks for holding her, Travers. Did you make arrangements?"

"Yeah. Meet me at Giza's in thirty minutes. Thorne will be there by then. It should be safe enough. It's way too early for most of these space scum to be up and about."

"Sounds good." Chase took her arm in a death grip. "I'll take Nessa back to the ship, then meet you there. Be very careful."

Sabin looked offended. "I'm always careful. It's the older ones I worry about. *You* be careful, old man."

Chase snorted. "You don't know Dansan like I do, Travers. Believe me, age and experience help when dealing with that criminal. Again, take great care."

"I will." Sabin headed back into the settlement.

Without a word, Chase turned toward the landing strip. He, too, walked rapidly, without regard for Nessa's awkward gait. Determined not to complain, she stumbled along beside him.

They had passed one building when he froze. Halting, Nessa looked to where his gaze focused, but she could see nothing but a cloud of dust.

"Someone's coming," he hissed in a low voice. "Quick! We have to get out of sight." He half-dragged, half-carried her back to the building they'd just passed and hauled her around the corner.

He squatted down, pulling her with him. "Stay close to the building," he whispered, then crawled forward to peer around the corner. He drew back quickly. "By the blazing hells. That's Brutus, one of Dansan's henchmen. What in the Abyss is he up to? Don't make a sound."

He pressed flat against the wall, forcing Nessa to do the same. She could see the cloud of sand signaling the approaching villain. The involuntary gasp that escaped her when Brutus walked past would have given them away if Chase hadn't clamped his hand over her mouth. She couldn't help herself. An Antek! Hulking and ominous, he lumbered by, unaware of their presence.

Chase leaned close to her ear. "Not another sound until I say," he whispered furiously. Nessa nodded. Releasing her, he inched to the corner and peeked around. "By the fires! He's headed for Giza's."

He sank back against the wall, glaring at her. "From now on, try to control yourself, before you get us killed. One more screwup like that and I'll gag you."

Nessa barely heard him. She stared toward the street, repressing a shiver. An Antek. She'd seen pictures and heard the gory tales, but seeing the real thing only brought the terrifying reality home. Anteks were barbaric brutes who carried out Controller orders efficiently and without mercy.

"Dansan's a Controller?" She blurted out, drawing the obvious conclusion.

"No. Dansan is a criminal—and far worse than any Controller." Chase slid forward and glanced around the corner again.

Her thoughts whirling, Nessa crept along behind him. "But you said Brutus works for Dansan."

"Brutus is a renegade Antek. Dansan employs an entire troop of them." Chase tensed. "He just went inside Giza's. Damn. It's too early. Something's wrong. I hope to the Spirit Sabin didn't go straight there." He reached back and grasped Nessa's arm. "Come on. I don't have time to take you to the ship. You'll stay at Moriah's until Sabin or I come for you."

Sensing his urgency, she didn't question the abrupt change of plan. She slipped out quietly and followed him to Moriah's, still trying to make sense of Anteks pledging allegiance to a non-Controller. To the best of her knowledge, all Anteks underwent Controller mind-indoctrination, as did officials and leaders of all planets; as did all agents—including shadowers. How could an Antek break free of the formidable Controller domination?

Chase stopped in front of the mercantile. "Get inside." He motioned toward the building, then turned away.

"Where are you going?" she called after him.

"To find out if my partner just walked into a trap.

Now get." He strode toward a building gatercorner across the square, pulling a phaser from his holster as he went.

Nessa hadn't noticed the pyramid-shaped structure before. Since it had a huge *G* emblazoned on the sand-colored wall facing her, she assumed it must be Giza's.

She started up the mercantile steps, her gaze focused on Chase. Catlike, he moved onto the covered walkway edging the pyramid and vanished around the side. She took another step, prepared to go inside, when a movement caught her eye, drawing her gaze back to Giza's.

Two massive Anteks prowled from behind the pyramid, then stomped off in the same direction Chase had gone, into the dimness of the covered pathway. Terror exploded through her body, trapping her breath. The impulse to flee burst over her; a need to escape as far as possible from the nightmarish Anteks.

She looked around wildly. Where could she go? Moriah couldn't offer sanctuary against two Anteks. But these Anteks didn't work for the Controllers, more rational reason interjected—or so Chase had said. They worked for some criminal named Dansan. Nessa's thoughts lurched in another direction. Both Chase and Sabin might have just entered an ambush.

Hideous scenarios flashed through her mind. Anteks torturing Chase; killing him. No! She couldn't lose Chase—not now. She tried to ignore the concern unfurling inside her, to convince herself that she only cared because she needed Chase for transport to Intrepid. Yet whatever the reasons, she knew she had to help him.

Nessa scurried down the steps and across the expanse to Giza's, halting only after she was safely in the shadows at the base. She slid her knife from her boot, then pressed against the wall, waiting for her labored breath to calm. Hearing voices to her right, she inched in that direction.

Reaching the corner, she glanced around and saw light from an open doorway about four meters away. The voices grew louder, although still indistinct, as she inched farther toward the entry. Just outside the door panel, she crouched down.

"Well, Brutus, what say you about our prize?" a deep but distinctly female voice asked.

"We pleased, Dan-san. Always to serve you."

"Clever answer," the voice purred. "Here, have a reward."

A gruntlike snort followed. Nessa glanced over her shoulder, finding the area behind her deserted. Falling to all fours, she crawled to the panel frame and edged forward enough to see in.

An overpowering reek of filthy, hairy bodies assaulted her, and she pushed back a surge of nausea. Breathing through her mouth, she surveyed the cavernous room that was dimly lit by solar flares. Massive, thronelike chairs, ornately carved with bizarre designs, were scattered around like huts in a Shielder colony.

Six Anteks ringed the room, their eyes intent on a woman slouched high upon one of the huge chairs, which had been placed on the counter running along the left wall. Nessa's attention fixed on the Anteks in morbid fascination. This close, she realized how huge they were, nearly seven feet tall and of massive girth. Their snouts dominated their broad faces, making them look more beastlike than humanoid. Small, dull eyes peered out from beneath protruding brows. Short bristles covered their skulls, obscuring flush ear openings. At their necks, the bristles gave way to hairy whorls, which she guessed covered their entire bodies. And their rank smell—awful. Grimacing Nessa turned her attention to the woman seated on the counter.

The woman propped her booted feet upon an acrylic crate. Snowy white hair flowed over the woman's shoulders and down her back. Sharp, almost colorless eyes glinted in a pallid face devoid of any emotion. Reaching into a bucket beside her, she lifted a piece of bloody meat. "And you, Brutus. You caught the enemy. You get an extra reward." She tossed the meat to an Antek across the room, blood spraying in all directions.

Brutus caught it in midair and shoved it into a mouth full of sharp teeth. Another Antek rushed toward the bucket, but stopped short when she whipped up an electrolyzer rod. "Uh-uh, Keret. You've already had yours."

She must be Dansan. The Antek had called her by that name. Nessa studied the woman, unable to determine her age. Her body, sheathed in a snug silver flightsuit, appeared firm and muscled, but her face showed signs of age. "My, my, but we do have cause for celebration," Dansan cackled, casting a lazy glance to Nessa's far left.

Sabin. He was slumped over in a chair, appar-

119

ently unconscious. Electronic shackles bound his wrists together behind the chair, while others secured his ankles. Blood oozed from a cut over his eye and his flightsuit was torn.

Nessa barely restrained her gasp of horror. Then she almost gasped again when she saw Chase crouched behind another chair on the opposite side of Sabin. He must have sensed her, for he looked up, shocked, then signaled furiously at her to get away. He crept behind Sabin. Deftly, he snapped a decoder on the shackle lock, then slipped back behind the other chair.

"What should we do with our prize, soldiers?" Dansan's exultant voice echoed across the room. "Cut him up and have him for our morning meal?"

Snorts and hoots of approval met this comment. Horrified, Nessa watched the decoder, hoping it would quickly find the unlocking sequence, although she wasn't sure how Chase and Sabin could escape six Anteks and their leader. She thought she saw Sabin's fingers move slightly.

"Before we enjoy some sport with Shadower Travers, we need a drink!" Dansan swung her feet from the crate and leaped up. "Thorne! Where are you? You have guests. We want a drink." She pounded the electrolyzer rod against the counter.

"Thorne! Thorne! Thorne!" the Anteks took up the chant, stomping and pounding.

A little man scurried through a panel behind the bar. "This is highly irregular," he sputtered in a shrill voice. "I'm not open for business until twelve hundred hours."

Dansan's eyes narrowed to transparent slits. "Oh,

really? Now isn't that just too bad. You see, Thorne, the Ants and I are having a special celebration, in honor of our friend over there. And you know how the Ants like to celebrate. It occurs to me that if you give them drinks to keep them occupied, they won't tear up your place. Seems fair enough, doesn't it?"

Brutus lumbered up behind Thorne and grasped the little man's tunic, lifting him off his feet. "Fair, Thorne?" he grunted.

Thorne's face paled considerably as his feet kicked uselessly at the air. "All right, all right!" he gurgled. "For you, Dansan, I'm open for business."

"I'm so glad you share our enthusiasm over the capture of Shadower Travers," Dansan purred, then nodded to Brutus.

He dropped Thorne, who crashed to the floor, then scrambled shakily to his feet. "Drinks coming up." He hurried behind the bar.

Dansan strutted along the counter, looking down upon her henchmen. "So, who wants to 'play' with Travers first? How about you, Keret? Wasn't it your brother he killed and turned in, for a measly two hundred miterons?"

Keret growled and spun toward Sabin. Dansan swung up the electrolyzer rod threateningly. "I haven't given the go-ahead yet. How about you, Raik? Didn't he give you that phaser scar on your leg?"

"Drinks." Thorne announced, shoving a tray on the counter. A loud clink followed his announcement, only it came from Sabin's direction. All heads turned that way. Sabin remained slumped over his legs, but the shackles lay open on the tile. The decoder had obviously done its job.

Dansan leaped to the floor. "What in the Abyss—"

"Heads up, Sabin," Chase whispered loudly, skidding a phaser along the tile behind Sabin.

Nessa started when Sabin's head shot up. He snatched the phaser and leaped to his feet in one smooth motion. At a light-speed blur, he phasered the second shackle, right between his ankles, then rolled toward the entry.

"Get him!" Dansan screeched, and the Anteks scrambled forward. Chase threw his chair at two Anteks and rolled after Sabin. He and Sabin hurled themselves behind other chairs and opened fire, which the Anteks returned. Phaser beams exploded everywhere, burning chunks of wood from the chairs. Dansan dived over the bar to relative safety, with Thorne right behind her.

Nessa clutched her knife and scrambled to her feet, although she stayed clear of the panel and pretty much out of view. Turi hissed in alarm, but she didn't have time to reassure him. Three Anteks were down, and Dansan had fled through the rear exit. Two other Anteks engaged Chase and Sabin in a crossfire. The sight of Brutus maneuvering into position behind Chase sent shock waves through her.

"Chase!" she screamed. "Behind you!"

But he couldn't hear her over the din of the phaser battle. Brutus raised his weapon, aiming it at Chase's head. Nessa acted on instinct, calling upon skills she'd learned seasons ago. She hurled her knife, burying it in Brutus's back. He dropped the phaser and, with a cry of rage, whirled in her direction.

His eyes clouded with pain, he charged at her like a wild animal. Her heart exploded with adrenaline. She barely managed to sidestep the crazed Antek, for her rubbery limbs were uncooperative.

Turi scrambled from the pack, clawing her shoulder in the process. Brutus staggered, then regained his balance and hurtled toward her. She leaped back frantically, just as Turi let out a shrill yelp and catapulted himself through the air.

He landed on Brutus's face, biting and scratching.

"No!" Nessa screamed, rushing forward. "Turi, no!"

Bellowing, Brutus tore Turi off and hurled the lanrax across the room. He hit the wall hard and fell to the floor with a sickening thud. He twitched, then stilled.

"Turi!" Nessa tried to go to him, but Brutus grabbed her. He wrenched her arm and she gasped from the pain. He raised his hand to strike her, then froze, his eyes opening wide as a blast sounded behind him. A grunt escaped him and he fell to the floor, a gaping phaser wound next to the protruding knife in his back. Phaser in hand, Chase leaped over him and shoved Nessa toward the entry. Sabin followed.

"Let's get out of here." Chase dragged her through the entry.

"No. I can't leave Turi!" she cried, struggling against his hold. "I can't leave him!"

"He's gone, Nessa. Come on."

"You'd better hurry, if you're going to catch Dan-san." Sabin took her other arm.

She bucked and kicked, grief clouding her reason. "He can't be dead! Not Turi. We can't leave him! We can't."

"We have to leave—now." Chase didn't attempt to placate her further. Sweeping her up, he swung her over his shoulder and broke into a run.

They ran to Moriah's, where Chase borrowed a two-seat land skimmer. A stupor pervaded Nessa's senses, and she didn't protest when Chase hauled her into the skimmer, then jumped in beside her. As they sped to the ship, she sat frozen, her grief crystallizing around her heart. She didn't resist when Chase hustled her aboard and strapped her in for takeoff.

Turi was gone. One of the few lights in her life had been snuffed out.

Chapter Eight

Dansan had evaded him again. Vanished like vapor, probably into one of the numerous wormholes connecting the quadrant's vast expanses. Staring at the blank sensor screen, Chase kicked a console and swore profusely. *He'd almost had her!* So close.

Yet he'd failed—the story of his life.

His head and shoulder throbbed, but it was no less than he deserved. Each unsuccessful attempt to capture Dansan only served to remind him how he had failed his people when they had desperately needed him.

He touched his forehead and winced. His fingers came away sticky with blood. The cut wasn't serious but needed tending if he didn't want it to get infected. His wound from Saron had not had time to heal completely; it probably needed to be checked as well. He set the ships coordinates for

Star Base Intrepid, then headed to the lab to get some antiseptic.

When he passed Nessa's chamber's closed panel, he slowed. Blazing hells. Here he was, thinking only of himself. He hadn't even checked on her since she'd fled the cockpit after takeoff. He hadn't even stopped to consider that her daring action had saved his wretched hide, or bothered to thank her. He'd been too enmeshed in self-pity.

By the Spirit, he had turned into a selfish bastard.

For all he knew, she might well have a dislocated shoulder, after the way Brutus had wrenched her arm. Plus she'd just lost her only companion, wretched creature that it was.

He knew what it was like to lose everything.

He sounded the panel tone. "Nessa, may I come in?"

Silence. He pressed the tone again. "Are you all right?"

"Go away."

"I'm coming in." He opened the panel.

Slumped on the floor, she leaned against the side of the bunk with her arms around her legs. Her eyes, dry but stark with pain, stared toward the now empty plexishield case, where a half-eaten piece of bread lay on the bottom. She didn't acknowledge his presence.

"Nessa." He sank down beside her, not sure how to take her stoic, detached demeanor. She might be in shock. "Are you okay?" He cupped his hand against her pale cheek, then slid his fingers down against the pulse in her neck.

It was steady enough, but she felt abnormally

cool, and her ashen complexion alarmed him. "Does it hurt anywhere?"

Fixated on the case, she shook her head almost imperceptibly. Chase saw the blood then, oozing through slashes in the right shoulder of her tunic. When he touched the shoulder, she winced. "Is this the same arm Brutus hurt?"

"It doesn't matter," she whispered, her voice dull and flat.

Remorse and concern welled through Chase. "It does matter, Nessa." He took her cold hands, tugging her good arm away from her legs. "Come on. I'm taking you to the lab so I can treat your shoulder."

She tried to pull back. "I just want to be alone."

"Later," he promised, grasping her waist and lifting her to her feet. "But right now, captain's orders are for you to receive medical treatment. We'll take care of the pain, too."

"I don't need treatment. The pain doesn't bother me." She shoved against his chest, wincing again from the pressure on her injured shoulder, then quickly hid her discomfort.

Considering her leg, pain had probably been a familiar and constant companion. But Chase had no intention of her suffering more than she already had, especially since he bore the blame for this situation. If he'd only thought to take more precautions before leaving Nessa on the ship; if he'd been more alert and insisted on accompanying Sabin to Giza's . . .

The realization that even more people had almost

127

died because of him burned a path of self-contempt through his gut.

"This is not open for debate, Nessa. You can either walk to the lab, or I'll carry you. Your choice."

For a minute, he thought she would defy him. But she turned and limped slowly down the corridor. He followed behind, noting her awkward gait. She had pushed herself to her limits today—and saved his life in the process. Sabin was the only person Chase would ever expect to show such heroism on his behalf.

He shuddered as they entered the lab. Spirit, how he despised this room. The equipment, the medical supplies, the antiseptic smell—they all reminded him of his inadequacies. Even though he'd sworn to never set foot in a lab again, common sense had prevailed when he'd ordered this ship. He'd requested a fully equipped medical laboratory.

A shadower's occupation invited danger, and while he had little respect for his own safety, Chase refused to put innocent people at risk. If Sabin or a bystander suffered injury because of him, he wanted to have the tools for their treatment.

Nessa stood listlessly in the middle of the room, apathy dulling her expression. Taking a thermal blanket from the linen cabinet, Chase laid it on the table. "Take off your pack and your tunic. You can get under the blanket." He placed his hands into the wall sterilizer.

The sterilizer beeped off, and he turned back to find her clutching the tunic tightly. This promised to be a battle the entire way. He didn't know if her reluctance to disrobe in front of him came from feminine modesty or shame from her scarred leg, or both. If she only knew how many nude bodies he had examined—Chase exhaled his pent-up breath. Besides, he'd already seen *all* of her, although he wouldn't point that out.

"I can't treat those cuts through the tunic." He picked up the thermal blanket and handed it to her. "Now, slip off the pack and your tunic and wrap this around yourself, but keep your shoulders bare. I'll get the supplies."

He turned toward the medication cabinet. At her soft gasp, he spun around. Nessa clutched the pack that had carried the lanrax. Tufts of midnight blue fur clung near the top. She stared at the fur, her hands trembling, her face deathly white. "Turi," she whispered. "Oh, Turi."

Her anguish tore at Chase. He strode over and slid his arm around her. She raised startled but dry eyes to his. "It's okay to grieve, Nessa. It's all right to cry and even scream, if that helps."

Her eyes reflected the depth of her torment, but no tears. "I never cry. It's useless and weak."

She looked so vulnerable, so fragile, her body rigid with the effort to maintain her composure. But she hardly appeared weak. In fact, Chase admired her spunk and her courage.

Even with her physical handicaps, even after losing her parents, breaking down in space, getting caught up in a battle not hers to fight, she'd persevered. Even sustaining new injuries and then losing her only companion, she displayed amazing fortitude.

No, he'd never see her as weak.

"Put on the blanket," he said, turning away.

Nessa remained silent while Chase helped her onto the exam table and sterilized the gouges left by Turi, then bandaged them. She shivered with cold, despite the thermal blanket, and he lowered a heatwave light over the table. Her shoulder had not been dislocated or her arm broken; both were only bruised.

His medical scanner picked up a virus, the same one present the first two times he'd checked her. He didn't recognize the viral structure, but thousands of viruses existed in the galaxy, the vast majority harmless. Probably a cold incubating—although it was going to be a nasty one, if the proliferation of the cells were any indication.

He gave her a combination injection for shock, infection, and pain. The warmth and the medication would drain away her tension and pain. He watched as she quickly surrendered to exhaustion, falling asleep on the table.

Chase left her there, placing more blankets over her. He sterilized her tunic, although it was badly torn and would have to be replaced at the first opportunity. He placed the tunic beside her, but folded the pack, slipped it into an airtight plastic bag, and then put it in a cabinet. He'd sneezed repeatedly while he was treating Nessa because of that damn pack, and he'd been tempted to disintegrate it. But he decided that might upset her further. If she asked for it, he would return it to her.

After he cleaned the cut over his eye and tended his shoulder wound, he returned to his cabin. He shed and disposed of his ruined flightsuit and took a long shower. Then he collapsed on his bunk and slept, awakening several hours later.

He went to check on Nessa and found her leaving the lab, dressed in her tunic. "Hello," he said.

She gazed at him, her eyes huge orbs of distress in her small face. Her color had improved somewhat, but dark hollows lurked beneath her eyes. She dropped her gaze and started past him.

He blocked the path. "How are you feeling?"

"Better." She raised her caroba gaze again. "Thank you for taking care of my shoulder."

Chase steered her toward the galley. "It was the least I could do. Thank you for saving my life."

Nessa tugged against his grip. "I'd like to go to my cabin now."

"A stop in the galley first. You need some nourishment. Then you can go to your cabin and rest."

She remained withdrawn and distant as she drank the simple broth he prepared. Neither of them spoke until she rose from the table. He rose with her. "Let me take you to your cabin."

She offered no argument and he opened the panel, to her chamber, stepping in behind her. At the sight of the empty plexishield case, her body went rigid. Her hands clenched by her sides, she trembled visibly. Chase cursed himself for not thinking to remove all reminders.

"Here, let me get rid of this." He moved around and grabbed the case.

"No . . . wait." She stepped forward and lifted the lid. Reaching in, she picked up the half-eaten piece of bread. "He loved your bread," she whispered. "He'd never had fresh bread before."

By the Spirit. Chase set down the case and turned to her. "It's okay to cry, Nessa. Really. It's not a weakness."

"I *don't* cry," she insisted. Her fingers stroked the bread. "I shouldn't have left him. . . . What if he was still alive? What if he was frightened and needed me?"

He patted her good shoulder. "He couldn't have survived the force of hitting that wall. He never knew what happened. He didn't suffer. We had to leave when we did."

Nessa looked at him solemnly. "You had to try to catch Dansan."

Her voice held no recrimination. She could have blamed him for forcing her to leave her beloved pet behind. She could have railed at him for allowing his obsession with Dansan to take her only companion from her. But she didn't. Instead, she'd apparently accepted the harsh realities of a world that had never dealt her a fair hand.

Again, remorse at his own selfishness swept through Chase.

"I should never have left the ship." Nessa's voice shook. "If I hadn't been so stupid, Turi would be alive now." Her voice broke completely, and he gathered her against him.

"You didn't know," he soothed, although he knew he should be reading her the riot act for leaving the ship. But he didn't have the heart in the face of her guilt. He had enough guilt of his own to judge anyone else. "It wasn't your fault, Nessa."

"It was." A small sob escaped. Then another. "Spirit, but I never cry."

Chase pulled her closer. "Then now is a good time to start. Go ahead and cry, Nessa. It's okay."

The floodgates burst then, and she sobbed against his chest, wrenched by waves of grief and anguish. He swept her into his arms and sank onto the bunk, cradling her against him.

He just let her cry, holding her tightly and murmuring reassuring words. He suspected she cried for more than Turi's loss; perhaps for her parents, or her destitute circumstances. If the duration of the flood was any indication, she'd been stockpiling tears for a long time.

Finally, the storm spent, she burrowed against him quietly. Her hands clutched his flightsuit as if it were a lifeline. Chase stroked the damp curls around her face, an immense tenderness welling up inside him. He hadn't been needed like this, hadn't responded to another's suffering in a long time . . . a very long time. "Are you okay?"

She raised her tear-streaked face to his, her eyes reddened, but no longer so haunted. He found himself drawn into their dark depths as she slowly nodded. He caressed her cheek, soaking up the dampness there. Spirit, but she had the softest skin, like the petals of an Elysian starflower.

Of its own volition, his hand slid along her neck, feeling the erratic pulse there, then to her shoulder. Wondering if she was that soft all over, he slipped his fingers beneath her tunic and stroked her shoulder and the back of her neck. Velvet. His pulse quickened. Her sharp intake of breath told him she wasn't unaffected by the contact either.

"Chase," she whispered. His gaze dropped to her

lips—lush and trembling. Heat spiraled through him, settling in his lower extremities. He shouldn't do this, he told himself. He shouldn't. Leaning down, he touched his lips to hers. She didn't pull away.

Stop this now. You've both suffered tremendous stress, Chase's rational side argued valiantly. *She's vulnerable right now—and very innocent.*

But her tentative, sweet foray with the tip of her tongue, the sensuous feel of her, drove all rational thoughts from his head. Hormones took over, and he deepened the kiss. His hand slid down the outside of her tunic, cupping her breast. She pressed against him and he was lost. Tearing his mouth away, he kissed the softness of her neck, then moved his lips lower.

"Nessa, Nessa," he muttered against her heaving breast. Need bolted through him; need so sharp he felt as if he'd been hit by a laser blast. He clamped his mouth onto the soft mound, frantically tonguing the nipple through the rough fabric. She cried out in surprised pleasure.

More. He needed more.

Breathing harshly, he yanked her tunic open. Her small breasts were beautifully rounded, like dainty tarini fruit, perfectly symmetrical. The sight of her nipples beaded into tight nubs sent shockwaves to his manhood. He cupped one breast, rubbing his thumb over the nipple. She gasped again.

"This is also part of mating, Nessa," he murmured hoarsely. "Do you like it?" He moved to her other breast and fondled it. "Do you?"

She arched against him. "Yes. Oh, yes."

She wanted this, too. At least her body did.

Chase knew with certainty that if he slipped his hand beneath her tunic, he'd find her female core wet and hot, ready for his male invasion. He also knew he should slow down, initiate her leisurely into this new realm of sensuality.

But then she grabbed his hair and pulled his face up to hers. Her mouth found and mated hungrily with his. He tasted the salt of her tears, the desperation of her need. With a groan, he returned her kiss, tasting deeply, invading her mouth. He continued stroking her breasts and teasing her nipples. Her soft moans, her frantic movements against him, urged him onward.

He pulled her upright, slipping her tunic off and down her arms. She released him long enough to shake away her tunic, then pressed herself against him. Keeping their mouths sealed together, he pushed his hands between them, unfastening and tearing off the top of his flightsuit. She murmured a protest when he broke the kiss to stand and yank off his boots, then the pants.

He came down upon her again, kissing her eyes, her neck, her breasts, finally latching onto a nipple and drawing it into his mouth. "Chase!" she cried, thrashing beneath his relentless suckling.

Spirit, but she tasted sweet. He moved to the other breast, mouthing the nipple and sucking it until she stopped thrashing and clutched his head against her. The blood pounded like a raging tide through his body.

He moved his hand down her slender thigh. "Open your legs, sweetheart." Mindlessly, she

135

obeyed, and he stroked the soft flesh of her womanhood, reassuring her when she almost surged off the bunk. "It's okay, Nessa. Touching you everywhere is part of mating."

Sinking back, she allowed his intimate touch, moaning softly when he slid a finger inside. He lifted his head to watch her face as he moved his finger in and out. She was tight, virginal, as he had known she would be. Amazingly, her hymen was still intact. A distant part of him knew he should take her back into the lab and painlessly remove the membrane, as was so often done these days.

But as he felt her wetness increase around his finger, heard her panting helplessly while she instinctively opened her thighs wider and arched into the pleasure of his strokes, he couldn't wait any longer. He slid in a second finger and she moaned again. Stars, she was tight, but she was ready for him.

"Sweetheart, I'm coming inside now," he whispered, positioning his body over hers. "Relax, and let me in."

She raised her hips as he pressed his manhood against her. As gently as possible, he began the push inside her, slowly, so slowly, he didn't know if he'd survive. She cried out, arching in pain now instead of pleasure. He pressed through the barrier, then all the way in, and stopped. "Nessa? Are you okay?"

"No," she gasped. "No more." He had lost her. The pain of penetration overwhelmed the need of passion. She didn't utter another sound, but her nails digging into his shoulders and the tenseness of her body indicated her suffering.

He should withdraw, but all she'd ever known was pain. If he released her now, with only the memory of the pain and not the pleasure, she'd never let him near her again. Somehow, he couldn't bear that happening.

"Relax, Nessa, relax," he urged against her ear. "The pain will ease, I promise. Then there will be pleasure."

She shook her head violently, and he held himself still, straining with the effort. Brushing her hair from her face, he pulled back enough to kiss her gently, coaxing her tongue to dance with his. He touched her, caressing her breasts and stroking the sensitive nub between her legs. He waited, continuing his sensual assault, until she moaned again, this time with pleasure.

Then he moved inside of her, with painstaking, torturous slowness at first. He rocked her in the mesmerizing movements of mating, increasing the tempo, until she responded, lifting her hips to meet his. His control broke then, and he thrust hard and fast, urging her to go on with him. But as the momentary oblivion descended with the explosive release of his body, he knew she hadn't reached the summit.

He held Nessa close while his breathing returned to normal. She lay passive and silent in his embrace. He regretted that she hadn't shared the euphoria of climax.

Other regrets surged forward, especially when he lifted his head and looked into her closed face. Guilt gnawed at him. He had given in to his baser needs, taking advantage of a grieving, innocent woman-child.

He'd relinquished control to the odd attraction that had drawn him to her from their first meeting. Even worse, he'd hurt her, more than just physically. Lasting relationships would never exist for him. He couldn't offer her what she desperately needed: permanence, stability, love. Nessa deserved to be cherished and loved.

He was no longer capable of love—only hatred. And at this moment, he hated himself.

He stroked her hair back from her face. "Are you okay?"

She nodded, her eyes expressionless. Her usual reply, he thought, shifting his weight off and settling on his side next to her. He swept his hand along her collarbone, down across her breast and over her rib cage. He could span her tiny waist with his hands. He frowned when he saw the scars on her abdomen. Odd, but he hadn't noticed them before. Leaning forward, he studied the two scars, tracing his finger along their raised ridges.

Tensing suddenly, Nessa tried to push his hand away. Anger rocketed through him. He knew what those scars were. The result of sterilization—by an incredibly barbaric and crude method. Livid, he raised his gaze to her. "Who did this to you?"

"I don't want to talk about it." She shoved against him and rolled from the bunk.

Grabbing her wrist, he swung upright and pulled her back. "Who did this?"

138

Her eyes finally came to life, myriad emotions sweeping through them. "Please. I've had enough."

Chase stared at her, feeling the tremors in her arm. He released her wrist and she fled to the lavatory. She had retreated from him, mentally as well as physically. Her words drilled into his conscience.

She'd had enough.

Of pain, of isolation—of him, he was certain.

He hadn't even displayed enough stamina or restraint to ensure that she enjoyed her first sexual encounter. She'd suffered the discomfort, but not the enjoyment. If her reaction proved any indication, she wouldn't be anxious to repeat the experience.

The image of those scars jumped into his mind. He was beginning to wonder if Nessa had ever known any kindness. Her experiences had made her mentally tough, yet despite the obvious hardships she'd faced, she displayed an innate gentleness and concern for others. But now . . . would she ever let another man touch her?

Probably not, and the blame rested with him. How many had already suffered needlessly because of his incompetence? Disgusted with himself, Chase rolled from the bunk. Seeing the blood on the covering, he wanted to kick himself. He yanked off the blanket. No sense in letting Nessa see it.

He wouldn't come near her again. She deserved a real man, a capable man who had something to offer. Not him. He didn't intend to hurt her any more than he already had.

*   *   *

Nessa leaned against the shower wall, letting the spray wash over her. If only it could cleanse away her disgrace, her embarrassment . . . the memory of the shocking things Chase had done to her. And the astonishing, incredible sensations . . . and the way she'd enjoyed it—until he'd hurt her so badly. The information she'd read on mating had never mentioned the pain.

If it was like that every time, she couldn't understand why people would mate, except for the necessity of bearing offspring. Children. One thing she'd never have to worry about.

A searing ache filled Nessa's chest and she clutched her abdomen. She'd always harbored a fondness for children, always dreamed of having little ones who would return her love, even if she was a freak. That choice had been denied her. At least she couldn't pass on her physical defect to an innocent child.

But it hurt to be barren. To have nothing to offer, nothing to give. It amazed her that Chase had even chosen to mate with her. He wouldn't want to again, she felt certain. She thought of Moriah, with her stunning beauty and perfect body. She remembered how she and Sabin had looked at each other, their lingering touches. Surely Chase would prefer that, prefer a woman who was beautiful and whole; one who had something to offer.

Not a deformed female who had even been spurned by her own people. Chase's mating with her had been a mistake. He was too intelligent to repeat his mistakes. Nessa wouldn't risk further humiliation or pain.

She would avoid Chase the remainder of the trip.

Chapter Nine

Nessa rose early the next cycle, tired from a restless night. The horrifying mental picture of Turi crashing against the wall, intermingled with thoughts of Chase and her traumatic mating with him, had robbed her of sleep. She'd been relieved to find him gone after her shower, although the emptiness of Turi's case, along with a sense of profound loneliness, almost made her long for Chase's comforting presence.

Somehow he knew when she stirred from her bunk, because he rang her panel tone just minutes after she arose. Nessa stiffened, not ready to face Chase just yet. But she knew well enough that he'd enter her cabin with or without her permission.

She braced herself. "Come in."

He did, prompting her to take an involuntary step back. He always had that effect on her, his size crowding out everything else in her small cabin.

Dark circles accentuated his eyes, making him look as tired as she felt. "How are you feeling this morning?"

His deep voice brought unwelcome images of the two of them intimately entwined. She forced a breath into her lungs. "Fine."

He studied her intently. "You'll probably be sore for a few days. I brought you this salve. It will help ease any discomfort." He held out a tube.

Without looking directly at him, she took it. Fervently, she prayed to Spirit he'd leave now.

He didn't. "Nessa . . . Nessa, I'm sorry about last night. It should never have happened. I take full responsibility. It wasn't your fault."

Nessa saw no cause for blame. Chase had mistakenly mated with her, and now he regretted it. Simple—and understandable. "It's okay," she whispered through a tightened throat.

Chase stepped toward her, halting when she scooted away. "You don't have to worry about it happening again," he said quietly.

She knew it wouldn't. Not with Chase, not with anyone. She met his intent gaze with as much composure as she could muster. "I understand."

There seemed no need for further words, and with a brief nod, he left.

For the next few days, he appeared as anxious as Nessa to avoid all contact. Their only real discussions occurred when she didn't want to come to the galley for meals. He would have none of that. She was going to eat—with him—and that was final.

Even though Nessa avoided Chase outside of the stilted meals they shared, the computer drew her

142

like a magnet. With Turi gone, her cabin seemed even more stark and lonely. Chase had never removed Turi's case, and it served as a glaring reminder of her loss. To escape her grief, she fled to the cockpit, seeking comfort in the wealth of knowledge found in the computer.

Enmeshed in the IAR link, she learned of fabulous other worlds, while Chase stared stonily at the controls. Even as she tried to ignore his presence, Nessa found herself drawn to him. She sneaked furtive glances at his handsome profile, admiring the breadth and power of his shoulders.

Memories of his touch and the desire their mating had evoked filled her mind and sent strange sensations coursing through her body. She tried to push the disturbing feelings away, but every time she saw Chase, they surfaced.

He seemed unaffected by her presence, however, remaining aloof and distant. Bitterly, Nessa understood his coolness all too well. He wanted nothing more to do with her, with her ugly body and freakish seizures. Although she'd faced this scenario for ten seasons, had dealt with being spurned and ignored, somehow Chase's rejection hurt worse than the others.

So she buried herself in the computer, trying to push aside the ache that arose in her chest every time she thought about him.

She kept an anxious check on their destination. Thirteen days had passed since she'd been injected with Orana, almost half the time she had left. She should have been in Sonoma five days ago. Dark fears of not reaching Sonoma, of failing at her mission and then dying an agonizing death, nagged her. But she reassured herself with the knowledge that they would arrive at Star Base Intrepid in three days. She'd still have almost two weeks to get to Sonoma. So far, no signs of the disease had surfaced.

On the third day out of Calt, she slipped quietly into the cockpit. Staring at his terminal, Chase ignored her, as he had the past two days. Sliding into her chair, she immediately checked the destination screen, which she did every morning shift.

Shockwaves spiraled through her. Bold, ominous letters flashed across the a screen: DESTINATION: ELYSIA. Nessa stared at the words, dread settling in the pit of her stomach. Not only were they headed away from Intrepid, but Elysia was still another day away.

She gripped the console, trying to calm the ensuing panic. How could she convince Chase to take her to Intrepid without revealing the fact she was a Shielder? She stared at his stiff, unyielding back. No matter that he had treated her injuries, no matter what had passed between them, including the shared intimacy of mating, he was a *shadower*.

Capturing and turning in Shielders comprised many a shadower's financial mainstay. Controllers paid handsomely for Shielders, who could be identified by a simple blood test. Of course, shadowers couldn't go around the quadrant giving blood tests, which was why they frequently hired renegade Shielders. Traitors, like Sabin, who knew their own kind instantly, and who were granted immunity from destruction. Why Sabin hadn't revealed Nessa's identity remained a mystery.

Even if Chase cared enough for her to forego financial gain, he certainly wouldn't be able to override the formidable mind control implanted during indoctrination. It was a mental domination so powerful that it had enabled the Controllers to rule the quadrant for hundreds of seasons.

No, she couldn't tell Chase the truth . . . not even after lying naked in his arms. The insidious shadow of Controller influence infiltrated even the most private bonds. If Chase knew she was a Shielder, he would surrender to the inexorable compulsion to turn her in.

Gathering her courage, she rose and moved behind him. "Captain McKnight, I'd like to speak with you." She managed to keep her voice calm, but her control faltered when he swiveled around, his cool gaze locking with hers.

"What do you want?"

Clutching at the fabric of her tattered robe, she drew a deep breath and asked Spirit for a mighty dose of bravery.

"I want you to honor your word to take me to Star Base Intrepid. I want to go there immediately."

Nessa stood stiffly before him, glimpses of her pale flesh peeking through her torn tunic. The woman wanted to get to Intrepid as quickly as possible, and probably not just for that damned eclipse, either. She'd made it quite clear she wanted nothing further to do with him. Not that he blamed her. Yet even as he stared at her, his gaze coming to rest on her generous mouth, his body stirred.

He should be concentrating on second-guessing Dansan's next move, but he couldn't stop thinking about the velvety smoothness of Nessa's skin. Her cries of passion. Her incredible tightness around him as he'd initiated her into womanhood.

Knowing he'd been the first man to touch her so intimately affected him profoundly. The urge to possess her pulsed through him like a primitive litany . . . accompanied by an equally strong urge to protect her. He had to put an end to these dangerous feelings—and quickly.

At the next possible opportunity, he'd get Nessa to a star base—and out of his life. He'd been foolish to give in to temptation and head for Elysia. Marak had been among those who'd murdered his people, true, but he was merely one of Dansan's lieutenants, acting on her orders.

Besides, Marak was an idiot, leaving trails as clear as a nebula. Chase would easily get him sooner or later. But since he'd come this far toward Elysia, he'd go on and capture Marak.

Then he'd take Nessa to Intrepid. The sooner the better. She created a definite distraction from his goal.

Revenge. It was all Chase had left, his entire purpose for existing.

"Captain, did you hear me?"

He met her gaze. "I don't like ultimatums, pilgrim. I make the decisions on this ship and I give the orders. I have some business to take care of on Elysia."

Her hands clenched into fists at her side. "Keeping your word should also be your business, Captain."

Chase checked his rising temper. Nessa could rouse his emotions with alarming swiftness. "You seem to forget, pilgrim, that I'm a shadower. It's not my word that's important; it's my ability to track and capture criminals. The survival of the fittest—that's all that counts—not some misplaced code of honor. But my word is good. You'll get to Intrepid—when I decide to go there. Argue with me again and you'll finish the journey inside the brig."

He didn't like threatening her, but fear helped foster distance between them. He needed some way to keep her in line, for she exhibited a surprising determination and tenacity.

She paled, as she always did when he mentioned shadowers or talked about the brig. Her slight body trembled, and he wondered again at her fear of shadowers and being locked up. Silently she retreated to the relative safety of her cabin.

Chase turned back to the computer, feeling strangely alone.

Nessa released her safety harness and slowly left the cockpit. Already beside the hatch, Chase was checking his weapons. She watched the now-familiar routine, noted the remote expression blanketing his face as he mentally readied himself for the challenge ahead.

Why? she wanted to ask. *Why do you do this? How can you hunt living beings and turn them in for money?* Suddenly it mattered very much that Chase was a shadower, and not just because of the threat he posed. Shadowers were the scourge of the universe, the lowest of the low. She knew Chase to be more worthy than that. But Controller indoctrination destroyed free will—and the choice between right and wrong.

Chase strapped on a blaster, then slipped on a backpack containing a portable body wheeler. The enormity of his chosen occupation swept through Nessa. By the Spirit! She had lain with him, allowed him to touch her with shocking intimacy. She had yielded her body to a *shadower*. An odd trembling seized her and she steadied herself against the wall. She had to elude him and find a way to Sonoma.

"Captain McKnight, about my earlier suggestion—I could catch a transport here on Elysia."

Chase met her gaze, his eyes impassive. "I've already given my answer. The transports leaving Elysia are not safe for a lone woman. We'll only be here a day. After that, we'll head for Intrepid."

Day fifteen—time was rapidly diminishing—and she couldn't trust him. "But I read in the IAR that Elysia is a big trading center. Large numbers of people come here to buy and sell all kinds of goods. Surely commercial transports are available."

Chase shook his head as he pulled on blast gloves. "There's a lot you don't understand. Yes, many wares are sold on Elysia. It's been said that whatever could be desired can be purchased here. Which is why I can't allow you off the ship."

Nessa mulled over his odd words. "I don't know

what you're talking about. I don't plan to buy anything, except transport to Zirak."

Opening the portal cover, Chase scanned the outside landscape, as he always did. "Not just material goods exchange hands here. Bodies, souls, human dignity. They all go to the highest bidders. Greed and lust drive this marketplace."

He snapped the cover closed and turned back, sudden emotion flaring in his eyes. "Some claim Elysia is the most beautiful planet in the quadrant," he said, his voice edged with steel, "but its essence—its soul, if you will—is blacker than that of Calt, or Alta, or any of the penal colonies."

Nessa shivered, although not from cold. He must be referring to the slave trade openly practiced on Elysia. Yet how could that—or anything—be starker than Calt, or offer darker memories? Especially after losing Turi there. "I don't care what kind of transport Elysia offers. I must get to Zirak, and quickly."

His eyes narrowed. "Forget it, Nessa. I won't allow you to board an Elysian transport. I don't even want you walking around out there. And to make sure you don't leave the ship while I'm gone, I've reprogrammed the hatch. Only my code will activate it."

Too surprised to react, Nessa watched him swing open the hatch. "It's twelve hundred hours now. I'll be back here by sixteen hundred hours. We'll take off immediately." With those final, terse words, he left, the hatch slamming behind him.

She waited several minutes, then she tried to open the hatch. Nothing. Anger swept through her and she kicked the hatch, then winced and shook her throbbing foot. Damning Chase McKnight to the fires of the Abyss, she limped back to the cockpit.

In pure defiance, she sat in *his* chair and used *his* keypad. Accessing the PWL file, she pulled up her program . . . and froze.

She stared at the screen, her heart accelerating. Her knowledge of encryption technology had paid off. The password file had been decoded, obviously by this third program, which she had effected yesterday while Chase was exercising. With the push of a key, all of his security codes transmuted into legible alpha/numeric sequences, right before her eyes.

Excitement raced through her. Nessa considered all the possibilities these codes offered. She could unlock Chase's vault and help herself to his miterons. Or open his armory and take his weapons; even hijack his ship.

His ship . . . The prospect whirled through her mind.

With this ship, she could travel so swiftly to Sonoma, she'd be there within seven days. She fingered the controls, imagining how it would feel to be in command of such an incredible space vehicle. Then her conscience stepped in. She couldn't do that to Chase, not after all he'd done for her. He had no family that she knew of. He had nothing perhaps except this ship. She couldn't steal it. Not when a public transport to Sonoma was all she needed.

She sighed. Well, she could at least open the hatch now. She'd take one or two of Chase's weapons for protection. No one would bother her if she pointed a wave-based weapon at them. And Chase would never expect her to leave the ship, so he wouldn't be looking for her.

She printed off the codes, then began accessing and scanning secured files. Now able to open Chase's armory, she took a blaster and a phaser. She also found a knife, similar to the one she'd lost on Calt, which she slipped into her boot. She left the vault containing his miterons alone, not wanting to take more from him than she absolutely needed. Retrieving her bag of food from her cabin, she decoded and opened the hatch. With one last glance down the ship's wide corridor, she stepped out. . . .

. . . and into a virtual paradise. Nessa stared in awe at the scene before her. Green and lush, Elysia sprawled as far as she could see, an oasis of the senses. Massive palm trees jutted up from the rolling landscape, waving gently in the balmy breeze. The scents of exotic flowers growing everywhere in profusion intermingled with the delicious aromas of cooking food.

About two hundred meters away, the marketplace began, neat rows of brightly colored tents. Teeming masses of people packed the wide thoroughfares winding through the tent rows. Nessa heard the babble of voices, although she couldn't distinguish any words at this distance.

She moved toward the bazaar, attracted like debris to a black hole. No one seemed to notice her. Her tattered pilgrim's tunic wasn't out of place here, she realized, not in this melting pot of beings and costumes. Looking for signs to the transport base, she stepped into the melee.

Rows and rows of goods, a thousand times more than she'd seen in Moriah's mercantile, lined the tents. Merchants hawked their wares. Silks, weapons, food, clothing, computers—yes, computers! Animals, soundmakers and musical instruments, furniture, numerous items she couldn't even identify. Wondrous things!

Even in her hurry, Nessa slowed to look at the different merchandise. She'd never seen anything like this marketplace and probably never would again. When she spotted lanraxes for sale, she stumbled and almost fell. These were babies, their fur not yet long, but, oh, how they reminded her of Turi, with their chattering and hissing. They scrabbled about in a case, and the woman selling them wore gloves so they wouldn't smell her scent and bond with her.

A lump rose in Nessa's throat and hot tears stung her eyes. Stars! She'd cried more in the past four days than she had in ten seasons. Resolute, she shoved past the lanraxes, blindly shaking her head at the vendor's urging to buy.

Her spirits dampened, she hurried by the rest of the vendors. Beyond the stall area lay two gracefully curved white domes, painted with colorful, exotic symbols. Nessa realized they must be the Pleasure Domes. She had read about them in the IAR, but she was just beginning to understand what they offered.

Stunning men and women, dressed in sheer layers of silk, gyrated in sensual dances along the walkways leading to the domes. They beckoned to those passing, trying to lure them inside to enjoy every type of erotic, physical pleasure—for a price, of course.

Unbidden images of Chase's body over hers flashed through Nessa's mind. Pushing away the unwelcome thoughts, she skirted the domes. Relieved, she finally cleared the main market area, intending to stop someone and ask directions to the nearest transport station. Then she saw the slave section of the marketplace. She halted, riveted by the scene before her.

Nessa had read about Slaver's Square in the IAR, but she'd refused to dwell too long on the issue of slavery. So many people in the quadrant suffered under the cruel and abusive rule of the Controllers that the plight of slaves didn't seem any harsher than most. But the actual sight of the slaves, naked and bound by electronic shackles, brought home the horrifying reality in a way the computer couldn't convey.

Age, nationality, and sex seemed to have no bearing on who could be a slave. Small children, elders bent with age, white, black, orange, fur-covered beings, hairless beings; there were a variety of hapless slaves lined up in their shackles. They could only shuffle slowly; if they moved too far or too fast, the shackles issued a severe shock.

The slavemasters, dressed in glittering gold robes and jewel-encrusted sandals, ringed the slaves, threatening them with electrolyzer rods. Their leader, an obese man with a neatly trimmed beard, stood on the dais, calling out to potential buyers.

"Hear, hear, citizens! Come buy a slave! Buy as many as you wish—we have plenty to choose from. No reasonable offer will be refused. Why do your own fighting? Or harvesting? Or upkeep of your dwelling or ship? Slaves are an economical way to have all that tiresome labor done for you. They don't need much food or much space—they can sleep standing up. Our slaves are trained to see to your needs—and I do mean your *every* need."

People milled around the square, physically inspecting slaves as if they were animals. Nauseated, Nessa tore her gaze from the morbid scene. She tried to scurry by with her head averted, but the sudden sensation of another Shielder jerked her upright. Oh, no! Not Sabin. He couldn't be here. He just couldn't be.

She didn't see Sabin behind her. Yet the presence of another Shielder persisted, and she rotated full circle, lowering her eyes against the appalling rows of naked slaves, then scanning the moving crowds. Nothing, no one. Reluctantly, she turned back toward the slaves, finding the emanations the strongest from that direction. But she found the sight of squalid, broken-spirited humanity unbearable and quickly looked away again.

Even if a Shielder stood among those slaves, what could she do? She started in the opposite direction. Still the pull beckoned. Gritting her teeth, Nessa spun around and moved back toward the square. Edging around the crowd of potential buyers, she walked parallel to the line of slaves, not looking directly at them, but concentrating instead on the Shielder energy.

When the energy level surged, she turned and looked. Two children, a girl and a boy, weary and bedraggled, lifted their eyes and stared back at her briefly, then fearfully dropped their gaze. Shielder children, for sale as slaves. The realization impaled her like a laser sword.

Reluctantly, Nessa approached the children. The stench of filth and human waste almost overwhelmed her, but she pressed forward, inexplicably drawn to these children. The girl, not much smaller than Nessa, appeared several seasons older than the boy, and approaching puberty. They both had dark brown hair, horribly matted.

At closer range, she saw that bruises and welts covered their thin bodies. Intense anger swept through her. Only a monster could do this to defenseless children. She hated her helplessness in this horrible situation.

Spirit, what could she do?

Buy them. The thought hurtled into Nessa's mind. Of its own volition, her hand slid into her pocket and fingered her bag of coins. Four hundred miterons—all she had to get to her to Sonoma. The good of the entire Shielder race far outweighed the plight of two children, she reminded herself.

But to leave them here seemed unthinkable. She reached out, touching the girl's shoulder. The girl started violently, raising her gaze. Nessa stared into hazel eyes, dull with apathy and fear. "What is your name?" she asked, but the girl only shook her head.

"You there! No talking to the slaves!" A burly slave-master stormed toward her, gripping his electrolyzer rod. He stopped before Nessa, glaring at her.

"We only allow prospective buyers to examine our merchandise. Begone, beggar!" He looked as if he might use the rod on her, which made her even angrier. He was no better than an Antek.

"Who says I'm not looking to buy?" she snapped, her hand going back to her coins.

The slavemaster's eyes narrowed and he grabbed her roughly by her tunic front. "You, buying a slave? I find that mighty suspicious. You sure you're not an escaped slave yourself? Where's your master, girl?" He looked around to see if Nessa was alone, then dragged her forward. "Maybe I just ought to put you in the line."

She found her wits in time to grasp the blaster beside her coins and whip it out and against the man's stout belly. "I don't think so," she hissed.

The slavemaster released her so quickly, she staggered back. He raised the electrolyzer rod toward her, then wavered in the face of the blaster still aimed at him. "I don't know who you are, beggar, but get off this square before I call the authorities."

"Maybe I'm a Controller agent." Nessa didn't know where those words had come from, but she knew the Controllers used myriad different beings to infiltrate the quadrant as their eyes and ears. Apparently, he'd had an experience with an agent, for she liked the slavemaster's reaction.

"I meant no disrespect," he stammered. "Forget what I said about calling the authorities."

"How much for the two children?"

A calculating gleam stole into the slavemaster's eyes. Apparently the prospect of a sale overrode everything having just transpired. Business was business. "How much do you offer?"

Nessa considered a moment, mentally totalling her coins. Maybe she could buy the children and still have enough for transport. "One hundred miterons each."

"One hundred miterons?" he roared, all pleasantries forgotten. "You're not a beggar, you're a thief! Listen, girl, I don't care if you do work for the Controllers. I have to eat. I can get more than that for children at the Pleasure Domes."

Children in the Pleasure Domes? Sickened, Nessa knew she could not leave the Shielder children here, even if it took all her money to gain their freedom. Only one solution presented itself. She would have to return to Chase's ship and take some miterons from his vault. He could afford it, she told herself, ignoring the twinge of guilt.

"Two hundred each, then." She offered all she had, praying to Spirit the slavemaster would take it.

"Please, you insult me," he cajoled. "I have overhead, you know. I have to feed these slaves and shelter them every night. I need to get back at least what I have put into them."

Slaves that slept standing up couldn't take much room, Nessa thought. "I have only four hundred miterons with me."

He rolled his eyes in well-practiced, long-suffering resignation. "By the gods, I must have a sign that says 'Cheat me.' All right, all right. You drive a hard bargain . . . I'll take it."

He probably would have taken less, but Nessa

didn't care. She waited impatiently while he carefully counted every coin, then drew up the papers. The children were hers. She owned two slaves, a staggering thought.

"You're coming with me," she told the children, taking them each by the hand. They showed no emotion at her words, just plodded along beside her in absolute silence. She led them back toward the marketplace, although she didn't have any destination in mind.

Nessa hadn't thought any further than getting the children off the square. Now she realized she'd have to take them with her to Sonoma. She certainly couldn't leave them on Elysia. They appeared ablebodied, so they'd be welcome at the Shielder colony. But now she not only needed money to transport three to Sonoma, but the children had to have clothing and food.

Best to get on with it and go to Chase's ship. She had no idea what time it was, according to the ship's clocks, but only a few hours had lapsed since he left. If she hurried, she could get the money and find the transport station before he returned.

Chapter Ten

The children spoke not a single word on the way back to the ship. Nessa talked to them, apologizing for them having to travel through the crowds naked, enduring the curious stares and cruel remarks. "We'll purchase you some clothing as soon as I get more money. And we'll get you something to eat, too."

The children remained silent, and Nessa gave up all attempts at conversation. She felt a great sense of relief when they finally reached the ship. She ushered the children into the corridor. "Wait here. I'll be right back."

Retrieving her list of Chase's codes, Nessa punched in the vault combination and the panel slid open. She found a strongbox containing miterons and credit disks. Bypassing the disks, which could leave a trail, she scooped up two handfuls of coins, dividing them between her pockets and her boots. As she closed the panel, she heard pounding on the hatch.

"Chase! Are you in there, old man? I need to leave some things on board. Nessa? Are you there?" Sabin's voice boomed from outside.

Stars! What was he doing on Elysia?

Nessa hurried to the children, who huddled against the wall. Sabin would go away if he got no answer. He couldn't enter the ship with the hatch secured. She squatted beside the children. "Shhh. Don't make any noise. He'll be gone in a minute." Her warning appeared unnecessary; the children had yet to utter a single word, much less a sound.

A split second later, the hatch hummed to life and begin lifting. By the Spirit! Sabin must have Chase's code. Damn him! He always managed to show up at the most inopportune times. Spurred to action, Nessa whispered, "Come with me, quickly," and half-dragged the children to her cabin. "Stay here until I return."

She stepped from her cabin just as Sabin entered, carrying two packages. "Nessa! Didn't you hear me pounding on the hatch?"

She remained silent as he strode toward her. "Locked you in, did he? Smart man. Where is he? Still out there, hunting down that worthless cur, Marak?"

Nessa glanced at her cabin door, realizing she needed to draw Sabin's attention away from the area. "Yes, he's still out there." She slid past Sabin toward the cockpit, hoping he'd follow. "Did you need to leave those packages for him?"

He started after her, a quizzical expression on his

face. "Actually, *pilgrim*, these are for you."

"For me?" Amazed, Nessa halted, the children momentarily forgotten.

"Yes, for you. And I'll be damned glad to get rid of this one piece of baggage." Sabin paused, trying to balance a package that suddenly seemed to take on a life of its own. Nessa heard scratching and hissing. "By the Abyss. Here, take it." He shoved the package toward her.

She realized it was actually a hinged box, with heavy mesh on the top. The box vibrated in her hands and chattering came from inside. A futile hope taking root, she undid the clasp. A familiar head popped out, four jet-bead eyes gleaming at her. Turi!

"Turi! Oh, Turi," she cried, snatching him against her. "You're alive! You're alive." He burrowed against her neck, chattering and chirping. Intense happiness blazed through Nessa and she felt like shouting for joy. Sudden tears blinded her and she sought Sabin through the blur. "How?"

He cleared his throat and shifted uncomfortably. "Moriah found him after you and Chase left Calt," he explained gruffly. "He was near death, but she nursed him back to health. I thought—uh, well— no one else could handle the little monster, so I brought him back to you."

Nessa thought she might burst from happiness. "Thank you," she whispered.

Sabin cleared his throat again. "I didn't do it for you. That creature bit me three times, although he liked Moriah pretty well—" He halted abruptly, his eyes narrowing. "What the—?"

Pivoting around, he dropped the second package, his hand whipping to his phaser. Tension poising his body for action, he strode toward Nessa's cabin. No, no!

"Where are you going?" she cried, stumbling after him, half-blinded by Turi's fur. Ignoring her, Sabin opened her panel.

"Wait! What are you doing?" Desperately, Nessa tried to think of a diversion, but he had already disappeared into her cabin. Prying Turi from her neck, she followed, praying for a miracle. But she seemed fated to suffer bad luck.

Sabin stood glaring at the two terrified children cringing against the bunk. "What in the Abyss is this?"

He still held the phaser and the children cowered even more, covering their heads with their arms. Nessa stepped between them and Sabin, shoving his arm down. "Put your weapon away, shadower. Unless you're afraid of two innocent children."

He turned his blazing glare on her. "How did these Shielder children get on this ship?" Grimacing, he brought his hand to his nose. "By the Spirit! They smell worse than Anteks. I know Chase didn't bring them aboard. He'd never allow anyone—or anything—this filthy on his ship."

Nessa hadn't even considered the smell, or the germs. Frantic, she tried to come up with a convincing story. Sabin grasped her arm in a merciless grip. "Tell me why these urchins are in your cabin— and don't even think of lying to me, Nessa. If you do, I swear I'll cast the lot of you off the ship."

Not a bad idea, considering the sooner she and

the children left before Chase returned, the better. "I'll save you the trouble," she retorted, trying to wrest free of his grip.

"No, I think you'll tell me the truth." He shook her, clinking the miterons in her pockets. His expression turned even more thunderous and he plunged his hand into a tunic pocket. She struggled futilely to break free, and Turi lunged at his arm, but Sabin evaded him.

"You little thief," he growled at Nessa. "Stealing Chase blind as soon as he leaves the ship."

"I had money when Chase rescued me!"

Sabin patted the other side of her tunic. "Not two pocketfuls of miterons, I'll wager. Or weapons, either. I'll take those right now."

He held out his hand. Nessa had no choice but to comply, especially since he held an activated phaser in the other hand. Reluctantly, she gave him the blaster and phaser. He took them, then patted her pockets again to be sure she'd given him everything. He didn't know about the knife in her boot, thank Spirit.

He snapped the weapons she'd handed him onto his utility belt, shaking his head. "We'll get to the bottom of this, lady. We'll just wait right here until Chase gets back and checks his gold and his armory."

Desperation flooded Nessa. She kicked Sabin's shin as hard as she could. "You do that, shadower! And see these two children returned to Slavers' Square, which is where I found them. I'm not a thief! I only borrowed enough from Chase to buy the children some food and clothing and purchase us transport. I could have taken more, but I didn't."

She paused, heaving for breath. Staring incredulously, Sabin released her and rubbed his shin. "Borrowed? I suppose you were going to pay it all back?"

Quiet despair replaced Nessa's momentary frenzy. "Don't you care about anything other than yourself? Doesn't it bother you to see people enslaved and put in chains? Look at these children! They've been abused and starved. Unlike you, shadower, I do care, and I couldn't leave them there."

Sabin shrugged, slipping his phaser back in its holster. "What are you going to do with them?"

Nessa wondered how much to tell him. "Take them with me to Zirak."

"Next I suppose you're planning on converting them to your 'religion.' Spare me, *pilgrim*. I'm not some dim-witted Antek. *I* know you're lying through your teeth, even if Chase doesn't."

"I'll leave you and Chase to your miserable greed as soon as possible. And I'll take the children somewhere safe. That should be enough."

"I'll be happy to see you go," Sabin muttered, punching the panel control. "You and that damned lanrax." He strode through the panel before she could ask his intentions.

She started after him, but then she heard the hatch opening and Chase calling out, "Nessa! Where are you?"

Panic slammed through her. She closed the panel, then leaned against it, battling the waves of dizziness washing over her. Oh, Spirit, what to do? *What to do?* Chase must never discover the children. He would send them back to Slavers' Square and imprison her.

Tremors shook her arms and legs. Not that! She couldn't have a seizure now. She sucked in great gulps of air. Miraculously, the blackout never came. After a moment, the trembling eased. Pushing away from the panel, Nessa turned to the children.

"We have to hide you. Quick, in the lav!"

Chase entered the ship, carrying packages and towing Marak in the wheeled body harness. He saw Sabin in the corridor. "Travers! What are you doing here? I thought you were headed toward Verante." He sneezed violently and rubbed his watering eyes.

"And I thought you were headed for Star Base Intrepid, old man." Sabin sauntered forward to study the unconscious prisoner. "So you got Marak. What did you do to him?"

"Injected him with a knockout drug, so I wouldn't have to listen to his foul mouth." Chase shifted the packages, not adding that he'd also wanted time to do a little shopping. It galled him that he couldn't banish thoughts of Nessa, even while planetside hunting a vicious criminal. But she'd needed something else to wear, he rationalized. Then, when he'd passed that cursed vendor . . .

He sneezed again, swearing under his breath. He would have to take another allergy injection, as much as he hated it.

"Allergies acting up?" Sabin inquired.

Chase resisted the urge to beat the knowing smirk off his partner's face. Once while in the throes of a drinking marathon with Sabin, he'd made the mistake of confiding that he had allergies. A confession Sabin liked to lord over him.

"Shut up, Travers. Where's Nessa?"

Sabin jerked his head toward her cabin. "In her quarters. Why do you ask?"

Chase sneezed twice. "Because I need to unload something into a plexishield case—not that it's any of your concern." He headed for Nessa's cabin, Sabin right behind him. At the panel, he turned and glared at his partner. "Don't you have anything better to do? You could put Marak in the brig."

Sabin considered for a moment. "Nah. Plenty of time for that. Marak looks like he'll be out for a while."

Chase almost decided to wait until later, when Sabin was gone, before he unloaded his troublesome package. His partner didn't need to know he'd lost all sanity in a few moments at the marketplace. But another round of sneezing changed his mind.

"Why don't you just mind your own business and go back to your ship?" he muttered, sounding the panel tone.

Sabin shook his head, an infuriating grin splitting his face. "I wouldn't miss this for a thousand miterons."

Chase ignored him. "Nessa, are you in there? I have something for you."

"Wait! I'm coming." Nessa opened the panel, her face unusually flushed. "What is it?"

She sounded breathless and Chase eyed her critically. "Are you okay? Your face is red."

Her hand flew to her cheek and she seemed to

grow even more flushed. "Umm, I'm just a little warm." She grabbed her tunic and fanned it. "This robe is very heavy."

A pungent stench wafted into the corridor from her cabin. Chase wrinkled his nose. "What in the Abyss is that *smell*? It's worse than Marak's stink."

Nessa's eyes widened and she glanced at Sabin. "I do—don't know," she stammered. She edged out and shut the panel behind her.

A sudden sneezing episode racked Chase. "I brought you something. You can open it in your cabin."

Nessa appeared anxious. Probably Travers making her nervous. She always acted skittish around him. "It's too crowded in the cabin," she hedged. "Couldn't we do this in the cockpit?"

Chase found her behavior strange. He was starting to get very irritated, not to mention completely congested. "No!" he snapped, shoving the boxes at her. "Open the larger one *now*."

Her hands shaking, she fumbled with the clasp. He couldn't understand her reluctance. Didn't every woman like to get gifts? The box opened and a silvery head poked out; four shiny eyes looked around. Chase stood proudly, waiting for Nessa's pleased reaction.

"It's a lanrax," she said blankly.

"Yep, it sure is," Sabin agreed.

The female lanrax hissed at Nessa and slithered out of the box. It hung by its back feet, then dropped to the floor and scurried to Chase. It climbed his leg before he could react and settled against his chest. Nuzzling its cold nose against his

167

neck, it chattered happily. A violent sneeze left his chest aching.

"Get off me!" He tried to pry the lanrax loose, but it dug its claws into him. He finally peeled it off and held it away from himself by the scruff of its neck. "Nessa, take it."

Hesitant, she reached out and took the spitting and hissing lanrax. It sank its teeth into her hand. "Ouch!" Nessa dropped the lanrax and grabbed her hand. "It bit me."

The creature hightailed it back to Chase and started up his leg again. Blazing hells. This wasn't going as planned. "What's wrong with this thing?" he snarled, pulling it off his leg. "It's for you, Nessa. Take it, dammit!"

She stepped back, shaking her head. She obviously had no appreciation whatsoever for his gift.

"It doesn't want Nessa," Sabin pointed out. "It wants you, old man."

"Why in the Abyss would the creature want me? I hate the damn things!"

"Let me see if I can guess. Did you use gloves when you purchased this little critter?"

Glaring at his partner, Chase shook his head. Sabin sighed with mock heaviness. "That explains it, then. The lanrax picked up your scent and bonded with you."

A sick feeling settled in Chase's gut. "That's crazy! I only held it for a moment while I put it in the box—" A series of sneezes interrupted his protest. "That's not enough time for anything to bond. Nessa, is that plexishield case still in your cabin?"

An apprehensive look crossed her face. "I'm not sure."

"It has to be there. I never removed it." He opened the panel to her chamber.

"No! You can't go in there!" She grabbed his arm and tried to pull him back. "The case is occupied."

"Occupied?" He pushed past her, his gaze shooting to the case. There was Turi. No, it couldn't be. He stepped closer and the creature hissed. It sure looked like Turi. "How did he get here?"

"Sabin brought him," Nessa explained, still tugging on his arm. "Moriah found him."

Chase met his partner's amused gaze. "Gee, thanks a lot."

"Think nothing of it, partner."

"Now, could you please leave?" Nessa pleaded, glancing toward the lavatory.

"But what am I supposed to do with *this* thing?" Chase demanded, holding up the other lanrax. "I have to put it in the case, too."

"I'd think twice about that if I were you," Sabin advised. "If this is a female, you'll have lots of little lanraxes running around here in no time."

Chase groaned, then sneezed. Worse and worse. If he ever saw that vendor again on Elysia, he'd torch her stall. "Well, then, this *female* lanrax will just have to stay in Nessa's lavatory until I can replicate another case."

"No!" she cried, digging her nails into his arm.

The ungrateful wretch. Chase glared at her, all vestiges of patience gone. "What is the matter with you? You're not allergic to the cursed creatures. I say it's going to stay in your lav. Either that, or I'll euthanize the damn thing."

Nessa paled. "You can't do that," she whispered.

"I can and I will, if I can't find a way to un-bond with it," he snapped, pushing past her toward the lav.

Her grip on his arm tightened. "Put it in the case with Turi, then."

Was it his imagination, or did she appear frightened? By the Spirit! Why had he ever delayed in dumping her at a star base? "Not a chance in the universe, lady. Two lanraxes are two too many. And what is that horrible smell?"

Shaking Nessa off, he stormed to the lav. He punched the panel pad, ready to toss the lanrax in . . . and froze. Two naked children, covered with filth, cowered against the cleansing stall. The stench almost gagged him. He stared, trying to comprehend the impossible. Then rage exploded through his head, momentarily blinding him.

He whirled, dropping the lanrax and grabbing Nessa up by her tunic. "What in the damned Abyss are these . . . these *children* doing here, on my ship?" Anger coursed through him, robbing him of rational thought. He shook her. "I want an answer and I want it *now!*"

Gasping, she tried to pry his hand away. He didn't realize how close he was to losing control, until Sabin intervened, breaking his hold on her. "Whoa, partner. She can't answer if she can't breathe."

He dropped her like a hot brand, dragging air into his lungs. The rage receded from boiling to simmering. Her hand at her throat, Nessa backed away. He grabbed her shoulders and jerked her back. "Tell me what is going on here."

She shook violently and her eyes rolled up—the beginnings of a seizure. Cold, lucid control returned to him. Chase maneuvered her to the bunk and eased her down.

"Breathe, Nessa. Stay with her, Travers. I'll be right back."

He dashed to the lab, ignoring the lanrax clinging to his leg, and filled a hypochamber with medication. Grabbing his medical monitor, he returned to find Nessa in the throes of a seizure, Sabin watching helplessly.

"Stars," Sabin said, gladly yielding his place to Chase. "Will she survive this?"

"She'll be fine." The seizure appeared the mildest Chase had seen yet. She was obviously taking the medication he'd given her, and it must be helping, if her quick response to the injection gave any indication.

He gave her only enough time to awaken and orient herself before he allowed his anger to resurface. He pulled her up against the end of the bunk, his face a few millimeters from hers. "I want to know where those children came from and why they're on my ship. I want the complete truth. If I don't get the truth and get it now—you'll find the brig mild in comparison to the consequences."

Her eyes huge, she looked over his shoulder at Sabin. A nagging suspicion entered his mind and his head snapped around. "Do you know anything about this, Travers?"

Sabin shrugged nonchalantly. "Not much more than you do, old man."

Although he didn't totally believe his partner,

Chase let it go, returning his attention to Nessa. "I'm waiting for the answer."

She swallowed. "The children were being sold as slaves on Elysia."

He must have misunderstood her. "Slaves! How did they get on the ship?"

Slight tremors shook her body, and she averted her eyes. "I bought them."

Her voice was so low, he wasn't sure he heard right. "Did you say you bought them?" She nodded and his blood pressure rose several hundred points. "How did you manage that?" he bit out.

She stared at her hands clenched tightly in her lap.

"My patience is at an end, Nessa. Tell me everything *now*."

"I decoded the hatch and went looking for transport." She twisted her hands.

"For the love of—how did you decode the hatch?"

Her gaze shot up and she paled even more, if that was possible. "I—I . . . I stood at the hatch pad and entered combinations until I hit the right one."

Her tenacity amazed him. "Go on."

"Well . . . then I went to the market place. When I saw the children being sold as slaves, I couldn't leave them there. So I bought them."

She decoded the hatch? She left the ship against orders? She purchased *slaves?* Angry tension began pounding through his body. He checked the strong urge to shake her into oblivion.

"And just what did you purchase them with?" She began the hand-twisting routine again, and he clamped his hand over hers. "Answer me."

"My coins."

Sustaining belief became harder with each answer she gave. "You spent your transport money on slaves? How much was that?"

"Two hundred miterons each."

"Four hundred miterons? You spent *four hundred* miterons on *slaves?*"

A quick nod of her head sent Chase's blood pressure off the chart. He grabbed the bunk to keep from throttling her. "After spending all your money on slaves, what did you plan to use for transport to your all-important eclipse?"

"I don't know," she whispered.

The dam of restraint broke and fury rampaged through him. *"You don't know?"* he roared. "You leave the ship against orders, purchase two slaves with the only money you have, and *you don't know?* I'll tell you what you don't know, pilgrim. You don't know how much you owe *me.* I rescued you, treated your seizures, gave you food, and offered you transport to the nearest star base. Yet at every turn, you've defied me, lady. I've been lenient, but no more."

He grabbed Nessa's shoulders, lifting her off the mat and drawing her so close that her breasts brushed against his chest. He glared into her dark eyes, unconcerned with her obvious terror. "You owe me so much, you can't possibly ever repay me. Where I come from, that means I own you now. *I own you, body and soul!* You're *my* slave, to do with as I command. And if you value your welfare, and that of those two children in the lav, you'll do whatever I tell you, whenever I tell you. As a matter of

173

fact, I plan on working what you've cost me out of your scrawny hide. You'll be very certain that I'm comfortable and happy at all times. My every wish will be your duty. I hope this is very clear to you, because your life depends upon it. Do you understand me?"

She stared at him, her chest rising and falling rapidly. He dug his fingers mercilessly into her upper arms. "I said, do you understand?"

"Yes."

He shoved her away and rose, peeling the lanrax off his leg. Shaking with anger, he knew he'd better put some distance between himself and Nessa if he didn't want to commit mayhem. A long, stiff drink of Elysian liquor sounded damn good—no, make that damn necessary—right now. Spirit, he needed at least a bottle. And an allergy injection, he thought, as a paroxysm of sneezing hit him.

"I'm going to my cabin. When I come back out, you and those kids had better be cleaned up and run through decontamination." He stormed past Sabin, who offered a mock salute. "Get the hell off my ship, Travers."

He headed down the corridor to his own cabin and the oblivion alcohol could give. He needed escape from his own reprehensible past, as well as from the waif who'd managed to turn his life upside down.

Chapter Eleven

The silver lanrax scurried after Chase, the cabin panel closing with the finality of a death knell behind it. Nessa sagged against the bunk wall, filled with despair. Now what?

All she could think to do was take the children and flee, hoping Chase would be in his cabin long enough for them to get away. She pushed onto shaky legs, meeting Sabin's taunting gaze.

"Tsk, tsk. You lied to Chase. Told him you didn't know what you would use to pay for transport. And all the while, your pockets were stuffed with his gold."

"It's none of your business." She started for the lav.

His hand on her arm stopped her. "It *is* my business. And you're going to put the miterons back right now. If you don't, I'll be forced to tell Chase."

The thought of further incurring Chase's wrath

sent a shiver through Nessa. "I can't put the gold back. Don't you see? It's my only way to get the children and me out of here."

"No. You can't take an Elysian transport. It would be too dangerous. You're far safer with Chase. He'll get you to Star Base Intrepid. He'll probably even give you the money you need to go on from there."

Nessa didn't see how a public transport could be any more dangerous than the situation she now faced with Chase. As furious as he was with her, there was no telling what he might do next. "I'll take my chances on Elysia."

Sabin shook his head. "No, you won't, Nessa. My ship is next to this one, and I'm not departing until Chase does. I'll be watching the hatch, and I'll notify Chase if you try to leave. Put the gold back."

She felt like a helpless creature caught in a snare. "I have to leave," she insisted frantically. "I don't know what Chase—"

"Chase won't hurt you or the children," Sabin interrupted. "He's just very angry right now. Now, go put the gold back."

Her feet dragging, Nessa headed for the vault, Sabin right behind her. She didn't have his faith that Chase wouldn't harm her. Halfway down the corridor, she faltered and whirled around. "Then take us with you," she pleaded. "You can drop us off at a star base."

"And give you money for transport fare? I think not. I'm not a credit institution." Sabin pointed toward the vault. "Go on."

He just didn't want to help her. It was that simple. Anger flared. "Don't you care about anything but hunting people and collecting gold?" she demanded.

"Not really. Put the miterons back."

Filled with dread, she returned the coins to the vault. She wondered if she'd have a chance to retrieve them after the ship departed Elysia—assuming she lived to have another shot at escaping. At least Sabin didn't know about the coins in her boots.

He reached past her and entered a sequence of numbers on the vault panel. "That should keep you out for a while." He strode to the unconscious prisoner and wheeled him toward the hatch. "Tell Chase I took Marak to turn him in. Probably best not to expose the children to the likes of him. I'll also message him the new code on the vault. See you around, *pilgrim.*"

Panic flooded Nessa and she ran after him. "Please take us with you!"

He turned back, and for a moment his expression softened. "Believe me when I tell you Chase is your best bet. He talks a tougher game than he plays. Stars, I've seen him give medicine to a sick prisoner who was condemned to die. Mark my words, he'll help you with those kids." He stooped to retrieve the other package he'd brought.

"But—"

"Forget it, Nessa. You're not coming with me." Sabin handed her the package. "This is for you, from Moriah. She thought you might like it. It occurs to me it might help you with Chase."

Confused, Nessa stared at the plain package. "I don't understand."

"Just be nice to the old man. Really, really nice. I promise you, everything will work out okay. Don't forget to clean up those kids and go through de-contamination. That always puts McKnight in a good mood."

With a jaunty wave and a maddening smile, Sabin slipped through the hatch, taking Marak with him. Nessa decided she hated him. Then she thought about him returning Turi. Well, maybe she didn't hate him. But he was a selfish, greedy man.

A noise down the corridor drew her attention. The silver lanrax scratched and pawed at Chase's panel, chattering pitifully. She sighed and scooped up the lanrax, holding her by the scruff so she couldn't bite. "Come on; let's put you where you can't bother the captain."

She went to her cabin and turned the lanrax loose after closing the panel. The children hadn't moved from the lav. She squatted beside them. "It's okay. Those men are gone now. You're safe and no one is going to hurt you again. What are your names?" They stared at her silently with terror-stricken eyes. Nessa began to wonder if they were truly mute, unable to speak.

"Okay, then. Let's get you cleaned up. Have you ever had a shower? I'm going to turn on the water in this stall. You stand in the water and get wet, then you rub soap on yourself and your hair."

At least they were agreeable, stepping into the stall at her urging. But they just stood under the water, and Nessa ended up washing them. It took three soapings to get the matted crud out of their hair, and two scrubbings to get the grime off their skin. Their nude bodies didn't bother her; she'd taken care of younger children from the time she was nine seasons of age until her seizures had begun.

The boy looked young, perhaps six or seven seasons of age. The girl appeared on the verge of crossing into adulthood, her body just beginning to show signs of the changes that would make her a woman. She was quite pretty, Nessa realized, as the layers of dirt came off.

"Okay, that's enough." Nessa turned off the water and gently prodded the children to stand under the dryer. She herself wasn't talkative by nature, but she sensed she needed to keep up a flow of words. She hoped her tone of voice could convince the children she meant them no harm.

"We're going to the decontamination chamber now. All you have to do is sit on the bench and let special rays clean away any germs on your skin and hair. You can't even feel it."

They followed her docilely, but the boy balked at the entry. He stared into the small chamber, trembling violently. "It's okay. There's nothing to be afraid of." Nessa eased him through the panel, lifting him slightly.

He stood stiffly by the bench, the expression on his face one of absolute terror. He shook even more when Nessa turned on the sanitizing rays. She gathered both children against her, telling them over and over that they were safe. When they were through in the decontamination chamber, she foraged in the supply room and found two blankets to wrap around them.

"See? That wasn't so bad. I'll bet you're hungry. Let's get you something to eat." She took them back to the cabin, since she didn't know how to operate the food replicator in the galley. Sitting on her bunk, they watched, round-eyed, as she dug into her bag of supplies and brought out some of her hoarded bread and cheese. They stared at the food with obvious longing but seemed afraid to take it.

"This is for you." Nessa took the boy's hand. He started in alarm and tried to pull away. She pressed some bread into his hand. "It's yours." He looked at her, uncertainty in his hazel eyes, and she nodded. "Eat it." He finally took a tentative bite.

She did the same with the girl, placing bread into her hand. When she looked back at the boy, he had crammed the entire piece into his mouth, as if afraid she might take it back.

"I wish you could talk." She sighed in frustration. "Then I'd know whether or not you understand me."

Chewing some bread, the girl considered her a moment. "I can talk," she offered so softly that Nessa wondered if she'd heard right.

"What did you say?"

"I talk. Brand don't. He hasn't talked since the first time they used the rods on him."

By the Spirit! The cruelty some beings displayed defied belief. Nessa leaned forward. "So his name is Brand?"

The girl nodded.

"And what is your name?"

"Raven."

"What pretty names. Is Brand your brother?"

"Yes, mistress. I take care of him. Sometimes I take the rod for him."

Nessa felt a catch in her throat. She knew Jarek would have watched over her in the same situation. Spirit, how she missed him.

"I'm not your mistress, Raven. I'm your friend. You can call me Nessa. Now, eat some more bread and cheese. If Brand sees you eating, maybe he won't be so afraid."

Both children ate more, but Nessa limited the amount, afraid they might get sick if they consumed too much. Then she noticed their eyelids drooping and realized how exhausted they must be.

She patted the bunk. "Lie down. You can sleep as long as you like."

They both looked amazed. "We're not allowed, mistress," Raven explained in her soft, singsong voice. "We sleep on the floor or against the wall."

"You are allowed to sleep here now," Nessa insisted. "I order you to."

She finally convinced the children it was all right, and they snuggled down on the mat. They fell asleep quickly, dropping off in the instant, boneless way children enter sleep.

Now what? Nessa wondered, standing and stretching. *Chase.* An odd shiver skittered through her. She would have to deal with him sooner or later. He said she would be his slave, do his bidding. She didn't know for sure what he meant by that, although she readily conceded her indebtedness to him.

Perhaps she should ask him if he needed anything. She could help him clean the latest cuts and scratches on his face, as she had helped him with his wounds from Saron.

Actually, going anywhere near Chase was the last thing Nessa wanted to do, but she'd never been a coward. She preferred to meet her fate head on.

Her gaze fell on Sabin's package, which she'd dropped by the lav. Curious, she retrieved and opened it. Her breath caught on a soft gasp. Inside lay the Saija silk robe she had admired in Moriah's mercantile. She lifted the garment cautiously, afraid it might snag on her rough hands. The rich russet fabric shimmered as it cascaded toward the floor.

Nessa had never seen any apparel so beautiful, much less ever dreamed of owning such. Stunned, she luxuriated in the faint woodsy smell inherent to Saija silk, in the satiny sensation upon her hands. Amazement, then gratitude, swept through her at the thought that Moriah had sent this wonderful gift to her, Leonessa dan Ranul, an outcast.

The package contained a few more items. Moriah had also included an elegant brush-and-comb set and a small vial of sweet starflower oil. Emotion tightened Nessa's throat. She had a friend! An honest-to-goodness friend. Why else would Moriah have so generously sent these items, if not in friendship?

Touched, Nessa started to fold the robe, but then she paused, staring at it. She needed to face Chase. Her own tunic hung in tatters around her. She could wear the robe. Maybe, if she looked as pleasing as possible, Chase wouldn't be so angry. Maybe, if she wore something special, he might find her a little bit appealing. She quickly rejected that last thought. She would never be pretty. But she would be far more presentable in the robe than in her rag of a tunic.

She had gotten in the shower with the children, then gone through decontamination, so she was clean. Decided, Nessa shed her tunic and boots, then dabbed a small portion of the starflower oil on her body.

She slipped into the robe, enthralled by the feeling of the silk against her bare skin. It fit her small frame so well, she decided Moriah must have had it cut down in size. The neckline scooped lower than she had realized and the robe split at each side, midway up her thighs. Not that it mattered—she wouldn't have parted with the robe for anything just then.

Taking her new brush, she brushed her hair until it crackled with static. She set the brush down slowly. She had delayed as long as she could. With a prayer that her improved appearance would soften Chase's anger she took a deep breath and left her cabin. The silk swished around her legs, exposing them with each stride. Nessa slowed her pace to better control the exposure.

Her courage faltered when she faced Chase's panel. He had been so furious with her. Perhaps later . . . no. She would need his help with the children. She didn't know how to use the food replicator. He could get proper clothing for them. Best to make amends as quickly as possible. She sounded the tone.

Nothing. She sounded the tone again. Nothing.

183

"Captain McKnight, are you all right?" He didn't answer, and alarm twinged through her. She punched the panel control, entering his cabin cautiously. Having never been inside before, she didn't know what to expect.

Chase's cabin was twice the size of hers. Bare, white walls gave the room a stark appearance, softened only by a case full of reading disks. A massive exercise machine took up one side of the room, and a control console and computer lined the wall directly opposite the entry panel.

Turned partly away from her, Chase slouched in a large, high-back chair, his booted feet propped on the console. Clutching a half-empty bottle against his bare chest, he didn't bother to look at her. "What do you want?"

"I came to see if you needed anything." Nessa paused, hating the telltale nervous quiver in her voice. "Or if you need assistance, like cleaning the cuts on your face."

"Oh, yes, that's right. You're my personal servant now, aren't you? My slave, I believe. Well, right now, *slave*, I just want you as far away from me as possible. Preferably on a planet on the other side of the quadrant."

Obviously, his mood had not improved. "I'm sorry I bothered you." She turned to go.

"Wait. You don't leave my presence until I dismiss you. Is that clear?"

"Yes."

"Yes, *what?*"

Nessa bit her lip, not sure what he wanted her to say. "Yes, captain?"

"No, no, no. A slave must do better than that. I expect you to say 'Yes, *master.*' Say it, slave."

She wondered fleetingly if he were drunk. His voice didn't sound slurred. *"Say it!"*

She thought of the children, of her mission. "Yes, master."

"Ah, but I do like the sound of that." He took a drink from the bottle, then set it on the console. Wiping his mouth with the back of his hand, he finally looked directly at her. His eyes widened, his perusal drifting downward, then back up.

"By the Abyss! Where did you get that robe?"

His intense, predatory gaze made her suddenly uncomfortable. That, and the sight of his bare, muscular chest. "Moriah sent it to me—"

With a thud, his booted feet hit the floor. He swiveled the chair and faced her fully. "Take it off."

"What?"

"I said, take it off."

Nessa recognized the expression on his face. He'd had it when he kissed her the first time, and when they mated. Sabin had also mirrored that same expression when he looked at Moriah. Panic and an odd excitement whipped through her.

"What?" she asked inanely, unable to say anything else. The pounding of her heart made it difficult to think clearly.

His molten gaze swept over her again, heating her blood. "You heard me, *slave.* Do it."

The breath seemed frozen in her chest as she reached for the seam seal. Tension hung heavy in the room, a tingling, anticipatory tension. She

185

pulled the seam, opening the robe halfway down. Shaking, she began to free her arms.

"Slowly. Take it off slowly."

Spirit! The way he was looking at her made her feel weak and hot all over. She thought of the men and women dancing in front of the Pleasure Domes, of the erotic energy they radiated. An instinctive, feminine awareness blossomed within her. This was the energy of mating, the excitement, the primal pull between male and female.

She was afraid. Afraid of the pain, afraid of exposing her deformed body, afraid of the intensity between her and Chase. But another part of her, the female core of her, throbbed with a need she'd never before experienced.

Remembering the sensual movements of the women at the Domes, she slowly slid one arm from the sleeve. Then, oh so slowly, despite her trembling, the other arm from its sleeve. She allowed the robe to slither down, clutching it over her breasts. Chase gripped the arms of the chair, his breathing suddenly labored.

"Come here." His voice sounded hoarse, guttural. She moved toward him, still afraid. "Closer."

Feeling exposed and vulnerable, she stopped before him. His pupils were dilated, his facial muscles taut, as his gaze branded her from head to toe.

Then he grabbed her, pulling her forward. She stumbled against him, hampered by the robe. He yanked the fabric up, baring her legs. Lifting her onto his lap, he settled her on her knees, spreading her thighs and forcing her to straddle him. The movement bunched the robe around her waist.

She gasped, feeling the hardness of him pressing between her legs. In an instant, his mouth was on hers, his tongue demanding entry. He pried her hands from her chest, and the robe slid down to pool around her waist. His hands covered her breasts and she gasped again, reeling from the rampaging sensations slamming through her body.

Chase tasted different, but not unpleasant. It must be the liquor lending that heady flavor to his mouth. She found herself wanting more of the taste of him and twined her hands through his hair. With a groan, he slid one large hand behind her head, holding her still while he plundered her mouth. His other hand squeezed and stroked her breast. Every sensation became incredibly acute, especially the pressure of the burgeoning hardness against her most private female place.

Her breath grew erratic, surging between each frenzied heartbeat. She no longer cared that mating would hurt. Coherent thought fled, reality blurred, until the only point of reference became sensation. The feel of Chase's hand on her fevered skin, the feel of his heaving chest beneath her fingers, of his flat, puckered nipples; the sound of his groans when she touched them.

Then his hand slid lower, and she arched up on her knees with a cry. He held her there, drawing a sensitive nipple into his mouth, as he stroked and teased between her legs, coaxing an alarming wetness.

By the Spirit! Surely she was undeserving of such pleasure, would die from the intensity of it. But she didn't. Instead, she spread her legs wider, and his

187

fingers stroked even deeper, and she cried out his name.

Groaning as if he was in intense pain, Chase withdrew his hand and fumbled with his pants. Then the startling boldness of his manhood invaded her, and panic surged through her. She thrashed upward, but he grabbed her waist and pressed her down upon him.

"No, sweetheart, don't fight it," he panted hoarsely. "It won't hurt as much this time, I promise. Just relax—oh, Spirit!" With another groan, he threw his head back as she sheathed him completely. He froze, gulping great breaths of air.

Nessa felt stretched further than was possible, and it hurt, although not as much as before. But escape appeared futile; Chase held her waist, keeping them firmly joined. She sagged against him. "I don't like it," she whispered.

He chuckled huskily. "Ah, sweetheart, but you will. I'll make sure you do."

He moved against her, small rocking motions at first, which emphasized how deeply he was embedded inside her. "Kiss me," he murmured, capturing her mouth with his. As the kiss distracted her, he lifted her, then pulled her down, showing her the motion. Automatically, in spite of the discomfort, she followed his guiding movements, using her legs.

It became faster, more urgent, as a tension built inside her, as he held her hips and met every stroke. Reality retreated, all awareness centered on the give and take of their bodies, of reaching for some unknown pinnacle. Vaguely, she heard Chase's guttural sounds, her own low moans. Suddenly, he surged upward, crying out. Then he sagged against the chair with a mighty sigh.

Pulling her against him, he rubbed her back, taking several deep breaths. He swore. "I'm like an untried adolescent with you. I'm sorry, Nessa, but I couldn't hold out. You're so tight, and the liquor didn't help any."

Nessa didn't understand what he was talking about. She hadn't found relief from the tension, although Chase obviously had. Something must be wrong with *her*, probably another result of her seizures.

As passion ebbed, embarrassment set in. She had done it again—allowed him to touch her in shocking ways, allowed him into her body. And he had probably expected it, since she owed him so much. She burned with humiliation at the thought.

"Are you okay?" he asked quietly.

Why should he be concerned, as long as his needs had been met? She pushed against his chest, disengaging their bodies. He let her go, and she scrambled off the chair. Her leg, stiff from her position in the chair, buckled, but she caught her balance.

"I'm fine." She fought a sudden rush of tears. What was the matter with her, to allow this to happen again? Trying to untangle the robe twisted around her middle, she limped toward the entry.

"Nessa, wait! Did I hurt you?"

She paused by the panel, keeping her back to Chase. It was foolish to be upset, even if he had mated with her just to ease his lust. Having now experienced sexual need herself, she could understand the urgent, primal drive to find release—even with someone as undesirable as herself.

"Nothing's wrong. I need to check on the children. You'll be glad to know they were bathed and decontaminated, just as you ordered—*master.*"

She fled then, to the safety of her cabin, away from him, away from the shame.

Nessa entered her cabin, finding the children sound asleep. They hadn't even changed positions. Poor little ones. At least, as able-bodied Shielders, they could find acceptance in a Shielder colony. They wouldn't be outcasts, and they could live useful lives, something she was beginning to fear would never be a possibility for her.

Numbly, Nessa stepped out of the robe. Smoothing the beautiful silk, she folded it carefully. She rubbed her throbbing leg, then went into the lav and stared at the mirror for a long time. No change, not even after the earth-shattering upheaval she'd just experienced in Chase's arms.

She was still plain and drab, with ordinary brown hair and eyes the color of dirt. Her body was still thin, without enticing curves; it was still scarred. But she didn't exhibit any of the changes indicating Orana either; the bloodshot eyes and the hemorrhaging beneath the skin, heralding the approach of death.

Sighing tiredly, she stepped into the shower, needing to wash away her encounter with Chase. But the warm spray couldn't remove the memory of his possession, nor the fears she'd been holding at bay. Time was running out.

Just as she reached for the soap compound, the stall door swung open, bringing a gust of cooler air with it. "I'll do that." Startled, she looked up into determined gray eyes. Chase stepped into the shower, forcing her back, and closed the door.

Surprise tightened her throat, but she managed to find her voice. "What are you doing here?"

Very deliberately, he pumped some soap into the palm of his hand. He looked at her, his eyes heated, and moved toward her slowly. "Taking care of unfinished business."

"What business?"

Not answering, he stepped closer. His advance forced her toward the back of the stall, where the wall halted her uneasy retreat. His eyes locked with hers, Chase pressed one hand against the wall near her head and leaned forward. "A slave may not leave without her master's permission. Did you ask my permission, slave?"

Before she could answer, he began leisurely soaping her breasts. Oh, Spirit. They reacted immediately, swelling beneath his touch.

"Did you ask my permission to leave?"

"N-n—no," she stammered, riotous sensations inundating her body.

Chase slid his hands to her abdomen. "Another thing you need to learn—a bed partner never leaves immediately after mating. Not from *my* bed." He massaged soap over her abdomen, then traced soapy circles along the tops of her thighs.

She shook her head to clear the sensuous cobwebs. "We weren't in your bed."

"We will be." He slipped his hand between her

thighs. "But first, I'm going show you how it should be between a man and a woman. You're going to experience the full pleasure your body can give you."

He lowered his mouth to hers, and her will no longer belonged to her. She clung to him, as he proceeded to demonstrate exactly what he meant.

Chapter Twelve

Nessa battled her way out of a deep sleep. Disoriented, she struggled to focus on her surroundings. Odd, but she'd always been a light sleeper. . . . Memory fragments drifted through her groggy mind—the children, Sabin, Chase. *Chase!* She bolted upright, the cover slipping to her waist.

The air against her bare breasts drew her surprised attention to her nakedness. Oh. Full memory returned in a rush. She pulled up the cover, looking around the room. Chase's cabin . . . Chase's bunk. She hadn't dreamed it.

She hadn't dreamed the wild mating in his chair, or the mindless fervor in the shower. The heat rose in her face at that last memory. Spirit, but he had been relentless in his determination to give her pleasure, and she had been . . . totally shameless. Even worse than her wanton behavior was the fact that he had been witness to it, although at the time she'd been too caught up in the throes of his wickedly knowing caresses to care. But she'd been mortified afterward.

She'd never slept beside anyone before, but Chase insisted. The children were in her bunk and the third cabin was being used for storage. He hadn't let her put on clothing, either, claiming he wanted to feel her bare skin against his, wanted to *look* at her. That had been a lie, for nobody in their right mind would want to see her body.

She didn't mind looking at him, though. Never had she seen a masculine body so powerful and well muscled. Just watching him stirred indecent urges.

They hadn't mated again, but he had curled around her, pulling her against him. She'd found the feel of his hard body pressed against her, the intense heat he generated, oddly comforting, yet, at the same time, alien and distracting. Chase had fallen asleep quickly, but she'd lain awake a long time before exhaustion claimed her. The fact that he'd left the bunk without waking her testified to her weariness.

Nessa pushed her tangled hair from her face, wondering at the time and where Chase might be now. She didn't relish any encounters with him today. She rose from the bunk, stiff and sore, well used for providing his pleasure. While she probably should be resentful, she grudgingly admitted he'd certainly demonstrated the desirability of mating.

Her clothing had been left in her own cabin, so she pulled the cover off the bunk and wrapped it around herself. Opening the panel, she peered cautiously down the empty corridor before making a dash for her quarters. She slipped into her cabin and stopped short in surprise.

Chase sat on the edge of her bunk, scanning his medical monitor over Brand. Huddled in the middle of the mat, the boy stared fearfully at the monitor. Raven crouched on the floor nearby, watching anxiously. Nessa's protective instincts went on full alert and she stepped toward the bunk. "What are you doing, Captain?"

He glanced up, his cool gaze skimming her, pausing at her bare legs before moving to her face. "I'm just checking the children over to make sure they're okay."

"Oh." Feeling rather foolish, she looked around the room, searching for her tunic. Not finding it, she moved closer to the bunk to observe. Chattering in welcome, Turi performed a flip when she passed his case. "They went through decontamination yesterday, if you're worried about germs."

"I'm not concerned about external bacteria." Chase laid down the monitor and picked up an item with a light at one end. "But I want to know if I need to worry about diseases or parasites. I'm going to look in your ear, Brand."

Brand drew back, trembling violently. Chase paused, lowering the instrument. "This won't hurt you. It has a special light on it, so I can see into your ear. Would you like to look in my ear first?" He offered the instrument, but Brand retreated even farther.

Chase considered a moment, then glanced at Nessa. "Tell you what. Why don't I check Nessa first? Then you can see exactly what I'm going to do, and that it doesn't hurt."

Brand's gaze cut to her, although he didn't give any other response. Chase beckoned. "Come here, Nessa."

She certainly didn't want him checking her, especially since she wore only a blanket. "I need to find my tunic," she hedged.

His gaze swept her again. "Your old tunic is gone. I put it in the disintegrator."

His words took a moment to register, and when they did, panicked outrage swept through her. With her tunic gone, the silk robe became her only item of clothing, and after last night, she didn't intend to wear it around Chase. "You destroyed my tunic? That was all I had—"

"You have another article of clothing, as I recall," he interrupted. "And I bought you some tunics while I was on Elysia."

That stopped her tirade midstream. Amazed, she snapped her mouth closed, but not for long. "You purchased me clothing? Why?"

"Because you needed it," he replied brusquely. "Now, get over here, and that's an order . . . Nessa."

He didn't say the word *slave*, but she caught the implication. He'd been quite clear about her new status when he found the children, as well as during their passionate encounters after that. Resentment burning in her chest, she clutched her blanket more tightly around her and walked slowly to the bunk.

Chase patted the mat. "Sit."

She sat stiffly, staring straight ahead. He pushed her hair behind her ear, the warmth of his hand sending small shocks through her. The cool metal pressed into her ear and he leaned so close, she could feel his breath on her face.

"Hmmm, very interesting. Pretty dirty in there."

Dirty? She scrubbed her ears whenever she took a shower. She turned to glare at him, but he deftly moved to her other side and held her head still while he examined the second ear.

"Wow. This one's even dirtier. And not a lanrax in sight."

Lanrax? Her gaze snapped to Chase's face. He grinned broadly and winked at Brand, who quickly averted his eyes. A soft giggle escaped Raven. Why, he was teasing, trying to put the children at ease. She'd never seen him really smile. His face lit up, his eyes glowed, and he looked incredibly handsome. Her breath hitched.

"I need to check your throat. Open wide."

Resigned, she allowed him to shine a light into her mouth. "I can see your dinner from last night, all the way down in your stomach," he declared solemnly. "You had bread and cheese." That seemed to catch Brand's attention. Even though Nessa knew it was just an educated guess, she found Chase's act charming. It revealed a side to him she hadn't known existed.

"Time to lie down now." Before she could react, he swung her legs onto the bunk and pushed her onto her back. "I'm going to press on you in a few places, to see if you've swallowed any weapons lately."

Raven smiled outright at that, and Nessa found it pretty funny, until Chase ran his hands over her breasts. Her breath caught, and a rush of sensations flooded her body. She caught him watching her, his eyes dark with a predatory gleam.

"Nothing there—at least, no weapons," he said, his voice deeper. He slid his hands lower and gently pressed his fingers down her abdomen, coming alarmingly close to the apex of her thighs. "Is it sore . . . anywhere?" he asked softly.

Searing heat flowed through her lower body, reminding her of last night, in the shower. . . .

With a gasp, Nessa grabbed his wrists. Her gaze locked with his, as a startling current flowed between them. She wanted to insist that he move his hands, to tell him he was hurting her, say anything to stop his touch, to stop the swiftly rising desire.

But the warning in his eyes reminded her of the children, and their fears. She realized, even as his presence threatened her on a number of levels, that he meant the children no harm. He appeared to possess a surprising amount of medical knowledge, knowledge that had benefitted her and would help the children. Forcing the breath from her lungs, she relinquished her grip on his wrists.

Approval flashed in his eyes. "Nothing there, either." He removed his hands. "You're done, pilgrim."

His calling her *pilgrim* jarred Nessa, reminding her that the children knew she was a Shielder. As she sat up, she made a mental note to speak with Raven and Brand when they were alone and emphasize the need to keep their identities secret.

"You were very good." Chase reached toward a plate of caroba Nessa hadn't noticed until now.

"Here." Taking advantage of her surprise, he slipped a piece of caroba into her mouth, then turned to Raven.

"Since Brand still seems a little nervous about this, why don't you go next?" He offered his hand to the girl.

She looked at Nessa uncertainly. Nessa nodded reassuringly. "It's okay, Raven. Captain McKnight won't hurt you. I'll sit next to you while he checks you."

Hesitant still, Raven climbed onto the bunk, holding her blanket tightly. Her fears were quickly calmed by Chase's soothing and kind manner. She even giggled when he announced with great amazement that she had a kerani in her right ear. That earned her a piece of caroba, which she had apparently never had, judging from the rapt expression on her face when she tasted it. She willingly lay down for the physical part of the examination.

Nessa watched Chase's hands moving gently over the girl. They were beautiful hands, strong, yet able to comfort with their touch. Able to stir all kinds of sensations . . . Spirit! She had to forget about what had passed between them. With a great effort, she forced herself to concentrate on the questions Chase was asking Raven, and the girl's diffident replies.

"Do you know how old you are, Raven?"

"Twelve seasons, master, I think."

"Have you started your menses yet?"

Raven appeared baffled by his question. "What, master?"

"Your cycle, the flow of blood once a month." He

paused, observing her confused look. "Probably not. Don't worry about it right now. There, we're done. And you're in good shape. You get another piece of caroba."

Raven crouched by the bunk again, slowly eating her treat. Chase offered his hand to Brand. "It's your turn." Shaking his head vehemently, Brand scrabbled into the corner of the bunk.

Chase picked up a piece of caroba. "Tell you what, Brand. I'll give you this so you can taste it and see if you like it. When you want more, you let me know. Then I get to check you out, and you get more caroba." He placed the treat in the boy's hand.

Nessa was touched by his patience and understanding with the children, with his caroba rewards for their cooperation. There would have been no tolerance of such behavior, even with good cause, in a Shielder colony. How odd that Chase, a shadower, a member of a group infamous for ruthless actions, showed such compassion.

He rose from the bunk. "We'll have the morning meal in a little while. But first, Nessa and I need to talk." He indicated a package on the shelves. "Those are your new tunics. Put one on and join me in the cockpit."

He gathered his medical equipment, then, much to Nessa's disappointment, retrieved the plate of caroba before he left. She could have used it to fortify herself for the coming confrontation, having no delusions as to the nature of the discussion.

She retrieved the package from the shelf, once again astonished at the generosity her new acquaintances had shown her. After going seasons without luxuries of any kind, to receive several offerings within a ship's cycle seemed overwhelming.

The package contained two tunics, one a deep, rich brown and the other a forest green color. Nessa knew instinctively that they would complement her coloring. She fingered the cloth, which was much softer than her pilgrim's tunic. Why had Chase purchased such fine-quality clothing for her? She'd needed another tunic desperately, but he could have gotten something a lot less expensive.

No use second-guessing him. Picking the brown tunic, she headed for the lav, where she found the silver lanrax curled mournfully in the sink. "Poor little creature," she told it, even though it hissed at her intrusion. "You would love to be close to Captain McKnight, while I'd like to stay as far away from him as possible."

But as the memory of last night resurfaced, Nessa knew that wasn't entirely true.

Chase was entering navigational commands when she entered the cockpit. She waited quietly while he finished, dismayed to realize they had departed Elysia and she hadn't even been aware of it. Now she could only hope their destination had been set for Star Base Intrepid. She didn't know if he would allow her further access to the computer, so she'd have to wait to check the destination screen secretly.

After a few moments, he pushed away from the console. Swiveling around, he eyed her, his gaze cold. The man who'd gentled two terrified children had reverted back to the ruthless shadower.

"Would you care to offer an explanation as to why you so blatantly defied my orders yesterday?"

Nessa forced herself to meet his steely gaze. "It wasn't my intention to defy orders, Captain. I only wanted to find transport to Zirak. The time before the eclipse is growing short."

"As is my patience, pilgrim. Twice now you've given your word that you would obey orders, and both times you failed to do so. Are you a liar, perhaps?"

Irrational anger flared at his blunt accusation. After all, she *had* lied about virtually everything. She'd been raised to believe that honor came before all else, yet Nessa knew her falsehoods were justified. "Not a liar, Captain. Just desperate. My people have sacrificed much for me to be able to participate in the ceremony of the eclipse."

"And was it desperation that led you to buy those children—or did you act solely on impulse? Did you even plan any further than buying Raven and Brand and bringing them on board my ship?"

She refused to admit her action might have been rash. "I planned on taking the children with me to Zirak. Then we could return to . . . Delsan together. My people will accept them." Chase had her so shaken, she'd almost forgotten her story. She warned herself to tread carefully.

"But now you have no money. How do you propose to earn transport passage for three people? And not only to Zirak, but home from there."

Realizing she had her hands clenched together, a dead giveaway of her tension, Nessa forced them to her sides. "I don't know. But I couldn't leave those children on Slavers' Square. I just *couldn't*. So punish me if you will, but don't take it out on them. I'll do whatever it takes to earn our passage. Anything you want me to do—cleaning, inventory, computer research, navigation. Anything."

His brows shot up. *"Anything?"*

Embarrassment set her face on fire. At the same time, pain jolted her heart. She'd known their mating had been a mistake, but to think it might be in payment of her debt to Chase wounded her deeply. Spirit, she could work in a Pleasure Dome if that was the case—except no one there would want her services.

But pride insisted she see this painful situation through. Determined Chase would never know her true feelings, Nessa drew a deep breath. "I'll do whatever is necessary for my survival and the survival of those children."

He scowled, apparently not happy with her answer. "I'll remember that, pilgrim." He spun the chair back around from her, and vehemently punched some pads.

It suddenly occurred to her that if Chase truly considered her his slave, he would see no reason to pay her for whatever services she performed. Desperation twisted her insides.

"What about the children?" she asked.

"What about them?"

"What are you planning to do with them? Will you allow them to go with me?"

His shoulders tensed and he raised his head. "I haven't decided yet."

"But what would you do with them? How could

you properly care for them, leading the life of a— of a . . ." She halted, appalled at what she'd almost said.

"A shadower?" he finished for her. "You should have thought of that before you so rashly purchased them."

Oh, Spirit, he meant to take them from her. Already, she felt an inexplicable bond with the children. They needed her. And she needed them. He spun back around just as her leg buckled, forcing her to grab the console for support.

"For Spirit's sake, sit down before you fall down," he growled.

She complied. "The children . . . are they all right?!"

Chase nodded grudgingly. "They appear to be in good health, although I need to examine Brand more closely. From their general condition, I'd say they hadn't been slaves very long; half a season, perhaps."

Even half a season seemed far too long to Nessa. "Why can't Brand speak? Raven said he used to talk."

Concern filled Chase's eyes. "It's probably not a physical condition, but a psychological one, caused by trauma. Hopefully, when he begins to feel safe, when the memories start to fade, he'll talk again."

Nessa leaned forward anxiously. She remembered so little about taking care of children. "How can we reassure him that he's safe with us?"

"By our actions. With patience and kindness, a lot of affection, and a lot of touching. We need to hold and hug the children as much as possible."

His statement seemed odd to her. Shielders did not customarily show much affection toward one another. "Why touching?"

Pensive, Chase stared toward the starboard portal. "Because human touch is healing. Even with the incredible medical advances of our age, nothing can surpass the power of loving, physical contact."

Physical contact. Nessa had certainly learned how electrifying that could be. She cleared her throat. "Is Raven okay?"

"Physically, she's fine. Emotionally, she appears to be dealing with her slavery experience better than Brand, although we might see signs of delayed post-traumatic stress. From her physical development, I suspect she'll be entering the transition into womanhood soon. She's going to need a mother figure. Someone to explain menses, to prepare her for the changes she'll go through."

A sudden memory bombarded Nessa, the memory of when her own cycle had started. She'd been terrified because she'd had no idea what was happening to her body. She'd been alone, without parents, for more than a season, when that happened. Jarek had been the one to explain she wasn't dying, only growing up.

She vowed to herself that that wouldn't happen to Raven. "I'll take care of Raven. I'll explain everything to her."

Chase steepled his fingers beneath his chin. "You're barely out of childhood yourself. What do you know about being a mother?"

She never would know—at least not as a biological mother. The painful reminder blazed through

Nessa. "Giving physical birth to a child doesn't automatically make a woman a good mother," she retorted, battling the ever-present bitterness from her own mother's desertion. "I do understand children. I used to take care of the younger ones in our clan, until—" The overwhelming memories kept her from continuing, and she bit her lip.

"Until your injury." Chase watched her, a wealth of understanding in his eyes.

Nessa looked away. She preferred his anger over his pity. "Please, let me help care for Raven and Brand. I'll talk with Raven about the coming changes, and look for some information she can read on the computer."

He considered for a moment. "All right. But understand this, Nessa. If you overstep your bounds one more time, your time will be spent pacing the brig."

Rising, he pulled her from her chair. "Come on. We're going to the galley."

"Why?"

"I'm going to show you how to operate the food replicator. I'm assigning you all galley duties—cooking and clean up. Then, after the morning meal, you can take the portable sterilizer and disinfect the ship. No telling what microorganisms you and the children tracked in, and I don't know if the air filtration system will catch it all."

So her duties were beginning. Nessa wondered just how far those duties would go, especially tonight. Anticipation hummed through her body. Disgusted and shocked by her reaction, she forced all thoughts of last night from her mind.

She was a Shielder, with a crucial mission to complete. She couldn't entertain a carnal attraction for anyone, much less a shadower.

Operating a food replicator proved to be a fairly simple process, and Nessa learned the basics quickly. Within half an hour, she was able to produce simple items like bread, cheese, and a dark tea Chase liked. Learning the program codes for the myriad other items the replicator could create would take a little more time.

They brought the children into the galley for the meal. Chase wanted them to become comfortable moving around the ship instead of burrowing in Nessa's cabin like frightened animals.

Before the children left the cabin, he fashioned makeshift tunics out of their blankets. He made Brand's first, cutting a hole for his head, then slipping the blanket on poncho style and tying it at the little boy's waist with a piece of rope. He did the same for Raven.

In the galley, Brand huddled in his chair, eating very little. Chase wrapped his leftovers in a napkin for him. "This is your food," he told Brand, "so you can take it with you, and eat whenever you want. But I expect you to begin eating more during our meals in the galley, okay?"

Observing this, Raven picked daintily at her food, then eyed Chase expectantly. "Oh, do you want me to do the same for you, Miss Raven?" She nodded shyly, and he complied, earning a small smile.

Watching him with the children, Nessa felt a lump rise in her throat. He seemed to understand their fears and insecurities and went out of his way to assuage them.

Chase explained to the children that he expected them to spend the morning shift with him or Nessa, not in their cabin. Raven seemed to have attached herself to Nessa, clinging to her tunic and following behind her like a shadow. But when Chase gently picked up the shaking Brand to go to the cockpit, Raven darted after them. She watched over Brand just like Jarek had watched over her, Nessa thought with a pang.

She cleaned the galley, then lugged the wheeled sterilizer from the supply room. Chase came into the corridor to show her how to operate the unit.

"Here's where you turn it on," he explained. "Aim this nozzle at the floor, ceiling, walls, all surfaces. It sprays an antibacterial mist that dries instantly. Do every part of the ship, except the cockpit, decontamination, and the laboratory. They have built-in sterilizing systems."

It took almost two hours for Nessa to complete her assignment. When she returned to the cockpit, Brand lay curled in Chase's lap, sound asleep. Raven sat in a chair pulled next to Chase, her feet dangling a good foot from the floor. As Nessa approached, she saw the girl had also fallen asleep, her head sagging sideways.

"I was trying to show them the different controls and how they worked," Chase admitted wryly. "As you can see, they found me fascinating."

Nessa nodded toward Brand. "How did you get him in your lap? He won't come to me."

"I told him one of his duties was being a lap

warmer. I still had to lift him up here. He's not ready to make any advances on his own."

Her heart warming dangerously, Nessa leaned down to study Raven. She noted the dark circles beneath the girl's eyes, and strong maternal instincts surged through her. She had the overpowering urge to wrap her arms around Raven and rock the fragile girl until she felt safe.

Surprised by her strong reaction, she jerked her head up to find Chase's discerning gaze upon her. Her emotions all jumbled, she felt her face grow warm. She straightened. "What else do you want me to do?"

He leaned back in his chair, shifting Brand. "Contact the computer at the sector Controller base on Odera and download the latest location reports on wanted offenders. It will take some time. The communication link codes are in the Odera file."

The one computer assignment she couldn't possibly enjoy, knowing Shielder names would probably be in the downloaded file. Nessa went to her seat and began the process.

A while later, as she sat waiting for the transfer to be completed, she heard the soft padding of small feet. A sleepy-eyed Raven stood beside her chair, watching silently. Remembering Chase's recommendation, Nessa patted the space beside her. "Come sit with me."

Raven moved closer, then hesitated. Reaching out, Nessa gathered the girl into the chair with her. She kept her arm around Raven, explaining how the computer worked. When the download was completed, Nessa glanced over at Chase. He seemed occupied, so she quickly checked the destination screen, which read: DESTINATION: STAR BASE INTREPID.

Relief swept through her. Chase was finally keeping his word. But once they arrived there, would she be able to come up with enough money for transport for three? She'd have to start decoding the new vault code, just in case.

Pushing aside those concerns for the time being, Nessa pulled up more interesting files to show Raven. The girl found the pictures of the strange creatures and the many planets in the quadrant fascinating, but admitted she couldn't read. Resolving to teach her at the first opportunity, Nessa read some of the stories to her. She also located some information on puberty and shared it with Raven, watching the girl's reaction. Raven kept looking from the screen to Nessa in astonishment. Nessa assured her that the information was true—Raven would soon undergo these amazing changes and become a young woman.

She had never felt so needed, especially when Raven cuddled closer and rested her head on Nessa's shoulder. Nessa wanted to hold the girl close forever, and protect her from the despair and fear that constituted an integral part of a Shielder's existence. But she knew she could only help Raven prepare for the world that awaited her.

The rest of the day passed uneventfully. Nessa prepared the midday and evening meals, with some further instruction from Chase, but all of the cleanup fell to her. She didn't complain, accepting her duties, grateful she wasn't in the brig instead.

As the ship cycle waned, the children grew

sleepy, worn out by the stress of a new environment. Chase and Nessa tucked them into Nessa's bunk, then watched them drop into sleep. When they were deeply asleep, Chase completed his examination of Brand. He also gave both children immunization injections, which didn't seem to disturb them in the least.

Nessa watched him gather his equipment, filled with both anticipation and dread. What now? Would he expect her to mate with him, as part of a slave's duties? She knew he couldn't possibly find her very attractive, but she now realized such considerations didn't matter if the mating need was strong enough.

She didn't want to mate under those circumstances. Pride and dignity demanded she refuse such an arrangement. Yet she might not have much choice in the matter. Not only was time on the Orana incubation growing short, but now the fate of two innocent children complicated the situation.

Chase closed his equipment case and stepped back from the bunk. He held out his hand to Nessa. "Come on, let's go to bed."

Chapter Thirteen

He must be going crazy. He knew better than to allow this senseless attraction toward Nessa to go any further, Chase told himself. He'd been sure that she felt the same attraction, until now, when he could feel her shaking as they walked toward his cabin. Was it from fear or desire?

She deserved to be in the brig, after the stunt she'd pulled yesterday. And that constituted the *least* of the damage she had caused.

In truth, Nessa's presence on his ship had broadsided him emotionally, in more ways than one. Her medical problems had necessitated frequent visits to the lab, a painful reminder of his miserable failure as a physician.

The colossal mistake of giving in to the lure between them and making love had further complicated the situation. Blazing hells. Why did she have to be a virgin and why, by the Spirit, why, did that fact affect him so profoundly? He'd reacted like some primitive cave dweller from Trion, feeling protective and possessive toward her. As if she belonged to him now.

Then she'd brought the children onto the ship. Those little waifs had immediately yanked on Chase's heartstrings. For three seasons, he'd managed to lock all feeling away. But now his carefully constructed wall was cracking. Spirit, but it hurt to feel again. Unresolved grief, anger, and guilt, safely buried until now, deluged him like a flash flood.

Not even competent enough to capture the one person responsible for his personal hell, how had he handled these emotions? By exploding at Nessa, shaking the life out of her, then losing himself in her exquisitely tight sheath. Which he wanted to do again—starting right now.

Granted, last night should never have happened—and wouldn't have, if not for the influence of the liquor. But the alcohol had weakened his guard just enough—and Nessa had looked so damned sexy with that robe clinging to every curve.

She looked apprehensive now, as they entered his cabin, but he would make certain she enjoyed the actual act of mating tonight. He should have stayed away from her after their first encounter. But he hadn't. The damage was already done, he rationalized, so why not find comfort in each other's arms? It had been so long for him . . . so very long.

He'd told Nessa the truth about the healing power of touch. Holding Brand today, Chase had wished for someone to hold him, to smooth away the terrible memories, the stark loneliness, if only for a short while. It was foolishness, because nothing would ever eradicate the reality. Still, he yearned for the momentary oblivion he seemed to find only with Nessa.

As the panel slid shut, he unbuckled his utility belt, tossing it on the console. He sank into his chair, swiveling to watch Nessa while he removed his boots. She remained by the panel, her eyes wary. It wasn't quite the look of the eager lover.

"What are you thinking, Nessa?"

She averted her gaze to the bunk, her hands balled up. "I'm not used to sleeping with anyone."

Good. He'd be the only one with that honor. Watching the rapid rise and fall of her breasts beneath her tunic, Chase felt himself hardening. He tossed his boots to the side. "Sleep wasn't exactly what I had in mind."

He stood and approached her. Her gaze snapped back to him, her eyes widening. The rich brown of her tunic emphasized the golden glow of her satiny skin. Her eyes, dark whirlpools of emotion, swirled him into their depths. By the Abyss, but he thought he might explode right then. He clamped down mentally, determined to master his body.

When he felt he'd regained a modicum of control, he spread his arms invitingly. "Why don't you undress me?"

Her gaze skittered down him, pausing at his straining erection. "Is that an order?"

Irritation cooled his ardor, if only a few degrees. Why was she so reluctant, given the extent of her sensual nature? He knew firsthand how incredibly responsive she was, how capable of enjoying his caresses. She'd come to him eagerly enough before; she had come apart in his arms in the shower.

Maybe she still felt shy in this new sexual arena and just needed encouragement.

He leaned forward and pressed his mouth to hers, teasing her lips with his tongue. "Consider it an order, if you wish," he murmured.

She stiffened, but her hands slid to the top of his flightsuit seam. He buried his face in her hair, inhaling the fresh scent as she pulled the fabric off his shoulders and down his arms. When his arms were free of the sleeves, he pressed his hands against the panel on each side of her head and captured her mouth again, this time plundering the sweetness inside.

Her hands fluttered helplessly before flattening on his bare chest. The contact was electric. *Touch me. Nessa. Touch me. Make me forget.* Blindly, he sought her breast and claimed it.

She broke the kiss and sidestepped, gasping for breath. Chase reached for her, but she evaded him. Baffled, he stared at her, noting her obvious reluctance. Squaring her shoulders, she met his gaze. "Do you wish me to finish undressing you . . . master?"

Master? His passion-fogged brain struggled to make sense of her actions. *Master?* Why would she call him that, with such a harsh tone, unless . . .

Realization speared through him, evaporating the sensual haze like a photon torpedo. She considered mating with him a requirement of her duties. The duties slaves performed for their masters.

Hadn't she said earlier she'd do anything to earn transport passage?

Understanding washed over him, with much the same effect as a cold shower. His mind cleared rapidly. If his guess was correct, last night had not been the mutual explosion of passion he'd assumed, but simply reluctant participation on Nessa's part. Rape—if he wanted to be technical.

And in the shower, she'd been too inexperienced and helpless against his sensual onslaught not to respond, albeit unwillingly.

Blazing hells. What else would she think, after the words he'd hurled in anger last night? He could rescind those words easily enough, but to what end? It wouldn't change the fact that she didn't want to lie with him. Hadn't wanted anything to do with him since he'd blundered through her first sexual experience.

Frustration roared through him and he pounded his fist against the panel. He'd never forced himself on any female, and he'd always despised those shadowers who raped their female prisoners.

He'd just sunk to their ranks.

"We're not finishing anything," he growled, striding to the console and grabbing up his half-empty bottle from last night. While he was at it, he yanked open the cabinet above the console and took another.

He stormed back to the entry, the top part of his flightsuit flapping against his legs. He glared into Nessa's startled eyes. "You're safe from me, do you understand? *Safe!* I won't make any more advances toward you."

He headed for the cockpit, where he could lock himself in and find the oblivion he'd been anticipating earlier.

Only it wouldn't be in Nessa's arms.

Nessa stared after Chase, totally confused by his actions. For a few moments, she'd been certain he planned to mate with her. Now she didn't know whether to be relieved or disappointed. Her mouth still tingled from his passionate kiss, and her body hummed with stirring sensations. She should be relieved, she told herself firmly. She didn't want to be chosen for mating solely because she was available and owed him a great debt.

But she wouldn't have to worry about that possibility. Apparently Chase found her so repulsive, he couldn't even force himself on her.

She shouldn't be surprised, especially after seeing the abundance of beautiful, gifted women in the quadrant. She shouldn't feel the hurt, not after ten seasons of rejection, not since Chase had made his disinterest clear from the first mating. His actions last night had been influenced by the liquor, nothing more.

She knew all that, understood it on an intellectual level. Yet she still found it hard sometimes to accept her shortcomings as a woman. To accept the fact that no man would ever find her attractive, that she could never bear children.

The reality didn't ease the heaviness in her chest right now, or the tightness in her throat . . . or the ache in her heart.

Reality didn't allow her the luxury of self-pity or

self-centered desires, either. She should thank Spirit for forcing her to remember the crucial goal at hand.

Eleven days. Cold fear crystallized inside her. Only eleven days remained before the Orana began actively invading her body.

And they were still two days from Star Base Intrepid.

Knowing Orana wasn't contagious until the final stages, Nessa slept with the children, curled protectively around them. They stirred early, stretching with the precious innocence of youth before they awakened fully. They blinked in sleepy surprise to see her in the bunk with them. She cuddled them close for a few minutes, discovering Chase had been right. Touch *was* healing, for the giver as well as the receiver.

An hour later, Nessa faced the food replicator in the galley, studying program codes. She heard Chase calling her. She stepped into the corridor as he headed from the cockpit toward his cabin. "Yes, Captain?"

He paused, glaring at her through bloodshot eyes. "Replicate some of that black tea we had yesterday. Make it strong. Bring it to my cabin—and be quick about it!"

She nodded, and he trudged to his cabin, swaying slightly. Nessa suspected he'd drunk all that alcohol last night and would pay for it today. On second thought, *she* would pay for it today. She replicated the tea and carried it to his cabin. He didn't answer the tone, so she entered cautiously. He wasn't in sight, and she could hear the shower. She left the tea on the console and returned to the galley.

Chase appeared some time later, while Nessa and the children were eating the morning meal. He didn't look quite as pale, although red still tinged his eyes. She rose and pulled out a chair for him. "Can I get you something to eat?"

Scowling fiercely, he shoved away the chair. "No, no food. The very thought of it sickens me," he growled. "Just make me another cup of tea and bring it to the cockpit. Don't take too long. And keep the noise down!"

He stormed from the galley, leaving Nessa relieved to see him go. Raven looked up, her mouth trembling. "What did I do wrong?"

Nessa leaned down beside her chair. "You didn't do anything wrong, sweetness. What makes you think that?"

Raven shivered. "Master is mad. I did something wrong. Will he use the rod on me?"

Nessa fought the distinct urge to go hit Chase. "Captain McKnight is just tired this morning, and he's grouchy. That's all. He's not mad at you. And we never, *never* use the rod on this ship."

When she glanced over and saw Brand rolled into a tight ball, she mentally amended that last statement. She might just use an electrolyzer rod on Chase if he upset the children like this again.

Several minutes passed before she convinced Brand that Chase wasn't mad at him, and there weren't even any rods on the ship. She didn't know if the child believed her, but at least he sat upright in the chair again.

Catherine Spangler

She made more tea and took it to the cockpit. Chase ignored her when she set the tea beside him. "Captain McKnight, I'd like a word with you, please."

He didn't take his eyes from the wanted offender screen. "Later. I don't want to be disturbed right now."

Nessa blew out a frustrated breath. "You terrified the children in the galley this morning."

He dragged his gaze from the screen, his brows drawing together as he scowled. "By the Abyss! All I did was ask for a cup of tea."

Staring into his haggard face, guilt besieged her. He'd done so much for her, only to be repaid with trouble. He'd been wonderful with the children.

"I know you didn't mean to," she tried to explain, "but your tone and your scowl made them think you were mad at them."

His brows drew even closer together. "I do not scowl. And I don't have the time or patience to deal with overly sensitive women and children."

His unreasonable mood annoyed her. "Well, you frightened them. They thought you were going to use an electrolyzer rod on them."

"Right now, I don't give an Antek's rear what they thought," Chase snapped, anger flaring in his eyes. "I have a ship to run, and I don't want to be bothered."

She held on to her temper. "You have good cause to be angry, Captain. I know I've been a troublesome burden. But please, wait to reprimand me when the children aren't around."

"I don't need you telling me how to conduct my

affairs. Now, get moving. Bring me an entire pot of that tea, then sterilize the damn ship again. Are those orders clear?"

She resisted the urge to kick him. "Yes, Captain. Perfectly clear." She left the cockpit, pondering his angry mood and deciding liquor had a strange effect on some people.

She took the children to the relative safety of her cabin, then fixed Chase's tea. She spent another two hours sterilizing the ship. After that, she and the children remained in the cabin.

Nessa told stories and introduced Brand and Raven to Turi. Displaying a surprising acceptance, he even allowed the children to pet him. After Turi had been safely returned to his case, they let the silver lanrax out of the lav, coaxing her over with scraps of bread. She proved to be gentle enough, daintily accepting the bread and chattering when Brand tentatively touched her. They decided to name her Lia, after one of Elysia's silver moons.

Having no desire to deal with Chase again, Nessa slipped furtively to the galley for the midday and evening meals. She brought the food back to the cabin, and they enjoyed a picnic on the bunk. The cycle slipped by pleasantly. When the children's eyelids began to droop, she herded them into the shower, then into bed.

Just as she was tucking the cover around them, the tone sounded. Nessa straightened, her heart speeding up. What could Chase possibly want now? Reluctantly, she padded to the panel and opened it.

He stood there, dark shadows beneath his eyes.

"I wanted to tell the children good night. May I come in?" he asked quietly.

He didn't seem angry. Nessa drew a deep breath. "Of course." She stepped back for him to enter.

The children watched his approach, apprehension in their eyes. As Chase reached the bunk, Brand squeezed his eyes shut and rolled into a ball. Raven drew the cover up to her trembling chin.

Chase sat on the edge of the bed. "I didn't mean to frighten you today," he began, his deep voice pitched to a soothing level. "You're both good children, and I'm not mad at either of you. I know this is hard for you to believe, after the way you've been treated, but we do not punish anyone on this ship by hitting or shocking them. If you do something wrong, we will discuss it and decide on a fitting discipline. But I promise you, no one will hurt you in any way."

He offered his hand to Raven. "Okay?"

Tentatively, she placed her hand in his. "Okay," she agreed.

Chase reached over and rubbed Brand's back. "How about you, Brand?"

Brand made no reply, and Chase patted him and rose. "Good night. See you tomorrow."

He paused by Nessa, his gaze capturing hers, and for a brief moment she thought he might say something. But he simply nodded and left.

The next morning, everything seemed to be on an even keel again. Chase joined them for the morning meal. Appearing more rested, he ruffled both Brand and Raven's hair before he sat down. Nothing was said about the day before. After the meal, he went to the cockpit to check for incoming transmissions, which he did first thing every cycle.

The children remained in the galley with Nessa, helping her clean. Raven proved to be an able helper, and such a joy, an inseparable shadow who tugged frequently on Nessa's tunic. She returned Nessa's hugs now, and even slipped her delicate hand into Nessa's for reassurance. Brand didn't offer any affection, but neither did he resist.

Chase's serious voice came over the intercom, startling all three of them. "Nessa, could you come to the cockpit, please? Leave the children in your cabin for now."

He didn't sound angry, but Nessa's internal alarm clamored. Something felt wrong. She ushered Brand and Raven into her cabin, giving them pieces of bread to feed the lanraxes.

Smoothing her tunic, she hurried to the cockpit. Staring out the portal, Chase appeared to be deep in thought. He turned at her entry, and her heart skipped when she saw his resolute expression. Uneasiness snaked through her; she sensed he was about to convey unwelcome news.

He gestured to her chair. "Sit down."

She sank into the chair, her hands seeking each other in her lap. Tension stiffened her spine as she watched Chase consider his words. He met her anxious gaze, regret in his eyes.

"I want to apologize for my aggressive physical behavior toward you. I realize I took advantage of your emotional state the first time we mated. That should never have happened. But more unforgivable was the second time, since you made it quite clear you had no desire to repeat the experience. That night in my cabin, I was not . . ." He paused and cleared his throat. "Thinking clearly, and I wasn't aware of your reluctance."

Nessa sat mystified, trying to grasp his meaning. She realized he was talking about the two times they'd mated, but he made no sense. She hadn't been aware of expressing any reluctance to mate with him. At least, not until she thought he expected it because she owed him.

True, she'd been fearful, of the pain and of exposing her scarred body, but not unwilling. She hadn't even thought of resisting, especially during the heated frenzy Chase's touch had triggered. But he didn't need to know that.

Chase sighed and leaned forward. "Nessa, I never intended to obligate you sexually in any way. I know I said you owed me whatever I wanted, but that didn't mean I expected you to mate with me against your will. I wouldn't demand that of anyone, not even in payment of a debt. I said some foolish things in anger. I apologize."

Her brow furrowed, Nessa mentally reviewed his words. He had just told her he hadn't expected her to mate with him, unless she chose to. But if he didn't think it her duty, and if he didn't find her appealing, why would he even approach her? Shock prompted her to blurt, "Then why?"

He shook his head, not comprehending. "Why what?"

Chagrined by her impulsive question, she averted her gaze.

"Tell me, Nessa."

She needed to better control her reactions. Questions still burned in her mind, but she didn't really want to delve into Chase's reasons for mating with her. She had no desire to risk further humiliation or reminders of her lack of appeal. She rotated her chair away. "It doesn't matter, Captain. There's nothing to apologize for. I'm not upset about . . . what happened."

A long moment of silence hung between them before Chase said, "All right, then. There's something else I need to tell you."

His voice held the tone that had alarmed her earlier. Nessa pivoted around. He sat back in his chair, watching her. "I might as well inform you directly, since you always discover our destination on your own. We're no longer headed for Star Base Intrepid."

She felt as though the breath had been knocked from her body. By the Spirit, no! So little time remained. "You can't do that!" she gasped, rising from her chair. "I have to get to Intrepid. I have to!"

Chase's eyes took on the cold, distant look she both dreaded and hated. "I must go to Odera on urgent business. Not that I have to explain my decisions to you."

Shaking, she came around the console to the side of his chair. "What about my business? It's urgent, too. And you gave your word. Several times now."

His face hardened into a mask of determination. "My business can't wait."

Her heart threatened to burst through her chest. "Neither can mine, Captain."

"I've checked the date of your eclipse on Zirak.

It's not for ten days yet. We'll arrive at Odera to-morrow, and depart within one ship cycle. Three days to Intrepid, four days from there to Zirak. You'll make it, just as I promised. Assuming you can purchase passage."

That would get her to Zirak in nine days. Then she still had to get to Sonoma, another two days. She grabbed Chase's arm. "I must be there sooner, to prepare for the ceremony."

His icy gaze bored through her. "Sorry. I can't get you there any sooner."

She tightened her grip on his arm. "But why? What is so pressing you can't take me to Intrepid first?"

He pried her hand off his arm. "It's not your concern, or your place to ask. I won't have my actions questioned. You're dismissed from the cockpit."

He stood, towering over her. "Go on."

Nessa dug her nails into her hand to resist the urge to grab him again. "Captain, please! You don't understand."

He gripped her shoulders and lowered his face close to hers. "What don't I understand?"

She saw no compassion or gentleness in his eyes, only a fathomless wall of indifference. The eyes of a shadower, predator of all Shielders. She couldn't reveal the truth to him. Not even after all the intimacies between them; not even after his tender care of the children.

For ten seasons, she'd endured the bitter lash of betrayal from her own people. How much swifter and harsher would the treachery be at the hands of a shadower? Especially a shadower under the influence of Controller indoctrination.

"You don't understand honor," she retorted.

Rage flickered in his eyes, and his grip on her shoulders tightened painfully. "Honor? You question my honor—you, who lied to me on at least two occasions? You, who refused to obey orders? You have a lot to learn about honor, lady."

He released her so suddenly, she staggered back. "Leave the cockpit. Now."

Nessa fled to the corridor, leaning against the wall to catch her breath. A sense of doom threatened to suffocate her. She wasn't going to make it to Sonoma in time. Not only would she suffer a hideous death, but her failure could result in the annihilation of her people. Unless she came up with another solution quickly, one that would enable her to travel directly to Sonoma without further delay.

Unless . . .

She hijacked Chase's ship while he was on Odera tomorrow.

Chapter Fourteen

Nessa paused outside Chase's cabin and nervously smoothed her robe. She didn't have to go through with it. She could still change her mind.

Oh, but she wanted this.

She wanted to feel the sensual excitement Chase roused when he kissed her, when he touched her. Wanted to again enjoy the incredible explosion of pleasure she'd experienced with him in the shower. A part of her felt mortified at these wanton urgings, while another part of her longed for one last time in Chase's arms.

After tomorrow, she'd never again have that opportunity. Even if she arrived at Sonoma in time, and survived the Orana, she wasn't foolish enough to expect any man to be interested in her. But Chase had mated with her twice and apparently had planned to a third time. He had been willing to join his body with hers, even if strictly out of sexual need.

She'd replayed the odd conversation with him to-day over and over in her mind, yet she didn't really understand what he'd been trying to say. So he might well reject her tonight.

But still . . . this could well be her last chance to experience mating. Taking a deep breath, Nessa sounded the panel tone.

"Come in."

Her hand shaking, she punched the pad and the panel slid open. Chase lounged back in his chair, a scanner line moving down the rows of words on the monitor before him.

He glanced up and his hand froze on the scanner control. He stared for a long moment, taking in her robe. Tension radiated from his stiff posture. "What do you want?"

Spirit, what do I say? Forcing air into her con-stricted chest, Nessa stepped into the room.

"I want . . ." She paused, desperately seeking the right words. Her heart pounded in her chest, rever-berating in her head. Licking her dry lips, she tried again. "I'm here to . . ." Failing miserably, she re-leased a frustrated sigh.

Chase came out of the chair. "What is it? Is some-thing wrong? Are the children all right?"

"Everything's fine," she assured him hastily. "The children are asleep, and—well . . ."

It was no good. She had no appeal, no seduction skills. Helplessly, she stared at him. He had gone utterly still, watching her with an intensity that both frightened and excited her.

"Why are you here, Nessa?"

She reached deep for her lagging courage. "To be with you." Spirit, even her voice shook.

"To be with me? What exactly does that mean?"

Best to say it outright. "I want to mate with you."

His eyes flared, then narrowed. "I told you today I don't expect or demand sexual favors. Go back to your cabin."

In spite of her pride being rapidly shredded, she pushed on. "I understand that. I'm here because I *want* to mate with you."

She took a step closer, and his whole body tensed. He grasped her shoulders, moving her back. His steely gaze bore into her eyes. "This won't change my mind about Odera."

He hadn't rejected her outright—at least, not yet. Reaching up, she slid a trembling hand down the seam of his flightsuit, opening it to his waist. "I'm not trying to change your mind about anything."

He removed her hand. "Then *why* are you here? You've made your distaste for mating quite clear."

With startling insight, Nessa realized that Chase doubted her desire for him. He saw her inexperienced attempts at seduction only as ploys to get his cooperation. In an odd way, he needed reassurance just as much as she did. That knowledge gave her a surge of confidence.

She inhaled deeply, nurturing a heady boldness, and moved closer. "I *do* like mating."

Bravely, she parted the seam edges of Chase's flightsuit, her breath hitching at the sight of his bare chest. Magnificent. She slid her palm over his breast, savoring the heat and the increasing beat of his heart. "I want to do it again."

He drew a shuddering breath. "You're playing with fire, lady."

Her breathing stopped entirely, and a heated rush flowed through her veins, pooling low in her belly. Wicked desires, fueled by mental images of the Pleasure Domes, lured her to press her lips against his chest. "I'm not afraid of fire," she whispered.

Beneath her mouth, his heart pounded fiercely, as a new tension seemed to radiate from him. Grasping Nessa's chin, he tilted her face up toward his glittering gaze. "This is not a game," he grated roughly. "If you stay, it will be on my terms."

His harsh voice only served to heighten the desire twining through her body. "Terms?"

"You'll be completely mine tonight. You'll give yourself freely. No pretenses, no false modesty. And you'll stay with me until morning. No running away."

She should be frightened by his words, by the ultrapredatory expression in his eyes. But, Spirit help her, she only wanted him more. A growing feminine perception led her to the realization that mating, like anything else in life, should be give and take. "What about *my* terms?"

His hand moved from her chin, threading through her hair and tilting her head back farther. "Your terms?"

Nessa pressed both palms against his chest. His skin felt tantalizingly smooth and warm. "I'll do what you want, but in return, you'll have to give yourself freely to me."

The lines of his face sharpened as his scrutiny burned into her very soul. Releasing her head, he took her hand and slid it down over the bulge of his manhood. "Then finish what you've started."

The feel of him through the flightsuit momentarily distracted Nessa from her own rising passions. Amazed, she explored the hardness of him. "How does it get so big? Does it hurt?"

"Sweet Spirit have mercy," Chase groaned, pushing against her hand. "Let's save the biology lesson for later." He released the seam of her robe, running his finger down to where the seam ended, right at her belly button. Slipping his hand beneath the fabric, he slid it along her belly, then lower. Nessa gasped and grabbed his arms, her legs threatening to buckle.

"So you like mating, do you?" His free hand worked the robe off her shoulders.

She tried to gather her scattered thoughts as he withdrew his hand from between her legs. "Y-yes."

"Let go of me for a minute," he said, tugging on the robe. She did, and the robe slid off her arms and down her body, into a silky pool at her feet. "Now step out of it."

Nessa did as he commanded. The cool air swept over her heated skin, almost painful against her hardening nipples. But then Chase's hands were there, cupping her breasts and making her forget completely about being cold.

He backed her toward the bunk and tumbled her onto it. Finding herself sprawled across the mat in a very exposed position, she struggled to get up; but he stopped her with his hand against her shoulder. "No. Don't move. I like looking at you."

Feeling extremely vulnerable, she sank back. He peeled off his flightsuit, all the while staring at her body. Unable to look away, she stared back. He was large and powerful all over, but her first good look at his jutting manhood drew her attention. Amazed by its size, she remembered the pain of the previous joinings, and alarm reared inside her.

Just then, Chase sat on the edge of the bunk, running his hands along her thighs. He parted them, ignoring her automatic resistance, his gaze focused on her most private part.

A heated flush spreading across her face, Nessa tried to close her thighs, but he tightened his grip. "Don't. You shouldn't be embarrassed, Nessa. You're beautiful all over."

He leaned down, kissing her injured thigh, gently moving his mouth over her scar. Appalled, she battled the futile urge to yank the cover over that hated scar, to hide its ugliness from Chase. But then his lips moved higher, and logical thoughts evaporated. His hair fell in a golden veil over her leg and abdomen, sending whispering sensations through her body.

His breath scathingly close to her female flesh startled her, and she jerked against him. "All right, little innocent." With a frustrated groan, Chase raised himself up. "No sense shocking you too much at once." He smiled shakily. "Perhaps later."

Crawling onto the bunk, he stroked his hands up her abdomen and claimed her breasts, teasing the nipples with his thumbs. "So soft," he murmured. "So perfect."

His husky words were as potent as his touch. Desire careened through her, so intense, Nessa let out a little cry. She twisted toward him, grasping his shoulders as an anchor.

He settled beside her, pulling her close. She pressed against him, feeling less exposed and blessedly safe. Cupping her face up to his, he kissed her, deeply and thoroughly. She could do this all night, she thought, savoring his taste, the suggestive feel of his tongue stroking hers. She was disappointed when his mouth left hers, but only momentarily. His lips moved to her chin, her neck, her collarbone, the slope of her breast. His mouth hovered there. "I intend to find out," he whispered, his breath sending rippling chills across her skin, "exactly what it is you like so much about mating."

He kissed his way to her nipple. "Do you like this?" He drew it into his mouth and suckled. Nessa dug her fingers into the mat as waves of sensation spread through her breast, somehow mysteriously traveling lower.

"Yes," she gasped.

A moment later, he lifted his head, his searing gaze taking what little breath she had left. "I'll bet you like this." Nudging her thighs apart again, he stroked her sensitive, feminine flesh.

Heat and need flooded her. "Chase!" she cried, writhing against his hand.

"And this." He slid a finger inside her, moving it in and out.

Hurtling way past the point of modesty or pretense, she spread her thighs wider, totally of her own volition this time. "Yes. Oh, yes!"

He gave a low laugh. "I thought you might. Spirit, you're hot and ready for me." His voice sounded strained. "I want you so badly, I think we'd better finish this *now*."

Claiming her mouth in a drugging kiss, he positioned his body over hers. Inundated with a need so aching, so intense and overwhelming, Nessa forgot her earlier fears, focusing only on the feel of Chase's manhood seeking entry into her body. She arched against him, urging him inside.

Even so, he entered her carefully, then stopped. It wasn't enough, and frustrated, she wiggled against him. He groaned. "Does it hurt?"

She shook her head against his chest. "No."

"Good." He pressed deeper, filling her completely, then withdrew. He returned to fill her again. And again. Nessa experienced no pain this time, only incredible pleasure. She found herself moving with Chase's rhythm, meeting each thrust, urgently seeking more. He seemed to understand what she needed.

"Pull your legs back," he instructed hoarsely. "That's it. Stay with me, Nessa."

Gasping, she pressed her head against the mat, enmeshed in the sensations engulfing her entire body. Vaguely, she heard a woman's cries, as if from very far away.

Were those sounds coming from her? Shocked at the sudden realization, she clamped a hand over her mouth. "No." Chase drew back, prying away her hand. He twined it with his and pressed it against the mat. "Sounds of enjoyment are part of mating. Come on, sweetheart. Let me hear how good it feels."

He increased his tempo, driving hard and deep, and her inner muscles tightened around him. Nessa gave up worrying about the sounds that flowed from her throat as readily as he moved inside her. Instead she surrendered to the mounting tension within, to the delicious, building anticipation.

Then she exploded in an ecstasy so fierce and intense, she wondered if she'd died and gone to Haven. She cried out as shockwaves of pure pleasure radiated from where she and Chase were joined, spreading heat and light through her entire body.

A moment later, he cried out as well, heaving and shuddering. Then he collapsed upon her, his breathing ragged.

They lay that way for some time. Utterly boneless, Nessa didn't mind Chase's weight pressing her down. In fact, she savored the sense of warmth and security his body offered. Eventually, he shifted off her, drawing her against his side and guiding her head to rest against his shoulder. She fit there perfectly, she thought dreamily.

Shards of pleasure still tingled within her body, gradually subsiding to a relaxed glow. The force of the physical release astounded her, as did the total contentment left in its wake. Even more surprising, a sense of intimacy lingered between them, as if the act of baring one's body to someone else bared one's soul as well.

She stirred, and Chase drew her closer. His fingers stroked soothing circles down her back and on her rear. Touch certainly had its benefits. Nessa felt so peaceful, so protected with Chase's arms around her, she wished she could stay there forever, forget about Orana . . . and her plans for tomorrow.

His warm hand grasping her chin jolted her from her reverie as he lifted her face and kissed her. He took his time, his tongue leisurely stroking hers before he withdrew to feather light kisses on her lips.

"So you really do like mating," he murmured, radiating masculine satisfaction.

Oddly shy now that the mindless passion had receded, she lowered her eyes from his triumphant gaze. "I told you I did."

He chuckled softly. "Still embarrassed, after what we just did? Better get used to it, Nessa, since I'm certain we'll be doing it again very shortly."

"We will?" She looked at him in wide-eyed surprise, not at all sure such an eruption of passion could possibly happen again so soon. "Is that what most people do when they mate?"

Chase grinned wickedly. "Some. Unless one of the partners runs anyway and hides in the lav—or the shower. But I don't think we'll have that problem, do you?"

Nessa realized he was teasing her, like he had done with the children. A giddy warmth filled her, leaving her lighthearted and playful, feelings she'd left far behind ten seasons ago. She smiled back. "Oh, I don't know. That could prove to be very interesting."

His eyes widened. "Why, you little tease. Come here."

He pulled her on top of him. Her breath caught

at the feel of her nipples rubbing against his chest; at the twitch and expansion of his manhood against her belly. Heated need flared again, sudden and urgent.

Chase held her face between his hands, his molten gaze sending sparks along every nerve in her body. "Do you know what happens to impudent females who tease their bed partners?"

Her heart raced erratically as erotic images flashed through her mind. "What?"

"This." He pulled her face down and kissed her hard, his tongue mating with hers. "And this." He turned her onto the mat, his hands moving over her body, igniting flames and leaving her breathless. "And this."

"Are we going to mate again now?" she asked breathlessly, reeling from his sensual onslaught.

He slid over her, settling his hardness between her legs. "What do you think?"

A surge of feminine power, as old as the universe, thrummed through Nessa. "I think not." She shoved against him, pushing him onto his back as she came to her knees. "Not until *my* terms are met. Not until I do this." She ran her tongue over one bronze nipple, emboldened by the sharp intake of his breath.

"Do you like this?" she asked, amazed at her own audacity, yet enjoying herself immensely.

"Yes! Oh, yes," he squealed in a mock falsetto.

He so surprised Nessa that she laughed and hit him with the pillow.

Chase stilled, pushing the pillow out of his face. He studied her, his gaze suddenly serious. "That's the first time I've ever heard you laugh."

When was the last time she'd felt so joyous, so free? Nessa couldn't remember.

"I like hearing you laugh. Do it some more." He started tickling her.

"No! Stop!" She tried to squirm away. But he pursued his assault relentlessly. They tussled a few minutes, Nessa laughing and gasping for breath at the same time.

"Please! I surrender," she finally pleaded, her voice hoarse.

"You surrender, do you?" he asked silkily, radiating male dominance. "So we're back to my terms, are we?"

Taking a moment to catch her breath, she shook her head. Stroking her hand down his abdomen, she whispered, "We're back to my terms."

Heat flooded his eyes, and he rolled back, pulling her over him. "Since you insist, I won't argue with you. Now, where were you?"

Passion returned with startling swiftness. "I think I was here," she whispered against his chest.

Boldly, she ran her hands over his body, making the heady discovery that he liked being touched as much as she did; that she could render him vulnerable and incoherent with her mouth and her fingers. That the power wielded in mating could indeed be a mutual give and take, a safe haven where no emotional barriers were needed.

When both of them were about to come apart, he lifted her to straddle him. Surprised, she found herself poised over his manhood. He found the entrance to her body, and she slid down over him, sheathing him so deeply, surely he must be touching her solar plexus, where her soul resided. She moaned, stretching, adjusting, closing around him.

His glittering gaze imprisoned her and she forgot to breathe. "Remember the chair?" he grated. "Just like that, Nessa. Ride me. You're in control now, lady. You have me at your mercy." He demonstrated what he wanted, moving her hips with his hands.

Taking up the motion, she threw her head back, lost in sensation. Oh . . . yes . . . oh, she liked being in control . . . very much. Liked Chase's fevered encouragement, how he touched her everywhere as she moved on him.

And the ensuing explosion . . . oh, Spirit. . . .

Sometime later, when rational thought returned, she found it fascinating that the second mating could be every bit as good as the first, perhaps even better. And the shared intimacy even deeper. She cuddled against Chase, too exhausted to move. Beneath her, the sheets felt cool and damp.

"We're sweaty," she said with some surprise.

"Yeah, we are," he agreed, his voice laced with satisfaction. His hand slid over her breast. "We'll have to take a shower later."

She tilted her head to look at him. "I don't know if I have enough energy."

His eyes gleamed in the semidarkness. "Oh, you will, sweetheart. Just give me a little time to . . . recover. Then we'll take a long shower together."

His unmistakably sensual meaning edged through her lethargy. "Oh, Chase, I can't possibly—"

"Sure you can," he interrupted. "Trust me on this, Nessa."

An hour later, she found out Chase was right. She also discovered there were many ways of finding pleasure in a cleansing stall.

Much later, curled in the sanctuary of Chase's arms, she acknowledged to herself that their intimacy had forged inexplicable emotional bonds. Resolutely, she prepared to sever those bonds tomorrow. She'd carry the memory of this night with her always, but her time with Chase had come to an end. She could delay her mission no longer.

After tomorrow, she'd never see him again.

"How much longer until we get there?" Raven asked. She shared a chair with Nessa as they read a computer file on novas.

"An hour, sweetness," Nessa answered, only half of her attention on the girl. Tension knotted her insides as she thought about her plan.

She looked over at Chase, who had Brand snuggled in his lap. She stared at Chase's muscular arm, wrapped securely around the boy. This gentle, nurturing side of Chase fueled the guilt already burning inside her. But she held to her resolve, reminding herself how little time remained. So very little. Panic reared every time she thought about her crucial predicament.

Her tension increased as they approached Odera. Chase began his usual pattern of withdrawal, mentally distancing himself in preparation for his foray onto the planet. He appeared an entirely different person at these times—a frightening glimpse of the shadower.

They strapped in to enter Odera's orbit. All too soon, the ship skimmed over the planet's surface. Chase brought them down on the pad with barely a tremor, then cut the engines. He released his harness and stood. "Nessa, come with me."

She rose and followed him to the hatch. He began inspecting and strapping on his weapons. "I'm securing the hatch with a new code, one you can't decode. Take warning: Don't even try. There's no public transport on Odera, if you did have passage money. I don't expect to be planetside long. If I find you gone when I return, I'll leave without you. Is that clear?"

He acted as if last night had never happened. Perhaps it meant nothing to him. She could grow to despise this cold, indifferent side of him, Nessa thought. Only she wouldn't be around long enough. She looked into his eyes, disheartened by the hardness she found there. "Very clear, Captain."

Where was the man whose heated touch set every nerve in her body on fire? Who had melded his body with hers, laughed and teased with her, then held her securely through the night, protecting her from the demons haunting her?

She wanted to see him one last time, before . . . before he turned against her for good. Of its own volition, her hand lifted to his face, tracing the square line of his jaw, feeling the warmth and pulse of the man.

"Take care out there . . . Captain."

Surprise flashed in his eyes. His hand covered

hers, then gently, he clasped it. He moved her fingers against his lips before lowering her hand and releasing it. "I intend to. And you behave, Nessa. I'll be back before you know it."

No, you won't, Chase. Good-bye. I hope you forgive me someday.

Nessa watched him stride through the hatch. He turned to look at her, then punched the outside control. The hatch lowered shut. A surprising moisture seeped into her eyes. Ruthlessly, she reminded herself of all that depended upon her success. She couldn't dwell on her feelings for Chase. It was time for action.

She hurried to the control room. "Raven, I replicated a plate of caroba for you and Brand. It's in the galley. Take it to the cabin to eat. I have some work to do."

Obediently, Raven slid from her chair. Taking Brand by the hand, she led him from the cockpit. Nessa delved into the computer, bringing up the PWL file and, with it, her decryption program. She printed off the codes she needed, then used them to access Chase's communications records.

She quickly found what she sought: a message from Sabin, received the day before.

DANSAN HAS BEEN SEEN ON ODERA. GO TO THE NEBULA AND ASK FOR KANT. SABIN

Dansan again. Nessa wondered at Chase's obsession with the woman. Perhaps she had an unusually high bounty on her head. Pushing aside her speculations, Nessa contacted the sector Controller base on Odera. Using Chase's identification code, she sent a written communication to Odera's command center. Her message was certain to get Chase arrested.

Guilt at having him detained inundated her. But delaying him would help guarantee her successful escape. Besides, he could easily prove his true identity with hand and voice prints. The arrest would only slow him down.

Nessa turned her attention to starting the engines and preparing for take off. The controls responded smoothly to her touch. Once again using Chase's code, she contacted base command and received permission to depart. She called the children back into the cockpit.

"Something has come up, and we have to leave Odera immediately," she explained. "You need to get back into the safety harnesses."

Raven's eyes widened. "But what about Chase?"

"He's been detained on business. He'll catch up with us later."

After strapping the children in, Nessa sank into Chase's chair. His body heat still lingered there. Remorse, and the old, familiar, aching loneliness swept through her. Granted, she had Raven and Brand, but she entertained no delusions about any mate in her future. No man would ever find her desirable. Her nights with Chase would have to provide memories for a lifetime.

Her heart beating wildly, she activated the hoverlifts, and the ship rose from the pad, listing a little. Rough vibrations shook the cockpit, demanding her complete concentration. But her seasons of flying reconnaissance missions with Jarek paid off. Righting the ship, she guided it into position to break away from Odera's gravitational field. The children watched silently.

No turning back now.

Minutes later, they sped toward freedom. The navigation plotter provided the coordinates for Sonoma, which Nessa fed into the flight controller. She released her harness and unhooked the children.

Raven immediately returned to her computer screen, while Brand went to stand by Chase's chair. He remained there, his gaze anchored to the chair, as if he expected Chase to return at any time. Nessa's initial adrenaline rush gave way to a sudden onslaught of fatigue. She rubbed her aching neck.

The computer's calculations indicated that it would take six days to reach Sonoma by the most direct route. Surely that would be soon enough. She still had eight days before Orana's incubation was complete, as best she could tell.

"Come on," she told the children. "Let's go replicate the midday meal. Then we'll play with Turi and Lia."

"Can't we wait for Chase?" Raven asked. She hadn't connected taking off with leaving him behind.

"No, sweetness. Chase is going to stay on Odera for a while."

"He's not coming with us? But it won't be the same without him." A crestfallen expression filled Raven's face.

No, it wouldn't be the same. Nessa willed the

Catherine Spangler

emptiness inside her away. "He has his business to attend to, and we have ours. We're headed to a Shielder base."

The topic of Chase fell by the wayside as Raven absorbed Nessa's last statement. "A Shielder colony?" She danced from foot to foot. "Maybe our mother and father will be there."

Nessa didn't think so, having pieced together what must have happened to Raven and Brand from Raven's jumbled descriptions. Their colony had been attacked by Anteks, who had apparently proceeded in their usual manner. The adults were slaughtered, but no one bothered to hunt out the children who escaped into the hills. They would die from starvation or exposure soon enough.

The Anteks didn't particularly care if slave traders moved in after the destruction of a colony, looting and taking young victims to sell as slaves. True, they were Shielder survivors, but the life expectancy of slaves precluded the possibility that many would reach adulthood. And if they did—well, they were still slaves.

"I don't know if we can find your parents, sweetness," she told Raven. "But if we don't, then you'll have a new home in the colony."

"With you? If I can't have my mother and father, then I want to be with you!"

Raven's vehement declaration warmed Nessa's heart. But she knew the girl would be better off with someone who could take proper care of her; someone who was a respected member of a colony.

Someone not infected with Orana.

She tried to shrug off her despondency. Exhaus-

246

tion pulled at her. A good night's sleep would help. "Come on, let's go eat," she urged, offering her hands. Raven came readily, but Brand dragged from the cockpit, turning to stare at Chase's chair one last time. He reminded Nessa a little of Lia, moping after Chase. She urged the child from the room.

Later that evening, Nessa watched the children slip into slumber. Would sleep come that easily to her? Exhaustion hung on her like armor, and sweat beaded her forehead. The ship felt too hot, so she went to adjust the temperature controls. Odd, but they remained at their usual setting.

With a sigh, she returned to her cabin. She couldn't bear the thought of using Chase's cabin, of sleeping alone in that wide bunk. She'd squeeze in with the children. Entering the lav, Nessa stared into the mirror. For a minute, all appeared normal. Then she noticed the telltale redness of her eyes.

The first indication of Orana.

Shock reverberated through her. Oh, Spirit, no! She had eight days—*eight days!* The Orana couldn't be manifesting this early. Unless she'd miscounted the days. Or perhaps the stress and uncertainty of her situation had speeded up the progression of the virus. Moot considerations, at this point. Bloodshot eyes, aching body, fever—all pointed to one thing, and one thing only.

She had active Orana.

Chapter Fifteen

Chase entered the Nebula, a recreation club for the Anteks and other workers stationed on Odera. The sector's Controller base generated the planet's only industry, the arid surface having nothing to offer. At this early time of day, few beings lurked around.

Chase knew his size and race made him an obvious outsider, drawing unwanted attention. He wore his visored helmet to hide his face, and displayed his weapons in plain view. He'd certainly be recognized as a shadower, not uncommon on Odera, but hoped his identity would remain anonymous. He didn't want Dansan forewarned.

He scanned the room before entering, then strode to the bar. The bartender, a woman of indeterminate age, eyed him boldly as he approached. She was attractive enough, yet a world-weary cynicism hardened her features. She probably earned a lot more off duty than when she served drinks.

"Can I help you?" she purred, placing her hands on the counter and leaning forward, her overly-generous breasts pressing against her low-cut tunic.

A vision of smaller breasts, nestled perfectly in his hands, flashed through Chase's mind. Blazing hells! Even here, when he must be deadly focused, memories of Nessa encroached on him. He forced them away.

"I'm looking for Kant."

"Oh." Disappointment flashed through her artificially tinted emerald eyes. "He's over there, drinking himself into a stupor, as usual. Can't imagine why you'd have business with the likes of him."

Chase looked where she pointed, seeing a hooded figure slouched over a drink. He hadn't expected a Shen, a member of a cultlike group that practiced an ancient religion based on magic. They usually kept to themselves, following Controller directives without protest.

They were not totally reclusive, however. Shens often gravitated to where money could be made. Chase knew a group of them worked on the base. But they weren't known to frequent the bar, because their religion prohibited drinking. Obviously, this Shen had forsaken that philosophy.

Chase approached the man warily, watching everyone around him. He stopped at the table. The Shen didn't move or acknowledge him in any way. "Kant?"

"Are you McKnight?" The low voice snaked from the shadow of the deep hood.

"Are you Kant?"

The man lifted his arm, and Chase tensed, his hand going to his blaster. But the Shen gracefully waved a long, slender hand toward the opposite chair. "Sit, McKnight."

His hand still on his weapon, Chase slid into the seat. The tunnel of the hood prevented him seeing his contact's face, which didn't sit well with him.

"So, you're seeking Dansan?"

The voice sounded sober, contrary to what the bartender had told Chase. He wouldn't reveal any information without confirming his contact first. It might be a trap. "Show yourself, Shen."

The Shen raised his hands, slowly pushing back the hood, revealing the face of a young man with ebony hair and pale blue eyes. "Greetings, Mc-Knight. You don't trust me?"

"I don't trust anyone."

"Moriah said to tell you she hopes you liked the robe."

Moriah. He should have known. A heated flush flowed through Chase at the reminder of Nessa in that robe, and their subsequent lovemaking. He saw her moving with innate sensuality upon him, her eyes closed, her expression rapt as passion overtook her. Even then, she'd radiated an aura of sweet innocence.

Jolting back to the here and now, Chase quashed the memory. It was time to focus on the matter at hand. So Moriah had provided this lead on Dansan. At least he knew the report was legitimate, and that he could trust this contact. He raised his visor and leaned toward Kant.

"Yes, I'm interested in Dansan."

Kant lifted his hood onto his head and again hunched over his drink. "She's on Odera to hire new henchmen. Word has it, some of her soldiers were put out of action on Calt."

Temporarily, anyway. Chase didn't use the kill setting on his phasers, choosing instead the highest stun level, which inflicted only surface wounds. He only turned criminals in; he left the killing to the more sophisticated methods of the Controllers. They had execution down to a fine art.

Kant's statement made sense. Dansan liked to persuade susceptible Anteks to desert rank and work for her, offering unlimited looting as incentive. Chase figured she must have some method of counteracting the standard Controller mind indoctrination, or she wouldn't be so successful at luring Anteks away.

She seemed to take perverse pleasure in doing it right beneath the Controllers' noses, and he couldn't understand why they offered no bounty on her. They only paid for the hapless creatures she recruited. Once an Antek had defected, his fate was sealed; he could never return to the Controllers without facing the death penalty.

"Where is she right now?"

"In the barracks at the north end of the compound."

Her audacity amazed Chase. He placed a pouch of miterons on the table.

Again a slender hand snaked out, slipping the

pouch beneath the table. "She's a bold one, isn't she? But most of the troops are at the midday meal. The only soldiers at the barracks are those being disciplined. Dansan will find willing defectors there. One more thing—she's dressed like I am."

A Shen tunic would be a good disguise, especially with the Shen's presence on the base. "Thank you, Kant. And thank Moriah for me when you communicate with her next." Chase rose, snapping down his visor, and headed for the barracks.

The north barracks edged the far end of the dusty compound. He kept his helmet on as he approached, his hand resting lightly on his phaser. Reaching the barracks, he skirted around the building to check the layout. Two entries, one at each end, no windows. No brush for cover, but some crates lined one side of the barracks.

Deciding Dansan would stay near the rear entrance, in case loyal soldiers returned, Chase opted for that entry. Standing to one side of the panel, he pried it open a few inches with his weapon. He glanced in, and there she was. She had to be the one figure in the Shen robe, talking to a small group of Anteks in Disciplinary Detention.

DD, as the Controllers called it, consisted of being stripped naked and held spread-eagled against a metal wall by use of magnetic shackles. The punishment could last days, with only water for sustenance. Humiliation was heaped upon the discomfort, as the DD wall was always in the midst of the barracks, and the offenders suffered metal and physical torment at the hands of the other occupants. And yet it was far better than other punishments the Controllers meted out.

Chase watched as Dansan leaned toward the Anteks on the DD wall, gesturing dramatically. The sight brought a flood of memories pounding into his gut.

He recalled Dansan speaking eloquently to the leaders of his colony, Torin, promising that her new discovery would enable them to access the precious veins of iridon running deep underground. A brilliant research scientist, she had developed a compound that dissolved the hard layers of shale over the iridon, without damaging the ore itself.

She offered a cooperative effort to mine the ore and share the profits. But her real intent proved to be treachery. She had engineered a deadly virus that swept through the colony, resulting in almost total devastation. . . .

Chase jerked, battling rising nausea. Spirit, but his futile recollections might allow his prey to get away. He had her in his sights, and she was unescorted, because her Antek guards didn't dare set foot on a Controller base. Chase punched the control pad, and the panel opened fully. He started toward his nemesis.

"You there! Halt! Drop your weapon and turn around slowly." The guttural command came from directly behind him.

Chase froze in disbelief.

"Drop your weapon now!"

Carefully, he released his phaser and it fell to the ground. He saw Dansan look up, then back toward the other entry.

"Turn around."

His quarry fled through the entry. He had to stop her. Chase turned to find two disrupters trained on him by Antek guards.

"I have authorization to be here," he said tersely.

"Remove your helmet."

Damn! He lifted off the helmet and glared at the guards. "What's the problem here? I have proper identification and I'm an authorized agent."

His words bounced off the stupid Anteks like radar waves. "You will come with us," one demanded harshly. "And no sudden moves."

Dansan would be well gone before he got clear of these idiots. He longed to pound them into the dust. But the disrupters aimed at him convinced him of the folly of arguing further. Seething inwardly, he strode toward base control. Commander Domek would set this matter straight.

But it was several frustrating hours later before he even saw the commander. He spent those hours in a holding cell, pacing and cursing the fate that had allowed Dansan to get away once more. The guards hadn't even bothered to look at his identification, or verify his palm or voice prints. He'd gone straight to holding.

"Captain McKnight. What a surprise to see you here." Commander Bron Domek stood on the other side of the force field, eyeing Chase with some humor. Only half Antek, he possessed reasonable intelligence, although he had the physical bulk of the species. Chase frequently transported prisoners to Alta for the commander, a courtesy to foster his freedom to roam the quadrant.

Domek grinned broadly. "A good thing the females on base didn't know you were being held. They'd have rushed the center."

"Very funny," Chase muttered. "Why the hell am I being detained, Commander?"

Domek shrugged. "I have no clue. I just returned from border patrol, and I'm meeting with Lieutenant Etan immediately. We'll get to the bottom of this. But I can't release you until I know what's going on."

He left Chase to stew another hour before sending a guard to release him. By then Chase could barely contain his fury. As he entered Domek's office, he forced himself to greet the commander, although he wanted to tear the place down.

"Have a seat." Domek turned toward the cabinet behind his massive desk. "How about a drink?"

"I hate to be rude, Commander, but I'd really appreciate an explanation of what happened today, if you don't mind. I'm a little short on time." And very short on temper, although he refused to show it.

Domek poured himself a generous drink. Chase knew the soldier imbibed frequently; alcohol made life on an isolated Controller base more bearable. Sinking into his seat, the man downed a healthy portion before answering Chase. "To be honest, McKnight, I'm still not certain what happened. I can only guess. I suspect someone wanted you delayed for some reason."

Chase clamped a heavy reign on his anger. "Why do you say that?"

Domek slid a piece of paper across the desk. "This

communique came into the center today at eleven hundred hours."

Totally mystified, Chase read the message.

Be advised I have tracked a wanted offender to Odera. His name is irrelevant, as he goes by many aliases. He has blond hair and gray eyes, and is supposed to be meeting with a man named Kant at the Nebula today. Detain him for transport to Alta. Chase Mc-Knight.

Stunned, Chase stared at the paper. Who had done this? And who, besides Sabin and Moriah, even knew he'd been headed for Odera?

Ugly suspicions reared their heads. He'd worked with Sabin for over two seasons now; he'd watched the man's actions closely, as he made it a policy never to trust anyone. But he'd never uncovered any reason to doubt Sabin. He didn't know Moriah quite as well, although Sabin swore she could be trusted—

"The message had your transmission code on it," Domek broke into his thoughts. "And we picked up your ship's homing signal when it came in. It had to be sent from your ship."

Sent from his ship? Disbelief slammed through Chase as the implication became clear. Nessa. She must have sent the message. But how?

Suddenly, things began falling into place. Nessa's skill on the computer. Her ability to decode his hatch. He'd believed her when she'd claimed she'd just gotten lucky and hit the right combination by trial and error. A rash assumption, considering he'd used a five-digit code, virtually impossible to determine randomly—without a computer.

She must have decoded his PWL file. Damn him for a fool!

For a moment, his anger obscured all reason; then his thoughts whirled in another direction. Why would Nessa have done this, unless . . . Chase leaped from his chair.

"I must get to my ship right away."

"I'm afraid that's not possible, McKnight." Domek took another long drink before meeting Chase's burning gaze. "Your ship received permission to take off four hours ago. It's long gone from here."

Another wave of fury roared through Chase, obliterating everything but thoughts of Nessa's treachery. All this time, he'd thought her an innocent. He'd accepted her into his bunk last night, believing she really desired him. He'd fallen for her large dark eyes and trembling lips.

The lying, conniving, little bitch.

"I have a request, Commander Domek," he ground out, battling for control over his rage. "Please report my ship stolen to all Controller bases. And for it's return, along with the *live* capture of the thief, I offer a reward of two hundred fifty thousand miterons."

"Do we *have* to go in there?" Raven asked, her voice quavering. "Why are you wearing that cloth over your mouth?"

Nessa sighed, inundated by a barrage of emotions. Battling debilitating fears, she prayed to

Spirit to help her take care of everything before she entered the advanced stages of Orana.

"I explained this to you. I'm sick. I don't want you or Brand to catch my disease, so I can't come close to you or touch you. This is a surgical mask over my mouth. It will help to keep the germs from spreading."

"What do the germs look like?"

Ah, the innocence of the child. "They're so small, you can't see them, sweetness. Now, please, get into the decontamination chamber."

"But why?"

Exhausted, Nessa leaned against the wall. Not wanting to panic the children, she had to remain calm and patient, even though she felt like pounding the walls and screaming. "Decon will kill any germs that might have gotten on you and Brand."

Raven considered a moment; then her eyes lit up. "Then if you go through de—con—tamation, all your bad germs will be dead!"

If only it were that simple. "The bad germs are also inside me. The decon rays can't go in there."

"Would they go in there if you opened your mouth? The rays could go in your stomach, like Chase's light did."

Nessa smiled at the memory of Chase examining her to reassure the children. "No, sweetness, it won't help. Please, no more talk. Go on in, and don't come out until I call you. Turi and Lia are already in there, so you can pet them."

Raven's mouth quivered, but she obediently took her brother's hand. "Come on, Brand. Don't be afraid."

Brand drew back, shaking his head vehemently. The terror in his eyes tore at Nessa's heart. He'd probably been locked in a small room for transport as a slave, and the fear lingered. She tried to think of an enticement to get him to enter the chamber, as she didn't dare touch him.

"You can have some caroba when you come out," she offered.

His little body trembling, Brand just stared at the floor.

An idea occurred to Nessa. "Chase will be so proud of you when he hears how bravely you entered decon."

His head came up at that. He thought about it a moment, then stepped through the panel. Heaving a sigh of relief, Nessa secured the panel and started the cycle. What to do next? She rubbed her aching forehead, trying to decide.

First, she had to consider getting Raven and Brand somewhere safe before she lost her faculties. Sonoma was the closest known Shielder colony, but could she make it there in time? Further computer research on Orana had revealed that the symptoms could appear up to seven or eight days before the victim succumbed to the final stage. But that offered no guarantees, with Sonoma almost six days away. Nessa wasn't willing to risk it.

Star Base Intrepid, the closest highly populated settlement, was less than three days away. It appeared the best option. Since Nessa couldn't just leave the children there, she'd have to find someone to take care of them.

Sabin. His name leaped into her mind.

She immediately rejected the idea. Sabin was a shadower. There had to be another solution. But where to take the children? Nessa thought of Moriah. She had been kind and generous. Perhaps she would take Raven and Brand. No, Calt was too far away, almost as far as Sonoma, and in the opposite direction. There must be someplace, with someone, where Nessa could safely leave the children.

She searched through the computer files, frantic to find a solution, and coming up again and again with only one solid possibility: Intrepid. But she couldn't leave the children there alone. They'd quickly fall prey again to slavers or end up in the Pleasure Domes. Nessa wrestled with alternatives, coming up repeatedly with one workable answer—Sabin. He presented the only logical choice. He was a Shielder, he already knew about the children, and he might be close enough to meet her at Intrepid in time.

But he was a renegade, she argued to herself. A traitor who hunted his fellow Shielders. Or did he?

He'd never revealed her identity to Chase, as far as she knew. He hadn't told Chase about the children, either, and he had returned Turi. She had to believe he possessed a good heart, even if he was a shadower. And because he was a Shielder, he was immune to the psionic brain waves of the Controllers, so he couldn't possibly be indoctrinated. The only thing which would impel him to turn the children over to the Controllers would be greed for gold. Nessa could only hope Sabin's conscience would win out.

At this point, she had absolutely no choice. She

was too afraid of the children contracting the Orana to risk keeping them with her for the six-day trip to Sonoma. She had to leave the children at Intrepid, with Sabin. She'd just have to trust him, and pray that he wouldn't betray them.

Going to the cockpit, she entered the coordinates for Intrepid into the flight controller. Then she sent a message to Sabin.

TRAVERS, MEET ME AT STAR BASE INTREPID IN THREE SHIP CYCLES. I'LL SEND THE TIME AND LOCATION LATER, MCKNIGHT

After that, she dragged out the portable sterilizer unit and sterilized Chase's cabin and lav. She wanted the children to stay there the remainder of the trip. They'd have more room, plus the computer to entertain them.

She prepared several days' food, along with some caroba. She used sterile gloves, but planned to run the food through decon as an added precaution. Then she went to the decontamination chamber intercom.

"Raven, Brand, are you all right in there?" She peeked through the portal, to see Brand huddled next to Raven on the bench. Turi and Lia were curled together beneath the bench.

Raven waved at the portal. "We're fine."

"Listen, I'm going to slip some food through the door, then run the cycle again. When it's done, I want you and Brand to carry the food and the lanraxes straight to Chase's cabin. Don't go anywhere else. Stay in the cabin until I tell you. Okay?"

Obviously baffled, Raven nodded. "Good girl," Nessa praised her. "And Brand, you're being very brave. I can't wait to tell Chase. He'll also be pleased if you take care of his cabin while he's gone."

Raven smiled, and even Brand seemed to brighten. Staggering with exhaustion, Nessa sterilized the rest of the ship, working her way to the cockpit. She wanted the corridor to be as clean as possible when the children went to Chase's cabin.

When she was done, she contacted them from the cockpit. They did just as she asked, going straight to Chase's cabin. Then she went through decontamination herself, hoping to kill any external germs that might be on her. At that point, exhaustion claimed her, and she fell asleep on the bench, alone and terrified.

Chapter Sixteen

Chase contacted Sabin from Odera, asking his partner to meet him. Commander Domek offered Chase transport on a ship headed for Alta, which he planned to take as far as the rendezvous point with Sabin, two ship cycles out.

There would be two long days, providing ample time to think. It was far too much time; thoughts of Nessa and her treachery pounded Chase mercilessly. Other thoughts, memories of Nessa lying beneath him, crying out in passion, warred with the knowledge of her betrayal. Too much time to feel pain he had successfully managed to channel the past three seasons into the hunt for Dansan.

Up until now.

What had possessed him to allow Nessa to get too close, to fool him? He could only guess her seeming innocence and the long months of loneliness had weakened his ever-present guard.

Catherine Spangler

But he learned quickly from his mistakes, and he never repeated them. He knew Nessa's true nature now. She'd be much easier to hunt down than the cunning Dansan. And she would pay for her treachery.

He was relieved to see Sabin when their ships finally docked, even if the idiot acted his usual irritating self.

"So you lost your ship, did you, old man?"

"Could you be serious for once, Travers?" Chase snapped, tempted to pound the smile off Sabin's face.

"Hijacked by a mere female—and a cripple at that."

Chase snagged the front of Sabin's flightsuit, dragging him up until they were face-to-face. "I do not find this situation funny in the least. Don't tempt me to rearrange your features."

"I know," Sabin responded quietly. "But if taking it out on my hide makes you feel better, try it. Just be forewarned—I'll thrash you back."

Travers always managed to mirror his fowl moods back at him. Chase released him. "Sorry. By the Abyss! How could I let myself be taken in by her? I fell for her story like an Antek. I only hope she's headed for Zirak. Because if she's not, I'll have to wait until my ship's signal is picked up. I have that frequency in another hidden program file. Maybe Nessa won't think to look for it."

"We might not have to track the homing device." Sabin straightened his flightsuit. "I've already received a message from Nessa."

264

Chase grabbed him again. "*You what?* What are you talking about?"

With a pained look, Sabin pried Chase's hands away and straightened his garment once more. "The day after you contacted me from Odera, I received a message with your transmittal code, signed with your name. It requested that I meet you at Star Base Intrepid in three ship cycles, which is now one cycle away. Nessa must have sent it."

What the hell was she up to? Wondering if Sabin might somehow be involved, Chase stared at his partner suspiciously. "Why would she want to meet you?" Was it his imagination, or did a brief expression of guilt cross Sabin's face?

"I don't know why." Sabin paused, then added, "For certain."

"What do you mean by that?"

"The only thing I can figure is that if Nessa sent that message, she must be in some sort of trouble. So she contacted me because she had no one else to turn to. She would have to hope I didn't know your ship had been stolen."

"I don't give a damn if she is in trouble, or even if her life is at stake," Chase growled. "Because she's going to be dead when I catch up with her anyway. Where and when did she want to meet at Intrepid?"

"The message said I would be contacted with that information later."

Chase glared at Sabin in frustration. "You have set the coordinates for Intrepid, haven't you?"

Sabin flashed his usual cocky grin. "Of course, partner. I'm as intelligent as I am good-looking."

Chase snorted. "Then we're in trouble. How long until we reach Intrepid?"

"One and a half ship cycles. We'll have to take steps to ensure that Nessa doesn't panic and leave before we get there."

"I'll take care of that." Chase headed for the cockpit. "I'll send a message to my ship, using your name, informing Nessa it will take an extra half-day to get there. Then I'll send a message to the authorities at Intrepid. Once my ship docks, it's to be detained until we arrive. Nessa's not getting away from me."

"She could dock at any of over fifty landing bays," Sabin pointed out. "She might be in and out before anyone tracks the ship."

Chase halted and faced his partner. "So we'll set two traps for her. One at the arranged meeting site, the other at my ship, which I *will* locate. I repeat, the lady will *not* escape me." Then, annoyed by Sabin's concerned expression, he snapped, "And why the hell should you care what happens to her? She deserves whatever punishment the Controllers mete out to her."

His partner watched him solemnly. "Are you really going to turn her over to the Controllers? That's a guaranteed death sentence."

Chase's insides knotted. Could he really do that to Nessa, after all that had passed between them? She had tended his wounds, even saved his life. She'd surrendered her virginity to him with a startling passion. She had touched him in the darkest hours of the night, a healing touch, gifting him with a few priceless hours of forgetfulness.

He hardened himself against the rush of emotions sweeping through him. Spirit, but he couldn't let Nessa's inexplicable allure leave him vulnerable to betrayal. Not again.

But could he turn her over to the Controllers and a certain, agonizing death? No . . . probably not.

He would deal with her himself. And it wouldn't be pleasant.

Nessa circled the ship on a wide berth from Star Base Intrepid's orbit. Certain Chase would report his ship stolen, she wanted to spend as little time on the planet as possible. She had taken precautions, however, locating the ship's homing frequency file. She reset the frequency, matching it to Sabin's ship's frequency, having also found that record in the files. Since Sabin and Chase's ship were marked only with standard Controller agent symbols, few would be able to tell their ships apart.

Rubbing her aching neck, Nessa pushed the intercom button. "Raven, how's it going in there?"

"Okay. But when can we come out? Is Chase back yet?"

The same two questions Raven always asked, several times a day. Every time she mentioned Chase, a heated rush of emotions inundated Nessa. Memories of the amazing explosion of sensations when they mated, of lying securely in his arms afterwards, of gray eyes that seemed to bore into her soul; all lodged in her mind, refusing to be exorcised.

She reclined in Chase's chair. As she had grown increasingly weaker, even walking between her cabin and the cockpit drained her. She'd made a pallet on the chair, spending most of her time in the cockpit. From there, she could run the ship and talk to the children. Fortunately, the Orana had not progressed to the advanced stages. No hemorrhaging or delirium—yet. Nessa pushed that thought aside.

"No, sweetness. Chase isn't back. But we'll be landing on the star base this afternoon."

"We will?" Raven's voice quivered. "Please don't make us go with Sabin. We want to stay with you."

"Oh, Raven. You can't stay with me. You might catch the virus. Sabin will take you to a Shielder colony. You'll have a new home."

"I don't want to leave you. I can take care of you and make you well."

Closing her eyes, Nessa battled the overwhelming desire to sleep. "I know you would take good care of me, sweetness. But I can't allow you to get sick, too. What's Brand doing?"

"He's playing Black Hole on the computer. I taught him how," Raven replied, pride evident in her voice.

"Good for you. What are Turi and Lia doing?"

"I think they're mad at each other. They've been fighting a lot, rolling around and making funny noises."

Nessa suspected the two weren't fighting at all, but didn't bother to correct Raven. Sabin would just have to find homes for some baby lanraxes. It would serve him right if all of them bonded with him. She almost laughed at the thought, except any movement hurt now.

"Listen, Raven, two packs, two surgical masks, and some miterons are in decon right now. I'm going to sterilize the corridor again before we land. Right after we dock, I'll ask you and Brand to carry Turi and Lia to decon and put them in the packs. You can each carry one. Then you'll put on the masks and we'll go out on the base. Okay?"

"Okay. . . . What if I don't remember what to do?" Once again, Raven sounded close to tears.

A lump clogged Nessa's throat and tears of her own filled her eyes. *No time for self-pity*, she told herself fiercely. *Save your energy for surviving and getting to Sonoma.*

"I'll remind you. Now, why don't you go play on the computer with Brand?" She turned from the intercom to compose her message to Sabin and arrange a meeting. Computer files detailing the Star Base Intrepid had helped her determine the safest place to meet. The CTC, Central Transport Center.

Intrepid's main terminal for public transport arrivals and departures, the CTC was the largest and busiest site on the base. Nessa studied a schematic of the terminal, pleased to find numerous entrances, as well as myriad private communication and meeting alcoves. She chose her meeting site carefully, then composed a message for Sabin.

TRAVERS, MEET ME AT THE CTC TODAY AT 16:00 HOURS. WAIT BY THE TRAMS TO TRANSPORTS FOR SECTORS TEN THROUGH TWELVE. I'LL FIND YOU. MCKNIGHT.

Sabin responded within minutes.

MESSAGE RECEIVED, OLD MAN. TRANSMIT YOUR OR-
BIT AND LANDING COORDINATES, SO WE CAN DOCK
TOGETHER. I HAVE SOME CARGO TO TRANSFER.

Nessa considered replying, then decided to ignore
the message. Let Sabin think she hadn't received it,
or that her return reply hadn't reached him.

She implemented procedures for entering Star
Base Intrepid's orbit, this time using Sabin's identification code instead of Chase's to request air
space. Her request granted, she dropped into orbit,
then began her descent to the surface.

Within an hour, she had landed the ship, wincing
when it slammed against the docking lock. Her
landing skills were a little rusty. She had chosen
one of the larger and busier landing bays. Hopefully, anyone looking for the ship would be looking
in bays on the more deserted area of the base.

Unhooking her harness, Nessa intercomed the
cabin. "Raven, we've landed. Did you and Brand
stay on the floor with the pillows, like I told you?"

"Yes, Nessa. We only bumped a little bit."

"Are both of you okay?"

"Yes."

Nessa exhaled a sigh of relief. She'd worried
about the children not having safety restraints for
the landing. The ship responded somewhat roughly
to her inexperienced handling; not nearly so
smoothly as when Chase manned the controls.

"Good. It's time to leave the ship. First, take
Brand and the lanraxes to the decon unit. Put the
animals in the packs and slip them on your backs.

Put on the masks, making sure your noses and mouths are both covered. Then attach the bags of coins on the inside of your blankets. The hooks are already on the bags. There's also a piece of paper, a letter to Sabin. Fold it and take it with you. Do you understand?"

Raven sniffed tearfully. "Yes. Then what do we do?"

"I'll meet you in the corridor. Remember, don't get close to me." Nessa pushed out of the chair, weak and shaky, praying to Spirit for the energy to see the children safely into Sabin's care. She hadn't told him much in the note—only that she could no longer keep the children with her, asking him to find a good home for them.

Perhaps she should have warned Sabin of the possibility of Orana. But since the virus didn't become highly contagious until the final stage, when hemorrhaging began, she thought it safer not to tell him. He might deduce she was headed to Sonoma and track her there. Even if she had already become contagious, hopefully her precautions had prevented the children from contracting the disease.

Slipping on her mask, Nessa tucked her maps of Intrepid and the CTC into her tunic pocket, along with a phaser. Extra miterons jingled in her other pocket, as the computer had readily deciphered the new code on the vault.

She reached the decontamination unit and saw the children inside, their masks on. Raven was obediently pinning the bags of coins on the inside of hers and Brand's blankets. Nessa hoped Sabin would buy the children some tunics and boots. She opened the door and stood back. "Come out when you're finished. Raven, don't forget the letter for Sabin."

Raven entered the corridor, Brand behind her. The girl stared at Nessa, her mouth trembling. "Please, can't we stay here?" she begged. Clutching the back of his sister's blanket, Brand kept his gaze on the floor.

Nessa pushed aside her own inner torment. "No, sweetness. More than anything, I want you and Brand to be safe. Chase wants that, too." She leaned against the wall a moment, drawing a deep breath. "Come on. Let's go."

With Nessa walking slowly to conserve her limited energy, they eventually reached a tram connection. Normally, she would have been avidly observing the sights and sounds of an active star base, but not today. Intrepid was actually a natural planet that had been commandeered as a base because of its central location in the quadrant. To give it appeal, the developers had planted numerous species of trees and plants, representative of all the planets in the quadrant, along the myriad tram routes. Each landing bay had nearby visitor complexes offering lodging, food, entertainment, and anything gold could purchase. A festive, if not commerical, atmosphere made Intrepid appear more like a vacation spot than a major shipping and transportation exchange.

But Nessa didn't have her usual enthusiasm for seeing all these wonders. Getting to the tram pickup point sapped most of her energy. Having to send the children away further dampened her spirits.

She insisted on sitting several rows behind Brand and Raven as the tram sped them to the CTC. Their surgical masks drew curious stares, but the star base had such a melting pot of cultures, no one paid them much attention.

They finally arrived at CTC. Nessa knew the terminal was busy, but nothing prepared her for the crush and movement of so many bodies in one place. A teeming crowd packed the enormous building. The children edged toward her, and she tried to move away, but the press of the people propelled her against them. Lia squealed in alarm, which set Turi off as well.

"Try not to touch me," Nessa gasped, to no avail. The children couldn't move away from her. She tried to remain calm, reminding herself, as she had repeatedly the past few cycles, that the Orana shouldn't be very contagious yet. She didn't want the children getting lost in this crowd anyway.

They huddled against her, panicked looks on their faces. "It's okay," Nessa reassured them. "Hold on to my tunic if you have to. Just be sure to wash your hands as soon as you get to Sabin's ship. If he has a decontamination unit, make sure you use it."

They worked their way within sight of the meeting place. Buffeted by the crowds, Nessa had little strength left. She got the three of them over to a wall, where she leaned back and surveyed the area. She didn't see Sabin; but then, they'd arrived almost an hour early.

The time had come. *Spirit, give me strength,* Nessa prayed.

"All right, now," she said, struggling to keep her voice even. "See those lines of people waiting for trams over there? And see the computer terminals next to them, where people are purchasing transport? That's were I want you to wait. Right at the end of the terminals."

Raven clutched Nessa's tunic even tighter. "Then what?" she sobbed, tears streaming down her face.

Nessa's own tears threatened to overflow. "Then . . ." Her voice broke and she struggled to regain her composure. "Then you wait until you see Sabin. The instant you see him, go to him. Be sure and give him the letter. Tell him I've already left the star base. Don't tell him anything else."

"Are—are you leav-v-ving now?" Raven wiped at her face.

"Don't touch your face until you wash your hands." Nessa wrapped her arms around herself to keep from hugging both children. "No, sweetness, I'll be nearby until I see you're safe with Sabin. Just don't tell him that. He might try to find me; then he might get sick, too. Can you do that? Say I'm already gone?"

With another sob, Raven nodded. "Do you think Chase will be mad at me for not telling the truth?"

Nessa closed her eyes against the sudden vision of Chase's face. "No, Raven," she whispered, "he'll understand. Now, go. Please!"

"But—"

"Just go!" Nessa made her voice as stern as she could. "Do it—now."

Her head hanging dejectedly, Raven turned toward the terminals, glancing back one more time. Then she trudged away, Brand trailing behind her, clutching her tunic.

All at once, Brand turned and scrambled back toward Nessa. He stopped a few feet away, his gaze locked on her face. "Nesss—Ness-ssa," he stammered. "No go."

His first words. A band tightened around Nessa's heart, threatening to squeeze the life from it. She called on all her self-control to hold back the tears.

"Oh, Brand, Chase will be so proud to know you spoke." Pressing against the wall for support, she forced a smile. "But you have to go, so you'll be safe. Chase wants you to."

Raven came up behind Brand and took his hand. "We love you, Nessa," she said, the truth of her words shining in her eyes. "We'll never forget you."

No one, not even Jarek, had ever said those words to Nessa.

She would never hear them again.

She could hardly see Raven and Brand's precious faces through the tears slipping down her face. "I love you, too. Now go. *Please go.* And be good for Sabin."

Raven nodded and took Brand's hand. He went, but kept his head turned toward her. "Nessa," he said again.

Trembling with fatigue and emotion, she watched until the children reached the end of the terminal counter. They took their masks off, then stood there dutifully. Nessa looked around, noting a recessed entry about fifteen meters away. Edging along the wall, she worked her way to the corner of the entryway, then waited there.

She longed to sink to the ground and rest, but then she wouldn't be able to see the children. Digging deep, she found the strength to remain standing, supported by the wall. She didn't have to wait long. Sabin appeared a short while later, fortunately coming through another entrance.

He looked around the tram area, his dark brows drawn together. He didn't notice the children, but Raven knew him. Nessa had refreshed her memory with his picture, kept in Chase's personal computer file.

Sabin looked down with a start when Raven tugged on his flightsuit. He leaned forward and listened intently for a moment. Taking the paper from Raven, he glanced up, his eagle gaze scanning the CTC. Nessa slipped around the corner, then peered back. Sabin was reading the note. He looked around the terminal again, then squatted by the children and talked with them, Raven replied, while Brand kept his usual focus on the ground.

Assured that she'd done the best she could, Nessa exited the building. Now, if she could only make it to Sonoma in time. She managed to get on the next tram to her landing bay, and sank gratefully into the seat. She forced herself to remain awake on the ride to the bay. She would have plenty of time to rest on the trip to Sonoma.

She made her way slowly from the tram drop-off to Chase's ship, heaving a sigh of relief when she finally reached it. Stumbling inside, she closed the hatch and pulled off her mask. *Have to stay alert just a little longer,* she told herself, limping toward the cockpit.

She punched the entry pad and the panel slid open. Starting in, she halted abruptly when she saw the blaster pointed at her. Raising her gaze, she came face to face with Chase.

"So, we meet again, you scheming liar."

Chapter Seventeen

"Chase!" Nessa gasped, feeling the blood drain from her face. Not trusting her trembling legs, she clutched the entry frame for support.

"Nessa!" Chase mocked, his eyes scorching her. "You seem surprised to see me. I can't imagine why, this being my ship and all."

Logical thought scattered. She met his scathing glare, knowing she'd find no mercy from him. "I'm sorry."

His brows rose. "Sorry? You're sorry? Somehow, I find that hard to believe." He strode forward and grabbed her arm with his free hand, keeping the blaster aimed at her chest. "How in the universe did you think you could get away with stealing a ship?"

Waves of dread washed over her, but she didn't feel the familiar tremors that normally signaled the approach of a seizure. This once, she wished she could seek haven in unconsciousness, but she'd

Shielder

faithfully taken the medication Chase had given her.

"You would have gotten it back. I only intended to take it as far as So—Zirak." Spirit, but her thoughts seemed increasingly harder to focus.

"I'm sick of your lies." Chase jerked her toward him. "Come on."

Maybe the Orana would kill her before the Controllers tortured her. Maybe she could use her knife to end it before she became so delirious that she disclosed the sites of Shielder colonies. But she didn't know if she had the strength to reach for her boot. . . .

"No, this way," Chase snarled, dragging her down the corridor, away from the hatch.

Surprise seeped into her mind. He wasn't taking her off the ship. "Where are we going?" she asked, stumbling and falling against his back.

He halted and whirled around. "What in the Abyss is wrong with you?" He shook her hands away, scowling fiercely. "Spirit! You're burning up with fever. You look awful."

Nessa reached for the wall behind her, hoping she wouldn't collapse then and there. "I'm fine."

"Like hell! But you know what? I don't give a damn if you're dying. Only that you live long enough to experience how I treat scum of the universe. Come on."

Dragging her to the first brig cubicle, he thrust her inside. He glared at her, hatred heating his eyes to a molten steel. She's seen them that color before, when he had touched her in passion. Now his gaze

279

seemed to hold only loathing. The reality of his feelings struck her like a blow.

She sank onto the bunk, trembling uncontrollably. "What are you planning to do?"

A bitter smile flashed across his face. "You'll find out soon enough. But for now, you'll be incarcerated in the brig. You're my prisoner. At my mercy, my every whim. Be afraid, pilgrim. Be very, very afraid."

He stepped back, his hand going to the control panel. The barely audible hum indicated that the force field had been activated. Just then, a heavy pounding vibrated the hatch. Chase looked down the corridor, his eyes narrowing. "I need to see who that is."

He glanced back at Nessa, the sneer returning to his face, twisting his handsome features. "I'll be right back. Don't go away."

She heard the determined stride of his boots down the corridor, leaving her alone in a living Abyss. She collapsed across the bunk, curling into a ball.

She had failed. Her people were right—she was simply a worthless scavenger, incompetent and undeserving.

How long would it take her to die? she wondered.

Chase knew Sabin wouldn't be pounding on the hatch. His partner had the code and always entered as if he owned the place. Probably the authorities, having heard of the reward offer and then spotting the ship. Too late. Chase would be collecting the reward himself. In flesh.

Even now, Nessa amazed him. Spirit, but she was a good actress. Managing to seem truly sincere, looking at him with fear-filled eyes, acting weak and helpless. How many people had she conned? She probably wasn't a pilgrim at all, just a thief.

She hadn't faked her virginity, though. Or coming apart in his arms. And she appeared genuinely ill. She needed medical treatment. Concern tried to snake its way in and defuse his fury. Angrily, he shook away the undermining thoughts and feelings.

Nessa had proven herself a liar, a thief, and only Spirit knew what else. After acting like Brand and Raven brought out every maternal instinct within her, she'd dumped them at the first opportunity. Thank Spirit they were in Sabin's capable hands. Sabin had contacted Chase from the CTC, so he'd known Nessa had headed back to the ship alone.

Anger welled up anew. She would get hers—he'd make sure of it. But he might treat her illness first— just to be sure she was alert enough to experience the full force of his wrath.

He snapped open the portal cover and studied the Anteks standing outside. He hated dealing with the slow-witted beings, but since they were Controller agents, he had to show them at least a pretense of respect.

Putting aside the blaster, he opened the hatch. "I'm Captain Chase McKnight, owner of this ship. I just reclaimed it from the thief."

The three disrupters focused at his chest didn't waver, their red active lights blinking ominously. Only the Controllers would condone using weapons as inhuman and destructive as disrupters, Chase thought, disgusted—or use Anteks as their watchdogs. The rank odor of the three facing him did nothing to lessen his revulsion of them.

"Hands up, citizen," ordered one. "Step outside the ship."

He had no choice but to cooperate. Inwardly seething, Chase moved forward, arms raised, and allowed an Antek to run a scanner along his body. Satisfied, the Antek stepped back and nodded to the first one, apparently the team leader. The leader inclined his head toward the hatch, and his two subordinates lumbered inside Chase's ship. He knew they would search every inch, a right that had always infuriated him.

They'd search Nessa, too, and probably take her into custody until they could check her identification. Vengefully, he hoped it scared the stuffing out of her. The Antek's treatment would be only a taste of what he had in mind for her.

"Produce your identification," the leader demanded, his weapon still trained on Chase. He took the disk Chase offered, checking the seal, which showed no evidence of tampering. Then he studied Chase, his beady eyes more cunning than those of most Anteks. "You will come with me now. We will see about this disk."

His credentials could easily be checked on the portable computer unit strapped to the Antek's belt. Standard operating procedure. "Why don't you check it here?" Chase suggested, barely containing his anger.

The Antek grinned, a feral sneer showing yellow, decaying teeth. "I prefer to wait until we get to the command center."

Chase gritted his jaw. Fine. Let the bastard play his intimidation game. He'd check out, like he always did, but he hated this watchdog routine the Controllers seemed to enjoy. Just their way of reminding the quadrant's inhabitants who was in charge. He strode toward the trams, ignoring the Antek breathing down his neck. The sterile, pristine landing docks bustled with activity; ships landing and departing, mechanical repairs being done, pilots discussing trade and passenger runs.

How like the Controllers, to always present the appearance of a perfectly ordered and run quadrant, with Intrepid as a prime example, when cruelty and corruption formed the foundation. It was a foundation based on blood and despair. Chase shook his head at the irony.

He found he wasn't the only suspect with an armed escort riding the tram to Command Headquarters. The Anteks had been very busy today. At least his wrists and ankles weren't shackled like most the other prisoners' were. Disgusted, Chase rode in silence, staring out at the profusion of greenery and vivid blooms, but not really seeing it. His thoughts focused on the moment he would be cleared to return to his ship—and to Nessa. She would regret ever having crossed him.

When he and his smelly companion finally reached Headquarters, Chase was roughly shoved into a holding cell. The brutish Anteks enjoyed their physical power. They had to, Chase thought sourly, since they lacked any real intelligence.

The tiny holding cell reeked, probably from the slime coating the floor and the walls. Very little light from the corridor infiltrated the dimness—probably just as well. With nothing to sit on, Chase opted to remain on his feet.

He resisted the urge to pace, not that he had the space to do so. Instead, he saved his energy for more important things—such as taking Nessa apart when he got back to the ship. And designing a more secure PWL file. It amazed him that she'd been able to breach his security, especially with his ship equipped with the most sophisticated computer system available in the quadrant. But then, he'd underestimated her on more than one occasion. That wouldn't happen again.

A guard deactivating his cell's force field drew his attention. He stepped to the entry, ready to retrieve his ID disk and return to his ship. He halted, annoyed to see a second guard, and two disrupters trained on him again.

"What's the meaning of this?"

"You will come with us," one Antek intoned, his voice as dull as his eyes.

"Why? Where are we going?" Chase demanded angrily.

A disrupter jabbed in his direction silenced him, and he walked ahead of the guards. Why hadn't he been released? Surely they had checked his identification by now. But as they shoved him into another, larger cell, indignation turned to concern.

This sure as hell looked like an interrogation room—and boded no good.

"Hey!" He whirled as one guard activated the force field. "What's the meaning of this? I demand to speak with your superior."

But they ignored him, leaving him to pace and fume for another hour, before the base commander finally appeared, along with three Antek guards carrying electrolyzer rods.

Grossly overweight, the commander wore the dark brown uniform of a higher official. A black sash stretched taught across his protruding belly, displayed his rank decals and his recognition awards. His bald head looked small compared to the rest of his body. He was not an Antek—but then, few highly ranked officers were; the breed was easy enough to dominate mentally, and generally not intelligent enough to make important decisions.

"Why am I being held?" Chase demanded as the commander and his guards entered the cell.

The commander's pale, watery eyes fixed on Chase. "Don't play the fool, Slade," he growled, sauntering forward. "Did you think you wouldn't get caught? No one evades the Controllers for long."

His words baffled Chase. "Slade? My name is Chase McKnight. I'm a registered Controller agent. I gave you my identification."

"Really, Slade. Did you think we wouldn't actually check the disk? I'm too smart for that. Now you will answer some questions about your illegal operations."

Chase refused to retreat as the four surrounded

him. "I'm Chase McKnight. If you really checked my ID disk, you'd know that."

The commander's mouth thinned. "Then you must have given me the wrong disk." He spoke into his wrist comlink, then gestured toward the observation monitors inset in the walls. "Watch the screen, Slade. Your disk is being put into the system now."

Chase looked toward the video display. A moment later, his picture flashed on the screen. Beneath it, the statistics listed him as Galen Slade, wanted for embezzling funds from major Controller business interests. The reward offered for his capture: fifty thousand miterons.

He gaped at the screen, shock barrelling through him. Someone had altered his identification records. It could have been done at the main Controller base at Alta, or any of the regional headquarters that received updates from Alta and transmitted them to smaller bases and Controller agents.

Records being altered at Alta seemed a remote possibility. More likely, the deed had been done at a regional facility . . . such as Odera.

Nessa! The suspicion kicked him in the gut. Nessa. She had the skill to bypass security and manipulate computer files. And she had obviously put them to use for her own selfish means.

The force of her betrayal sent him reeling. It hadn't been enough for her to simply have him arrested and steal his ship. His heart thudded painfully in his chest, his lungs constricting until he battled for breath.

Oh, no. Nessa had gone for total destruction of her prey.

Just like Dansan had.

The pain of Dansan's treachery surfaced, as vivid and real as if it had happened only yesterday, instead of three seasons ago—the old wound was now ripped open by Nessa's betrayal.

"Now, where were we?" the commander broke into the melee of Chase's thoughts. "Time for you to answer our questions, Slade. By force, if necessary."

They closed in around Chase, but his focus remained on his internal pain. He'd sworn no one would ever be able to double-cross him again. No one would ever touch him emotionally or get close enough to hurt him again.

But Nessa had.

After they crudely searched her and confiscated her knife and identification disk, the Anteks took Nessa to a brig at the command center. The immediate adrenaline rush she'd experienced had provided the energy necessary for her to march to the trams, two disrupters focused on her back. She wondered what they did to ship thieves, although she suspected the Controllers had only one penalty, encompassing all crimes.

Death.

At this point, she thought, sinking wearily to the floor of the bare brig into which the guards had shoved her, it was only a matter of how her death occurred. Either at the hands of the Controllers or the Orana—whichever came sooner. The fever had begun to glaze over her fear of dying, but it hadn't abated her feelings for Chase, or the hurt generated by his actions.

She loved him.

She knew, with every fiber of her being, that she loved him.

Having never experienced much love in her life, her feelings overwhelmed her. She loved Jarek, of course, and Turi, and had begun to love Raven and Brand. But those feelings were platonic and maternal, not the intense emotional and physical cravings inundating her whenever she thought of Chase.

How could she love a shadower, a man who threatened the existence of her people, her entire reason for being?

Only Spirit knew. Yet the fact existed: She loved Chase. He had looked at her with nothing but condemnation in his eyes, then turned her over to the Anteks. On one level, she knew his reaction was logical. She *had* stolen his ship—but it had been only when all other options had failed.

But on a more emotional level, she had hoped he'd look deeper for the reasons behind her action, be willing to listen, and forgive. She'd hoped he loved her in return. How foolish. She need only look in a mirror or suffer through a seizure to be reminded that she had nothing to offer.

Sounds outside her cell drew her attention. She rolled to a sitting position, her heart pounding, as three Anteks heaved Chase into the chamber. Groaning, he stumbled, then collapsed on the floor.

A fourth man, obviously not an Antek, stepped to the entry.

"Your partner in crime, returned to you," he gloated.

Nessa stared at Chase, appalled by the welts visible on his face and through his torn flightsuit. She raised her gaze to his tormentor. "But why—"

"He had an aversion to answering questions. I'd advise you to cooperate when it's your turn."

"But he's a shadower. He works for the Controllers," she protested, perplexed and alarmed.

A sneer quirked the man's face. "We're not fooled by that story. Our system provided a positive identification on him. We know who he really is. And he will answer our questions eventually, probably the next session."

The man took a threatening step closer. "As for you, your identification is also false. There are no corresponding records, either to your ID disk or your voice and hand prints. Your turn at questioning is coming, citizen. I'd begin now, but more pressing matters demand my attention."

He stepped back, and a guard activated the field. Nessa scrambled awkwardly across the cold, slimy floor to Chase. Horror knotted in her chest as she gazed at his puffy, bruised face. Gingerly, she touched his cheek, drawing back when he moaned. Oh, Spirit, this was all her fault.

She forced herself to her feet and over to the container of rancid drinking water in the corner. She jerked at the hem of her tunic, trying to tear off some fabric, cursing her weakness. Finally, she used her teeth and ripped a strip loose. She dipped it in the water, then returned to Chase.

Cradling his head carefully in her lap, she battled her own shakiness while she dabbed gently at the welts on his face. She didn't worry about him catching the Orana, because the latest research reported in IAR indicated that the virus had been engineered solely for Shielders. They appeared to be the only ones susceptible to its heinous destruction.

After a few moments, Chase groaned and stirred and opened his eyes. He looked at her, confused and unfocused at first. Then recognition chilled his gaze.

"You!" he spat, twisting away and sitting up. "The bastards must have killed me, and I'm in the bowels of the Abyss." He groaned again, pressing his hands to his chest and wincing. "Spirit, I hurt too much to be dead."

"What did they do to you?"

His head snapped up, his furious gaze impaling her. "Why should that matter to you, traitor? You did this with your computer manipulations. You should be well pleased." A mocking smile appeared on his grim face. "Except it backfired on you, didn't it?"

His pain, both mental and physical, shook her to the core. She reached toward him. "Chase, I'm sorry—"

"Save it," he snarled. "Shut up and get out of my sight, before I decide to put you out of my miserable existence." He turned from her and, rising, staggered to the water.

The force of his hatred shuddered through Nessa. She'd made her choices, and she'd have to live with them, live with the emotional pain ravaging her now. Crawling to the corner near the entry, she huddled there, shivering from internal chills and the damp stone floor. The horrendous stench of the brig threatened to gag her.

That faded as the need to stay alert declined, and she surrendered to her weakened condition. She dozed off, drifting through disturbing images and memories. The tread of boots and harsh voices stirred her from her stupor, and she forced her heavy eyelids open.

"Move along, citizen!" a guttural Antek voice ordered. Nessa watched several sets of booted feet cross her line of vision of the corridor, two of them shackled and shuffling slowly.

"We're going as fast as we can," hissed a voice . . . a familiar voice.

She roused herself enough to sit up and study the men passing by. One of them stumbled and turned to glare at the Antek who had shoved him. Shock reverberated through Nessa when she saw his face. Jarek! Jarek here, in this prison.

Gasping, she scrabbled up the wall to stand and stare after them. "Jarek," she whispered to herself, knowing she mustn't get his attention. He would only worry about her, when he needed to get himself free. Any shred of hope that had been remaining in the universe for her disintegrated at that moment.

"Someone you know?" Chase asked bitingly from behind her.

She turned slowly, still stunned, to face him. He sat against the opposite wall, his arms resting on his upraised knees. She didn't answer, but he must have seen the truth in her face.

"Obviously, this one didn't fall for your lies. After all, you still had your virginity when you plied your wiles on me."

She pushed back the pain his jab generated. She had to think, to concentrate. There must be some way she could help Jarek. Chase would certainly never offer assistance, even if she could trust him.

"By the fires! You look like you've been in the Abyss," he snapped. "Go back to your corner, before you fall down."

She couldn't do that . . . she had to think of a way to help Jarek first. . . . But the heat burning her body threatened to disintegrate her. Eyeing the water container longingly, she staggered toward it. Those few steps sapped her remaining energy.

She sank down by the trough and rested her face on the edge, willing the strength to drink. Not even the odor from the less-than-clean water bothered her.

"What the hell is wrong with you?" Chase snarled from behind her.

He slid one arm across her midriff and helped her raise up. Cupping the other hand, he dipped it into the water and lifted it to her parched lips. She slurped it, as weak as a baby lanrax. He repeated the offering several times, until she sank back against him with a sigh.

"You're burning with fever." He lowered her to the stone floor.

Tepid water splashed against her face and chest. She lay there, too exhausted to move, while he sloshed more water from the container onto her. Why was he helping her? she wondered.

He ripped open the front of her tunic, exposing her burning skin to the dank air. Startled, she opened her eyes and stared at his granite face. He met her gaze, his eyes blazing with a barely restrained fury. Unable to confront the condemnation she saw there, she closed her eyes again.

More water dribbled across her chest and down her rib cage. She could feel the steamy heat rising from her body, smell the musty odor of disease. Several more handfuls of water drenched her thoroughly before Chase closed her tunic.

She curled onto her side, drifting in and out of awareness, her thoughts shifting from Chase to Jarek. She just needed to rest, to conserve her strength, she told herself. If she managed to get released, then she could take action to help Jarek.

A sudden spasm of chills jolted her from her daze. She wrapped her arms around herself, shivering uncontrollably. Her eyes flew open when Chase's arms slid around her. He hauled her against him, pressing her face against his chest and throwing one leg over both of hers to keep her still.

His heat seeped through her damp tunic, counteracting the coldness wracking her body. Even though her grogginess, she understood he did it only to head off the danger from a chill contracted after a high fever. His next embittered words verified that fact.

"Spirit help me, but I don't even know why I'm doing this. You will pay for your lies and treachery, Nessa. I promise you that."

She was already paying, and it was a higher price than he could begin to imagine.

She must have slept eventually. The scream woke her, intruding into the welcome oblivion. She jolted awake, bewildered.

"No!" the tormented voice cried. "No, not Chandra! She can't be dead." A groan echoed through the chamber, then, "No! Not another one. Spirit, you have to help me. Help me save them . . . no, no!"

Chase. Finally recognizing the voice, Nessa sat up. Clarity returned, and she remembered where she was. Chase lay nearby, thrashing, the agonized cries tearing from him. Her heart pounding, she crawled to him. He twisted into her, knocking her sideways.

"Chase! What is it?" Panicky, she struggled up and edged back to his side. She stared at his contorted face. His eyes were closed. "Chase?"

"Somebody, please. I need help. Isn't there anyone who can help?" he moaned brokenly. "I can't . . . can't do it."

He cried out again, his voice fraught with grief and despair. Nessa realized he must be in the throes of a nightmare. His torment knifed through her, and she wrapped her arms around his struggling body.

"Chase. You're okay. It's just a dream." Using all her limited strength, she held on to his heaving body. She continued talking, soothing him, as she had Raven and Brand, until he finally stilled with a shuddering breath.

She sank back, barely maintaining her hold on him. Trembling, he sagged against her, resting his head on her breast. Shaking as well, she stroked his hair, damp with sweat. She reveled in the feel of him. One last chance to touch him, to trace the strength of his face.

Suddenly he stiffened, full awareness returning. He lifted his head, his eyes narrowing. "Get away from me." He pushed to his feet and moved to the opposite end of the cell.

An arrow of pain pierced her soul. Wishing she could go back in time and do something—anything—to have prevented this situation, she whispered, "You don't know how sorry I am."

"Save it for another fool." Leaning against the wall, he dropped his face into his hands. "Spirit, I haven't had that nightmare in two seasons—" He paused, looking up and impaling her with a look of pure loathing. "Damn you, Nessa. Damn you to the corners of the galaxy."

His curse was unnecessary. She was already damned.

And the man she loved would never forgive her.

Nessa gathered enough strength to crawl to the opposite corner, where mental and physical exhaustion finally claimed her. Some time later, a boot prodded her awake. "Up, citizen. The Commander is on his way."

Disoriented, she gaped at the Antek looming over her. He prodded her again. "Up." Then he lumbered toward Chase, but Chase had already awakened and risen to his feet.

She pulled herself upright along the wall, praying

her stiff, weak legs would support her. The room tilted alarmingly. Closing her eyes, she tried to draw a deep breath into her lungs, instead receiving jabs of pain.

Two more guards preceded the base commander into the cell, flanking the entry. Behind the commander, Sabin sauntered in. Until this moment, Nessa had never dreamed she'd be glad to see him. *Please get us out of here.*

"I understand you're Chase McKnight," the commander said to Chase.

"I told you that yesterday," Chase grated out.

The commander seemed unconcerned. "Ah, well, one can't be too careful, now, can one? But your partner here contacted Commander Domek, who identified you from a visual. Then we ran your disk through the main computer at Alta, and you came up clean. Apparently your records were altered on Odera."

Chase shot Nessa a damning glare. "I assumed as much."

This news staggered her. Someone had planted condemning computer records on Chase, and he obviously blamed her. No wonder he displayed such hostility. No sense trying to tell him she hadn't altered those records. He'd never believe anything she uttered now.

He turned toward the entry. "Come on; let's get out of here."

Nessa started to follow, but the commander flung out his arm, blocking her. "She's not leaving. Her identification is false. I can't release a possible criminal."

Chase turned back, his gaze sweeping her, cold and calculating. "This one's mine. She's a wanted felon, all right. I've been hunting her, and I claim bounty rights. I'll take her to collect the reward. But first, I have some personal business to settle with her."

At least he didn't plan on leaving her behind. Relief swept through Nessa, even though his expression told her quite clearly that his business with her would be very unpleasant. At least she could try to help Jarek now.

The commander eyed her, taking note of the slime covering her bare legs and arms, her torn tunic. "If you're sure," he grunted, disgust evident in his tone. "Aren't you going to shackle her?"

Chase stared pointedly at the commander. "It seems my utility belt was confiscated yesterday. Travers, would you do the honors?"

Sabin raised his brows but stepped forward, unhooking from his belt the electronic shackles every shadower carried. Nessa stiffened but didn't resist when he snapped them onto her wrists. She noted that he didn't tighten them much or activate the shock mechanism.

"Should I do her legs, McKnight?" he asked.

Chase's glittering gaze speared through her. "That's not necessary. She can't run."

With a grunt, the commander turned and strode through the entry. The guards, then Chase and Sabin, followed him. Nessa limped behind the group, trying to catch up with Sabin, who trailed the others. Extending her bound arms, she managed to grasp his flightsuit. He glanced over his shoulder at her, his expression none too pleasant.

"Keep your filthy hands off me," he hissed.

"I have to talk to you." She kept her voice low, so Chase wouldn't hear.

"By the Abyss, I don't want to talk to you. You look like the walking dead, and you smell even worse."

"Please. This is urgent."

Exhaling loudly, he slowed, letting Chase and the guards get farther ahead of them. "Come to think of it, I *do* want to talk to you. What were you thinking when you hijacked Chase's ship? And why did you dump those children and two ill-tempered animals on me? Just *what* is going on?"

He took a step toward her. Remembering the Orana, she backed up hastily. "Are the children okay?"

"They're just fine. What did you think? That I'd leave them there at the CTC? I didn't, but I should have. All they've done is mope and cry for you and Chase. Spirit preserve me!" He stepped forward again, and Nessa moved back. His eyes narrowed and he raised a hand toward her.

"Don't touch me."

He dropped his hand, glaring at her. "What is the matter with you?"

"I saw my brother entering this center as a prisoner."

For a moment, she thought she saw a look of compassion cross his face. "I'm sorry, Nessa." Then his usual mask of nonchalance returned. "Why are you telling me this?"

Her legs trembled, reminding her that they

wouldn't hold up much longer. She was terrified she might sign Jarek's death warrant if she told Sabin too much; yet she was filled with dread that Jarek's fate might already be sealed. She would have to trust this renegade Shielder. She had no one else to turn to.

"He's an able and skilled squadron commander. He's also next in line as Council head in our colony."

Sabin's gaze sharpened. "What colony?"

Nessa hesitated. She had to risk Jarek's life in order to help him. She didn't have to place an entire Shielder colony in jeopardy. "I can't tell you that."

He muttered a curse, then grated, "And your brother's name?"

"Jarek."

Sabin considered a moment. "Chase gave your last name as Ranul. I would assume your real name is Nessa dan Ranul. Am I correct?"

Again she hesitated. If Sabin knew her real name, then he'd know Jarek's. Jarek had always been secretive about his forays against the Controllers. For all she knew, her brother had a price on his head. But if he did, he was as good as dead anyway. Not only that; once he arrived at Alta, they'd perform the standard blood test, and ascertain immediately that he was a Shielder.

She nodded. "Yes. That's my name." Her strength gave out, and she staggered, almost falling. Sabin reached for her, but she jerked away. "No! Don't touch me!"

He frowned. "The way you're acting, one would think you have—" He froze, a look of horror spread-

ing across his face. "By the Spirit! You have Orana!"
He stumbled back from her.

"Lower your voice." Nessa glanced around, relieved to see the others some distance away. She
looked at Sabin wearily. "I'm sorry you're exposed,
but I pray it's not contagious yet. I just didn't want
the children to catch it."

He took another step back, understanding dawn-
ing in his eyes. "Is that why you brought them to
me?"

Nessa tried to focus her rapidly blurring
thoughts. "Yes. Now about my brother—"

"What's going on there?" Chase's voice cut in angrily.

Sabin turned his head. "Nessa's ill. She needs medical treatment."

"So?" Chase strode back down the corridor,
highly aggravated by the fact that Travers and
Nessa had seemed so chummy lately. Not that he
was jealous, he told himself. Damn, but Nessa
looked even worse today. Cloud-white skin, dark
circles beneath bloodshot eyes. "Why should I concern myself with a ship and computer larcenist?"

Amazement crossed his partner's face. "You
mean she's the one who tampered with—"

"I know she is." Chase locked his gaze with
Nessa's, making his intent of retribution clear. "And
she'll get hers. But right now, all I want to do is get
the hell out of this Abyss—even if I have to carry
her to speed things up."

He reached for her, but she staggered away, looking toward Sabin, her eyes beseeching. "Please help him," she pleaded hoarsely.

Chase's irritation flared. He grasped Nessa's arm. "Help *who?* What's going on here, Travers?"

Sabin hesitated for the briefest moment. "She's concerned about Brand. Wants me to find a good home for him."

Feeling an inexplicable pang at the mention of the mute little boy with huge, sad eyes, Chase pulled Nessa closer. "I want to discuss the children with you later, Travers. Right now, we're leaving. Be still, Nessa!"

He swung her into his arms and headed up the corridor, toward the commander and his guards, who watched them suspiciously. After a brief struggle, where she tried to look around his arm at Sabin, she sighed and went limp, resting her head against his chest.

By the Abyss! She still burned with fever—hotter than the sands of Calt. Her sweat-drenched hair clung to her pale face; the dampness of her tunic seeped through his own clothing. Panic resurfaced. She needed treatment immediately—only he didn't know for what.

"What is going on here, McKnight?" the commander demanded. "And what's wrong with her?"

"As I said, Commander, I have some personal grievances against this prisoner." Chase glanced at Nessa, his chest tightening. Her eyes closed, her breathing ragged, she appeared to have surrendered her grasp on consciousness. Only her clenched hands indicated otherwise. "She has the

Alberian flu. You'd better be sure all your men are up to date on their immunizations."

The soldiers drew back quickly. "Then get her out of here," the commander barked, retreating with his men.

"Gladly," Chase muttered. He glanced at Sabin behind him. "Let's go."

Sabin shifted back, his dark eyes unfathomable. "You go on, old man. I have some business to take care of here."

"What business would you have in this hellhole?"

"I need to settle a debt."

So did Chase, with two different women.

"You do that, Travers." He paused, bitterness warring with other, unidentified emotions. "Catch up with me later. I want a report on Raven and Brand."

He wanted to see the two children, assure himself that they were all right. He missed Brand's warm little body settled on his lap, the boy's soft sigh as he leaned against him. . . . He didn't need this! He strode toward the entry.

"McKnight."

Chase turned back to his partner. "Yes."

Sabin inclined his head toward Nessa. "She's really sick."

Chase's insides churned with a myriad of feelings. Concern, anger, resentment—and fear. Dread, actually, and a familiar sense of helplessness. "I can see that, Travers," he snapped. "What do you expect me to do about it?"

"You seem to know a lot about medicine."

Not enough. Not nearly enough. "I know a little."

Sabin watched him, as if trying to discern his deepest secrets. "Are you going to help her?"

Chase looked down at Nessa. She appeared truly unconscious now, her sagging hands almost sliding from the shackles. Her arms and legs were filthy with the slime from the brig. She felt so small and fragile in his arms. She'd lost weight she couldn't afford to lose.

He couldn't let her die. Even after what she'd done to him, he still cared for her, drawn to her by inexplicable, emotional bonds.

Yet she was no better than Dansan. She had been willing to destroy a life. It didn't matter if it was one life or hundreds, the criminal intent was the same.

And she had betrayed *him*, just as Dansan had.

He had tried to curse her last night. He wanted to hate her . . . but he couldn't.

Even now, all his instincts screamed for him to protect her, take care of her. His vows of healing bound him, even though he'd turned his back on his profession three seasons ago. As much as he tried to believe that part of his life was over, he never seemed able to leave it completely behind.

"I'll do what I can," he told Sabin. "Contact me later."

Chapter Eighteen

Heaving a sigh of relief, Chase entered his ship. Nothing else had delayed him. Still, Nessa had not stirred, which concerned him. Bypassing decontamination, he carried her to the laboratory and placed her on the table. After removing the shackles, he ran the monitor over her, cursing at the readings. The virus he'd detected a few weeks earlier had proliferated like wild keranis. It appeared to be a nasty one.

Apprehension paralyzed him, as harrowing memories flooded him, taking him back three seasons. He'd battled a demon virus then. And he'd failed horribly.

This virus seemed the likely cause of Nessa's symptoms—and a possible threat to her life. No . . . not again. Stop! he told himself firmly. The odds of her having a virus as deadly as the Ramos virus Dansan had engineered were minuscule. He just needed to draw some blood and analyze the virus, then compound a treatment.

He sterilized his hands and slipped on gloves. As an added precaution, he donned a surgical mask, although he'd already been well exposed to whatever she had. Taking Nessa's arm, he swabbed away the grime with antiseptic solution, discovering the blotches weren't all dirt. Surprised, he cleaned her arm again, his alarm escalating.

Large, ugly bruises lined her arm, mottled and purple beneath the surface. It looked like hemorrhaging under the skin, but he couldn't tell to what extent. He cleaned one leg, finding similar bruises. Checking beneath her tunic, he discovered more. They hadn't been there last night. By the Spirit! What was this virus?

He drew blood and placed it in the centrifuge. Then he woke Nessa with a stimulant injection, wanting to evaluate her mental faculties. As she stirred, he ran the monitor over her again, noting the abnormal readings. She stared up at him, confusion reflected in her eyes.

"Where are we?" she asked, struggling to rise.

"In the lab. Lie still." Chase pushed her down, then retrieved a blanket from the cabinet.

She grabbed his wrist as he spread the blanket over her, her dark eyes huge. "Where is Sabin?" she rasped.

She'd asked for Travers the minute she regained consciousness. Why should he care? Sabin could have the lying traitor. Chase pulled away from her grip. "He had some business to attend to." Taking a hypochamber, he filled it with a coagulant and a

fever-reducing compound. He'd start an intravenous strip after he got her cleaned up.

"Oh," she sighed, sinking back and closing her
eyes. Seconds later, they flew open. "Have we left
Intrepid yet?"

"Not yet." Chase deftly injected the medication.

Her eyes followed him like heat-seeking missiles.
"I must get to Zirak. But I have to talk to Sabin
first."

He resisted the urge to slam his fist into something. "I have no idea where Travers is. He could
have departed by now, for all I know. As for Zirak,
I'm afraid you're in no condition for a pagan lunar
celebration."

Nessa pushed up, panic etched on her face. "I
must get there. It's crucial." She drew a deep
breath, her body trembling.

It always came back to reaching Zirak. Nothing
else had ever mattered. Yet nagging doubts diluted
Chase's anger. Nessa had treated his injuries, saved
his life. What had compelled her to alter his identification file, when she had already taken his ship?

Had she hoped it would merely delay him getting
free on Odera? Perhaps she didn't understand the
Controllers, how they operated. He wanted desperately to believe she hadn't known what she was doing. But he suspected she did.

"Is getting to Zirak as important as staying alive?"
he snapped.

She started to reply just as the hatch tone reverberated through the chamber.

"That's Travers now." Removing his mask and

gloves, Chase headed for the entry panel. "I'll get him. You stay right there."

He strode down the corridor, ready to deck Sabin. But a terrifyingly familiar figure brought him up short.

Heading for the cockpit, Dansan whirled around when she heard Chase. They stared at one other. Chase battled the flood of memories and pain he always experienced when he encountered this soulless being, when he stared into eyes containing no shred of human decency.

Dansan's evil aura lingered so strongly around her, he asked himself for the hundredth time how he and a whole society could have been so blind to the monster within the woman.

Regaining his wits, he reached for his blaster, then remembered he'd removed it before he'd been arrested the day before. Not that it would have done him much good, he realized, staring at the disrupters Dansan's two henchmen had trained on him. He was damned tired of having weapons pointed at him.

"Well, well," Dansan drawled, her pale eyes glittering. "McKnight. What are you doing here? I heard you'd been detained at base command."

She couldn't have known he'd been arrested. Unless she had spies planted at the command center, a likely possibility.

"This is my ship. Why wouldn't I be here?" he countered, stalling to formulate a game plan. His blaster. By the hatch, where he'd laid it yesterday. He stepped toward the hatch, halting when Dansan's guards tensed and raised their weapons slightly.

Dansan strutted forward, her tight flightsuit showing off every curve of her muscular body. She kept herself in top physical condition, but her age had begun to show in her face. Face replacements only worked so many times.

"I expected you to be delayed much, much longer," she crooned in her throaty voice.

Even with contacts at base command, she couldn't have gotten to Intrepid this quickly unless she'd already been headed here. Chase inched toward the hatch. "How did you know I was on Intrepid?"

"I have my sources, McKnight. Even after all this time, you continue to underestimate me."

Oh, no, he'd *never* underestimate the evil of which this woman was capable. "So you thought you'd check out my ship—maybe even take it?"

Her cool gaze scanned the corridor. "It's a nice ship. I wouldn't mind adding it to my fleet."

A nagging suspicion snaked into Chase's mind. Dansan never did anything by chance, so she must have believed he would be delayed a while. "What made you so certain I wouldn't be returning to my ship any time soon?"

Her gaze met his, diabolical, cold. "Let's just say I arranged your detention. Although I rather expected you to be detained on Odera."

Realization slammed into Chance with the force of a rocket launcher. Dansan possessed almost as much knowledge about computers as she did genetic engineering. *She* must have been the one who had altered the records on Odera, not Nessa. She probably had his voice and hand prints recorded somewhere, probably procured during their dealings on Torin. Oh, she was cunning.

She'd had ample opportunity to access the computer data base on Odera, as the authorities hadn't known of her presence there. He hadn't thought to tell them; he'd assumed she'd fled. Not that anyone would have arrested her. Fury rose at the knowledge that this woman had successfully infiltrated every level of government and society with bribes and threats.

"Is that why you altered my identification records?" he demanded. "To confiscate my ship?"

"Your ship would have been a side benefit, McKnight. I just wanted to put you out of action for a while."

So, Dansan *had* altered his records. He'd accused Nessa without ever giving her a fair chance. Pushing aside his remorse, Chase prodded for more information. "Why put me out of commission, Dansan? I thought you enjoyed the challenge of pursuit."

"Perhaps I enjoyed outwitting you for a time. But I grow weary of looking over my shoulder at every turn." She strolled forward and ran a finger down the front of his flightsuit. Her nose wrinkled. "My, my, aren't we filthy. What's this? Welts, dried blood? Hmmm, I don't mind a little sweat, and I do so like the taste of blood. I might be persuaded to prolong your miserable life a while longer."

Nausea roiled inside Chase. His nemesis, this close, and he could do nothing to her. She'd lusted after him even when they were supposed allies, working to mine the iridon. Then, he'd refused her advances politely but firmly, not attracted to her in the least. Now, hatred and revulsion filled him. He battled the urge to wrap his hands around her treacherous throat, knowing he'd be killed on the spot if he did.

Unable to touch her, he glared into her eyes. He found no light, no spirit in those dispassionate, icy orbs. Only greed and death.

"Tell me, why don't you have a price on your head, like the common criminal you are?" he asked, slipping closer to the hatch.

"You just don't get it, do you?" she sneered. "Everyone has his price, McKnight. *Everyone*. Including the all-mighty Controllers. They wanted a way to destroy Shielders, and I supplied it. They willingly provided Shielder prisoners for my experiments. Once I isolated the chemical providing Shielder immunity to mind domination, all I had to do was create a virus that would bond with their unique DNA. The Controllers were most grateful. They wouldn't dream of disposing of me. They might need my services again."

She'd created Orana! The revelation stunned Chase. He'd heard that a viral strain had been decimating enemies of the Controllers, and it seemed she was responsible. Using her twisted genius, Dansan had engineered Ramos and then Orana, simply for money—knowingly setting in motion the destruction of at least two groups of people.

And yet, it seemed she would continue on unpunished. Was there no justice in the universe?

A blinding flash of white-hot rage barrelled through him. There damn well would be justice. With a bellow, he charged Dansan, knocking her into the nearest Antek, who crashed backward.

Chase hit the floor and rolled toward the hatch, kicking the legs out from under the second Antek. Leaping to his feet, he swept up the blaster and whirled toward Dansan. Too late. He faced the disrupter she aimed at him.

"Drop it," she hissed. Behind him, he heard the two Anteks staggering to their feet. He didn't stand a chance if he tried to fire. He dropped the blaster.

Her face twisted with contempt. "Your so-called weapon wouldn't have hurt me anyway, McKnight. Your blasters don't begin to compare to a disrupter, and everyone knows you keep your 'toys' set on stun."

Chase's chest heaved and his heart pounded from the impotent rage roaring through him. He balled his fists and drew a deep breath. "Unlike you and the Controllers, Dansan, I don't have to scramble the brain and nervous system to control my prisoners."

She shook her head, her eyes gleaming. "Such a bleeding heart, Dr. McKnight. I'll bet you wept over those fools on Torin. But your weakness is my advantage. You could never kill me. That would be murder, and you swore to protect life."

Her taunt hit its mark. Chase had never killed anyone, although he supposed he could if it was in absolute self-defense. As many times as he'd dreamed of finding Dansan, of placing a blaster to her head and blowing her evil mind away, he'd always known he could never murder another being in cold blood.

Like a predator closing in for the kill, she stepped closer. "No, you'd never kill me. I always wondered what you planned to do with me if you ever actually caught me. But I know what I'm going to do with you. If I happen to be in an amorous mood, I might enjoy your body for a while, before I inject you with the Ramos. Then I plan to watch you die, McKnight. Slowly, in agony, like the rest of your witless clan."

An insidious coldness congealed in his chest. He felt oddly detached, as if he was watching the scenario from a video screen. He knew he'd rather die fighting than give this madwoman the satisfaction of watching him go insane. As he prepared to launch into drastic action, a movement to his left caught his eye.

Nessa. She sidled quietly along the corridor, a phaser clutched in her hand. He could see her trembling. She'd get her fool self killed. Before he could react, she raised a shaking arm toward the Anteks behind him. Just then, she stumbled, drawing all attention to herself.

Chase seized the distraction. He hit Dansan with a high kick to the chest, hurling her across the corridor. She stumbled into the brig cubicle on the other side. Nessa fired the phaser at one Antek, as Chase whirled and punched the second one. The first Antek slumped over, a phaser wound in his chest.

Chase dove for his blaster. The second Antek charged with a roar just as he scooped up his weapon. The brute slammed into his back and he went down, the breath knocked out of him. He managed to roll again, his blaster in his hands. As he rolled, he kicked the Antek in the groin, and Dansan's henchman screamed in pain and lurched away.

Halfway to his feet, Chase froze when he saw that Dansan had gained her footing inside the brig cubicle and had her disrupter trained on him. Hatred set her face in an ugly mask, and her white hair swirled wildly around her face.

"This weapon is at the highest scramble setting, McKnight. It won't kill you immediately. You'll experience the total disruption of all signals to your brain and nervous system before you die. You'll hallucinate your worst nightmares, while your tortured nerve endings will have you writhing and screaming in agony. It will take a while, but you'll die eventually. Good riddance, McKnight."

Everything seemed to happen in slow motion then. Chase saw Dansan's finger slide over the discharge button. At the same time, he heard Nessa gasp, "No!" and saw her lunge for the brig control pad. His hand tightened on his blaster in a futile race to beat Dansan to the first shot. He saw Nessa hit the force field pad just as Dansan discharged the disrupter.

The flash momentarily blinded him. Dansan's scream of pain reverberated down the corridor. He blinked his eyes to clear his vision. She writhed and twitched on the floor, moaning, then stilled. He didn't spare more than a cursory glance her way. The force field had amplified her disrupter beam as it rebounded. He could do nothing for her now.

He whirled as the Antek he'd kicked rose and charged again. Raising his blaster, Chase shot the Antek in the shoulder, and he crashed to the floor, paralyzed. Dropping his weapon, Chase turned his attention to Nessa.

She'd saved his life again.

Her huge eyes fixed on his face, she slid slowly down the wall. He rushed to her and eased her down into his arms. She stared at him, fever glazing her eyes.

"Is she dead?"

He glanced at the inert form in the brig. Dansan's absolute stillness verified what he already suspected. She posed no further threat to anyone. He'd waited for this moment for three seasons. Now that it had arrived, he felt nothing. No joy, no release . . . nothing. "Yes, she's dead."

"She created viruses to kill people," Nessa whispered through parched lips.

Hundreds of people, Chase thought grimly. The cost in human life hadn't even been important to her, just the monetary gain. "She won't murder again." He brushed Nessa's hair from her face. "Don't try to talk any more. We'll get you help."

Gazing at his face, she lifted a shaking hand to his cheek. "Too late . . ." She paused, gasping for breath. "Take care of the children. Chase, I—"

"What in the Abyss happened here?"

Chase whirled to see Sabin stepping over the unconscious Anteks, followed by another man. "Where the hell have you been, Travers? Dansan and her henchmen decided to help themselves to my ship. Nessa's not injured, but she collapsed. I need to get her into the lab."

The man with Sabin leaped across the bodies and strode over. "Nessa!"

She jerked in Chase's arms, reaching toward the man. "Jarek! Oh, Jarek, you're all right."

A wave of jealousy hit Chase as he stared up at the dark-haired young man looking at Nessa with open emotion on his face. Jarek leaned toward Nessa, but Sabin pulled him back. "Don't get too close."

"Thank you, Sabin." With a sigh, Nessa went limp in Chase's arms. The stimulant injection had long since worn off, and only sheer determination had kept her conscious.

Chase didn't have time to question whom Jarek was to Nessa. He gathered her in his arms and carried her to the lab. By the time he placed her on the table, tremors were shaking her body. He covered her and lowered the heatwave light, then began cleaning her arm to apply an intravenous strip.

From the entry, Sabin cleared his throat. "Chase, we need to talk to you about Nessa's condition."

His partner rarely called him by his first name; something in his tone caught Chase's attention. He shifted his gaze to Sabin. "Just what do you know about this?"

Sabin gestured to the man beside him. "First of all, this is Jarek san Ranul. He's Nessa's brother, and he can tell you more than I can."

Nessa's brother! A sense of relief swept through Chase, but he didn't have time to ponder it. He looked at the serious young man. "Then tell me, and quickly. She's running out of time."

Jarek looked at Nessa, grief contorting his face. "She has Orana. She was injected with it almost one moon cycle ago."

"What?" Chase laid Nessa's arm down and stepped toward Jarek. "*Orana!* But—only a Shielder can contract it. That means—" He whirled as the full implication hit him, and he stared at the inert form on the table.

A Shielder! Nessa was a Shielder.

Stunned, he spun back around and looked from Sabin to Jarek, then back to Sabin. His partner nodded, confirming the staggering truth.

"Who did this to her?" Chase growled. Ready to take someone apart with his bare hands, he strode toward the two men in the entry.

"It's not what you think," Jarek said hastily. "She volunteered as a live host to carry the virus. She was taking it to—to a medical laboratory for analysis."

"To Sonoma?" Chase asked quietly but received no response. He knew no honorable Shielder would ever reveal a base or colony location to a non-Shielder. He had just happened to stumble on the facility at Sonoma once but had never exposed its location. He had no intention of participating in genocide.

Jarek paled even further. "Don't worry," Chase assured him. "I won't reveal the base location. I have no quarrel with Shielders."

"Then you won't turn Nessa or Jarek in?" Sabin asked.

"I'm not planning on it."

Sabin cleared his throat. "Why not? The indoc-trination—"

"Never took," Chase interrupted, understanding Sabin's implication. "I went through the required procedure, like all other agents, but not before I'd undergone steps to protect me from mind domi-nation. I'm not a big fan of mind control."

He sobered, turning back to Nessa. The pieces were falling into place. Her desperation to reach Zirak, only a few days from Sonoma, as quickly as possible. A desperation finally reaching such great proportions that she'd stolen his ship. "Why didn't she tell me? I would have taken her directly there."

"You're a shadower, old man. She was afraid to tell you." Sabin moved beside him. "You have to help her, Chase."

Orana. A virus reputed to be every bit as atro-cious as Ramos, created by the same twisted ge-nius. And if Dansan had employed similar genetic traits, then the virus mutated at regular intervals, making it virtually impossible to find a treatment.

Panic slammed through Chase, sucking him into an undertow of painful memories, dragging him back in time. . . . The bodies everywhere, over-flowing the infirmary into the corridors, faces twisted in agony. All the while he rushed here and there, trying desperately to tend to the ill and at the same time create a counteragent to the virus rav-aging its victims. Every time he thought he had the cure, the insidious strain changed again.

"Chase, help me," his sister Chandra had gasped,

clinging to his hands, writhing uncontrollably on the mat. "I know you can help me. You're the best . . . the best."

But in the end, her sightless eyes had stared up at him, a mocking reminder of his colossal failure to save *any* of its victims. His parents, his brother, his best friend, all dead. He had failed them all. The only ones spared besides himself were those few who had been away on a trade mission.

He never knew for sure why the disease hadn't claimed him. The most plausible reason was that he hadn't drank from the communal water supply into which Dansan had dumped the virus. He preferred Merlain spring water and always kept a supply on hand. Once the virus had manifested, he'd taken further precautions, using masks and gloves.

He'd turned his back on medicine the day the last body had been lowered into the unforgiving ground. Swearing vengeance on Dansan, he'd promised the remaining colony members he'd bring her back to stand trial for her crimes. He'd begun a pursuit that had taken three seasons. And now . . .

He stared at Nessa, her frail body wracked with chills. Terror threatened to consume him; his heart pounded fiercely against his chest. She couldn't die on him. Not now, not when he was just beginning to realize how much she meant to him, how very much he needed her. But the apocalypse at Torin haunted him, immobilized him with fear.

"I don't know if I can help her." He turned anguished eyes to his partner. "I'm not capable."

Sabin's dark gaze bored into Chase's eyes. "I think I know your *real* identity. If you're who I suspect you are, *Dr. McKnight*, you're more than capable. You were galaxy renowned once."

Chase looked at Nessa again. Fear tormented him—fear he would fail her as he had so many others. "I don't want her to die, but I don't know if I can save her."

Sabin clasped his shoulder. "What happened on Torin was a horrible tragedy, but it wasn't your fault. Are you going to let the past keep you from saving Nessa?"

It wouldn't be the past that hurt Nessa; it would be his own incompetence.

"You are her *only* hope, Doctor. And Raven and Brand's." Sabin nodded at Chase's startled look. "Yes, they're Shielders. That's why Nessa brought them to me, hoping they wouldn't contract the Orana from her. And Jarek has been exposed. He needs the vaccine as well."

Pausing, Sabin drew a deep breath. "I need the vaccine, too, Chase," he added quietly. "I'm a Shielder."

Chapter Nineteen

"Nessa. Wake up, Nessa."

Heaviness engulfed her, weighing her down in a surreal stillness, although the welcome darkness seemed to be receding. Light encroached on the edges of her consciousness, but she didn't want to wake up, didn't want to remember. . . .

A faint hum vibrated over her forehead. "Leonessa dan Ranul! Come now, I know you can hear me. Open your eyes."

Only her father had ever called her by her full name. Her father! A blooming hope nudged her toward the light. After all these seasons, he'd come to help her.

"Captain San Mars . . . Father," she rasped. Her throat was so dry. "You've come! You're accepting me back." She struggled to awaken, but sudden dizziness swept her back into the darkness.

"I'm not your father, Nessa. Open your eyes."

She knew that commanding, arrogant voice from somewhere . . . no, she didn't want to wake up. If she did, the pain would return—an insufferable agony burning through her limbs.

Instead, she chose to sink deeper, floating through vague memories, memories of a voice calling to her, refusing to let her drift away, even when the pain had been intolerable. Memories of a cool, wet cloth stroking her burning skin, of the soothing touch of hands against her face. A touch that had been intimate and familiar. . . .

A warm hand slipped beneath the covers, clasping her much cooler hand and squeezing gently. "Nessa, look at me."

She didn't want to leave her cocoon of warmth and safety, of blissful oblivion. She shook her head.

"Still trying my patience." Amusement tinged the deep voice. "Don't make me take drastic measures."

The hand holding hers released it, then slid along her rib cage and over her breast, settling there in a blatantly possessive gesture. That got her attention, pulling her toward full awareness. She stirred, half-opening her eyes.

The form before her blurred, cleared, blurred. Chase. She squeezed her eyes shut. It couldn't be Chase. He hated her now. Besides, she must be dead. The Orana . . . Her groggy mind struggled to function. The virus! Her eyes snapped open.

Above her, Chase grinned, his hand still on her breast. "Good, your heart rate is up. I should have done this sooner."

Nessa closed her eyes again, not certain whether she'd entered Spirit Haven or the Abyss. Would

Chase be awaiting her in Haven as a reward, or in Abyss as a punishment?

The pain and the fever were gone, so she must be dead. But her body felt solid—and stiff. Perplexed, she shifted, wincing at the soreness of her backside. Did the dead feel discomfort? Drawing on her last conscious memory, she remembered the Orana had been too advanced for her to reach Sonoma in time.

"Nessa, don't shut me out. Open your eyes, sweetheart."

Sweetheart? Maybe she'd been granted entry to Haven. Hopefully, she reopened her eyes. Chase was still there, and he didn't look angry. But lines of strain etched his face, and dark circles lay beneath his eyes. She thought she saw relief in their smoky depths. His hand slid from her breast to stroke the hair back from her face.

"Where am I?" she croaked.

He laid the medical monitor down and took her hand again. His other hand remained against her face. "You're in my cabin."

Surprised, she shifted her gaze from him, noticing for the first time the familiar surroundings. Perhaps Haven duplicated a dead person's last environment to make them feel welcome.

"I moved you here this morning. You've been in sick bay—the medical lab actually—until now.

Spirit, she couldn't make any sense of this. "The medical lab?"

"We're on Sonoma, Nessa. I kept you on the ship because it has better facilities."

"But the Orana—"

"Is gone. Your body fought it off, with a lot of help."

She blinked, trying to comprehend his words. "Then I'm not dead?"

"Of course not. Wait a minute."

He rose and strode away. His motion made Nessa dizzy, and she closed her eyes. She heard a clunk, some hissing and snarling, then Chase sneezing. Returning, he sat on the edge of the bunk and took her hand. She felt the softness of fur beneath her fingers, heard an excited chattering. Turi!

Her eyes flew open. "Turi." He scrabbled across her chest and burrowed into his favorite place beneath her chin. She stroked the silky body. "Oh, Turi."

Chase sneezed. "Does he feel real?"

Turi's reassuring heartbeat thudded beneath her fingers. "Yes."

"You're alive, Nessa. And you're going to recover completely. Thank the Spirit."

She was alive! If she'd had any energy, she would have shouted for joy. She couldn't believe she'd been cured. "How?"

"It's a long story, and you need to rest." Chase pried Turi away, holding him by the nape of his neck so he couldn't bite. Sneezing several more times, he returned the lanrax to his case.

She watched him, her momentary exhilaration dulling with fatigue. She was so confused, had so many questions . . . so tired.

Chase loomed over her. "Sleep now, Nessa. We'll talk more later.

No sense in arguing with him, she thought drowsily, already drifting away. The covers were pulled up around her. "Sleep," his voice rumbled near her ear.

As she slipped back toward oblivion, one thought dominated. She was alive ... she was alive ... alive. . . .

Nessa awoke with a start, more alert this time. Glancing over, she saw Chase by the bunk, slumped down in his massive chair, sound asleep. Beyond him lay the familiar shapes and wall units indicating that this was indeed his cabin. She hadn't been hallucinating—she really was alive!

She lay in the glow of relief, luxuriating in the feel of the silky covers, of being able to draw a full breath of sweet-smelling air. Even with her body sore and aching, it felt wonderful to be alive.

Her mind much clearer, she tried to trace from her last conscious memory to here. She couldn't remember much, only being very ill. She was certain Chase had somehow been responsible for her survival, although the method eluded her. If he knew anything about Orana, then he now knew she was a Shielder. And if they were on Sonoma, he knew about the Shielder colony there as well.

Perhaps she should be alarmed, but every instinct told her that Chase wouldn't turn them in to the Controllers, even if he was a shadower and had undergone indoctrination. Perhaps he was too intelligent to be affected by it. His actions did illustrate a difference from others of his profession. For whatever reasons, he had always seemed to be pursuing specific people, not just anyone with a price on his head.

Nessa sighed, fatigue already returning. She watched Chase sleep, drinking in every detail, memorizing his features. He looked tired, and badly in need of a shave. His hair lacked its normal glossy sheen, and his flightsuit was badly rumpled.

Love wrapped around her heart. She would cherish every memory of their time together for as long as she lived. She didn't understand the inexplicable bond that had brought them together in passion, but she knew it had been temporary. Permanent matings were for other women—whole women. No man would want her.

She sat up gingerly, every muscle in her body screaming in protest. Waves of dizziness swept through her, and she leaned back until the spinning stopped.

Chase stirred and mumbled. His head lifted, then dropped back down. Tenderness welled inside her. Reaching out, she brushed his hair back from his face and stroked his cheek, feeling the rasp of a beginning beard.

He stirred again, then jerked awake with a start. "What—" His gaze snapped to her. "Nessa! You're awake."

He rose from the chair, the muscles of his powerful body evident beneath his flightsuit. Her breath hitched.

"How are you feeling?" he asked, leaning over the bunk and placing his hand against her face.

"Okay," she whispered shakily.

"Let's see how you're doing." Retrieving the medical monitor, he scanned her.

She lay quietly, content to watch him. She found the play of emotions on his handsome face fascinating—first concern, then concentration as he read the monitor, then immense satisfaction. His intense gaze flashed to hers, taking away what little breath she had left.

"I think you'll live."

Although he spoke the words lightly, Nessa sensed his deep relief. Without thinking, she raised her hand toward him. He took it, settling on the edge of the bunk.

"I thought we were going to lose you."

She nodded her agreement. "I was afraid it was the end."

"Volunteering to be injected with Orana was an incredibly brave thing to do. You're quite a lady."

The pride in Chase's voice warmed her soul, but Nessa knew bravery had little to do with it. Desperation and despair had motivated her actions. "I'm not brave. It was the only thing I could do for my people."

"For a people who had turned their backs on you?" he asked, a quiet anger underlying his voice.

Staring at her hand nestled in his, she sought to avoid that subject. "How did you know I'd been injected with the Orana?"

"Your brother Jarek told me."

Acute joy swept through her. "So he's all right! I didn't dream seeing him on the ship after all. Sabin must have gotten him out of the prison."

Chase chuckled. "My partner has the most amazing connections. I believe he decided to collect on a gambling debt to get your brother free."

She owed Sabin more than she could ever repay. "What about the Orana? Is there a cure now?"

"Yes. Thanks to you, a vaccine is being replicated in Sonoma's medical laboratory. It should be ready in another day or so."

"Thank the Spirit!" She indulged in a feeling of triumph. A moment later, a thought occurred to her and she struggled upright. "The children! I forgot all about them. Are they all right?"

He pushed her back down. "Take it easy. They're fine. They don't appear to have contracted the Orana, but they'll get an inoculation as soon as the vaccine is ready. Raven told us everything you did to protect her and Brand. You were right to take them to Sabin. Matter of fact, you did everything right *except* stealing my ship instead of trusting me enough to tell me the truth."

So he was still angry about that. "Oh," she said in a small voice. "I was afraid to tell you because you—you were—"

"A shadower," Chase growled, his voice laced with frustration. "By the Spirit, lady, after all that passed between us, you should have known I would never harm you."

The heat rose to her face, and her gaze skittered away from the accusation in his eyes. "But with Controller indoctrination, you'd have no choice but to turn me in."

"I wasn't indoctrinated."

She stared at him, amazed. "You weren't? But how did you avoid that?"

"Before I underwent the procedure, I put myself through extensive autohypnosis to make my mind resistant to outside hypnotic suggestions. As an added precaution, I injected compounds into my body that temporarily interfered with neurotransmitter activity in the brain and helped block the Controller's psionic brain waves."

Chase lowered his face close to hers. "So the indoctrination didn't take. I certainly wouldn't have brought you to Sonoma if it had. Do you believe me?"

Nessa's instincts had already banished her doubts, but hearing his explanation still relieved her. "Yes."

His eyes glowed warmly. "Good. Then it's time you start trusting me, lady." He released her hand and stood. "Are you feeling up to visitors? You're no longer contagious, and I know two children who are very anxious to see you."

Her spirits lifted at thoughts of Raven and Brand. "I want to see them, too. Can they come now?"

In answer to her question, Chase went to the console and punched some pads. "Travers, are Raven and Brand with you?"

Sabin's disgruntled voice came loud and clear over the com. "Where else would they be, old man? Leeches, both of them."

"Quit complaining and bring them to the ship. Nessa's waiting to see them."

"Well, son of an Antek. We'll be right there."

Moments later, the panel slid open. "Nessa! Nessa!" Letting go of Sabin's hand, Raven ran across the room, but stopped short of the bunk, suddenly uncertain. Nessa held out her arms. "Come here, sweetness. Give me a hug."

The slender girl crawled onto the bunk and burrowed against her. "I thought I'd never see you again."

Nessa's arms tightened around her. "I missed you and Brand. I hope you behaved for Sabin."

"Oh, we did." Raven's head bobbed up and down emphatically.

Brand moved hesitantly toward the bunk. "N-e-sa."

"Brand, you're still talking." She held out a hand. "Come here, little warrior."

"Oh, he's talking all right." Sabin nudged the boy forward. *"Chase, Nessa, Chase, Nessa.* That's all I've heard."

Brand turned and grinned at Sabin, the first time Nessa had ever seen him smile. "Sabin."

Sabin's mouth fell open. "Well, I'll be—" He stopped abruptly and ruffled Brand's hair. "Get over there, you wild little kerani, and see Nessa."

A moment later, Brand cuddled against Nessa's other side. Both children looked wonderful, their coloring healthy, the haunted look gone from their eyes. The welts and bruises were almost completely faded. Squeezing them gently, Nessa savored the warmth of their vibrant bodies.

"What have you been doing on Sabin's ship?"

"Playing a bunch of computer games," Raven said. "Brand is really good at Black Hole now. Sabin gave us lots of caroba. And he let us jump on the bunks all we wanted."

"He did?" Nessa patted Brand's back. "Did you jump really high, Brand?"

He nodded, his face hidden against her shoulder.

"Did you fall off?" she teased. He shook his head.

"He did, too!" Raven scoffed. "But I didn't—not even once."

Suddenly silent, the little girl grew pensive. "Sabin told us our parents are probably dead," she murmured.

Nessa shot a glance toward Sabin, who nodded.

Since Raven and Brand had to be told eventually, she realized he had probably done the best thing. She hugged the children tighter. "I'm sorry."

"I miss them," Raven said.

"Me miss, too," Brand echoed, although Nessa wondered how much he remembered of his parents.

They were all quiet a moment, then Nessa noticed Turi had plastered himself against the side of the plexishield case. He watched her longingly. "Where's Lia? Is she on Sabin's ship?"

"Yes. Her case is in our cabin," Raven answered. "Sabin was pretty upset when he saw her and Turi playing together, so he made them stay in different cases. I guess that made Lia sad, because she's gotten really fat."

"How interesting." Nessa glanced at Sabin, who rolled his eyes in disgust.

"Yeah," he muttered. "Now we're going to have a frigging lanrax colony. But it will be McKnight's problem soon, because I'm bringing the little tramp—I mean Lia—back here."

"I don't think so, Travers. I don't intend to take allergy injections the rest of my life. However, I know a vendor on Elysia who might relieve you of a few lanraxes," Chase offered.

"Go jump in the Abyss," Sabin growled.

The children giggled, and Nessa smiled at him. "Thank you for taking care of Raven and Brand. And I hear you rescued my brother. I can never repay you."

"Yeah, you owe me big time. Don't worry, I'll collect."

The gold grubber. However, she strongly suspected there was more to Sabin than met the eye—

330

much more. "By the way, where is Jarek?"

"He's meeting with Sonoma's leaders. He'll be here later." Sabin sauntered closer, his gaze assessing. "You look a lot better than you did the last time I saw you. Lucky for you, Dr. McKnight here knows his way around a medical laboratory."

"Doctor?" Nessa's head pivoted to where Chase leaned against the console, scowling at his partner. He'd changed into a clean flightsuit, but he still needed a shave.

"Yep. McKnight is a physician. If it hadn't been for him, you wouldn't be here."

Amazed, she couldn't tear her gaze away from Chase. Still scowling, he advanced toward Sabin. "Why don't you shut up, Travers?"

Suddenly, everything came together. How Chase had treated her seizures and her shoulder; his interest in her leg injury. The ship's laboratory, with all the advanced medical equipment. "I should have known," she mused. "You saved my life."

Chase looked at her, his expression impassive. "I can't take the credit for that. The Sonoma lab contributed a lot toward finding a treatment."

"But he kept you alive during the trip to Sonoma," Sabin explained. "And he had isolated the virus components by the time we arrived. The lab here had the equipment needed to complete the process, under Chase's supervision."

If Chase was such a competent physician, then why had he chosen the path of a shadower? The closed expression on his face indicated that he didn't wish to discuss the subject further. Confused, Nessa snuggled Raven and Brand closer.

"What about the Orana? What happens next?' she asked.

Chase visibly relaxed. He returned to his chair by the bunk. "Sonoma's lab is making up batches of the vaccine. Tomorrow or the next day, it will be shipped out to Shielder colonies everywhere."

Concern furrowed her brow. "But how can you do that without being caught? The Anteks search almost every ship traveling the main sectors."

"Ah, but we have a secret weapon." Sabin sat on the edge of the bunk. "Moriah."

The fatigue seeping through her made Nessa wonder if she'd heard right. "Moriah?"

Sabin nodded. "Best damn smuggler in the quadrant. Or used to be, actually. Now she oversees a whole squadron of runners, all of them women. They're the best in the business—and a great source of information."

Disbelieving, Nessa looked from Sabin to Chase. "Really?"

Chase nodded. "Really. Moriah's an amazing lady. She's offered to get the vaccine delivered—for a price, of course."

"But most Shielder colonies have no money to spare. How can we pay Moriah?"

"Shhh." Leaning forward, Chase placed a reassuring hand on her arm. "Don't worry about that. You did your part. Sabin and I will take care of the rest. Besides, Sabin is in a special bargaining position with the lady."

She sank back, suddenly exhausted. Taking Chase's advice and not worrying about anything held a tremendous appeal right now. After a little nap, she'd think about all this new information.

Cuddling the children closer, she had just closed her eyes when she heard the panel open.

"Nessa."

The familiar voice brought her instantly alert. Her brother stood by the bunk, looking incredibly handsome, the smile on his face brighter than a nova.

"Jarek!" She disengaged from the children, clumsily struggling to sit up. "Oh, Jarek."

He sank onto the bunk, gathering her to him for the second time in her entire life. She clung to him, needless of her soreness. Vaguely, she was aware of the children scrambling out of the way.

"I thought we'd lost you," he grated. "If it hadn't been for Dr. McKnight, we would have. Thank the Spirit he was there."

"I thought I'd lost *you*, when I saw you at the prison," Nessa mumbled against his chest. "I was terrified. I begged Sabin to help, even though I didn't know if he could be trusted."

Jarek drew back to glance toward Sabin, his expression amused. "Imagine not trusting san Travers. You, and about all the other women in the universe."

Sabin snorted and shook his head.

Nessa found her brother's attitude puzzling. "Of course I didn't trust him. He's a shadower."

"I've known san Travers a long time. He's obnoxious, but he can be depended on."

"You two know each other?" She looked from one to the other, amazed.

"Sure do." Sabin leaned against the wall, his legs crossed at the ankles. Raven pressed against his side, obviously comfortable with him. "San Ranul and I have engaged in a few forays against the Con trollers together."

"He's also contributed a huge amount of gold t the cause," Jarek interjected, gently easing Ness. down.

"He has?" Her gaze returned to Sabin. H shrugged and studied his nails. No doubt about it— there *was* more to the man than met the eye.

"He's a loyal Shielder," Jarek assured her.

Her thoughts whirled from sensory overload. " don't know what to think about all this."

"We've all had a lot of surprises," Chase saic dryly. She turned her head as he lifted Brand of his lap and stood. "Enough, I think, for one day Nessa looks tired, and I want her to rest. You car visit her again tomorrow."

She hated to see them leave, but her eyelids were drooping.

"Good-bye, sister." Jarek leaned down and kissec her cheek.

The children scampered over for a hug. "Bye Nessa," Raven said.

"Bye," Brand echoed.

Sabin surprised her with a quick kiss and a wink "Don't forget you owe me." He held out his hands to Raven and Brand, and they took them without hesitation. "We'll come back tomorrow."

"Good-bye," she murmured drowsily.

She remained awake long enough to drink some broth and visit the lav, then collapsed back into the bunk. Her last conscious memory was of Chase covering her and running the scanner over her.

A physician, she thought. Imagine that. . . .

Chapter Twenty

Chase soon declared Nessa well enough to resume normal activities. She had free reign of the ship, and although she tired easily, she drew energy from the sheer exuberance of being alive.

The vaccine had been produced en masse, and Jarek and Sabin had taken it to a rendezvous point where Moriah's runners would pick it up. They wouldn't be given exact Shielder colony locations, but they'd deliver the vaccine at nearby drop-off points. The Shielders would take it from there. It seemed Nessa's mission was drawing to a successful conclusion.

Now what? she wondered.

Jarek would be returning in a few days, and she guessed she'd travel to Liron with him. A part of her wanted to return, to see her home; also to see if her success had altered her status with her peo-

ple. Another part of her yearned to remain with
Chase.

It was a senseless, unrealistic hope. She had
nothing to offer any man. She was still plain and
thin—even thinner, since being ill; still deformed.
He certainly hadn't shown any further interest in
her, although he'd been civil enough.

He'd saved her life, taken care of her, hovered
over her, insisting that she rest and eat properly.
But his actions had been those of a physician—professional, competent. His eyes never had that sexual, predatory expression when he looked at her.
He hadn't kissed her, had made no advances of any
kind.

Perhaps he'd never forgiven her for stealing his
ship, yet he didn't seem angry about it. Heaviness
settled around Nessa's heart. She needed to accept
the obvious and move on. She planned on taking
Raven and Brand to Liron with her, hoping Chase
would agree they'd be best off in a Shielder colony.

Right now, the children were sound asleep in her
old cabin. She continued to stay in Chase's quarters. He'd been sleeping there as well, on a nearby
floor pallet.

Nessa gazed around the familiar cabin. She'd
miss this chamber, miss the memories here. She
looked at the chair, the heat rising to her face. *Don't
think about it,* she told herself. *Stop wishing for the
impossible to happen.* With a sigh, she went to
bathe. She'd also miss the unlimited electricity and
water.

She took a long shower, the hot water easing
some of her still-aching muscles. Finally, she shut

off the water and stepped from the cleansing stall.

Her heart leaped wildly when she saw Chase lounging against the sink. He wore a thick terry robe, belted around his firm waist. The robe fell to his knees; his strong, muscular legs were bare below it.

Nessa stared at him dumbly, her heart still pounding.

"You took long enough," he said huskily. His gaze scanned her and she belatedly remembered her nude state.

She looked around and located her tunic, tossed carelessly by the panel. "I didn't know you were waiting to use the lav." She edged toward the panel.

He smoothly stepped between her and the panel. "I was waiting for you."

It was there, in his eyes—that predatory look. Her breath froze. "I—I—For me?"

He reached out and traced a trail of water trickling down her breast. She bit back a gasp as her breast swelled, the nipple puckering almost painfully. The water dripping from her hair and down her face reminded her that she was soaking wet. "I need to dry off." Spirit, couldn't she think of anything better to say?

Chase's gaze moved slowly from her breasts to her face. Molten silver flames burned in his eyes. Unbelting his robe, he slid it off his shoulders. He wore nothing underneath, and her knees went weak at the sight of his powerful body—his very aroused, powerful body.

She staggered back as he stroked the robe against

her arm. "Steady, now," he murmured. "I'm goin
to dry you off."

Unable to think clearly, she pressed her palm
against the corner of the stall for support as Chas
dried her with the robe. He did her arms, then he
face, then blotted her hair. All the while his intens
gaze burned into her eyes, until he lowered the rob
to her breasts.

His gaze moved to her nipples, and he rubbe
them with the soft fabric until Nessa threw he
head back and moaned softly. Kneeling, he slid th
robe to her legs, nudging them apart and bringin
the robe up the inside.

Her legs trembled like leaves fluttering in th
wind, and heat rushed through her lower abdomen
Swaying, she grabbed at the wall. When he move
the robe to the most acute source of her heat, sh
clutched blindly at his shoulders.

"Chase."

The robe fell to the floor and he slid a finger in
side her. Lightning flashed through her. She cried
out, her nails digging into his skin. With a groan
he pressed his lips to her belly.

"I want you," he grated out. "Now."

Her thoughts tailspinned. No time for wondering
why, or even if she should. She wanted this—
wanted him—desperately. "Yes," she whispered.

Sweeping her into his arms, Chase carried her to
the bunk. The covers were cool beneath her damp
fevered skin. Light from the lav filtered into the
room, casting shadows on his face, taut with desire
as he lowered his mouth to her breast.

He kissed and licked away the remaining mois

ture from her skin, flowing down her body like Saija silk. Spirit, but she needed more, needed the bliss of Haven that only he could give her. The tremors rippling his body told her his need was just as great.

Caught in the throes of an uncontrollable urgency, she writhed beneath him. When he spread her legs and kissed her most private place, the intimacy and the utter pleasure stunned her.

She dug her fingers into his hair. "Chase!"

He slid over her, capturing her lips with his. Holding her face between his hands, he plundered her mouth, and she responded in a sensual duel of tongues. Groaning, Chase tore his mouth away.

"Spirit, I can't wait any longer. I have to be inside you." Positioning himself, he entered her in one smooth stroke. She arched up to meet him.

He plunged deeply, driving both of them toward the precipice. So fierce was his possession, Nessa could only hold on and go where he took her. Hard and fast. Again and again.

High . . . So very high . . .

She cried out, her body jerked upward by a rush of sensation packing more force than a torpedo. Through the shockwaves, she felt Chase stiffen, heard his cry of release.

He collapsed with a ragged sigh. Limp and drained, Nessa welcomed his weight. A moment later, he rolled onto his back, pulling her against his side. His chest rose and fell rapidly beneath her cheek.

What had just happened? She was still too new and inexperienced in this arena to understand why

Catherine Spangler

Chase had mated with her. Perhaps uncontrollable lust, or a release from the stress of the past cycles. She didn't have a clue, although she wouldn't have traded the experience for anything.

"All you all right?" His voice rumbled beneath her ear.

She nodded her head. "Yes," she whispered. "Are you?"

He chuckled and stroked her back. "Oh, yes. Very, very all right. Spirit, but you're so soft."

He continued stroking her, and a pleasant lassitude stole over her. His body felt relaxed beneath her. It occurred to her that this might be the perfect time to share her plans. Her stomach knotted at the thought, and the heaviness returned to her chest, but she had to tell him sooner or later. It might as well be now.

"Chase?"

"Hmmm?" His hand moved to cup her backside in a possessive manner.

Hot tears stung her eyes, but she blinked them back. "Jarek will be returning in a few cycles."

"Yes. So?"

She inhaled a quick breath, then said the words quickly. "I'm returning to Liron with him. I plan on taking Raven and Brand with me."

His hand jerked, his fingers digging painfully into her bottom. "No."

Panic swept her, stealing her breath. "But I must keep Raven and Brand with me! They need me. They're Shielders. They should be with other Sh—"

340

"No! Raven and Brand aren't leaving. Neither are you."

"But—What?"

Chase rolled her onto her back, taking her chin in his hand. A determined expression molded his face into stern lines. "Why did you mate with me tonight?"

Surprised, she tried to marshall her forces, which had scattered to the four corners of the quadrant. "W-what?"

"You just surrendered your body to me, let me do whatever I wanted. You spread your legs and welcomed me inside you, then exploded around me. Why? Did you hope to gain something from it?"

His blunt statement shocked her. "Of course not." She paused, unwilling to bare her heart to any more pain. He didn't need to know she loved him, not when he didn't return that love.

His tawny eyebrows drew together. "No? Then let me ask you this: Why did you come to my cabin the night before you hijacked my ship? Was your sweet seduction a tactic to distract me from your thievery?"

She bit her lip, staring into determined gray eyes. "No," she whispered, the memories of that night crumbling her resolve. "I—I thought I would never see you again. I thought it was our last chance to—to be together." She tried to turn her head away, but his grip on her chin tightened.

"I didn't think so. I did at first, when you took my ship. But the more I thought about it, I realized you had nothing to gain by mating with me that night.

I was hell-bent on going to Odera, and that provided all the opportunity you needed."

He trailed a finger down her breast, circling the nipple, which beaded instantly. "I also realized your physical responses to me couldn't be faked. You wanted me, as badly as I wanted you."

Nessa closed her eyes against his perceptive gaze. So, she wanted him. That probably stroked his ego to no end. "Lust is not enough," she murmured.

"At first, I thought physical attraction might be all that lay between us. But then, when I thought you were slipping away from me . . ." He shuddered. "Spirit, if I had lost you . . ."

Nessa's eyes snapped open, her attention fully riveted on him. Emotion glittered in his eyes. "My life would have been plunged into darkness."

She stared at him, not comprehending. "Why?"

A tender smile curved his sensuous mouth. "Because I love you, Leonessa dan Ranul. That's why."

Her illness must have affected her hearing. "What?" she asked lamely.

His hand cradled the side of her face. "I love you. You are *not* going to Liron with Jarek. You're not going anywhere. As soon as you're completely recovered, we're getting married. I don't care how— Shielder lifemate vows, Elysian orgy, Shen joining ritual—doesn't matter to me."

Shock dulled her reaction. Maybe she *was* hallucinating. Maybe this was really Haven after all. . . .

"By the Abyss," Chase growled. "Don't just stare at me like I'm an Antek. Answer me."

He loved her? "An-answer what?" she stammered.

His expression grew thunderous. *"Will you marry me?* You can't tell me you don't feel something for me. Not after tonight."

A flush spread through her body. "Well . . . umm, I do."

Chase scowled. "You do what?"

Please don't let this be a dream. She forced air into her lungs, then turned her heart loose. "I love you."

A smug smile spread across his face. "And?"

"I'll marry you, if you're sure you want someone like me."

She found herself crushed against his chest. "Nessa, Nessa. You're beautiful, caring, and brave."

"I already told you. I'm not brave."

"Yes, you are, Nessa, remarkably courageous. I'm the coward."

Incredulous, she pushed away to look at him. "You? You're a shadower. You've hunted some of the most dangerous criminals in the universe. You're one of the bravest men I know."

His expression turned pensive, and sadness palled his eyes. "No, sweetheart. Facing my feelings terrified me. I didn't want to feel the pain, so I buried it. To keep it at bay, I turned to hatred instead. My only focus for the past three seasons has been hunting down Dansan and her goons."

Compassion and a strong yearning to hold him in her arms and comfort him pooled in Nessa's heart. "What did she do to you?"

Chase sank back, pulling her against his side again. "Not just to me—to an entire people. It's a long story, but I want you to hear it. I may have assumed too much. You might not want to marry me after you know about my failures."

Her fingers tightened on his chest in protest, but he continued on. His voice sounded far away, almost as if he were entering another time and place.

"Dansan was a brilliant physiopathologist and geophysicist. She approached the leaders of my colony on Torin with a plan to speed up the mining of iridon. She had developed a chemical process that would remove the top layers of shale rapidly, without damaging the iridon beneath. Until then, it had taken months to mine even a modest amount of iridon.

"She proposed to share the process and oversee the operation, for an even split of the iridon. She convinced our leaders of her integrity, and they agreed. Then . . . then she betrayed us."

He paused, tension emanating from him. "She developed a deadly virus—Ramos, we called it— and dumped it into Torin's water supply."

Nessa gasped, horror slithering through her stomach.

"Everyone in the colony at the time caught the disease—everyone but me. I didn't drink the community water, because I had a supply of Merlain spring water."

He drew a ragged breath. "The virus raged through the colony. It was merciless, inflicting terrible suffering before death occurred. The sick and the dying were everywhere. I tried to formulate a cure, but the Ramos kept mutating. In the end . . ." His voice broke and his grip on Nessa's shoulder tightened.

She could feel his pain, could imagine what he

must have gone through. Tears filled her eyes and trickled down her cheeks. "Oh, Chase."

"In the end," he continued, his voice shaking, "they all died. I couldn't save anyone. All my medical training was worthless. I failed them all."

Nessa threw herself across him, holding him tightly. "Spirit, how horrible. But it wasn't your fault. You know that, don't you?"

He remained silent for a long moment. "I kept thinking if only I'd known more about viruses, if only I'd stayed calmer instead of panicking, if only I'd been able to get one jump ahead of the Ramos. If only I could have saved *someone*."

The last pieces to the puzzle clicked into place. "So you turned your back on healing and became a shadower instead."

"Yeah." Chase clutched her tightly to him. "Dansan and her soldiers took as much iridon as they could transport and hightailed it to this quadrant. The only way I could pursue them without interference was to apply for a shadower entitlement, which I did. I picked up other wanted criminals here and there to keep from drawing suspicion. They were space scum anyway, and didn't need to be terrorizing innocent people."

Nessa lifted her head to gaze at him wonderingly. "You turned away from healing. But you treated my seizures and my shoulder. You gave me medicine. And you examined the children. Why?"

He gently wiped the dampness from her cheeks, a rueful expression on his face. "I tried to stay away from medicine. I hated entering the ship lab. Then you came along, with that damned lanrax, and I

found myself in there more and more. Then you
brought Raven and Brand on board, and I worried
they might be carrying disease or parasites. It became harder and harder to avoid medicine."

"Then I got the Orana and you saved my life," she
said softly. "You even created a vaccine against it."

He smiled at her then, and a dizzying relief swept
through her. That smile somehow told her that he
would be all right. With Dansan gone, he could put
the past behind him.

"Yes, I did. And I realized something that really
surprised me. I missed working in a medical laboratory, analyzing diseases and formulating cures. If
I hadn't been so worried about you, I would have
enjoyed what I was doing."

A blossoming hope took root. "Then you won't
continue as a shadower?"

Chase slid one hand along the side of her face.
"Would it bother you if I did, *Shielder?*"

She nodded solemnly.

Humor glinted in his eyes, and he pressed her
head down for a kiss. A long moment later, he released her. "No, little Shielder, I'm definitely not
going to remain a shadower. It wouldn't do to hunt
my mate's people, now would it?"

Her heart swelled with joy, yet nagging doubts
remained.

"Are you sure you want to marry me?" She almost
succeeded at keeping the telltale quaver out of her
voice.

"Are you sure you want me?" Chase countered.

"But my seizures and my leg—"

"Don't mean anything," he interrupted fiercely.

"They don't matter, but we can do something about them, if you wish. It's your spirit and courage I love, those huge, dark eyes of yours, that sexy mouth."

She pushed away, amazed. "My mouth is sexy?"

Chase leaned over her, his eyes heated. "Oh, yes, sweetheart. Very sexy. And I have lots of ideas on how you can use it."

He kissed her again, with more urgency this time.

They were married ten ship cycles later, in a Shielder lifemate ceremony, with Sonoma's Council head, Captain san Kincaid, officiating. They wanted Jarek and Sabin to stand with them, so they waited until the two had returned from delivering the vaccine to Moriah's runners.

Nessa wore a stunning overrobe made from cream-colored Saija silk, with matching slippers. Chase looked breathtakingly handsome in a royal blue tunic and leggings, the uniform worn by healers throughout the quadrant. Both outfits were wedding gifts from Moriah, who had returned to Sonoma with Sabin.

Nessa had been surprised to learn that Sabin and Moriah were mated. But now, knowing that Sabin was a man of many mysteries, she suspected time would bring even more interesting revelations. And she was glad to see that her two new friends obviously loved each other very much.

Raven and Brand were there, wearing new tunics and boots for the occasion. Also present, Turi and Lia watched from their cases, each adorned with interwoven cream and blue ribbons. Turi showed off outrageously, chattering and performing flips, while Lia's advancing pregnancy necessitated that she sit regally through the event.

The weather on Sonoma cooperated in full, so they held the ceremony outside on a small rise, with striking, multicolored mesas rising up behind them. The midafternoon sun drifted through wispy clouds, contributing a magnanimous warmth. The balmy breeze ruffled their hair in a gentle caress.

Even though they exchanged traditional Shielder lifemate vows, Nessa and Chase didn't give each other the customary leather bracelets. Not knowing where their travels might take them, they decided against wearing obvious Shielder adornments. Instead, Chase presented Nessa with an enormous, rare topaz crystal on a gold chain. She gave him a crystal starburst pin, the starburst being the universal symbol of the healer.

Moriah had procured both gifts on their behalf from her remarkable storehouse of goods. She'd also brought toys for the children, much to their delight.

Raven and Brand stood beside Nessa and Chase while the vows were said. They both squirmed with excitement. Right before the ceremony, Nessa and Chase asked the children what they thought about living with them permanently. The answer was an enthusiastic, jumping up and down, squealing "Yes!"

Gazing into her new husband's glowing eyes, Nessa feared her heart might burst, so great was her happiness. She still found it difficult to believe Chase found her desirable, although he'd certainly shown strong amorous tendencies these last ten cycles. Just the thought of their bed-play curled her toes and fanned flames of desire throughout her body.

"Wife," he murmured, leaning down.

"Husband," she breathed, stretching upward and wrapping her arms around his neck.

Their lengthy kiss held the promise of a long, sensuous evening ahead.

"Ahem! Really, old man, you need to reserve your strength for tonight," Sabin observed. When Chase ended the kiss to glare at him, Sabin shoved him away none too gently. "Besides, Jarek and I want a chance to kiss the bride."

Taking Nessa into his arms, he gave her a kiss that seemed a little too long to be brotherly. "Take good care of the old man and the kids," he muttered gruffly. "They're lucky to have you."

Somewhat breathless, Nessa smiled at him. "Thank you, Sabin, for everything. It appears I was wrong about you."

He grinned. "Probably not. You're the only one I haven't managed to fool."

She shook her head, not falling for his smoke screen for one instant.

"Don't believe a word he says," Moriah advised. Dressed in a gorgeous gold brocade overrobe, her copper curls glinting in the sunlight, she drew the eyes of every male in the colony. Not even Sabin's possessive glares could stem the admiring glances. Seemingly oblivious to the stares, Moriah smiled at Nessa, her amber eyes sparkling.

"I adore happy endings. I knew Chase wouldn't be able to resist you in that robe. But that was just trimming. Don't you ever doubt for a minute how beautiful you are, both inside and out." She hugged Nessa tightly and whispered, "But just for fun, I brought you a special robe for tonight. It's very sheer, guaranteed to drive Chase wild."

As if he needed any encouragement, Nessa thought, returning Moriah's smile. "Thank you for everything, Mori. I've never had a friend before, but I'm proud to consider you one."

Moriah's eyes glistened with a suspicious moisture. "The feeling is mutual, my friend. We have to stick together to keep these men in line."

"Nessa."

"Jarek." She turned to her brother and accepted his kiss upon her cheek.

"I'm happy for you, sister. Chase is a good man. Take care of yourself. May joy be your shadow."

She forced back the tears. After ten seasons of refusing to cry, it seemed she was forever tearing up. "You also. Spirit watch over you and protect you on your trip home."

He stepped back, taking her hand and offering it to Chase. "On behalf of my family, I entrust Nessa into your keeping. Cherish her and guard her well."

The warmth of Chase's hand enfolded hers and he drew her against him. "I'll take good care of her."

"Nessa. Chase. Happy," Brand proclaimed without a single stutter, cuddling against them.

Raven joined them, pressing close to Nessa. "Can we call you mother and father?" she asked shyly.

Her heart in her throat, Nessa looked at Chase. Smiling broadly, he nodded.

"Of course you may," she answered. "We're your parents now."

"Okay, Mother," Raven chirped.

Laughing and crying at the same time, Nessa knelt down and hugged both children to her. All these many seasons, she'd been adrift and alone, with no true home, and no one but Jarek to call family.

And now . . . now, she had everything she could possibly hope for.

Thank you, Spirit, she whispered in her heart.

Epilogue

Nessa paused outside the assembly hall, trepidation edging out the excitement of returning home. She took another look at the barren terrain and the gray haze drifting around the distant rock formations.

The fine mist in the air dampened her hair and face, and a brisk wind rippled her cape. This time, however, her heavy tunic and leggings, along with her overcape, blocked out Liron's unrelenting chill.

Around the compound, Shielders halted any pretense of working, their gazes riveted on Liron's visitors. No one had spoken to her or stepped forward in greeting, although she hadn't seen the old derision or loathing in their expressions. A few had even nodded grudgingly at her and Chase.

Nessa turned and faced the assembly hall's huge double doors. No reason to delay further, yet she hesitated. What if nothing had changed? What if she received the same humiliating treatment she'd endured for ten seasons? She would hate to be disgraced before Chase and the children. As if sensing her anxiety, he caught her hand and squeezed it reassuringly. "Shall we go in?"

Offering an encouraging smile, Jarek pulled open the door. Taking a fortifying breath, Nessa entered with Chase by her side. Raven and Brand and little Celene followed behind, each clutching a lanrax pup from Lia's litter. About four seasons old, Celene was the sole survivor of a Shielder colony that had been decimated by Anteks. Sabin had found her and brought her to Chase and Nessa. She'd been with them one lunar cycle now.

The flickering solar lanterns threw odd shadows on the stone walls, doing little to dispel the dimness. A familiar musty odor wafted through the cool interior.

At the far end, the Council members sat upon the raised dais. Captain Ranul san Mars stood before the dais, waiting to greet his guests with traditional Shielder formality. Beside him stood Meris and Elder Gabe san Ardon. Nessa had eyes only for her parents as she and Chase walked toward the group. Drawing another deep breath, she quelled her nervousness. She kept her back straight, her head high. She walked evenly, without a limp, thanks to Chase.

He had used tissue samples from her normal leg to generate new muscles for her damaged leg. Physical therapy and exercise had strengthened the restored leg. Two laser surgeries had eradicated the outside scarring. Her leg now appeared normal.

She no longer suffered seizures, either. Chase had fine-tuned her medication until her condition stabilized.

A lot of physical changes, yet Nessa realized the greatest change had occurred within herself. Part of maturing, she decided, lay not in material accomplishments, but in knowledge and spiritual growth. Through Chase, she'd learned that physical appearance didn't determine the true depth of a person.

She fervently hoped that Ranul and Meris would see that truth as well.

She halted before her parents and Elder san Ardon, fisting her hands by her side. She addressed the Council head first, as was the custom. "Captain san Mars."

His eyes impassive, he nodded briefly. "Leonessa."

She swallowed. "I present my husband, Dr. Chase McKnight."

The two men clasped hands, locking gazes, each assessing the other. Ranul broke the silence first. "I understand we owe you a great debt, Doctor."

"That honor goes to your daughter, Captain. Without her amazing bravery, the Orana virus would still be rampant."

Ranul's gaze returned to Nessa, and she tensed. "So I've heard. My thanks, Leonessa. Job well done."

The genuine pride in his voice warmed her. She hoped those simple words represented the first step toward reconciliation. At a loss for words in response, she nodded her acknowledgement.

Never shy, Elder san Ardon stepped forward, openly beaming. He grasped Nessa's shoulders. "By the Spirit, but you did well, girl. A true Shielder, through and through."

Astonished, she stared into the elder's eyes, finding acceptance and approval there. "Thank you, sir."

He turned to Chase. "And you, Doctor. I understand you formulated the antidote to the virus and got it distributed to the Shielder colonies."

Chase smiled ruefully. "Again, I must decline that honor. The lab on Sonoma replicated the vaccine, and your own Commander san Ranul here, along with Commander san Travers, transported the medicine to runners. I only assisted with the process."

"You did more than that," Jarek protested, speaking for the first time. "You saved Nessa's life, and you isolated the components of the virus. All Sonoma's technicians needed to do was feed the information into their computers and compound the calculated formula."

Chase shrugged, and Elder san Ardon slapped him on the back. "It was a big assist, young man. We thank you."

"I'm glad I could help." Chase turned to Ranul. "Captain, we've brought more Orana vaccine and other medical supplies. With your permission, I'd be happy to attend any colonists who need medical treatment."

"Your offer is appreciated and accepted."

Chase's hand on Nessa's back nudged her forward. "Uh, Captain, we also brought some new computer equipment and software. If it's all right I'd like to install it while Chase sees the colonists."

Surprise crossed Ranul's face. "I didn't know you had knowledge of computers."

"Father," Jarek intervened, "who do you think patched our old system every time it went down? I allowed Nessa access to the computer from the time of her injury. She's become very proficient at programming."

"I'll vouch for that," Chase added, winking at her.

Ranul sighed, his gaze settling on her. "I can see there are many things that slipped my notice over the seasons. Again, my thanks, daughter. Your efforts are welcome."

He'd called her "daughter," and his eyes had reflected warmth. Nessa's heart swelled, yet one more hurdle remained. She faced her mother.

"Meris."

"Daughter." Meris stared at her. "You're looking well."

Daughter. A word Nessa had dreamed of hearing again these many seasons. Not in this tentative, groping manner. In her dreams, it had been spoken loudly, with laughter and tears and perhaps even touching. But this was a start, more than she could realistically hope for.

"Mer—Mother," she stammered, saying that word for the first time in seasons. She gestured to the children, who had watched the proceedings with wide eyes. "These are my adopted children: Brand, Raven, Celene, these are my parents, Captain san Mars and Lady Meris. And this is Elder san Ardon."

"Hi," Raven said in a small voice.

Brand hid behind his lanrax. Celene smiled shyly.

Meris studied them, myriad emotions flitting across her face. Finally, she leaned down. "What have you got there? Looks like desert krats."

"Oh, no, Lady Meris," Raven protested. "These are baby lanraxes."

"Lia's babies," Brand added. "She had four."

Pride welled through Nessa. With lots of love and encouragement, Brand was talking more and more. The little boy proved to be a bright and apt student, as did both the girls.

"Lanraxes?" Meris snorted. "Just more mouths to feed."

"We don't have to feed them," Raven explained. "Lia does that."

A small smile eased onto Meris's weathered face. "Does she, now? Well, you do remind me of another little girl I once knew."

She patted all three children, then rose to her regal height. Her gaze fixed on Nessa, steady, accepting. "And *she* grew into a fine young woman."

Overwhelmed, Nessa blinked back a rush of tears. She groped blindly and found what she sought—the warm strength of her mate's hand. Chase. Her rock, her anchor . . . her husband, her love. He pulled her tightly against him.

"Yes, she did, didn't she?" he said proudly.

Nessa looked up at Chase, then at the children, who watched her with adoration in their eyes. She already had everything she really needed. In time, the grudging acceptance her people offered might grow into something more. She hoped it would, but she no longer defined her existence by their favor.

Spirit had shown her true self-worth. It resided in the love reflected back to her from Jarek, and from her new family. Chase, Raven, Brand, Celene. They loved and needed her, and she loved them.

She was whole in every way.

DON'T MISS OTHER STARSWEPT FUTURISTIC ROMANCES FROM *LOVE SPELL!*

Nighthawk by Kristen Kyle. Determined to earn her father's approval, Kari Solis must capture the commander of the rebel forces wreaking havoc on their world. But she doesn't count on her plans being upset by a rogue smuggler—a handsome loner concealing a shadowy past and an even darker secret. Confronted by a dark menace, the two reluctantly join forces, igniting a firestorm of cosmic passion that takes them to a final battle—pitting the power of betrayal against the strength of their love.

_52184-9 $4.99 US/$5.99 CAN

Hidden Heart by Anne Avery. Determined to free her world, Marna has traveled to the planet Dilor with her own secret agenda. And her plans don't include being seduced by the first hard-bodied man she encounters. Although the enchanting beauty refuses to forget her mission, she can't deny the ache Tarl rouses in her. But the more Marna longs to surrender to unending bliss, the more she fears she is betraying everything she holds dear.

_52109-1 $5.99 US/$6.99 CAN

Futuristic Romance

Keeper of the Rings

Nancy Cane

"A passionate romantic adventure!"
—Phoebe Conn, Bestselling Author Of
—*Ring Of Fire*

He is shrouded in black when Leena first lays eyes on him—his face shaded like the night. With a commanding presence and an impressive temper, Taurin is the obvious choice to be Leena's protector on her quest for a stolen sacred artifact. Curious about his mysterious background, and increasingly tempted by his tantalizing touch, Leena can only pray that their dangerous journey will be a success. If not, explosive secrets will be revealed and a passion unleashed that will forever change their world.

__52077-X $5.50 US/$7.50 CAN

Futuristic Romance

Star-Crossed

Saranne Dawson

Bestselling Author Of *Crystal Enchantment*

Rowena is a master artisan, a weaver of enchanted tapestries that whisper of past glories. Yet not even magic can help her foresee that she will be sent to assassinate an enemy leader. Her duty is clear—until the seductive beauty falls under the spell of the man she must kill.

His reputation says that he is a warmongering barbarian. But Zachary MacTavesh prefers conquering damsels' hearts over pillaging fallen cities. One look at Rowena tells him to gird his loins and prepare for the battle of his life. And if he has his way, his stunningly passionate rival will reign victorious as the mistress of his heart.

_51982-8 $4.99 US/$5.99 CAN

Mine To Take

DARA JOY

He is full-blooded and untamable. A uniquely beautiful creature who can make himself irresistible to women. With his glittering green and gold eyes, silken hair, and purring voice, the stunning captive chained to the wall is exactly what Jenise needs. And he is hers to take . . . or so she believes.

___4446-3 $5.99 US/$6.99 CAN

Dorchester Publishing Co., Inc.
P.O. Box 6640
Wayne, PA 19087-8640

Please add $1.75 for shipping and handling for the first book and $.50 for each book thereafter. NY, NYC, and PA residents please add appropriate sales tax. No cash, stamps, or C.O.D.s. All orders shipped within 6 weeks via postal service book rate. Canadian orders require $2.00 extra postage and must be paid in U.S. dollars through a U.S. banking facility.

Name_____
Address_____
City_____State_____Zip_____
I have enclosed $_____ in payment for the checked book(s).
Payment <u>must</u> accompany all orders. ❑ Please send a free catalog.

THE WHITE SUN
STOBIE PIEL

Sierra of Nirvahda has never known love. But with her long dark tresses and shining eyes she has inspired plenty of it, only to turn away with a tuneless heart. Yet when she finds herself hiding deep within a cavern on the red planet of Tseir, her heart begins to do strange things. For with her in the cave is Arnoth of Valenwood, the sound of his lyre reaching out to her through the dark and winding passageways. His song speaks to her of yearnings, an ache she will come to know when he holds her body close to his, with the rhythm of their hearts beating for the memory and melody of their souls.

___52292-6 $5.50 US/$6.50 CAN

The Midnight Moon

STOBIE PIEL

Dane Calydon knows there is more to the mysterious Aiyan
than meets the eye, but when he removes her protective
wrappings, he is unprepared for what he uncovers: a woman
beautiful beyond his wildest imaginings. Though she
claimed to be an amphibious creature, he was seduced by
her sweet voice, and now, with her standing before him, he
is powerless to resist her perfect form. Yet he knows she is
more than a mere enchantress, for he has glimpsed her
healing, caring side. But as secrets from her past
overshadow their happiness, Dane realizes he must lift the
veil of darkness surrounding her before she can surrender
both body and soul to his tender kisses.

___52268-3 $5.50 US/$6.50 CAN

Dorchester Publishing Co., Inc.
P.O. Box 6640
Wayne, PA 19087-8640

Please add $1.75 for shipping and handling for the first book and
$.50 for each book thereafter. NY, NYC, and PA residents.
please add appropriate sales tax. No cash, stamps, or C.O.D.s. All
orders shipped within 6 weeks via postal service book rate.
Canadian orders require $2.00 extra postage and must be paid in
U.S. dollars through a U.S. banking facility.

Name_____
Address_____
City_____State_____Zip_____
I have enclosed $_____ in payment for the checked book(s).
Payment <u>must</u> accompany all orders. ❑ Please send a free catalog.
       CHECK OUT OUR WEBSITE! www.dorchesterpub.com

Love ONCE & FOREVER
FLORA SPEER

Laura has traveled here, to this time before the moon has come to circle the earth, to embrace Kentir beneath the violet-and-ochre brilliance of the Northern Lights. In his gray-blue gaze, she sees the longing he cannot hide. His lips seek hers and find them. In his kiss she tastes the warmth of amber wine and the urgency of manly desire. She drinks deeply, forgetting that for them there can be no past, no future; for he is of a time that is ending, while she belongs to one that has yet to begin. Closing her eyes to the soft shadows of the lantern lights, she gives herself to him, determined to live out her destiny in this one precious night.

___52291-8 $5.99 US/$6.99 CAN